THE JONAS TRUST DECEPTION

by

AFN CLARKE

A THOMAS GUNN BOOK

CLARK*e*- BOOKS

The Jonas Trust Deception

First eBook edition published by Clarke-Books LLC in 2013
This print edition published by Clarke-Books LLC in 2014

Copyright Registered at the Library of Congress 2013

Cover design AFN Clarke
Cover background image © Pawish Tanachotpunyaphon|Dreamstime.com

ISBN: 978-1-938611-20-9

CLARK*e*-BOOKS
www.afnclarke.com

For My Brothers
Chris & Rick

ONE

Sea of Cortez – Baja Mexico – July 30th 2013

Somewhere in the back of my head behind the pounding jackhammer and piercing pain, a glimmer of light flickered unevenly.

Maybe a candle.

Maybe a reflection in a bathtub.

Maybe just an illusion drifting through a dream.

No. A nightmare.

An ordeal my shattered mind could not quite comprehend as it wandered through the twilight of semi-consciousness.

I'd been here before and knew the experience, the uncertainty, the gut gripping fear as fragmented parts of my mind fought back to consciousness; not knowing whether that consciousness would be the world I knew or the 'Other World', the existence beyond earthly life that I'd determined not to visit again any time soon.

The yellow light shimmered and wavered, then gradually steadied becoming clearer, whiter, seeming to envelop my world, jarring me back towards reality in a roaring swirl of foam.

Seawater filled my mouth, forcing its way down my throat, until my body screamed, and threw it back out in a wrenching coughing vomit, screwing my gut into an agonizing spasm, burning my lungs and searing my throat with burning bile. Tears of pain squeezed from my eyes as I waited for the wracking spasms to ease, the jackhammer still pounding out a rhythmical tattoo inside my skull as my swamped lungs worked hard in huge gasps, fighting for much needed oxygen.

Then slowly it dawned on me that I was drowning.

Dying slowly.

And for a moment I was tempted to drift off into its welcome arms that promised a release from this nightmare of pain and torment.

Another heaving retch, my body still trying to rid itself of the noxious

5

salt water before being swamped again in the curling racing foam. And somehow as I was drowning, courting death with a begging frenzy, I was also trying to gather my shattered wits and unravel the mystery of the moment.

'*A typical contradiction*', I could hear Julie's voice gently mocking me, as her face swam, undulating in the waves of my hallucination.

Sounds drifted back beyond the jackhammer. Soothing regular sweeping curls of breaking surf rolling past and a low thudding hum, counterpoint to my erratic gasps and intermittent coughs. A little closer to consciousness now, but still wrapped in a chaotic cocoon of noise and jumbled images.

Where? What? How? Vague memories just out of reach, snatched away on the wind.

Wind? Yes wind.

And water. Salt water.

The ocean.

If I could find the beginning, then I could work this out. Ravel some sense together and struggle out of this quicksand sucking me towards oblivion. I could feel death's hot acrid breath, the stench making me vomit again.

Trying to understand what had happened earlier, while drowning, were the ridiculous thoughts of a man preparing to die.

I shook my head and concentrated on the light and the dark mass that was pulling me slowly along. Instinct making me roll onto my back and feel for the half-inch nylon line that was attached to my harness. Hazy memories flickered; flashbacks that in some strange way anchored me to the present, helping me stay focused on the light.

When I saw the Bay-Cruiser in the San Carlos Marina for the first time, it was exactly as expected.

Forty-seven feet of flat bottom sit-at-the-dock and drink cocktails faux leather chintzy luxury. This boat would be a bitch in big seas, but at least the hull was strong and could cruise at seventeen knots in calm conditions. If there was anything approaching a storm I'd have to watch the rudder pintles as I'd found out when trying to cross the bar at Grays Harbor in

Oregon during less than perfect conditions in a similar boat. The pins had sheared and I'd steered with the engines alone, cursing through the spray and huge breaking seas that just wanted to pound the yacht into the rocks. It was sheer luck and anger rather than skill that got us through, and left me vowing never to set foot on another one of these again in my entire life. But there were reasons I was doing this now that had nothing to do with my love of the ocean.

The owner of this particular fibreglass ego-bucket was a tall man, obviously very wealthy, not because of the clean bronze tan, silk shirt and Armani sunglasses, but by his air of control, as if the world was his own personal playground. Having spent time on other people's multimillion-dollar yachts, I knew the type.

Hell, I was one of them with my own fifty-seven foot Fountaine Pajot Sanya catamaran.

He walked along the quay, stepped onto the transom swim platform and shook my hand with a firm dry grip. For a fleeting moment I thought that he looked more like someone who should own an upmarket expensive trawler type yacht, a Nordhavn 67 perhaps, instead of this piece-of-crap Bay-Cruiser. Tall, slim with a shock of grey hair and neat Van Dyke beard he looked like a European Archduke. Eyes almost impossibly blue, bright white teeth, handshake firm.

"Thomas Gunn no doubt. Good to meet you, I am Randolph Byron Moresby." Watching him step into the saloon I had the distinct impression he had never been on this boat before in his life. Again, just one of those old warrior insights.

"I'll be coming with you as far as Cabo San Lucas." He smiled, eyes remaining cold and disconcertingly direct.

"We'll be leaving in two days once I've checked the boat thoroughly," I replied easily.

Randolph Byron Moresby shook his head slowly, eyes never once leaving mine. "Tonight. We leave tonight. I have my jet waiting in Cabo and an important meeting to attend in New York." It wasn't a request.

Pushing a cart along the quay towards us was a middle-aged man with long lank sun bleached hair and a ragged beard, sweating in the heat of the day. Medium build with a slight beer paunch, he wore cowboy boots, a belt with a big brass buckle engraved with the initials 'CD' and a Stetson that looked ludicrous.

"Hola mi amigo ¿cómo estás? ¿Tomas Gunn?"

I stared at the man blankly as if I did not understand a word of Spanish. This may be Mexico but I wasn't going to play his stupid game.

"Hey apologies man, just kinda slip into the lingo when I'm in town. Chaz Duprés is the name. I'm your crew for the passage all the way to San Di..yea..go." The slow drawl completed the tacky caricature of a typical boat bum, but to my eye he just didn't seem to fit into the boating life at all. I'd been wrong before and would no doubt be wrong again, but there was a nagging feeling that he was going to be more trouble than he was worth. But I was here to follow Moresby, not worry about whatever motley crew his yacht management team had drafted for the passage.

I left Duprés to prepare the deck for passage and checked the engines. Within three hours we were motoring out of the bay into the Sea of Cortez in the late afternoon sunshine.

Randolph Byron Moresby sat on the settee at the aft end of the saloon, a sheaf of papers spread out across the table in front of him, reading steadily and making notations on a laptop. From my position in the galley I was able to study him without him being aware. He looked to be about fifty-six years old, fit and healthy and he carried an air of authority that some men have, that marks them as leaders. Next to his papers was an expensive bottle of Courvoisier L'Esprit Decanter Cognac, the glass in his hand, half full.

"Want a sandwich or anything?" I asked, helping myself from the galley fridge.

"No, thank you," he replied without looking up, fitting a small flash drive into the USB port. "Care for a glass?"

"Not while I'm working, thank you."

He nodded. "Good. If you'd have said yes I would have fired you, which would not have been a good idea as then I'd be stuck with that idiot you have for a first mate."

I left him alone and went back up into the pilothouse to find Chaz asleep in the skipper's chair, head lolling with the roll of the boat in the swell. I shook him awake as roughly as I could and felt like busting him in the mouth because sleeping on watch was the worst offence on a boat.

"Sleep when you're off watch. When you're up here you stay awake. Get it?"

He looked at me with a mixture of arrogance and dislike and stumbled from the chair, disappearing down the steps into the saloon. I could hear the muffled sound of voices above the dull roar of the diesels and the thud of waves as the Bay-Cruiser powered through the seas.

Settling into the Captain's seat, I took stock. So far the boat was steady with the autopilot keeping her on course. I watched as the seas continued to build, with a growing apprehension. I didn't like powerboats, I didn't trust powerboats and I'd be glad when the voyage was over.

Looking at the barometer I leaned forward and tapped the side, noticing that the pressure had changed a few millibars. A sure indication that very soon the conditions would be ripe for a chubasco.

I focused on pulling myself towards the black mass that I knew was my only hope of survival. Salt water filled my mouth every minute or two as the waves forced me under, but I kept pulling until I felt a solid surface. There was no time to feel a sense of achievement, for I knew I had to get onto that solid surface or die.

My bare feet felt the steel ladder dangling in the water, and my toes wrapped around the bars in an almost unbreakable desperate lock. But I had to unwrap them and climb, one steel bar at a time, until I could slide myself onto the roughened surface of the swim platform. Lying gasping for breath, spluttering every time another wave rolled across the transom. What had happened?

It was the quiet that woke me. No engine sound, just the slap of water against the hull. Staggering from the berth, I vaguely wondered how I'd got there. I felt as if I'd been on a boozing session for ten days straight and had to steady myself against the bulkhead in case I fell, as I unconsciously snapped on my safety harness. It was an automatic act from years of sailing. I waited for the nausea to pass, then went up into the saloon. It didn't seem right. I'd only had one beer and no Silver Patron chasers.

Something was very wrong.

Up two steps into the saloon and I could see the vague outline of someone who looked like Moresby, outside on the swim platform.

Suddenly he disappeared, falling off into the darkness. Lurching forward I stumbled and fell, struggled to my feet and staggered to the aft deck and the swim platform, clipping the safety line onto the padeye on the transom. I squinted into the darkness to catch any sight of the body, knowing it was futile in the utter darkness of the night.

Then everything went black as I was hit from behind. A familiar darkness that I'd experienced before.

The stern light stared at me unblinkingly. Even in my semiconscious state it was clear there was no one on board. As a delivery skipper, to have a passenger fall overboard was a career ender. To have two passengers fall overboard would be a full-scale criminal enquiry. I wasn't a delivery skipper by choice, but once again I wondered just who had set me up. What I did know was that my cover had been blown long before I boarded this piece of crap boat. And that created more questions that demanded answers.

Unconsciousness began to wash over me and yet somehow, instinctively, I dragged myself across the aft deck, through the open door into the saloon, and slammed the door shut behind me.

Then oblivion.

TWO

Three weeks earlier

The passage from the Mediterranean was fast, pushed along by the winds of a building hurricane system. We had detoured, spending a month idling in the Bahamas, followed by another fast sail across the Gulf of Mexico, a quick transit of the Panama Canal and yet another fast passage to Cabo San Lucas on the southerly tip of the Baja peninsula of Mexico, then a leisurely sail to La Paz.

After the Orange Moon business all I wanted to do was escape from the corrupt selfish cauldron of deceit our world had become, to the safe, comforting, secure place I knew it could be. I shrugged the feeling away. But the truth was, all I wanted to do was sail, dive, swim and enjoy my life. Baja was as good a place as any to drift into anonymity for a while with the woman I loved.

We dropped anchor and, after launching the Boston Whaler 110 Tender, motored across the harbour to present our papers to the Port Captain as a courtesy, even though we'd cleared into Mexico at Cabo. Capitan Ernesto Rodriguez stood as we entered and indicated seats opposite his desk. A tidily dressed, medium build, slim man in his late forties, with a shock of black hair, his smile was disarming, his pleasant manner tempered with a faint look of suspicion in his brown eyes.

"Welcome to La Paz."

"Gracias."

He studied the ship's papers, casting occasional glances at Julie who sat beautifully dressed in a casual yet immaculate white silk pantsuit, with a long sleeve top. I had persuaded her to leave the string of black pearls and black face Parmigiani Fleurier Toric Retrograde Perpetual Calendar watch in the safe. It was not a good idea to flaunt affluence at any time, and certainly not here in Baja. As a mark of respect to the Port Captain, I had also dressed up, something that few American cruising sailors thought to do.

"How long will you be staying, señor?" he asked quietly in perfect English.

"Through the summer. Three months, before we sail up to Santa Barbara."

"Most sailors come down here at that time."

I smiled easily. "We like to stay away from the crowds. Maybe next week or in a week or two we'll sail a little further up the coast. To Loreto perhaps."

"That is a wise decision. There is the possibility of a hurricane, señor. Costa Baja Marina is well protected, I myself have a boat there, but hurricanes are unpredictable."

"Gracias, Capitán. Seguiremos tus consejos."

He smiled at my Spanish, and nodded sagely, then stamped our passports and papers, issued the necessary permits and handed them back to me. "Disfrute de su visita a nuestro país. And if I can be of service in anyway, at any time, please do not hesitate to ask. My card." He stood, held out his business card, which I took, and shook my hand. He kissed the back of Julie's ceremoniously, and for a moment looked deeply into her eyes. "My wife thinks you are the most beautiful woman ever to grace the cover of Elle magazine, señorita. Which, I am unhappy to say, has cost me many pesos," he said laughingly. "She tells me to tell you that you are welcome in our home in Pichilingue. No doubt so that she may brag to the neighbours."

Julie laughed with him, enjoying the moment. "Gracias a su esposa para mí. Eso es muy bueno de ella. I am surprised she knew we were here."

"Gracias señorita, I will pass the message to her. And to answer your question, the Port Captain in Cabo San Lucas called me that you would be arriving."

We walked back to the whaler and slowly meandered back across the harbour to where *KOLOHE* was anchored. I had named her after the Hawaiian god Maui who was 'kolohe', meaning a mischievous rascal. It seemed to suit.

"You certainly made an impression on our Port Captain," I teased

Julie in sign. We'd had plenty of time on the voyage for me to pick up the rudimentaries.

"Best to keep on the good side of the authorities."

"Indeed."

Once aboard we 'upped' anchor and motored to Costa Baja Marina where our end-tie was waiting, as was the Dockmaster. Our rental car was ready and after securing *KOLOHE*, changing into casual shorts, tee-shirts and Tevas, we decided to drive to a palapa style restaurant on a beach nearby for a cheap early dinner instead of paying the exorbitant prices in the marina restaurant. I may be wealthy but $50 for a cup of coffee was absurd. We had better fresh coffee on board. To feel the hot late afternoon sun through the open roof was a delight. Julie lay back in the seat, eyes closed, savouring being on solid ground after two months at sea.

"My agent wants me to take the South African job," she said slowly, turning to watch my lips. I could see the anxious look in her eyes.

"When?"

"I leave in three days. Fly to LA, then Cape Town through London."

"Long trip. You could take the G550. Route through São Paulo."

"I want to spend a few days in London and see Dad before flying on," she said slowly. "Thought I'd travel incognito on my UK passport."

"Good idea." I paused and smiled, resting my hand on hers. "You need to go. You'll hate yourself if you don't."

"Patronising bastard," she said with a grin. "But I'll miss you every day."

"We can Skype."

"Yes we can."

"I'll let Paul know. Just in case..."

She nodded and we drove in silence, each knowing what the other was thinking. We wanted the past to be the past, but knew that was perhaps a wish too far.

The beach palapa style restaurant was exactly as I remembered. We dined cheaply on delicious fresh spicy jumbo shrimp on a bed of rice with a salad of avocado, corn, red bell pepper, jicama, diced tomatoes and crumbled feta cheese on a single Romaine lettuce leaf, complemented by a drizzle of honey-lime dressing. The taste was perfect, washed down with glasses of cold draught Baja Blond beer.

We ate, talked, laughed and let the past year drift away in the deep recesses of memory, but not without our ritual toast to Danny and our fallen friends. I missed my pal greatly, but I knew he'd just get pissed off if he thought we were self-indulgently bemoaning his loss, instead of getting on with our lives. After all, there was a sense of freedom now that Gunn Group Industries had ceased to exist, its assets 'disappeared' by the British Government. There was still the trust fund, which even if Radley knew about, he'd have a hard time getting his bureaucratic hands on.

Four days later and I was on my own. It was one of those sunny July days that you wish would never end. Surprisingly not too hot for this time of the year, with just enough breeze to keep the air circulating. And lazily floating in the warm waters of the Sea of Cortez, I felt as if I was lying in a bath.

You know what I mean, a perfect summer day that made life worth living.

All it needed was Julie to be here with me, but she wouldn't be back for two months. She was supposed to have had the operation on the damaged bones in her ears but was, to my mind, unreasonably reluctant and took the South African job instead.

The wind had freshened over the last few days, so I took Captain Rodriguez's advice, and sailed the catamaran up the peninsula towards Loreto, anchoring close to Morgan's ranch in the lee of a small rocky island that looked as if it belonged on Mars when the planet had water. The yacht would be far enough from the ravages of a hurricane here, or so I hoped. Morgan was also away on an assignment, so I was left to my own devices, secreted away where I thought nobody could possibly reach me and the oncoming hurricane would ignore me.

Of course when you have modern satellite communications, there is no way to remain a recluse unless you've switched off the system. I hadn't because I was waiting for my daily Skype from Julie. Usually she called around 2200hrs Baja time just as she was having early breakfast in her hotel, but today she was on a night shoot so we had arranged an earlier time.

It had been another lazy day swimming, cleaning the catamaran, and as the sun dipped behind the Baja peninsula, I cracked a cold Baja Blond and contemplated a meal of barbecued mahi-mahi with a simple tomato and avocado salad. Then the familiar sound of the Skype tone called softly.

"Hi sweetheart," I said as Julie's face peered at me from Cape Town.

"How's everything on the other side of the planet?"

"Quiet. I dropped anchor about three miles from Morgan's ranch by a small island." I carried the iPad mini through to the cockpit, switched to the back camera and panned across the stunning landscape as the sun set casting shadows across the island peak.

"Gorgeous."

I switched back to the front camera. "How's the shoot going?"

"Tedious, as always. Every time I say 'never again'..."

"...and every time you do it anyway."

She shrugged and grinned. "It's a living. And it's fun. Some of the time. Besides what else would I do? Laze around with a filthy rich boat bum?"

"There could be worse things." It was a stupid thing to say as I saw Julie's eyes cloud over for a moment. Sometimes I just wished I could keep my big stupid mouth shut.

"Guess so. Could be a boat bum on a dinghy," she laughed, banishing the momentary vividly unwanted memories of 'worse things'.

We continued chattering for another twenty minutes before she was called to the set, blew me a kiss and signed off.

These brief moments every day were bittersweet. While we talked and laughed it was as if we were in another world. And after we signed off, we were back in our own solitude with the feeling of sudden loneliness.

'Holy Mother of Mary pull your head out your arse. You could have gone with her.' I heard Danny's voice in my head and turned around, half expecting to see him lying back on the cockpit settee with a glass of Jameson.

"Fuck you, Danny," I shouted across the water, laughed and tapped the Pandora app on the iPad, selected Erik Satie, and relaxed as the beautifully delicate music of his composition Trois Gymnopédie floated across the deserted anchorage, thinking back to the small 'snug' off Danny's kitchen in his London house where we would relax after one of our adventures.

Inner reflection tinged with sadness does little to lighten the mood, so I shrugged off my innate Anglo Saxon melancholy, and set about preparing my dinner in the peace of the warm summer evening.

Nothing lasts forever. A stupid cliché that fitted the moment when my burn phone rang. I'd forgotten I even had it, or that it was switched on. Then I remembered that I had used it to call Morgan during the voyage as we approached Baja. It was still in the locker in the cockpit where I'd stowed it after our last conversation. The battery was low.

"Thomas. Thomas can you hear me?"

"Morgan?"

"I need your help."

Last December seemed a lifetime ago and images of Morgan helping me through my injuries jumped into my mind at the sound of her voice.

"Of course, what's up?"

"I need you to call Roshan for me." Her voice, usually so calm, strong and confident, was edgy. Fearful. "You know the number. Let him know where I am. It's important Thomas. Please."

"Okay," I answered slowly, the hairs standing up on the back of my neck. Another cliché but equally as true. "What's this all about?"

"I'll see you tomorrow night, ten o'clock..." Then the line went dead. There was no answer when I called her back, just the usual cheerful greeting and invitation to leave a message on her voicemail. Cut off as the battery on the burn phone died.

I knew that her job as an financial investigative journalist meant she often pissed off some embezzling banker or Ponzi scheme fraudster, who then decided to repay her journalistic diligence with threatening phone calls and late night visits from hired help. But what niggled in the back of my mind was whether her call for help had any connection with what I had asked her do a few months ago before we left the UK after the Orange Moon affair. I had asked her to check into the Griffin Trust, an outfit in Atlanta Georgia who had been involved with the International Security and Economic Council and a certain Ted Lieberman. When she returned from her current assignment she was going to fill me in on the details.

During the short conversation she had not told me where she was, just given me a cryptic clue as to where I might find out. Roshan was the name of her Arab stallion, so no way was he going to answer a phone call. My thoughts of a cold Baja Blond beer and barbecue tuna were going to have to wait.

Fate had cast me in a role I didn't want, but felt obligated to fulfil.

Julie and I owed our lives to her, so within two minutes I had a small Beretta tucked into the waistband of my pants at the small of my back with a spare clip in my pocket, and was powering *KOLOHE's* whaler towards the beach where Morgan and I drank to each other and said our goodbyes before I flew to Ireland seeking revenge so many months ago. Now, as darkness crept across the land and a new moon rose on the other side of the Sea of Cortez, Morgan was the one in trouble and I felt a sickening dread crawl around in the pit of my stomach.

Cutting the engine fifty metres from the beach I let the whaler quietly drift to shore, stepped out and took the anchor up the beach and wrapped the line around a torote tree before digging it into the soil. Leaving enough scope now the tide was falling so the tender could float in the shallow water and not be stranded. I didn't want to worry about having to try and drag it back into the water if I needed to leave in a hurry. I could see the outline of the house and to the right thirty metres beyond it, the stables partially hidden by low mesquite bushes, prickly pear cactus and torote trees that grew all around the property. But it was the momentary sweeping beam of a flashlight across the window of the study that caught my eye.

There are those moments when adrenaline floods through your body in anticipation and the urge to pee is strong, but it quickly disappears as deep seated training takes over, and the 'flight' response is rapidly replaced by 'fight'. There is a comfort, even a sense of excited

17

anticipation to enter the arena and defeat the enemy. For I knew instinctively that whoever was inside Morgan's house was not a friend.

The flashlight flickered again, telling me that the intruders were not concerned that anyone would see them. The nearest ranch was half a mile away, hidden behind a low ridge. I had to consider that there were at least two intruders so as to be prepared for any circumstance.

Closing on your target is a game of patience and stealth. A game I had played many times, some successful, others not. But I had an advantage of knowing the layout of the house and property intimately, and was banking on the intruders having to guess in their search for whatever it was they were hunting. The glimpses of flashlight told me they weren't as professional as they perhaps thought they were. I brushed the thought from my mind. Assuming would get me killed.

With the new moon behind me, I carefully circled around through the rough terrain and cactus until I was inland before approaching the house. That meant using the stables as cover. Roshan whinnied softly as I approached, then quietened as I let myself in through the back door and gently rubbed his nose. He nodded his head as if in understanding, and watched as I quickly made my way out through the front and circled around to approach the house from the west, pulling the silenced Beretta from my waistband. The intruders' Lexus SUV was parked in front of the deck as if they knew there was nobody home.

It was a good sign. They were far too comfortable and not expecting company.

That thought was almost my undoing.

I hadn't seen the driver hunkered down in his seat until almost too late. He was short, partially hidden by the headrest, so it wasn't until I was almost abreast the door, that I saw him the instant he saw me in the rear view mirror. He was dead before he had time to react, slumping sideways in the seat as the silenced 9mm round tore a hole in his temple, the suppressed Ingram MAC-10 machine pistol slipping from his dead hands. I slipped the Beretta back into my waistband and picked up the MAC-10, checked the magazine and saw it was full of subsonic 0.45 rounds, the right match for the suppressor. It was US military specification and a good close combat weapon, if somewhat inaccurate. In fully automatic mode you'd run through a thirty-two round magazine in less than five seconds.

Silenced weapons are good, but there is always the possibility that in the absolute quiet of the night, somebody might just hear it for what it was, and I couldn't take any chances. The MAC-10 suppressor worked very well. The bolt made more noise than the bullet.

I slipped off my deck shoes and carried them in my left hand so that the rubber soles didn't make any noise on the finished wooden floor inside the house. The front door was open and the flashlight beam flickered again as whoever it was moved from the study to the bedroom.

Lying in the hall was a body. I knelt down and felt for a pulse. There was none. A shaft of moonlight bathed the face of the dead man.

It was the doctor who, along with Morgan, had saved my life and repaired my broken body. While she was away, he would have been house sitting and taking care of the horses. Anger and sorrow fought for prominence, and I took a deep breath, forcing the emotions down and concentrating on the task at hand. I laid my shoes down next to the Doc's body.

My bare feet barely made a sound as I slipped down the hallway and crept towards Morgan's open bedroom door. The flashlight beam flickered across the floor and I could hear the intruder going through the shelves in Morgan's built-in wardrobe. I knew she kept a fireproof lock-box there, and heard the sound of it being pulled off the shelf and placed on the floor.

Two rounds from the MAC-10 hit the wardrobe door three inches from the intruder's head.

"Move and the next one goes through your brain," I whispered.

The intruder was smaller than I had imagined, then I realised it was a woman. On the floor beside her gloved right hand lay a Glock 9mm, which she had to lay down before lifting the lock-box off the shelf.

I moved forward quickly while she was still disoriented, and hit her behind the left ear with the butt of the MAC-10. She crumpled to the floor without a sound. From my experiences in Afghanistan with women suicide bombers, I knew that gender was no discriminator when it came to violence, and some of the worst offenders are women.

Hitting a woman is not something that I make a habit of; in fact I have an innate hatred of violence to women. But this one had a gun, and guns have only one purpose.

To kill.

And I wasn't going to end up dead.

I could have just shot her, but I needed to know why she was searching Morgan's house. What I already knew was that whatever she had been looking for wasn't in the house, it was in the stables with Roshan.

Her body was light but well muscled, as I found out when I picked her up and sat her in a chair by the window. Using the laces from her army style 'jump-boots' I tied her arms and legs to the chair then went back through the house, checking the rooms and retrieving my shoes.

Outside I searched through the Lexus. As I suspected the car was 'clean'. No registration document in the empty glove box and the lifeless driver had no identification, just several hundred US dollars in his wallet and about seven thousand pesos.

The GPS, however, provided a complete history of the SUV's travels over the past week, starting in San Diego, travelling north to a private residence in Santa Barbara, then a circuitous route around the east of Los Angeles to the border crossing point between Calexico in California and Mexicali in Baja. And then down to Morgan's ranch. My guess was that the vehicle had been stolen in San Diego and they had used an established route to bring it across the border. No doubt the Lexus would end up as the prized possession of a Mexican police or customs official. But I did wonder who they had to pay in Calexico to smooth the way. The GPS also yielded an address in Santa Barbara.

Back in the house, the woman was coming to as I returned. The light from the bedside lamp shone on her face. A trickle of drying blood ran down the back of her ear, matted her mousy brown hair and stained the collar of the white T-shirt she wore beneath the black jacket. I guessed her age at early thirties, and judging by the cautious but fearless expression in her grey/green eyes, this was not her first mission. Her full lips were partly open and the only thing that marred the beauty of her classic high cheekbones and strong chin was a fleshy slightly flattened nose. She didn't look Mexican, more East European with a touch of Asian and a vague recollection stirred at the back of my mind.

"Just what is it you're looking for?" I asked quietly, sitting on the edge of the bed and watching her as she gently tested the strength of my knots. Her eyes momentarily flickered to the Glock that still lay on the floor where she'd left it, and then back to my face.

"Who's asking?" Her voice was low and husky, gravelly almost. American accented with that hint of an East European inflection. Her eyes gave nothing away.

"The guy with the guns."

She shrugged slightly, looked away to the window and then stiffened as the telltale red dot of a laser sight reflected in the glass and centred on her forehead.

A split second before the window glass shattered, I kicked over the chair, sending her over backwards, the bullet catching her in the upper chest as the shooter adjusted aim. I thrust the MAC-10 through the broken window and emptied the magazine into the night.

It was over in moments. Pausing just to see if the woman was alive, I dived out of the smashed window and sprinted towards where I had seen the flash of the rifle barrel beside the stables. By the time I reached the gunman's position, Roshan was stamping in his stall and whinnying in terror. The rounds from the MAC-10 had peppered the wooden wall, and I could see a blood trail leading away towards the beach. Not stopping to check whether I had hit Roshan, I ran in pursuit. By the volume of blood, I guessed the shooter was not expecting such a swift reaction and had been in the open, trusting in the darkness.

The moon had risen high in the sky and bathed the land in a soft glow, enough to see the trail of blood. Ahead I could hear the shooter crashing into the cactus and mesquite, followed by a heavy thud and the sound of a person gasping for air.

By the time I reached him, he was barely conscious, bleeding out through the wound to his femoral artery. How he'd managed to run this far was surprising. Even more surprising was that I'd hit him at all. He stared up at me, tried to raise the VSS Vintorez silenced sniper rifle

- the preference of Russian Special Forces - gasped one last time and sighing, lay back and died. There was no identification on the body, so I took a photo of his face. The rifle's serial number had been ground off. A forensic lab could potentially recover it, but given the circumstances I couldn't make that happen, so I left the rifle with the body. The Policia Federal Preventiva (Federales) were going to have a lot of fun figuring out this mess.

What had started out as a wonderful day in paradise was ending like one of my constant nightmares.

Roshan had quietened down by the time I returned to the stable. He hadn't been hit with any of my wildly fired rounds from the MAC-10, and I breathed a sigh of relief, patted him gently, made soothing sounds to calm him and returned to the house.

The silence was deafeningly surreal in the silvery moonlight. Shooting stars arched through the night sky oblivious to the death below. Torote trees standing in rustling accusation with the slight breeze that blew across the peninsula from the Pacific.

It hadn't been a good night for the woman in the bedroom. First I'd slugged her and then she'd been hit in the upper chest by the round fired from the Vintorez rifle. I leaned down and picked her up, still strapped to the chair. She moaned and her eyes rolled as she fought to recover her senses. I tore open her jacket and gently cut open her T-shirt uncovering the wound. There was no exit wound, so the bullet had either exploded inside her, or ricocheted around and lodged somewhere only a surgeon could find. On her neck was a small tattoo of a butterfly.

I went back to the living room where I had spied the Doc's medical bag. He never went anywhere without it.

There was not a lot I could do except clean and bind the wound to stop the bleeding. And to be perfectly honest, I didn't much care about the woman's imminent death, just needed her alive long enough to answer some questions.

I hated that cold callous part of myself that extreme violence brought to the surface, but shrugged away the thought and sat down on the bed, cracked open a vial of ammonium carbonate and waved it beneath her nose. It would only be effective for a short time. She breathed in sharply, gasped and opened her eyes, panting rapidly.

"Why?" she asked, staring at me uncomprehendingly.

"I don't know. Maybe somebody doesn't want you talking. I need answers."

"This wasn't supposed to happen."

"No doubt, but I need to know who sent you."

"We don't get names, just the contract."

"From the house in Santa Barbara?"

Her eyes slid up to mine, alarm showing for the first time. "What do you know?"

"Your driver should have reset the GPS, or at least disconnected it."

"Who are you?"

"They didn't tell you? My name is Thomas Gunn."

She nodded slowly. "I heard about you." She tried to laugh but coughed instead. "The contract was to search the house and take out everyone who was here." She coughed again, this time blood flecking her lips and I knew her lung was punctured. She wheezed and her eyes started to close. I waved the vial under her nose and she snapped back to consciousness.

"So it was a hit," I asked roughly.

"We don't ask questions. Just carry out orders."

"You were expendable."

"He was probably aiming at you."

"The laser dot was on your forehead, not mine. You're a liability." I walked over, retrieved the Glock and smelled the barrel. It had been fired. I popped out the magazine and pushed down on the bullets. There was room for one more. "The man you killed was the only doctor for fifty miles. Now the local children will have no medical care."

"I don't care, it was a job," she repeated, coughed again and I could see she was fading fast.

"You're dying. You might want to think about talking. Perhaps help someone for once."

A weak smile flickered on her bloody lips as her eyes started to glaze. "I don't care about anyone."

"Nor does Marika Keskküla," I said deliberately, playing a hunch.

Her eyes snapped back into focus and I knew I was right. My stomach turned over in realisation that the danger Julie and I thought we had left behind was still with us. An ever-present spectre looming over our lives.

"She is too smart for you, Thomas Gunn. You..." she coughed again and flopped back in the chair, the spark from her eyes fading rapidly. "...are as dead as me." Blood gushed from her mouth and nose with her last breath.

I cut the laces off her wrists, laid the Glock in her dead hand and left the MAC-10 on the floor beside the chair. Then smeared some of her blood on the edge of the chest of drawers, as if she'd hit her head as she fell after being shot. Not very convincing in a thorough investigation, but from a cursory look the Federales might put it down to a drug deal gone wrong. It would buy me time to get to wherever I needed to be tomorrow night, before anyone thought to look for someone other than a drug dealer.

It took me an hour to find what I was looking for in Roshan's stable. Of course Morgan had given me the clue in our phone conversation, and had hidden the note in plain sight where only a child would see it; not some suspicious adult who was thinking of the safest and most devious of hiding places. The 'thing' out-of-place was an import licence for Roshan, which Morgan had partially tucked behind the nameplate on his stable door. It caught my attention because I knew her horses were bred locally in Baja at a well-respected stable. I carefully removed the paper from the door and unfolded it. There was enough light from the moon to see there was an address in East Los Angeles written on the back, a phone number and an odd doodle which I couldn't make out. I took a photo with my encrypted satellite phone.

Morgan had known she was heading into trouble before she left, and I silently shouted at her for not telling me earlier. My male ego rising to the front and cursing the women in my life who just went and did stuff they were ill equipped to handle.

Or so I thought.

Then I remembered the look in Julie's eyes as she shot Hamish.

But I was still very uneasy, especially because of tonight's episode.

After carefully checking through the house and grounds to make sure I hadn't left any clues that could identify me, including footprints from my bare feet, I took a circuitous route back to the beach. It took another fifteen minutes to sweep any signs of my presence from the sand using my T-shirt and a mesquite branch. I then retrieved the anchor and paddled the whaler about a mile offshore before starting the engine and slowly making my way back to *KOLOHE*.

At this time of year during the off-season, there were very few cruisers in the Gulf and none within a hundred kilometres of where the catamaran was anchored. And as this wasn't a great fishing location, there were no pangas anywhere to be seen either.

Even though the night was warm, with only a slight breeze, I shivered as the adrenaline dissipated from my blood stream. The after effects of the action gripping my body and soul.

Violence was an unwelcome part of my nature.

A part I didn't want.

A part I tried desperately to banish to the deep recesses of my psyche. There was so much beauty in the world and yet I seemed to be embroiled in the ugly desolation of Man's baser nature. But moaning about my situation wasn't going to help Morgan. There was a time limit and I had to get to Loreto and catch a flight to Los Angeles by late tomorrow afternoon.

KOLOHE sat calmly at anchor, stunningly sleek in the moonlight, a welcoming sanctuary from the madness of the last few hours.

Once aboard with the tender stowed and the fake import license tucked away in the 'secret' safe in the false wall behind my clothes in the cabin locker, I retrieved my secure phone, entered the address and number that Morgan had left for me, started the engines, raised the anchor, and set course for Loreto one hundred and sixty kilometres to the north. It was just before midnight and at a steady pace I figured I would make the sleepy Spanish-style town by midday.

It was the start of the mahi-mahi fishing season and as I powered north, I knew I would encounter the sport fishing vessels that ventured forth from Loreto as a precursor to the main fishing tournament set to begin in July. I turned north-east so that when I encountered the first boats, they would report that I was approaching from the east. Just another detail to avoid being placed near Morgan's ranch when the bodies were eventually discovered.

Sailing alone on a yacht in the middle of the night allows too much time for inner reflection.

I watched Julie lying on the cockpit settee, curled up on her side, long blonde hair cascading across the pillow as the light from the rising sun slowly bathed the ocean with a light orange glow, that gradually lightened to another glorious day. I wondered if she knew just how deeply I loved her. Something that I always seemed completely incapable of expressing.

"I can feel your eyes on me again Thomas," she murmured without opening her eyes, a slight smile playing on her lips.

"Nothing else to look at except water."

"Thanks for the compliment."

"I'll rephrase. There is nothing as beautiful as watching you sleep."

"Too late. You should have said that the first time." The smile broadened, but her eyes stayed closed. She had recovered about forty percent of her hearing, and if there was no loud ambient noise she could hear me speaking. Her surgeon had said that it wouldn't get any better than it was without the operation, but she stubbornly held to the belief that she would recover in time.

"Condemned by my own words."

"Indeed." She stretched, opened her eyes and looked out across the calm sea as we sailed comfortably at ten knots. "Mmmm. I smell coffee."

"I'll get it, you relax. Your watch starts in thirty minutes."

"Slave driver."

"Right. I let you sleep an extra hour and that's the thanks I get."

"I deserve all the sleep I can get after everything you've put me through," she teased with a laugh that was only half in jest.

"We have a saying in the army..."

"I know. Never volunteer for anything."

I leaned down, kissed her gently and went to the galley where the coffee roaster was just finishing its cycle. I ground the freshly roasted beans, poured them into the percolator basket, and set it on the stove.

"What do you want to eat," I shouted. There was no reply, so I went back into the cockpit and shouted again.

Julie turned lazily. "The usual. Parma ham and melon."

The memory stirred in my mind and I looked at the cockpit settee half expecting Julie to be there. Emotions were dangerous. A distraction when I needed all my attention focused on finding Morgan, knowing that I was already knee deep in the shit again, with three bodies on my conscience and seething rage at the needless murder of the Doc.

Contradictions abounded.

I didn't want to be forced back into the underbelly of a violent society, where murky individuals and devious agendas boiled beneath a seemingly civilised surface.

Some men are born killers. Some are trained killers and some have killing thrust upon them.

I still didn't know into which category I fitted.

The maudlin reflections weren't getting me anywhere, so I grabbed a Baja Blond from the cockpit fridge, downed it quickly and reached for another bottle. As I have already said, days alone at sea gave too much time for disturbing internal doubts.

Loreto is one of those idyllic sleepy towns that you imagine when yearning of a holiday away from the hustle and bustle of life. The truth, however, was a little different.

At this time of year the loud obnoxious sport fishermen from Southern California descended upon the town and small marina, intent on bagging the biggest and best mahi-mahi, sailfish, marlin or tuna in the Sea of Cortez. Earlier in the year it was yellow tail amberjack and roosterfish. To me, Loreto had turned into a tourist trap with a golf resort and panga rides to the islands. Understandable in a modern global economy, but it spoiled the quintessentially Mexican feel of the town with its ancient cave paintings, old Spanish architecture and stunning coastline.

On this day however, none of that mattered as I steered *KOLOHE* into the marina and went to see the Port Captain, presented my credentials, gave him Capitan Rodriguez's regards and let him know I had to travel to the USA for business for a few weeks. For someone who craved anonymity, I was making myself very visible. I'd managed to book an afternoon flight to Los Angeles and pondered whether to call Julie, wake her up and tell what was going on, then decided against it. She was busy and worrying about me would be a distraction she didn't need.

THREE

Driving a battered rental car from Rent-a-Wreck and dressed in a tatty baseball cap and clothes I'd bought at a thrift store, I hoped I'd blend into the background of seedy East Los Angeles. It is no place to be at night, especially alone and Caucasian, and I missed not having my trusty Glock; the price of having to fly on a commercial airline and not my personal Cessna Mustang 510 which, having been refitted with long range fuel tanks, was being delivered by a couple of Paul's friends to Phoenix airport in Arizona, where I figured it would be reasonably inconspicuous as part of a corporate jet leasing company that Julie's father, Professor Oldfield, had set up. I'd also arranged for him to buy an MD-902 Explorer similar to the one Julie and I had crashed.

What can I say? I liked the way it flew.

This one had two passenger seats removed making it a six seater, and an extra fuel tank added to give it a 450nm range, plus some extras like free-fall parachutes and emergency survival gear. Who exactly owned the aircraft was buried in the mind-boggling paperwork of offshore corporations and blind trusts.

I didn't like Los Angeles at the best of times, but at night the frantic polluted city took on a different tone, seeming more like a Middle East war zone than a modern developed American city. It was here in the gang-controlled ghettos where the comparison between the poor and the super wealthy came into stark contrast. The dividing lines could be as simple as from one side of the street to the other.

Gangbanger cars prowled the darkness full of young men without hope whose sole purpose was to kill. Drugs proliferated and the Mexican cartels held sway in the dingy darkness. The Global Financial Crisis didn't affect the people here, only their middle class neighbours who stared from their over mortgaged homes in fear of ending up in the ghetto. Police sirens wailed and helicopters flew overhead as occasional gunshots echoed through the dirty dark dry heat of the summer night.

'What on earth was Morgan doing down here?' I wondered. *'And what did a seedy Latino ghetto have to do with international high finance?'* More questions than answers.

A black 1955 Chevy Bel Air low rider cruised up beside me, and the young wispy moustached passenger looked across, daring a confrontation. I knew that he probably had a MAC-10 on his lap. I drove as if they weren't there. After a minute they accelerated down the street, bouncing the front suspension up and down on hydraulic rams. There was something unsettling about their appearance and in the rear view mirror I saw another low rider following.

It was a trap.

I slammed into the back of the black Chevy as it braked hard. Tried to reverse but was pinned in by the low rider behind. Running wasn't an option as the gangbangers spilled out of their cars and surrounded me, handguns and MAC-10s levelled. A couple of them looked out-of-place, more Caucasian than Latino, with a military style about them. The leader, a short wiry man in his late twenties, indicated for me to get out.

There are times in your life when you just know you're going to die.

This was one of them, and it made me angry.

"¿Qué diablos está sucediendo?" I shouted as loudly and aggressively as I could muster.

"Chill güey. Get in the car." He indicated the low rider and moved aside to allow me past. With guns levelled at me this was no time to argue.

Within moments I was sandwiched between two gangbangers who stared at me expressionlessly. In less than two minutes we pulled up to a sleazy rundown block of apartments in a lightless street.

"Out," commanded the leader and led the way with a flashlight, followed by two of his henchmen while the others stayed outside.

Sweat trickled down my back and I felt the hairs on the back of my neck standing up, convinced that this was where I was going to meet my end. I followed the man into one of the buildings. He stopped, turned to me, pointed down the darkened hallway and handed me his flashlight.

Morgan lay at the bottom of the stairs of the derelict fourplex. A pale, twisted, semi-naked caricature, her bare arms bent at impossible angles framing her head, a surprised expression on her face. Not angry, not frightened, just surprised. A politely bored surprise. As if I'd just told her that the price of soya beans had risen a couple of cents. Close by lay two East European looking men, each shot at point blank range in the back of the head.

Morgan was still alive, barely, looking up at me in confusion. Her expression cleared as I gently cradled her head and she smiled. Tears started in her eyes, then she whispered something I didn't catch. I bent down with my ear close to her mouth.

"Hal Gordon," she said distinctly. "Julie." Her voice trailed away to a whisper and she stared into my eyes urgently struggling to speak as blood burst from her mouth. "Bottom... Lost... track..." but she never finished the sentence and died, falling limp in my arms with a gentle sigh, and I felt my world crumble amid the trash and debris of a violent city falling apart at the seams.

In the distance police sirens wailed, rapidly closing in on us, but I wasn't going to leave her alone like some rejected piece of garbage.

"We go," the leader said as the sirens grew closer.

"Who did this?"

He shrugged. "Morgan say you to find out." He started to leave, stopped and looked back at me. "She was friend to me, Tomas. Find out."

"Who are you? How do you know my name?"

He smiled without humour. "Some people call us 'the Mexican Mafia'. I am called 'El Cobra Poco' by the Federales. It means 'The Little Cobra'. Not a very flattering name. Morgan tell me about you. She say you are to be trusted. Me, I trust nobody, but she was different. Betray her legacy and you betray me."

"She was my friend. Family."

"If you do not come with us, the police will take you. Then maybe the people who kill Morgan will kill you." He turned his head as the police sirens drew closer, then looked back at me.

"I'm not leaving her," I said emphatically.

He stared at me for a moment and nodded. "If you are alive by Friday, call me," he said quietly and pulled up his sleeve to reveal a tattoo that I was sure I'd seen before. "Someone tried to enter your boat in Loreto this evening. Without us you will never be safe. "¿Me explico?" He waited until I nodded that I understood his meaning perfectly clearly.

"Buena," he said and walked calmly away into the frenzied clamour of the Los Angeles night. Strangely, he and I were not so dissimilar. We both had a code, albeit different, but that code established a set of rules, which were precise and uncompromising. We understood trust and loyalty, and the penalties for breaking either.

I held Morgan in my arms and wondered again what she had been doing with the Mexican Mafia and why. The tattoo on El Cobra Poco's arm was the same as the doodle on the back of Roshan's fake import licence.

The Los Angeles Sheriff's Department, under whose jurisdiction East Los Angeles falls, is not renowned for being gentle with prisoners. Especially prisoners they suspect of being murderers. By the time I reached the East Los Angeles Station, I was pretty bruised and battered.

Two deputies sat in front of me in an interrogation room, contempt written all over their faces. I wondered if they were members of the infamous LASD gang 'The 3,000 Boys' or the offshoot, 'The Jump-Out Boys', whose beatings of prisoners were well documented. Violence and crime seemed to tinge every aspect of Los Angeles, from police brutality to corrupt city councillors and ruthless business people. What concerned me most was that this didn't look like a normal Sheriff's interrogation room. Not that I had first hand knowledge of the inside of a Sheriff's cell block before, but I had no doubt it was an interrogation room. Just not one to which 'normal' prisoners were brought. There didn't seem to be any cameras or recording equipment, and there were stains on the walls and floor I took to be blood.

"Your name is Thomas Gunn?" The deputy I took to be the senior of the two spoke roughly.

"You know it is. You have my passport. And I think I get a phone so I can call my lawyer."

They both sneered at me.

"Do you know the deceased?"

"I did. She was a friend."

"Piss you off did she? That why you killed her?"

"No. And no. And I want a lawyer."

"Get smart with me and I'll bust your mouth wide open," he growled and I could see he was itching to beat on me. "Why did you kill her?"

"I didn't. She called me and wanted to meet."

"In East LA. On that street?"

"That's right."

"Bullshit."

"No again." I could see I was getting to him by keeping my voice low, matter-of-fact, my manner calm and unthreatened.

"Admit you killed her."

"I didn't. And again, what don't you understand about *'I want a lawyer'*," I said and smiled.

It was the smile that did it.

He came across the table and slammed my chair over backwards, the handcuffs slicing the skin on my wrists as I hit the floor. Then he was kicking me in the stomach and back, I was half conscious before I heard the interrogation room door bang open, and loud voices.

Then I must have blacked out, for when I came to I was lying on a bed in a cell. The door was open and a black suited man, who I took to be in his early fifties, sat patiently watching me from the corner. He was slightly overweight with thinning sandy hair and grey blue eyes. The rimless glasses gave him the air of a doctor regarding a patient.

"My name is Robert Sutherland," he began in a soft but assertive voice. "You are Thomas Gunn, former British Special Forces Operations Group Officer and you're in a shit load of trouble."

"Pleased to meet you too. I think I prefer the goons, at least their brutality is honest. They're dumb and don't know any better." I stared at the two deputies who stood outside the cell itching to have another go at me.

Sutherland raised his eyebrows, perhaps a little taken aback at my comment considering the precariousness of my position.

"You're everything your file says you. Arrogant and uncooperative."

"That's all?" Just how he got hold of my file was food for thought. And the immediate thought was Radley. "I guess Jonathan didn't give you the entire scoop." I used Radley's first name to judge Sutherland's reaction. There was a momentary flicker in his otherwise expressionless eyes.

"The DA wants to charge you with First Degree Murder with Special Circumstances. A capital offence in California."

"But something tells me that isn't going to happen. Is it?" I countered, thinking fast. If my instincts were right, Radley was deeply involved in whatever was about to happen to me.

I was being played.

Again.

"You have dual nationality, so as a US citizen you are entirely in our hands, Mr Gunn." He smiled coldly.

"You have to love the Land-of-the-Free."

"Freedom comes with a price."

"Undoubtedly. And you're about to collect. But just who are you collecting from and why?" I paused and watched him carefully. There was a quietness about him that was faintly disturbing. He wasn't fazed by my stare and looked back unblinkingly. Then he did something that surprised the hell out of me.

His eyes flickered upwards briefly in warning and his lips pursed ever so slightly. If you weren't paying careful attention, you'd miss the tiny sign that told me to not say anything that might be picked up by the camera and microphone hidden somewhere in the walls or ceiling.

"The woman you are accused of killing was working for my department. That means you are under my jurisdiction."

"So you're a Fed." I lay back on the bed. "Say what you've come here to say, Sutherland. I didn't kill anyone."

"Perhaps you did. Perhaps you didn't." He stood and walked from the cell. "I'm having you transferred into my custody in the morning."

"Don't I get a phone call?" I shouted to deaf ears.

The cell door slammed shut and the deputies gritted their teeth, obviously under direct orders not to touch me. If Radley was involved then I had a certain level of safety, but as Sutherland indicated, that would come at a price.

There is something so totally desolate about sitting in a prison cell staring at the blank grey walls that, unless you've experienced it, you'll never understand. There is a finality and hopelessness that is almost beyond comprehension. A despair that sucks at your soul. My salvation was that I knew that my stay here was going to be short-lived, but what the future held was one big question mark. I had the distinct feeling somebody had put a ring in my nose and was leading me on a mystery tour with more questions than answers.

Left alone with just the usual sounds of dissatisfied inmates, clinking keys and slamming doors for company, I thought back to the frantic last few days.

Confusion would be an apt description of my state of mind.

What facts could I scramble together?

Several dead bodies at Morgan's ranch.

A small but ruthless Mexican Mafia gangbanger with the unlikely nickname of 'El Cobra Poco', who seemed as if he could be a strange ally.

And the mysterious Robert Sutherland.

What other questions remained?

There were many, starting with who would have wanted to kill Morgan? Everything went back to my request for her to investigate the financial dealings of the Griffin Trust and its Chairman Ted Lieberman.

How was the Mexican Mafia involved, if what Sutherland said about Morgan working for him was true?

I could just lie here all night long and create imaginary scenarios, but that wouldn't supply any answers, so I closed my eyes and concentrated on emptying my mind.

Sleep was what I needed.

It must have been two hours after the jail cell lights went out, that the goons came for me. Dragged me off the bed and frog marched me down the corridor to the back of the jail and down narrow stairs to a basement garage without saying a word. There was a nondescript cream coloured painter's van waiting with the rear doors open, and I was unceremoniously bundled inside. The goons climbed in the front seat.

I spotted the tail about ten minutes into the journey. A couple of guys in a late fifties Rambler station wagon. The goons had spotted it too, and the driver took a couple of exploratory turns. The Rambler stayed on our tail.

We stopped at traffic lights on Pico and La Brea and the Rambler pulled up two cars behind. The lights turned green and we stayed put. The '89 Corvette behind gave a couple of blasts to move forward but the goon driving the van didn't move. The lights changed to amber and the Corvette driver was turning purple with rage. On red we shot across the street leaving the Corvette, a BMW and the Rambler impotent at the red light.

Without my phone and the moving map display I was lost in the myriad of tiny roads that crisscrossed the hills, winding amongst the houses crammed into the area. Older Spanish style built on flat lots whilst modern houses clung tenaciously to vertical lots, some cantilevered out into space tempting fate and the laws of gravity. Anything for a view across the smoggy city.

Big billboards normally advertising the latest blockbuster movies now carried smiling photos of the Los Angeles Mayoral candidates.

A pudgy faced balding white man, JT Purdue, who promised a return to fiscal responsibility and *'cares about the People of the City of Angels'* and a moustached Latino Carlos Santos, who *'cares about Angelinos'*.

Sprinklers flickered across lush green lawns and palm trees swayed gently in the pre-dawn breeze. Sultry hot days heralding the Santa Ana's, the 'Demon Winds', that stirred dust and garbage, screeched through canyons and blew trucks over on the freeways. And sand whirlwinds mixed with brush fire smoke as the sun blazed into the sea casting red purple colours across the smoggy sky.

The narrow road wound tortuously around the contours of the hill and abruptly ended abruptly at the top. Black wrought iron gates defended a red brick driveway that arched a short distance to the front door of a beautiful white-stucco Spanish style house. The closed circuit TV camera must have picked us up, for the gates opened as we approached. The goons stopped the van at the front door, walked around to the back and let me out, uncuffed me and stepped aside.

The ornately carved wooden front door swung open as I approached, and a middle-aged Latin American woman in a crisp maid's uniform smiled and beckoned me inside. I was trying to decide if she was from Guatemala or El Salvador as I crossed the threshold into the hallway. The goons stayed outside as she led me to a room at the far end.

Sutherland sat at an antique Louis XV desk, in a room overlooking the canyon and the city beyond.

"Sit down, Mr Gunn."

He looked back at the file he was reading, and turned his leather swivel chair so that the light from the standing lamp to his right cast across the pages. Sutherland tapped the pages absentmindedly.

"Professional British soldier for seven years. British Parachute Regiment, Special Forces Support Group. Served in Iraq and Afghanistan. Wounded in action during covert deep penetration cross-border patrols on second tour. Sole survivor of a four man patrol..."

"I think we've already established that you have my file."

He looked across as if realizing suddenly that I was in the room. His slate grey eyes bored into me. Rage was building inside me like a capped volcano. He turned back to the file.

"You were given the opportunity of a desk job at the Ministry of Defence but chose to leave the service when you recovered from your wounds. High Altitude Parachutist, qualified pilot both helicopter and fixed wing - multi piston engine and jets - and you have particular talent for infiltration and assassination."

He shut the file with a snap and looked at me, the grey eyes devoid of expression. Sutherland wasn't finished with me yet. "What happened in East LA?"

"I've already told you. Morgan asked for a meet. When I got there she was dead."

"I am led to believe that you have ample financial assets. You are also wanted for a murder in Northern California and now for the killing of Morgan Alvarez."

"I didn't kill her," I said tiredly, already bored of this conversation. "Just get to the point and tell me what you want."

I glanced around the room. It was clean, sparsely furnished with the antique desk and comfortable leather armchairs on the bare redwood floor. No pictures on the wall but they weren't needed, for the window framed by a heavily styled Moorish arch dominated the room. This didn't seem like the kind of house a Government employee could afford. Strangely, there was not a computer in sight.

"I want you to work for me."

"Doing what exactly?"

"What you're good at. Gathering information and if necessary an assassination."

"So this is just your normal job interview. That's a relief, for a moment I thought I was in really deep shit, but I think I'll pass thank you very much. I've seen enough death and destruction for one lifetime."

Sutherland smiled thinly, looked past me and nodded briefly.

I turned at the sound of a woman's footsteps and got the shock of my life.

Julie walked into the room and threw her arms around me, tears streaming down her face. Joy at seeing her turned to anger as I rounded on Sutherland.

"What's she doing here?"

"Patience Mr Gunn. Patience. Be glad that Julie is safe."

"The US Government takes hostages now?"

"Nothing is as it seems. Be patient and I will explain," he said calmly, continuing as if explaining to a lecture hall full of University students. "The autopsy report on Morgan Alvarez revealed that she was held down, raped, then injected with enough cocaine to kill a horse before being thrown down the stairs."

There was a stifled sob from Julie. By the look on her face it was the first time she'd heard this. I was on my feet and halfway across the desk, determined to grind Sutherland's face to pulp, when I noticed the

357 Magnum pointed straight at my chest. One bullet would tear a hole in my back the size of a dinner plate.

"Sit down, Mr Gunn." He got up and walked around the desk, snapped the gun back into its holster and kept a safe distance from me. "Nobody knows about this little meeting of ours. Not even my bosses in DC. Just you me and Julie."

"And the maid, your goons outside and whoever brought Julie here from South Africa."

Sutherland shrugged and held up his hand, half closing his eyes as if trying to quiet a noisy child. "It all began five years ago. I was investigating the Banking scandal and glut of Ponzi schemes that infested Wall Street. It didn't seem to be anything new. It happens all the time and you know the stories. Everybody does. Over the years every lead I uncovered went nowhere. Until that is, I discovered a young woman, Keely Banks, who worked for a firm of stockbrokers in New York City. Not one of the biggest firms but they had some pretty large clients. Almost all overseas investors. She was putting together a small but solid portfolio when she was asked to hand over all her clients to one of the junior partners in the firm."

Sutherland walked back to the desk and sat down, swivelling his chair to stare out across the city as the sun began to break on the ridgeline of the Hollywood Hills. "One of her former clients lived in Los Angeles, so she took a leave of absence and came out here to find out what was going on. You see she wanted to get her clients back and take the portfolio to another Broker. Not ethical, but she was an ambitious woman. She tracked her client down, met with him, and two days later she was found dead in a Santa Monica apartment, apparently from an overdose of cocaine. There are witnesses who said there had been a pretty wild party going on, they used the word 'orgy'."

He stopped and sighed heavily. Frowning, his lips pursed.

"Twenty-five years ago, to my shame, I indulged in an indiscretion. A one night stand. I never saw the woman again and never knew she had twin daughters, one of whom she gave up for adoption. Keely Banks was my daughter."

Sutherland paused again, staring out of the window, lost in his own thoughts.

"There was a trail of what we now suspect as murders, but at the time officially recorded as accidental drug overdoses. All the victims were connected with investment banks." He turned his chair back to face us and leaned forward on the desk. One of the Banks involved in the transactions was headed up by a Ted Lieberman. You know the name Mr Gunn, because you asked Morgan Alvarez to investigate him."

"So you lied to me. Morgan wasn't working for you, you were investigating her."

"I want you on board Mr Gunn. God knows you're probably a liability but Mr Radley seems to think you're okay. How we know each other is a long and boring story, but the UK and the USA are allies and, contrary to belief, we do share information on occasion. He tells me you could sneak in and out of a full session of Congress, steal the microphones from right under the President's nose and nobody would know."

"He is prone to exaggeration. How is his ear by the way?"

"Healing," Sutherland said with a slight smile. I got the feeling he didn't like Radley much. That was a plus in his favour.

"None of this has anything to do with either Julie or myself. We are in the wrong place at the wrong time, and you pretty much told me that what you're doing doesn't have government sanction."

"Nice speech, but I know and you know that you want to find out why Morgan was killed."

Sutherland walked across to Julie and stood beside her. It was curious. Then gently touched her face and turned to me.

"One thing you don't know, Mr. Gunn, is that Julie is my daughter, Keely's twin sister."

I must have looked real dumb at that moment.

"We all have skeletons hidden away, Mr Gunn. As I said, I didn't even know I had twin daughters until I started investigating Keely's death. So you see, even I have a vested interest, over and above the call of duty, in discovering what happened and who did this. Call it atoning for my past sins if you prefer."

Sutherland went back to his desk and sat down.

I watched Julie and saw the pain and confusion etched in her face. I knew that Professor Oldfield had adopted her when she was six months old and we had never discussed who her real parents might be.

"We can't investigate this normally. We don't know where the rot runs or how high up the ladder. My personal belief is that some major government agencies are involved."

"Can you be trusted, Sutherland?"

"I won't risk my only surviving daughter's life, Mr Gunn."

"So you think that I can clean this up, all by myself?"

Sutherland watched me quietly. "I want to know why my daughter died and you want to know why Morgan was murdered." He paused again staring at me unblinkingly. "I think you're a resourceful man Mr Gunn. You know I cannot take this through official channels. There's no other way. If you do this, you and Julie are on your own. I can only run interference and share what I know. Maybe a little help here and there, but that's all. Mr Lieberman is very well connected, if somewhat of a recluse. Either he is in the clear, or he is not. Whichever it is, we still need to know what Morgan Alvarez found out about the Griffin Trust."

"This could get very messy."

"I've heard that about you. It is also why there is no official sanction."

"I want to talk to Julie," I said quietly. "Alone."

He nodded. I got up and left the room. Julie followed. One of the doors off the hallway led to a large living room, also with a huge picture window. Dust cloths covered the furniture, the floor immaculately clean. We walked to the window, our footsteps sounding hollowly loud in the quiet, and looked out across the canyon. I turned and faced Julie.

"Do you believe you're his blood daughter?" I signed to her, keeping my hands low and close to my body, aware that Sutherland would no doubt have cameras and microphones watching our every move.

"I don't know what to believe. He showed me the birth certificates and adoption papers," Julie signed back.

"They could be fake."

"I talked to my father. He was totally shocked but confirmed all the names, places and dates. You know what he's like with data. If there's something phony going on, he'll find it."

She followed me with her eyes as I moved around in a seeming distracted state, but actually trying to locate the camera and microphones. Finally I stopped in front of her again and looked deep into her green eyes, trying to fathom the woman I thought I was getting to know, seeing a different soul, one in torment and I wondered where her loyalties now lay. She held my gaze unwaveringly, knowing what I was thinking.

"I have to find out who killed Morgan. You know that, don't you?" I signed again.

"Yes. And I have to find out who killed the sister I never knew." She dropped her eyes. "This isn't easy for me, Thomas. I feel like my whole world has been turned upside down again."

"I understand."

"Do you?"

"I think I do."

"There is only us and my father, Thomas."

"Which father?"

I could see the hurt start with the tears in her eyes. But I had to know, and grasped her shoulders as she turned away, pulling her back and signing quickly.

"We have to be clear. Both of us."

"I only know one father."

I took her in my arms and held her tightly. There was no doubt in my mind as to Julie's strength of character under normal circumstances, if our lives could be considered normal in any way, but this was different. This was family. Blood. And there was still an uncomfortable niggle of doubt in my mind. In the depths of my being I was still a suspicious Special Forces soldier who never took anything at face value, not even from those I loved. That side of me fought with the carefree romantic adventurer I aspired to be.

Julie's expression changed as she looked at me, as if reading my thoughts.

"Don't doubt me, Thomas. Not now. Not ever."

We looked deep into each other's eyes for a long moment and I nodded.

"OK. Let's go find out what Sutherland wants from us."

Sutherland was pacing his office when we returned, looking somewhat annoyed. No doubt because he hadn't been able to hear our silent conversation. It confirmed my suspicions that he was not to be trusted.

"Your decision?" he asked abruptly.

"We're in."

"At some point the DA is going to want you back in his jurisdiction. I can only stall for a few weeks. Then he'll hunt you down, and probably me as well."

"No he won't."

Sutherland arched his eyebrows.

"You will make sure that he doesn't Mr Sutherland, otherwise we are out."

He nodded, but I could see the muscles in his jaw working hard as he clenched his teeth.

"What information can you give us?" Julie asked quietly.

"Very little. One thing did crop up. A client of the Griffin Trust wants a delivery captain to take his yacht from San Carlos in Sonora to San Diego, via Cabo San Lucas. Normally that would not be surprising, but I discovered some anomalies in some transactions in which the client, Randolph Byron Moresby, and the Griffin Trust have been involved. It was those particular transactions that both Keely and Morgan were investigating."

"So you have put my name forward as a suitable delivery skipper."

Sutherland inclined his head. "We created a website for you and ensured that Mr Moresby's representative assigned you the contract."

"When?"

"July 29th. That gives you about a week and a half to dig around and see what you can find. I'm sure there's much you are not telling me. After all, you were the one who sent Morgan after the Griffin Trust in the first place. And you were the one who exposed the extent of ISEC's involvement in the Pakhia debacle."

I didn't know if Sutherland accidentally slipped that piece of information to me, or whether it was deliberate. The only way he could have known was from Radley. Perhaps I'd made a mistake and used an unsecured phone. I couldn't remember. What I did know was that Sutherland and Radley were two-of-a-kind.

Both manipulative bastards.

"I also told Radley that I was finished with this stuff."

"The game's changed, hasn't it?" Sutherland said tersely. "This house is yours for the next two weeks. It's safe."

"And bugged."

Sutherland pursed his lips. It was his 'tell' when he was irritated.

"Take it or leave it," he said curtly.

"We'll take it," Julie cut in before I could tell Sutherland where he could shove his house. "If you clear the bugs. All of them."

Sutherland pursed his lips again, this time flaring his nostrils before answering. "I'll see to it."

"And no satellite surveillance," I added.

"For a wanted murderer you are in no position to make demands."

"And you're in no position to refuse. You want our help, stay out of our space."

He nodded briefly.

"What do you have on Randolph Byron Moresby?"

"Owns a company that manufactures electronic guidance systems for communications and military spy satellites. RBM Defence Electronics Corporation. He's a recluse and there is only one photograph of him." Sutherland pointed to another file on his desk. "That's all we have."

I picked it up and flipped through the pages. There was little information about Moresby in the file. A blurry twenty-year-old photograph of a man in a desert setting, and a brief bio. But the company information was detailed and seemed squeaky clean, as befits an organisation in the space industry. They also had extensive government contracts to supply systems for weapons and NASA deep space vehicles.

Sutherland rose from behind the desk and walked towards the door. "I'm a man of my word Mr Gunn. The surveillance systems will be deactivated immediately. Not for you, but for my daughter. She is what matters to me. You'll also find your personal possessions in the top draw of the desk along with the front gate remote." He paused and smiled slightly. "The DA was a little upset that his team were unable to crack your phone encryption. My phone number is on the desk. One more thing, Ted Lieberman's name has been offered as the next Chairman of the Federal Reserve. That is one reason this operation is 'off the books'. It could be extremely embarrassing to the Government." With that he left the room.

My passport, wallet and phone were as he said, in the top drawer. This particular phone had a biometric sensor Professor Oldfield had incorporated into the aluminium casing that was impossible to detect unless you knew exactly what you were looking for and had the right algorithm. The sensor also scrambled the GPS and all calls and text messages, using a constantly morphing algorithm to produce high frequency microsecond bursts, which could not be traced. Julie, Morgan, Paul and Professor Oldfield were the only people with a similar phone.

"Let's take a walk," Julie said taking my hand.

The house was high up in the Hollywood Hills, near the ridge that separated the San Fernando Valley from the Los Angeles basin. Houses clung precariously to the shifting sandy hillside under threat of sliding to oblivion with a major earthquake. Julie and I found a dirt path off the road that led to the rear of the house and up the hill to the ridge, where we found a suitable place to sit and stare out across the city towards to the ocean, half hidden in the smog haze. Jet airliners lined up in an endless stream on approach to LAX as Police helicopters buzzed over Hollywood.

"What happened?' Julie asked bluntly.

"Morgan called me just after you and I Skyped, wanting me to meet her in East LA." I told her the whole story of the intruders in Morgan's ranch, the seeming link to Marika Keskküla, and Morgan's last words. When I had finished, Julie was silent for a moment.

"I know Hal Gordon," she said slowly.

The day was full of surprises.

"How?"

"He's a film editor. A small documentary project I did a few years ago. He's a gentle soul with a bitch for a wife. How he could be caught up in this is unfathomable."

Of course she would know Hollywood film people, and no doubt a film star or two. Julie was so down to earth it was easy to forget she was a sought after fashion model at the top of her career.

Before she met me.

Sometimes I was so wrapped up in my own shit I forgot that her glamorous career made my life look very ordinary.

"So we have to meet Hal then."

"I'll give Caroline a call, she might know where he is."

"Caroline?"

"My Hollywood agent."

"Of course, how could I not know that?"

"And we need transport," she said ignoring me.

"That, I can arrange."

All it took was a call to my newfound ally, El Cobra Poco. I had his number from the photo I took of Roshan's fake import licence. He said he would have a 'clean' Porsche Carrera 4 delivered to the house in an hour. My second request intrigued him. I needed someone to sweep the property for bugs. Discreetly.

"I do not know how you managed to get them to release you Tomas," El Cobra Poco said, with the hint of an unasked question. "You are a resourceful man."

"I've heard that a lot lately."

"Please remember who your friends are."

"I never forget."

"Morgan did say you were Special Forces."

"Really."

"Indeed. Perhaps we have more in common than you think."

Perhaps we did. Killing being one thing that came to mind.

"Yes. Finding out who killed our friend and why."

He left my unasked question unanswered. It was one of those 'I know that you know something that I know you know' things.

"One more request. I need someone to take care of Morgan's horses on her Baja ranch."

"It is done."

Later in the afternoon the car was delivered and shortly after a food delivery truck pulled up with not only enough gourmet delights to fill the fridge and freezer, but enough sophisticated equipment to flush out any bugs Sutherland had left behind. I figured that if the Mexican Mafia couldn't find bugs, nobody could.

They discovered three. Two microphones and a camera.

As I suspected, Sutherland was not to be trusted.

I accompanied the men and made sure they didn't replace Sutherland's with their own.

Nobody could be trusted.

"So they are Morgan's friends?" Julie asked when Poco's crew left.

"Seems that they are. He'll leave a couple of 'Gardeners' behind. Our personal security detail."

"Is that wise?"

"They want answers and until we provide them they'll make sure nobody touches us. But just what their real motive for doing this is what concerns me."

FOUR

Caroline owned a multi-million dollar 'week-end' house on half an acre that was out of a nineteen fifties movie. Garish art deco colours, open plan layout and battered furniture making it about as comfortable as a dog kennel. With a little care and attention it could be extraordinary.

But it wasn't the house that was the attraction. It was the beach. A beautifully curving half moon shaped expanse of white sand, backed by the mountains and lit by the sun. It faced due south on the curving Malibu coastline and once the 'June gloom' marine layer lifted, soaked all day in a cloudless sky. A private sanctuary below the bluffs where the Pacific Coast Highway sped its way north, it was worth the one and a half hour drive through the snarling LA traffic.

When Julie called Caroline, she had immediately invited us to her beach party.

Being the anti-social animal that I was, I hated parties. Julie however was right at home, steering me past several movie wannabes to where Caroline was holding court, surrounded by a bevy of perfectly shaped hopeful future film stars. She spotted Julie and descended upon us like a hungry matriarch, wearing a flowing floor length dress that hid her ageing corpulent body, her shoulders seeming to join directly to her head, giving the appearance of a toad. On her arm, a young sun-bronzed beach bum whose eyes kept drifting off to stare at the bodies of other young sun-bronzed beach bums, their veneered teeth shimmering in Hollywood smiles.

"Julie. Darling. God, I thought you'd deserted us for good. Everyone has been so worried about you. You are so beautiful."

I sensed the bullshit, but Julie seemed immune to the overarching flattery. She'd seen it all before. Besides, we were on a mission and I knew just how determined she could be when she was focused.

"Caroline. This is Thomas."

"Hi." Caroline took my arm and smiled at Julie. "This *'The One'* sweety?"

Julie raised an eyebrow and looked at me with laughter sparkling in her eyes, enjoying my discomfort.

"Tell me what's going on with Harry. I heard you tipped a bowl of salad over him in Cecconi's the last time you were in town," Caroline continued.

"Harry's a graceless idiot."

"That's not very friendly. He's a very powerful producer with a lot of money backing him, that's why I put you together," Caroline said petulantly.

"Caroline, the man's a idiot. He doesn't know his ass from a hole in the ground and I'm not interested in money. I have too much money as it is."

"There's never too much money, honey, and I've got a contract. All you have to do is sign it. It's worth five million to you."

"And five hundred thousand to you."

Just like all thick-skinned Hollywood agents Caroline ignored Julie's remark, patted me on the arm as if I were a pet, smiled condescendingly and nodded down to the patio.

"Harry's trying to get the barbecue going. Do you mind helping him?"

For a moment all I wanted to do was say something extremely rude, but instead I smiled, got up, and went down to introduce myself to Harry. I could feel Julie and Caroline watching.

Harry staggered a little as he tried to light the briquettes. By the smell of him, he'd already downed half a bottle of scotch.

"Need some help?" I asked as cheerfully and politely as I could.

"Who the fuck are you?" he answered, his eyes trying to focus on me. "Another of Caroline's toy boys?"

"Actually, I'm with Julie."

"She's into stuck up British pricks now, is she, fucking whore?"

There is a certain amount of pressure that you can put on a man's testicles that is so excruciatingly agonising it does two things. First, the pain is so intense shock prevents the victim from screaming. And second, he passes out.

One moment Harry was standing grinning inanely at me, and the next collapsed into my arms. I laid him on the ground and glanced up at Julie who shook her head slightly, a resigned look on her face.

"I think he's had enough to drink," I offered with a shrug.

Several people who had been watching the little pantomime, smiled to themselves, among them Hal Gordon, who Julie had pointed out when we first arrived. He looked to be in his early sixties, and walked over chuckling happily.

"Where did you learn that?"

"Oh, just something I picked up."

"Very neat, he deserved it," he laughed and extended his hand. "I'm Hal Gordon, pleased to meet you..."

"Thomas, and likewise," I replied taking his hand, surprised at the firm grip.

Harry started to regain consciousness, sat up and vomited into a bank of geraniums. Then started to cry. Nobody paid any attention as he stumbled away into the house.

Hal turned as Julie joined us. "Hey Julie, good to see you again."

"Hal. You've met Thomas then."

"Indeed. You two together?"

"That's not for public consumption," Julie said easily.

"I won't breath a word."

"Hal also has a boat, Thomas. In Marina del Rey. You two have a lot in common," Julie said.

"Really, what kind?"

"Forty-five foot Californian Trawler. And yourself."

"Fountaine Pajot Sanya 57 catamaran."

"Sailor eh? Too much like hard work for me," he laughed easily.

"Not these days. Just push a button and up go the sails."

"Really. I'd like to see that."

As we talked, Julie skilfully steered us away from the press of noisy guests onto the beach. We strolled slowly along the crisp white sand.

"Listen you two, why don't you come to dinner tomorrow night. Marie would loved to see Julie, she's like a daughter to us, and God knows when you'll be back in town again."

"That would be wonderful, Hal. But please check with Marie first," Julie implored. "I know how she gets when she has to cook for guests."

"You're not a guest, you're family. But I'll check anyway."

We continued to walk and talk boats of which I knew something about, and films of which I knew nothing about. Hal bid us goodbye when we returned to the house, but Julie wasn't ready to fight the traffic back to the Hollywood Hills, so we meandered around the headland and onto the next beach.

The sun slowly sank towards the sea, an orange mass, distorted into a light bulb by the distant sea mist, high clouds orange red and white in colour bathing in reflected light. Surf pounded a steady rhythm in accompaniment to the departing day. Sand flies and odd jumping shrimp-like creatures played around our feet as we walked, a steady breeze, warm and friendly on our skin.

"You never talked about what happened in Baja after the helicopter crash," Julie's voice was soft and gentle.

I looked at her in surprise, the question obvious. "There's nothing to tell."

"Were you and Morgan lovers?" The question was a shock. I'd never even considered Julie would have thought that a possibility.

"No. Of course not." Why didn't I just tell her my life had fallen apart back then because I thought she was dead, instead of keeping silent?

She was quiet for a moment. We stopped walking and sat down in the sand.

"I'm sorry I asked."

"I feel I let her down. Was ungrateful to her for saving our lives. But I was also pissed off that she kept the secret that you were still alive."

"It wasn't her choice."

"Maybe."

She shrugged and shook her head, tousled hair blowing away from her face in the wind. "There's still so much I don't know about you Thomas Gunn."

"What do you want to know?"

"Anything you want to tell me. Anything. Whatever you want."

"This seems kind of strange. As if we're on a first date," I said a little self-consciously. "This glamour and glitz side of your life I know nothing about. But there's a side of my life you know nothing about."

"Does it matter after all we've been through?" Her smile was encouraging and she sensed the emotion building up inside and leaned towards me. Touching my arm. "You don't have to tell me about those days."

Her closeness and warmth were reassuring.

"It seems a long time ago and yet just like yesterday." What I'd experienced before in my life made the maniacal meanderings of tinsel town moguls unimportant. The lurking manic depressive in my soul hovering in the shadows, waiting to burst upon the scene and scatter the peace with the screaming madness of guilt and hatred. That was what I strove to bury.

Julie reached up and touched my cheek, softly running her fingers down through my trendy stubble, tracing the line of my chin, coming to rest on my shoulder.

"I'm sorry. I didn't mean to open old wounds." Her eyes were full of concern; breath butterfly wings against my skin, and desire began to burn in my gut, fuelling man's most primitive instinct.

"You know what I want to do?" I said quietly.

"Take me back to the house and make mad passionate love to me?"

"Exactly."

By the time we arrived at Hal and Marie's house on two acres on top of a hill in Malibu overlooking the Pacific Ocean, Hal was drunk and I understood why the moment I met Marie. Her lips were thin and pursed, with those shrewish wrinkle lines that rose vertically to her nose. In keeping with the Southern California lifestyle, she stayed in shape with a golden tan from years of sunbathing by the pool and hours in the gym every day. Her beady grey cold suspicious eyes were decidedly creepy.

"It's nice to see you Julie. A little short notice, but no matter," she said crisply, her small sharp eyes turning to me. "You must be Thomas.

Please come in."

Hal grinned, slightly unsteady on his feet. "Drink?"

At this point, a feeling of depression swept over me in waves, almost to the point of nausea. I sat listening to the cicadas and the coyotes, debating whether we should quietly leave or see the evening through. There was of course no choice; we had a job to do.

Music from the 1960s seeped through the house from a decade old CD player, tinny and thin.

"Here you go." Hal held two glasses of margaritas on the rocks, and walked past me to the rear of the house. "This way. We'll leave the girls to it."

I followed as he led the way around the side of the house to where a small, private patio afforded a panoramic view of Malibu and the ocean beyond. He sat down and I took a good look at him. Yesterday he was neat and tidy, as befitting a Hollywood party that was as much work as pleasure, but in his own home he let his long grizzled gunmetal grey hair fall to his shoulders instead of being tied back in a neat pony tail, and with the tie dyed T-shirt, baggy tan shorts and leather thong sandals he looked like a hippie throwback.

"Glad you could both come." He whispered quietly, sad eyes staring out at the view. "Mind if we sit out here a while?" He still stared out at the view, a nervous tick at the corner of his eye.

"Sure," I said, glad not to have to deal with Marie.

In the west, the sun crept out of sight into the ocean, casting a brilliant glow in the sky. Cicadas chirped and a slight breeze rustled the leaves and petals bringing forward the tangy smell of orange blossom. To the east the city lights twinkled tantalizingly in the smoggy evening haze.

"I know why you're here," he said unevenly.

"Oh," I tried not to sound too surprised.

"Morgan Alvarez. She told me to expect you." He drained his glass and stood up. "I'll get us some more." He shuffled off to wet bar off the living room, and returned a moment later with a large jug full of margarita. "Here you go." He filled our glasses and sat down.

"Morgan's dead," I said roughly. Deliberately trying to draw him out.

"I know. I heard."

"What else do you know, Hal?" My tone carried a hard edge.

"Not now." He glanced at the kitchen door. The sound of Marie's shrill voice knifed clearly through the balmy night air.

"Come to my boat tomorrow night. About nine." In his eyes there was the fear of a trapped man with no escape route and sure in the knowledge that he had run his course. "Listen, I invested all my life savings. About two and a half million. The whole bunch. It's gone."

"What did Morgan have to do with that?"

"I'll tell you tomorrow. At the boat. Not here." This time there was a harsh, urgent edge to his whisper, and he nodded his head towards the kitchen. "Marie doesn't know any of it." He drained the glass again and poured more. "I tell you Thomas, every morning I wake up and wonder what the hell I'm doing. This place is a mink lined trap. Take a look at the jerks like Harry who run it. Me? I'd like to up anchor and motor away across that big wide ocean we spend so much time looking at."

"Why don't you?"

"Because I'm just like every other asshole in this town. Pay me enough and I'll make my dick stand up and sing the Star Spangled Banner."

The 60s music switched off suddenly and a moment later lilting strains of Chopin filtered through from the kitchen, carried on the wings of niggling nagging conversation as Marie schemed and bitched. I felt the spider's web of unhappiness and spite that enveloped this house.

"Come by the boat tomorrow night. Dolphin Marina in 'D' Basin on the end tie. Look for *'GALWAY SPIRIT'*. Julie's been there. She knows."

Dinner was uncomfortable in spite of the delicious, perfectly cooked food. Marie was a gourmet chef but the worst kind of spiteful shrew, and I wondered why Hal hadn't left her years before.

"Because he's basically weak," Julie said, as we drove back to the Hollywood Hills. "She keeps the house going and a place for him to come back to after his little film dalliances."

"Sounds like a wonderful relationship."

"I guess it works for them," Julie said without humour.

"Hal told me he knew Morgan. Just how I don't know, but he'll meet us tomorrow night at his boat. Do you know where it is?"

"I went there once. I think I can find it."

My phone rang and I reached over and pressed the speaker button.

"Hey Paul," I answered recognising the coded number.

"Just arrived in Phoenix Arizona Thomas, how're things? Julie still in South Africa?"

"She's here with me. It's a long story. Can you get to LA by tomorrow night?"

"The Cessna's scheduled for maintenance tomorrow, so I'll drive. I've had enough flying for a while."

"Just get yourself here."

"There a problem?"

"You could say that. I'll fill you in on the details tomorrow." I gave him the marina location and hung up.

FIVE

The marina was quiet as I parked the Porsche in the lot near the slips where Hal's trawler was docked. Julie and I checked to see if we had been followed before leaving the car and walking to the unlocked dock gate.

Lights were on in *GALWAY SPIRIT* and the sound of Puccini's opera Turandot filtered through the open door. Hal sat in the saloon, head back, eyes closed, margarita in one hand tossing a baseball in the other. His eyes opened briefly, smiled at us and closed again.

The music finished but the ambiance stayed for a long time as we sat listening to the echoes in our minds gradually merge with the gentle slapping of wavelets against the hull. Hal opened his eyes.

"If the world could spin around the axis of my thoughts. And all the pain, frustration and torment dissolve in cascading colours of fiery joy. Then peace would descend to smooth the passage of my time." He slurred his words and tossed me the baseball.

"Who said that?" I asked, thinking he was quoting from some famous author I'd never read. I put the baseball on the saloon table.

"Me. I dabble a little in writing. Helps clear my head." Suddenly the fear was back in his eyes and the tension in his body, his shoulders slumped and he stared into the bottom of the glass then heaved another sigh. He helped himself to more margarita.

"Two and a half million dollars. Everything I saved, kept away from Marie's grasping fingers. She's got a pretty good idea I've been putting it aside, but she didn't know where or how much. Dean got me into it, said he was involved with some pretty hefty financing deals, raising money to make movies, underwrite commercial deals, a guaranteed return on all monies invested with huge profits..."

"Dean Stockton?" Julie interrupted.

"Yes. Bastard."

"Who's Dean Stockton?" I asked, completely ignorant of the

56

unsavoury personalities that infested Hollywood.

"Shock Jock. Has a really right wing Radio Talk Show. Makes Rush Limbaugh look positively insignificant. I met him once when he interviewed me," Julie answered softly, watching Hal pour himself another drink.

Hal downed the marguerite and poured another. "Dean showed me a lot of paper work and introduced me to a big money man who runs an International Investment Trust Fund, or something." His voice was a monotone as if all life had been sucked from his body. He sank into his own thoughts as he watched a yacht leaving the basin headed for a night cruise. "Dean said he'd made millions on the last transaction, so I invested a hundred thousand just to see. I figured I could afford to lose that. I made a fifty percent return, so went all in. Then I got a call from Morgan Alvarez."

"How did you know her?"

"I didn't. Never heard of her before. She told me she was a friend of Julie's and was investigating a number of Banks and Investment Funds, including the one Dean got me into."

Julie turned to me. "Morgan must have kept notes somewhere."

"Which was why Marika Keskküla's contractors were going through her house."

"I think it's time I had another talk with El Cobra Poco."

"Is that wise?"

I shrugged. "They won't touch us. At least not until they've got what they want, and I want to find out what that is. Although I have a pretty shrewd idea."

Hal moved uneasily in his seat and glanced away as both Julie and I looked at him.

"What's bothering you Hal?" Julie asked staring at him unwaveringly.

"Look, Dean told me not to worry, everything was working just fine and they just had the usual bureaucratic stuff to deal with, then the funds will be freed. So maybe we just wait. See what happens." His breathing had shortened and his tone had become whiney, like a little kid who didn't want to pursue the conversation anymore.

"I mention El Cobra Poco and you get pale and sweaty. Why is that?"

He glanced at us then looked around to see if there was anyone else within hearing distance. Satisfied we were alone, he turned back and leaned forward. "It's about the investment company. The Trust. Dean told me they also laundered money for the Mexican Mafia."

"And why the hell didn't you tell the police?"

Hal stood and leaned against the cockpit combing, watching the small inflatable putter its way back from the channel to its mooring, the girl languidly waving to us as she passed.

"Because Dean said they'd kill Marie if I opened my mouth. Jesus, this whole affair is scaring the hell out of me. Someone went through my office, I think my phone's tapped and I'm sure they're watching the house."

"Who?" I wanted to shake him, maybe beat the truth out of him, but I sat still, watching, waiting.

"I don't know who they are. The Mexican Mafia. Some secret Agency. I don't know."

"How much haven't you told us, Hal?"

He reached for the jug of margarita. His hand shook a little, drops falling onto the highly varnished surface of the table, which he wiped away with his fingertips, smearing a line of liquor across the table.

"I've told you everything."

"I don't believe you." My grey cells were clicking over faster than a dragster at full throttle.

Then he got angry. Red spots appearing on his cheeks, eyes burning with booze and fear. "It seemed like a great way to get movies funded. A little investment and ten times the return. Invest $2.5m and get back $25m. What's the matter with you both, for Christ's sake? I tell you my troubles and you start treating me like someone with a communicable disease. I thought you wanted to help. That's what Morgan said. She told me you'd figure it out because you're this big ex-Special Forces super hero. Well fuck you." He was standing, shaking, the drink slopping out of the glass.

"Sit down, Hal," Julie said quietly but firmly. "Now, we want the whole story. Who is really behind this? You said you'd do anything for a big pay check, so who's blackmailing you. We know it isn't the

Mexican Mafia. That's too easy. If it had, you'd have been dead as soon as they took your money. "

Now the fear was plainly visible. Eyes wide, face pale, hands shaking. Then he looked beyond Julie out of the saloon window, his eyes grew bigger and he started to cry.

The sound of breaking glass and the choked off scream were almost simultaneous as the dart struck him in the neck. His eyes grew wide and he coughed, tried to breathe and his face turned puce. Then his eyes rolled back in his head and he was dead before he hit the floor.

The second dart missed me by inches as I threw myself sideways grabbing Julie and pulling her to the cabin sole. Then I was out of the door into the cockpit before Hal's killer had made it onto the dock, but he wasn't so dumb either. He'd anticipated and was waiting. The third dart thudded into the cockpit coaming next to my cheek.

I rolled to my left and came up fast, just in time to see a second figure emerge from the shadows. My would-be killer collapsed in a heap and Paul checked his pulse, then turned to me.

"You and Julie okay?"

I nodded and climbed up onto the foredeck.

Paul looked up and shook his head.

"Hit him too hard. Neck's broken. What do you want to do with him?"

"Checked his ID?"

Paul nodded. "He's a professional. Nothing on him. Looks like a company man to me."

"Why would the CIA be involved? Doesn't make any sense. And on home soil?"

"Maybe this wasn't officially sanctioned."

"Or maybe it was. An unofficial department within the department. Some 'Black Ops' nonsense."

"Why?" Julie said. We hadn't noticed her standing in the doorway. She was shaking. "Hal's dead."

I stood and took her in my arms, holding her until she stopped shaking.

"I'm OK now," she whispered, stepping back and taking a deep breath.

"What do you want to do with the bodies?" Paul asked.

"Sutherland can deal with them," I said, looking at Julie.

She nodded quickly. "We need to check on Marie."

"You and Paul get back to the house and stay there. I'll deal with this and check on Marie."

"I'm coming with you," Julie said firmly, her chin jutting forward in determination.

"No. Not this time. I want you safe in the house with Paul."

She was about to argue, but then her shoulders sagged and she nodded. "OK."

Paul picked up the small compressed-air multi-shot weapon that looked more like a kid's toy than a real gun and extracted one of the darts. Its short thin hollow needle looked to have a milky white substance. "I've seen this before. It's a Batrachotoxin, ten times more powerful than Ricin. Kills inside five seconds. Killer walks in, removes the dart and walks away. All traces of the poison are absorbed in the body. Most pathologists wouldn't know what to look for and the puncture wound is too small for anyone to notice." He stood up and handed me the weapon.

We went back to the saloon. I laid the gas gun on the saloon table and picked up the baseball, tossing it my hand, looking down at Hal. He lay spread eagled on the floor, eyes open, terror still in his dead eyes. Paul gently pulled the dart from his neck and showed me the puncture wound.

"Can't see it in his beard stubble at all. What are you into, Thomas?"

"I wish to hell I knew. Julie will fill you in with what we know. We need somewhere to hide out. The Hollywood Hills house is too exposed. "

He nodded and grinned. "Already ahead of you. I had the aircraft moved to a strip near Tombstone. My friend bought an old abandoned airfield. Figuring on turning it into a pilot's oasis retreat at some point. It's just what we need. Somewhere nice and private."

"I guess your friend needs financial help with that," I said with a smile.

Paul shrugged sheepishly. "Nothing is free. Anyway, would you rather help one of us or a total stranger?"

"You know the answer to that."

He grinned. As ex-Special Forces, we belonged to an almost invisible 'club' that existed anonymously beneath the radar of public awareness. It had no borders except the ones we recognised. Duty and Loyalty.

We cleaned up as best we could, ensured everything we had touched was wiped clean, and then I called Sutherland.

"Radley warned me you'd leave a trail of bodies," he grunted.

"It is what it is Sutherland. At least you'll have the killer's body you might be able to identify. And the murder weapon."

"I want a full report."

"Later," I said and rang off before he could reply.

Julie sat on the edge of the settee and watched as I covered Hal's face with a tea towel from the galley. He was her friend and I could see she was finding it difficult to come to terms with his murder.

There were too many questions and seemingly no answers.

Just the murders of people we knew.

Then there was Marie.

I owed it to her to tell her what had happened. That's if I made it that far. If Paul was right and these were Government men, then we were in deep shit. But it didn't make sense.

If it was a sanctioned operation and the Feds were involved then all they would have to do to keep me quiet is throw me in jail. Hell, nobody would question it. A charge for tax evasion, rescind citizenship. There were numerous ways.

On a hunch I knelt down and searched through Hal's pockets, found his wallet and flipped through it. Apart from the usual credit cards, money and driver's license, I found a business card for Dean Stockton.

'My belief is that some major agencies are involved, nobody can be trusted,' Sutherland had said.

Federal agencies? Mexican Mafia? Investment brokers?

Supposing someone was skimming. Stealing the investments. Maybe a con. A sophisticated Ponzi scheme.

And supposing that someone was not a person, but the Government.

But why would the Government have to or want to skim? To finance some nefarious operation somewhere?

Like Iran, Iraq, Afghanistan. Syria maybe?

Or perhaps closer to home in Venezuela, Bolivia, or Chile?

So what was I looking at? The same scenario we'd uncovered in the UK? A rogue outfit in the Treasury Department? The CIA doing its own thing again, without sanction and with no knowledge from the top?

Questions. Questions. All feasible, but where was the answer?

The only reality was that someone was trying to kill us. Why? Because they thought I knew what Morgan had found out? Maybe they thought Hal had tipped me off. Every answer led to another question.

The deeper we got the more confusing it became.

Paul, Julie and I left the boat and walked to Paul's car. Once there, I slipped away into the shadows as they drove off.

Crawling through the parking lot on my hands and knees under normal circumstances would have felt ridiculous, but now it felt like it did back in Afghanistan on the Pakistan border, sneaking into a command HQ to set mines.

A Porsche Carrera 4 is a difficult car to slide beneath, so anything attached to the underside would be within arm's length and fairly easy to spot. As I was crawling under the car, shining the pencil beam across the floor pan and under the engine I thought it was a waste of time. They wouldn't use a bomb. They had tried to get me with Batrachotoxin. To leave no trace. So I switched my attention to anything that looked remotely like a tracking device.

I found it after three minutes search. Nothing stirred in the parking lot. Cars drove down the street to the Charthouse Restaurant. It was at times like this I wish I had an image intensifying night scope, then I'd be able to spot the killer's back-up. Then I had a thought. I slipped into the driver's seat, started the car and unclipped the convertible roof. As I reversed out, it slipped down. I love paddle shifters, it makes accelerating and cornering so much easier using left foot braking.

The stake out car was parked by the exit and the driver must have been dozing because I caught him unawares. I was almost past him by the time he got the engine started and the car moving. I hurled the baseball I'd brought with me from Hal's boat, hoping to God my aim was true. It flew through the open passenger window and hit the driver, who bailed out of his door maybe thinking it was a grenade. The Porsche complained as I slid it out of the parking lot onto the street and accelerated hard to the traffic lights, reaching them before they turned red, fishtailed around the turn onto Via Marina, kept accelerating hoping there were no Police cars, made the next two sets of lights and melted into the night traffic on Washington Boulevard, heading north-east.

It would be a good few minutes before the killer's partner got started back in pursuit. Maybe he'd take longer, thinking they had the tracking device and didn't need to hurry. I tossed it into the back of one of those old battered pick-up trucks Mexicans seem to favour for carrying around gardening tools and engine parts.

I took city streets all the way out to the Valley and then followed a zigzag route through to Topanga Canyon, just in case they had another car tailing me. As I drove, I configured the car's navigation system to find me a back route to Hal and Marie's house. The air was cool, the night clear and stars bright, but I wasn't enjoying it. Instead my eyes flickered down every side street and constantly roamed across the rear view mirrors.

Fifteen minutes driving and I found the narrow road that led up the mountain, bringing me out close to Hal's property. It was about a mile away across rough country, but I wasn't about to drive up and announce myself. There was a small dirt road that led out of sight of the main highway, so I drove down a few hundred yards and hid the car. Coyotes howled close by, and the scrub bushes rustled with the sound of nocturnal animals.

The moon shone in a cloudless sky, stars pin-pricking the black night, flashing aircraft strobes slowly vanishing amongst the myriad lights of the city that twinkled in the smog haze. I stood alone with the full awareness of my solitary presence, watching, listening, an observer not a player. From now on I was an outsider skating on the periphery, a skimming darting mosquito waiting to be squashed, and no one would mourn my passing. An expendable item, more useful in death than in life.

The thought was little comfort. I did not belong, therefore I need not conform. My death was inevitable anyway; it was simply a matter of time.

Ideally, the time should be long in coming, but if it came in the next moment, then it would be a brief flash of realization, of pain, then oblivion. Welcome, warm, comforting, an end to the pain and suffering. I'd been there before so death held no surprises, no fear, just disappointment for experiences unfulfilled.

So if I were to live on the outside, then I would determine my own destiny. I was back at war with the enemy within.

How many times I fell scraping elbows, knees and shins was a matter for the watching coyotes to figure. Every step was an uneven pathway to disaster, every bush a potential knife that tore through my clothing and scored bloody slashes in my skin. It took an hour and the pre-dawn glimmering light was beginning to gather the skirts of darkness and lift the night from the earth.

The house was quiet. No extra vehicles in the driveway or the roadway. The latches on the backdoor lifted easily and I was through into the kitchen.

Plates were piled unwashed in the sink, the refrigerator door open and a milk carton lay on its side, the contents pooled on the floor, a sickly smell filling the air. Somewhere a fan turned lazily on low. The power light on the CD player glowed dully and a tap dripped steadily onto a tilted pan lid.

Goosebumps rose in warning and the hairs on the back of my neck stood straight up, tickling against my shirt collar. Sweat dripped from my armpits and ran down the side of my chest. Death cloaked the house, filling every room, every nook and cranny, suffocating in its finality. Ordinary shadows became enemies with talon fingers that groped towards me.

I hadn't moved in three minutes, listening for any other sounds. Anything that would betray a presence, a danger. Anything even the slightest bit out of place. The hum of the refrigerator seemed deafeningly loud, a constant demanding noise. The boiler burst into life, settling to a steady low roar and hot water pipes ticked as they expanded.

I slowly moved towards the living room, the steadily increasing light casting eerie shadows across the antique furniture and Mexican masks that hung on the walls. A settee lay upturned, Chinese rug pulled up and thrown into a corner, books from the shelves scattered about the floor, torn as if someone had searched through every page, uncaring of the content, simply looking for something that was not there.

My instincts led me to the bedroom. Everything had been ripped from the shelves, desk dismembered and the old leather armchair and settee sliced apart, white calico stuffing lying strewn about the floor. There was dried blood on the floor, smeared across papers and against the wall.

A small bathroom extended off the study and joined with the bedroom. I pushed open the door and went through. The blood trail led through the bathroom and into the bedroom. If a tornado had been through the room, it would have left it in better condition. The mattress lay half on the bed, half off, ripped apart as were the pillows, feathers stirring as I walked slowly through. The window was smashed, blood stains on the jagged glass and window frame. Marie's naked, tortured body lay strapped stomach down across the table on the patio outside the bedroom. Her legs and arms were tied to the table legs with electrical wire and the back of her head lay between her shoulder blades, sightless eyes staring up at the lightening sky. They'd tortured, raped and then cut her throat. I'd seen it before but I wasn't immune.

I wanted to cut her free and cover her, but I knew I couldn't. All I could do was take photographs with my phone and leave. Quietly, without fuss, without anyone knowing I'd been there.

By the time I reached the car it was light, and I could see the dirt road I was on led down to a small, dilapidated ranch house. There was no sign of life. My feeling of exhilaration at being on the outside had given way to a cold clammy fear. I knew why they'd done that to Marie. It was for my benefit. They knew I'd go there. Maybe they had been watching. Perhaps not. Perhaps they knew that I'd spot them and would turn and run. And I still didn't know who 'they' were.

No. They wanted me to see her. They wanted to give me a graphically clear warning of what they would do to Julie. At this moment there was no point in trying to understand what was happening, it was just important to move one step at a time. I needed to flush out Sutherland somehow, see if he really was an ally or the puppet master, so I called him on my secure mobile.

"Where's Julie?" he asked immediately. Whether his concern was an act I had no way of knowing.

"At the house."

"What happened at the boat?"

"I would have thought your men would have figured that out."

He was silent for a moment. "Where are you now?"

"Nowhere that need concern you. I do, however, want to know why a Fed killed Hal and then tried for Julie and me."

"How do you know the killer was one of us?"

"Because you all dress the same way," I answered sarcastically. "How do you think I know? I can smell Government Operative a mile away. And whoever is behind this is after Julie and me in a big way. And it's then it's only one step to you."

"What aren't you telling me Mr Gunn?"

"They also killed Hal's wife tonight. Tortured, raped and nearly cut her head off. Mexican Mafia style." I was certain it wasn't the Mexican Mafia, but I wanted Sutherland's reaction.

He was silent for a moment and I could almost hear his brain ticking over at breakneck speed, accessing all the different answers he could give.

"I would agree with the style, but there's no reason for them to do that."

"Then what aren't you telling me Sutherland?"

"Nothing I haven't already told you."

This was getting nowhere, so I gave him the address of Hal's Ranch and hung up.

Next I called El Cobra Poco and told him to meet me at an all night diner I had seen on Ventura Boulevard near Topanga Canyon when I was driving to Hal's.

Then I called Julie.

"Marie's dead," I said coldly and heard Julie stifle a cry. I didn't have time to waste on preambles. "Pack your bags, you and Paul need to get out of there now. Tell Paul to take you to our private retreat; I'll meet you there. Make sure you're not followed." My little Mexican 'friend' would most certainly want to know where Paul and Julie were going and I was equally sure that Paul could shake any 'tail'.

By the time I arrived at the diner El Cobra Poco was already there, sitting at a table near the rear exit, his entourage outside. They nodded as I pulled up walked inside ordered a coffee and crossed to the table.

"You have been busy tonight my friend," the little man said with no humour. He was no longer the street gangster I met in East LA, but dressed in an expensive suit with neatly cut hair as befitting a young successful businessman.

I laid my phone on the table and turned it so that he could see the photograph of Marie. He stared at it, pursed his lips and breathed out slowly.

"I need to know two things," I said slowly. "One is your real name, I'm getting tired of referring to you as a 'little snake'."

He raised his right eyebrow, narrowed his eyes then relaxed and smiled. "Martinez. Eliseo Martinez. My first name means 'God is My Salvation'. And the second thing?"

"Just how much money did these guys take from your organisation?"

"Seven billion dollars," he answered without blinking.

"I can understand why you're upset."

"Now I ask you a question."

"Go ahead?"

"Do you believe we killed your friends?"

"No."

He studied me to see if I was lying. My acting must be pretty good because he continued. "Good. We understand each other. You and I both kill, but not because it is enjoyable. For me it is business. To kill somebody who is not an enemy like this..." He indicated the photograph of Marie and shook his head. "This is bad for my business, and that is why they do it. But you, why do they hunt you?"

"Because I am bad for their business."

"And you know who they are, these people?"

"Not yet. But I can tell you that someone called Marika Keskküla was responsible for killing Morgan Alvarez."

"I have heard the name."

"She sent a hit team to Morgan's ranch in Baja."

"I know. We found the bodies you left behind when we went to take care of the horses. It is clean now." He smiled suddenly, mischief dancing in his eyes. "I see we can still surprise you."

A part of me thought I understood we were on the same side, but whereas I felt what I did was morally justified he didn't bother with any form of justification. Was I the hypocrite? How could my desire for revenge be any different from his?

"You understand why we need you?" Eliseo asked cautiously. I noticed that he had lost his Latino street talk.

"Because perhaps some of your people on the 'inside' are not to be trusted. With the Feds focusing on me, they ignore you."

"We try to keep our 'legitimate' enterprises separate from our less than legal activities. That means we deliberately did not place any men inside in the US Treasury Department, or the Federal Reserve. Perhaps it was a mistake and we need to change that, but Morgan was convinced that your special skills would be best suited to reach our goal."

"You want your money back."

"I do not think we are alone in that. And besides as you said yourself, with the focus on you we fade into the background. What interests me is why they would focus so much on you."

"I thought Morgan told you."

"Some, but not all."

"Perhaps the less you know the safer we all are."

He nodded. "Perhaps. But I always like to know with whom I am working."

I sat back, appraising him from a different perspective. On the street he may behave like a typical Mexican Mafia gangbanger, but there was something about him as he sat before me now, that did not fit the image. I could see in his eyes that he knew what I was thinking.

"Like you, I consider there are not many ways to redress the social balance, particularly in my country. With political power comes corruption and sometimes the ballot box is not the answer."

"And drugs and human trafficking are?"

"Coca-Cola was so called because it originally used extract of coca leaves and was proclaimed a nerve and brain tonic. Prohibition caused much violence in the 1920s, until it was lifted. For many thousands of years, hallucinogenic drugs have been used in religious and spiritual ceremonies and then they were outlawed. We use the money we make selling drugs to Americans to pay for schools, medical facilities, and agricultural investment in our country. Things our government has failed to provide. I understand other cartels do not. We do not use drugs and we forbid the sale to our countrymen. Other cartels do not. As for human trafficking, I do not do that and if I find those that do, there is retribution."

"Like decapitating your enemies and leaving their bodies hanging from bridges for all to see?"

"We take responsibility. You killed three people in Baja, covered your tracks and left the bodies for others to find. Do you think there is a difference?" His question was uncomfortable. I could justify my actions in all sorts of ways, but did that give me the right to judge him? "At this moment, we need each other. And it seems, so does your Government friend, Sutherland. To misquote Charles Dudley Warner, war makes strange bedfellows."

"You are a complex man, Eliseo."

"It is a complicated world, Tomas. We both live in two moralities."

I stood and held out my hand. He shook it firmly. "I'll be in touch."

"This Keskküla person. Where can we find her?"

"When I know, so will you."

SIX

Once many years ago, before the army and everything that had ensued, I had driven Interstate 10 non-stop from LA through Phoenix to San Antonio Texas, stoked up on NoDoze caffeine pills. It's a long and boring drive, interspersed with magnificent desert scenery, and it was no place to be caught out in the open in the heat of a summer's day. The air conditioner made the drive bearable and I rued not having had the time to reposition the Cessna Mustang to Santa Monica. It was perhaps just as well, as right now Julie, Paul and myself needed to take a breath and evaluate our options.

The Interstate was patrolled by fixed wing aircraft and helicopters always on the look-out for speeding cars, so there were not many opportunities to floor the accelerator and drive flat out, but I did anyway, blasting across the southern tip of the flat Mojave Desert where it joined with the Sonoran Desert, some 300 kilometres south of were Julie and I had been shot down in the helicopter last year. But that was far from my mind as I mulled over the last week's events and pondered the future. I had so little information, and I wracked my brain to think where Morgan could have left her notes.

The conversation with Eliseo had thrown up another dimension, for which I was unprepared. Morality. I could see Danny shaking his head and saying, *'If you start worrying about that shit, you're a dead man.'*

I banished the thoughts from my mind and tried to think of every nuance of Morgan's phone call and last words, in case there was something I'd missed. The head injuries I'd sustained in Afghanistan and then last year in the helicopter crash, meant that sometimes when I was tired, my brain function slowed down. After two hours drive I stopped at a small gas station, stretched my legs and bought a twelve-pack of Arrowhead water. Then drove for another twenty minutes before taking a side road and finding a secluded spot on a dirt track behind a rocky outcrop, to rest and think.

Before Morgan died she tried to tell me something and I couldn't figure out what that was. Perhaps I'd misinterpreted what she'd said. Maybe just misheard. *'Lost track'* she'd whispered. But what did she lose track of? No amount of thinking helped.

Back on the road I drove to Quartzite in Arizona then branched off towards Yuma, trying to confuse anyone who might be attempting to follow. Day turned to night as I reached the turn off and drove for two miles before switching off the lights and ducking down a small side road. I waited for five minutes then resumed my journey, certain that the only way 'they' were going to track me was by satellite. I wondered if I was being overly paranoid, but given how my life had changed in the past year I couldn't take any chances.

An hour later I turned onto the road to Tucson. From there it would be country roads to the airfield southwest of Tombstone.

From the rough single lane road it was hard to see the airfield, the entrance just a dirt track leading to steel gates. At an elevation of nearly 1,380m (4,528ft) the airfield was cooler than the low-lying flatter desert of the Phoenix/Tucson area, and tucked on a narrow flat plain between two crescent shaped rising hills. The single strip of tarmac, 1,068m (3500ft) long looked in reasonable condition and long enough for the Mustang's take-off run. Two old weathered arched corrugated steel hangars sat side-by-side at the western end; with a large shed about seventy-five metres away that housed the refuelling trucks, one for Avtur and one for Avgas. On the ramp were just two old single engine aircraft. A Piper Super Cub and a 1940s Stearman PT-17 Biplane.

It was quiet, well away from Tombstone city and with no houses for a several miles. It was strangely lost in space and time, and I could see why it could be an attraction for owner/pilots to be able to fly in for a vacation away from the hustle and bustle of a big airport.

There were no signs of any cars, or the Cessna Mustang or MD-902 helicopter. I thought I'd come to the wrong place, and I drove around to the front of the hangars. The doors on the first one were open, but it was empty except for a battered Chevy pick-up. It was still early as I pulled the Porsche into the hangar, parked and stepped out, stretching my leg, which had stiffened on the long drive. Then I knew I was in the right place as I spotted a fresh honeydew melon sitting on the hood of the pick-up.

My exploration of the hangars was cut short by the sound of a vehicle approaching from the south. I cautiously peered out and saw a Jeep Wrangler slide to a halt by the first hangar. Paul and Julie got out as I walked across to them. Julie smiled, put her arms around me and held tight for a moment, then let go and introduced me to Paul's friend.

"This is Sarah Deakins."

"Pleased to meet you, Thomas," Sarah said, smiling broadly as she climbed out of the Wrangler. She was a medium height, slim half-caste woman in her mid thirties, with short brown hair covered with a large cowboy hat. She walked stiffly on a prosthetic leg, stirring dust trails as it dragged slightly. She shook my hand firmly, brown eyes set in her strong face, direct and full of mischief.

"Pleased to meet you too." I felt a little awkward.

"Paul didn't tell you anything about me, did he?" She laughed. "Lost the leg one night flying an MH-60 Black Hawk in Afghanistan. Just picked up a SEAL Team when we took some ground fire."

"What she won't say is that she flew back to base, landed in one piece and nobody knew she was shot to pieces until they had to lift her from the aircraft. For that she got a Silver Star," Paul said as he shook my hand.

She scowled and turned back to the Jeep. "Ancient history. I was twenty-five and stupid for adventure. Come on, let's go. I'll show you your accommodation and I need breakfast. Paul will bring the Porsche, you ride with me and Julie."

Sarah had already begun her 'pilot resort' idea with the first two of a series of unconventional houses built halfway up the southerly crescent shaped hill beside the airfield, hiding in plain sight. The 'Earthship' blended so perfectly with the landscape that it was impossible to see until you were close. Hidden from the road by the curve of the hill, it was constructed of old car tyres packed with earth and clad with adobe. It boasted photovoltaic cells for electricity, a deep water well drilled into the aquifer, and a view of the airfield and mountains beyond. Specially coated and angled window glass captured heat during the winter and reflected it in summer. There was no way I could see to reach the house, until Sarah pressed a button and hidden doors in the hillside below opened, revealing the house's own private aircraft hangar. Inside was the MD-902 Explorer.

"It'll be a bit of a tight fit for the two of them, but not bad eh?" Sarah said, as she drove into the hangar and parked the Jeep on a grid. Paul followed with the Porsche, the doors closing behind us, lights coming on automatically.

"Not bad at all," I breathed, the horrors of the last week falling away as I climbed out of the Jeep and stared at the gleaming cleanliness of the hangar floor. Set in the far walls was an elevator and beside it stairs to the house above.

I looked across at Paul who was smiling hugely. "The Mustang's in Phoenix," he said. "It's got another two days worth of maintenance."

Sarah led the way to the elevator and in moments we were stepping out into the open plan living room, dining room, kitchen. In front, by the wide windows that looked out across the airfield and the crescent shaped hill on the other side, were hydroponic plant beds where vegetables and fruit grew alongside flowering cactus and stubby desert plants. There were two bedrooms and two bathrooms. The furniture was simple, comfortable and the wooden tables in keeping with the environment.

"There's meat and chicken in the freezer, fresh veggies as you can see. Beer in the fridge and wine in the pantry. You'll be pretty self sufficient."

"Where do you live?"

Sarah grinned mischievously. "Where nobody can find me." She laughed heartily. "There's another one of these, the prototype just on the other side, about fifty yards away."

"How much?"

"For the house or the development?"

"Both?"

"One point two million for this house. Fifteen for the complete development," she answered crisply, watching me carefully. "You all wanna tell me what's going on? You didn't come out here to buy a house."

"Better you don't know."

Julie caught my eye and signed quickly. Sarah frowned. "What'd she say?"

"That I should tell you. You have a right to know."

"Too goddam right I have." She sat down on the settee. "Paul, get some coffee would you hon. Now tell me what I 'better not know' Mr Thomas Gunn."

So I told her everything, including how I met Paul. When I finished, she looked from me to Paul and Julie then nodded.

"I need something stronger than coffee." She got up stiffly, limped across to a wall cabinet and took out a bottle of Angel's Envy Kentucky bourbon, placed it on the table and returned for four glasses. She broke the seal, poured generous measures, then solemnly handed one to each of us. She raised her glass.

"Fuck the Feds. Here's to freedom and privacy. If I'm gonna have some asshole try and shoot my butt off, I may as well make it worth my while." She refilled her glass and sat back, looking back and forth between Julie and me. "Hell, life's been a little tedious lately anyway."

We drank quite a few more glasses before I told her Paul had intimated that she needed investment to complete the project, and I had the money. She studied me for a very long moment before answering.

"I tell you what. We all come out of this alive, we'll talk about it. Now let me show you something." At the back of the kitchen was a door leading to the pantry. It was surprisingly cool and at the far end Sarah opened a cupboard that nobody would have suspected concealed an arms cache.

Inside, were three shotguns, two M-16s and two handguns, plus two monocular night scopes for the M-16s.

"This is Arizona, Thomas. If you look like me people can get a little strange, if you know what I mean." She paused and glanced at me. "Bahamian/American in case you're wondering. My little sister Leila

74

still lives in Great Abaco in the Bahamas. She's the brains in the family. Does computer graphics stuff. Her specialty is reconstructing old black and white photographs digitally. Like who doesn't these days? Makes a bundle. Me, I like the desert, just like my uncle. Bought this place with money my mother left us. The ammunition is in a locked cabinet in the living room behind the bourbon," she explained as I took down one of the M-16s, stripped it and started to clean the working parts and barrel.

"Of course. Where else would it be?"

"Comedian, eh?"

"How's the electricity supply up here?"

"Pretty good. There's a back-up generator in the hangar with enough diesel to last over a month. Water's from a small aquifer I tapped into. The town doesn't want it because there's not enough water, so I have it all to myself."

I found a piece of cleaning cotton, threaded it into the end of the cleaning rod, wet it with a few drops of oil and pushed it through the barrel. The oil on the metal smelled good, comforting.

"You don't have a partner?" I said conversationally.

She gave me an '*old fashioned*' look. "Once. Before this." She pointed to her leg. "Sandra couldn't get used to it. We sounded like a music hall act anyway. Sarah and Sandra."

"I guess she didn't know a good thing when she saw it," I said, knowing that she was feeling me out.

She laughed delightedly. "I like you Thomas Gunn. Figured when I first saw you that you take people as you find them."

I stopped what I was doing and looked at her seriously. "Loyalty and Truth, Sarah. Loyalty and Truth."

Sarah stepped forward and kissed me full on the lips. "If I knew you existed I'd have gone straight a long time ago." And we both burst out laughing.

"My friend Danny would have loved you."

"I'll get the ammunition."

I put the rifle back together, worked the action a few times and then stripped and checked the magazines. There were two twenty-round magazines and two of thirty. Sarah brought back the boxes of ammunition with Julie's help. They contained high velocity rounds for the M-16 and several different grain cartridges for the shotguns including a box of solid shot and 10mm rounds for the Viking automatics.

"You still fly?" I asked as she cleaned one of the Vikings.

"Those little puppies out there on the apron ain't just for show."

"Helicopters?"

"Still keep current. You never know when some rich guy will show up with an MD Explorer," she laughed uproariously. "Who d'you think brought it down here?"

After I'd cleaned the guns and checked the ammunition, Sarah and I went back into the living room where Julie had set up her iPad and was checking the secure connection. She put her hand to her forehead and held it there a moment, eyes closed, then blinked and went back to work.

"You okay?" I asked in sign, sitting in front of her.

"Just a slight headache. Didn't get much sleep last night and the air's really dry."

"Need a Tylenol?"

"No it's fine." She smiled, then said aloud. "So what's the plan?"

Paul and Sarah glanced over waiting for me to reply.

"I need to pay a visit to Dean Stockton, find out what he knows."

"We need to pay a visit," Julie said emphatically. "I met him a while ago. Remember? And you have no idea where he lives."

I held up my hands in surrender. "Okay. Where does he live?"

"Santa Barbara."

I looked at her in disbelief. "Then I'm pretty sure I do know where he lives."

"How?"

"The GPS navigator in the SUV at Morgan's ranch. Her killer's went there."

There was stunned silence in the room.

At last Sarah spoke. "Better use the Mustang, it's too far for the Explorer," she said tersely and reached for her mobile phone. "I'll call the Cessna maintenance people, see if I can get them to finish tomorrow, then I'll run you up to Phoenix in the chopper. When you're done with this Dean feller, fly straight back here, but file for Phoenix. I'll fix it with ATC when you're in the air."

I went outside onto the deck and made a call to Eliseo. I needed a car waiting in Santa Barbara in the parking lot of a good restaurant I knew, as we couldn't afford to have our names on a rental agreement and I didn't want any cameras at the airport taking the license plate. I told him what I was doing, adding that it may yield information on Marika Keskküla. I didn't want the cartel getting pissed off with me. Having done that, I toyed with the idea of calling Sutherland and decided that could wait. The others joined me, Paul carrying a tray of Eggs Benedict and Julie with a pot of fresh coffee. We sat as the sun rose higher in the sky, talking about the development and enjoying a relaxed breakfast. For a brief moment forgetting the world outside this oasis.

It was good to be back in the Mustang, feeling the surge of acceleration as the two engines powered up and hurtled the little jet down the runway of Phoenix International Airport and into the late afternoon sky.

As we climbed out through the scattered clouds I relaxed, concentrating on the routine of flying the jet. Julie put her head back and sighed heavily. The headphones were good, blocking out all the engine noise, so she could hear me speaking.

"You okay sweetheart?"

"Yeah. Good. It's nice to be on our own for an hour or so."

"This stuff with Sutherland's really bothering you, isn't it?"

"Yup, really thrown me for a loop."

"Do you believe he's your real father?"

"A part of me would like to, but I get no connection. Nothing. I'd have thought I would have felt a bond." She looked over at me. "What do you think?"

"You might not like it."

"Tell me anyway."

"I'm cynical enough to think it's a ploy. He thinks he needs a way to drag me into his little drama and playing with your emotions will do that. Especially if you think you had a sister."

"He doesn't know me very well, does he?" she said grimly. "And even if it turns out that he is my real father, by some freak of nature, I still feel no bond."

"So what do you want to do?"

"Play his game until we find out who killed Morgan and Hal. Nothing else matters. Hell, at this point I don't even care if someone is stealing the Government blind."

"What about if it's the Government stealing us blind?"

"Okay. Let's poke the hornet's nest then."

Dean's house was at the head of a narrow canyon peppered with houses, where the steep road ended. It was partially hidden behind high adobe walls and an entrance arch with a classic double-door wooden gate. Drooping wisteria grew up the walls. Old olive and orange trees gripped the side of the hillside.

Julie parked the car and walked up to the door. There was modern intercom on the wall. She pressed the button and waited.

Nothing happened.

Twice more she pressed the intercom and still nothing happened. I pulled the business card from my pocket and dialled the number. Somewhere inside the house a phone rang interminably until I finally disconnected the call. It hadn't even clicked through to voice mail.

"Curious."

Julie peered through a small grid in the door. "There's a Mercedes in the driveway. Perhaps he's taken a trip."

"Maybe. But this doesn't feel right to me."

"The house has a very expensive security system, so I wouldn't advise breaking the door, or climbing the wall," Julie said warningly, as I looked up at the gate arch.

"Let's see what's at the back then."

Julie and I walked around the wall, on what seemed like a narrow trail that emptied out onto a fire road winding around the back of the property. We walked on until I spotted a break in the brush, leading to the rear wall of the property. From where I was standing it looked as if

I could climb along the steep hillside until I was adjacent to the wall closest to the back of Dean's house, then clamber across the branches of an olive tree onto the roof.

Daylight began to fade as the sun disappeared behind the mountain, and with the darkness came a drop in temperature and a rare but welcome rain shower. Drops peppered down through the branches, disappearing into the soil as they hit.

"Are you thinking what I think you're thinking?" Julie whispered in my ear, startling me.

"Don't do that. I was figuring how to get in."

Every alarm system is designed to stop people entering from the ground. Through doors and windows. Very few places, except for commercial properties, had the roof wired. Dean's house was no exception.

Julie scrambled onto the roof a great deal more easily than I, then together we felt around the edges of the tiles. They were loose and we lifted them easily and stacked them neatly into the guttering, until there was an area big enough to take my body. Then I cut through the felting and thin roofing board with my sailing knife.

Fifteen minutes after we had climbed the tree we were inside a bedroom. Ceiling plaster had fallen over the bed. A film of dust lay over the furniture and the room had a musty smell.

"This is weird. I heard that Dean's a 'neat freak'," Julie whispered.

The door led out onto a wide landing that overlooked the hallway and living room. Two standing lamps, one in either corner of the room, were on, as was the outside light illuminating the courtyard. I could see a chocolate brown Mercedes SLS AMG Roadster parked by the front door.

The floorboards creaked under foot as I moved slowly down the stairs followed by Julie and crossed the hallway to the open door of what I could see was the study. She stopped beside me in the doorway and instinctively put her hand to her mouth. Lying beside the desk was a body with what looked like a 9mm hole in his forehead; eyes still open and a surprised look.

"It's Dean," Julie said quietly.

I'd seen the modus operandi before, at Morgan's ranch, and it was pretty clear that the girl who killed the Doc also killed Dean, but there was something about Dean's face that didn't look quite right to me, so I leaned down and touched the irregular looking patch of skin by his left ear. The killer would have been too busy to notice it. Gently I peeled off the silicone mask.

"That's not Dean," Julie whispered, turned, walked to the living room and sat down, eyes closed, breathing deeply.

Dean's desk didn't reveal much of anything. The desk had been cleared and there were no files in the cupboards, so I sat down and tried to access the laptop. My computer skills are reasonable but not up to the task, so I went into the living room and knelt in front of Julie.

"I need help with his computer. You up to it?"

She opened her eyes and nodded. "I'm okay. Just a bit of a shock, that's all. I expected it to be Dean and it wasn't. Who would do that? The face I mean. Why?"

"Somebody's idea of a bad joke maybe. Or perhaps Dean wanted somebody to think they'd killed him."

Julie followed me back to the study, sat down at the desk and typed vigorously for what seemed like way too long for me. Then she stopped and stared at me.

"Stop pacing for God's sake and go find something to shoot while I do this," she said irritably.

Suitably chastened I searched through the rooms, which looked as if they hadn't been lived in for some months. Dust covered the surfaces, and the fridge in the kitchen contained moulding food and sour milk. On the coffee table was a booklet from the Healing Spirit Hot Springs Resort near Murrieta. It was not covered in dust and my sixth sense began to prickle the hairs at the back of my neck. I picked up the booklet and flipped through the pages. The resort was a revamped version of New Age nonsense. They charged exorbitant amounts of money for mud baths, hot springs, rainwater therapy, whatever that was, and meditation sessions with a non-denominational *spiritual healer*. I put the booklet in my pocket.

I was still trying to put the pieces together when I heard a soft explosion. It was so gentle that at first I didn't realise what it was, until smoke started to seep from the settee.

"Julie. Time to go," I shouted, running to the front door. There was another soft 'whooshing' sound and flames started to flicker from the settee. "Come on."

Then there was a moment of déjà-vu.

The incendiary device exploded just as we entered through the roof. We had been told that it was a good sniper position covering the route into the alley between the shabby apartment blocks in the town. The terrorists had a habit of using innocent people's houses to congregate, threatening the locals with a slow painful death if they didn't cooperate.

Obviously our intelligence was seriously flawed and now it was a question of how the hell to escape. Danny looked at me, grinning as usual.

"Forward or backwards mate?"

"Go back and we're dead," I replied, looking at the burning rafters that were our only escape route and wondering if they would support our weight before they burned through completely.

"What you waiting for then?" His grin was driving me crazy as I tested the rafter and then walked across, staring down into the forty-foot drop to the burnt out floor below. "Just like the trainasium," he laughed as he sent the next soldier across.

"I swear to God I'll swing for you, Danny."

"You'll have to survive this first."

I felt the rafter start to crack beneath my feet...

"What are you waiting for," Julie shouted as she came running, Dean's laptop in hand, snapping me back to the present. We ran outside slamming the door shut behind us, and sprinted to the gate as the automatic security lights lit up the courtyard.

"Keep your head down," I yelled and quickly slid the bolts on the wooden gate and slipped out into the road. Within twenty seconds we were driving down the road as behind us flames flickered in the upstairs windows.

"Dean has to be pretty desperate to pull off a stunt like that," Julie offered as we turned onto the main road, driving slowly so as not to attract attention.

"Or scared to death. Who would torch a multi-million dollar mansion unless their life means more than money?"

"Dean's pretty slippery, but I never would have thought he'd murder someone."

"Did you get anything off the computer?"

"No, it's got a very sophisticated asymmetric encryption, so I'll have to talk to my Dad. That's why I brought it with me."

"I trust you mean the Professor?"

"If I didn't need a pilot to get me back to Tombstone, I swear I'd shoot you and dump you on the side of the road," she said with feeling.

I glanced across to see if she was smiling, and luckily she was, because I'd seen what she could do with a handgun at close range.

"Yes ma'am."

We laughed, letting the tension dissipate as the sound of sirens grew louder and fire trucks sped past us. But there was an unsettling feeling at the back of my mind that we were being played in the same way as a cat plays with a mouse. Suckered into a scheme that left us exposed, compromised and vulnerable. It didn't take a rocket scientist to figure out that it all had something to do with the Orange Moon affair in London, which I thought we'd left behind us. But just how the pieces fitted together was still eluding me.

I knew one thing. If you're being led, the only thing to do was follow. I had to trust the skills I had been given, and at the same time keep Julie and Sarah safe.

We left the car where we'd found it and I called Eliseo to thank him.

Sarah had minimal runway lighting. Basically just two lights at each end. The approach to runway 24 was between the two eastern spurs of the crescent shaped hills. Her friend in the Phoenix ATC quietly routed us through the city's airspace to Tucson using a fake identifier and then we were on our own.

The flight instruments in the Mustang were comprehensive, with terrain mapping through the GPS system, so once we dropped out of radar sight I could thread my way through the hills at fairly low level until it was time to turn onto final approach and line up on the runway. With nearly a thousand hours in the Mustang I was comfortable flying her into the narrow strip, confident there was ample room to stop, even if I overshot the threshold a little.

As it was, we touched down right on the numbers and coasted down the runway, slowing to turn off on the apron and taxiing past the old aircraft and hangars to the lights from the open 'Earthship' hangar. The little jet bounced along the rough, hard-baked ground until I slowed it down to walking pace and eased to a stop. Sarah was waiting with an oversized golf cart to tow it into the hangar.

"Nice flying." Sarah gave Julie a hug and patted me on the back, chuckling softly. "Not bad for a Limey bastard."

"Good to see you too."

Upstairs Paul was busy assembling more weapons he had commandeered from somewhere. "How'd it go?" he asked, without looking up.

"Another body and an encrypted laptop."

"Dean?"

"No. It seems our Mr Stockton planned a disappearing act."

"Huh."

The smell of fresh coffee permeated the little 'Earthship' from the percolator bubbling on the stove. It felt safe and secure here, tucked away in the remoteness of the Sonoran Desert.

"Coffee anyone?" I asked, seeing the four mugs laid out and knowing the answer.

Julie was busy on her iPad messaging with the Professor and took the mug of steaming coffee without looking at me, sipped gratefully then smiling as she waited for a reply. "What about Sutherland?"

"I'm going to set up a meet."

"Don't you have that so-called yacht delivery in two or three days?"

"I do. Question is, do I meet him before or after."

Julie pursed her lips, glanced at her iPad. "I think after. Without Dean's key, Dad's having a tough time getting around the encryption on the laptop. He says most of the information is in *the cloud*, hidden on different servers around the world that keep changing every thirty seconds. If he can discover the key, he thinks he can figure out the decrypt algorithm and consolidate the information on one server."

"But that's going to take time."

"Correct."

"Guess I'm going sailing then. Or to be more precise, trawling with Randolph Byron Moresby."

"How long will it take?"

"Five days maximum."

"I should be coming with you."

"That would blow my cover, wouldn't it? Besides, it's just an intelligence-gathering mission. This Moresby guy doesn't know me from a hole in the ground."

Julie didn't look convinced and I was wondering whether I shouldn't have some backup. I wanted Paul to stay here and I was not sure just how far I could stretch Eliseo's goodwill, unless I had some solid evidence for him.

Sarah came up from the hangar where she'd been drooling over the Mustang. "Nice bird, Thomas. When you're done with this nonsense, you can take me for a spin."

"Gladly," I said smiling. Then tossed her the booklet I'd picked up at Dean's. "Know anything about this place?"

She looked it through and shook her head. "No, but I might know some people who do. Want me to fly you down to San Carlos in the chopper tomorrow? Made the trip a few times ferrying rich fisherman from Tucson."

"Sure."

In the morning Julie busied herself on the computer, while I packed some things for the trip. Taking a weapon with me was out of the question. If the Federales found it, they'd lock me up and throw away the key.

Sarah insisted I fly so she could watch and critique my rusty skills. She was enjoying herself way too much but I didn't care, relaxed and comfortable to be in the air again. The Sonoran Desert from Nogales to Guaymas is pretty boring. Lunar type landscape, with fractured pinnacle peaks jutting from the flat plain past Hermosillo until the mountains crowded together on the last leg to San Carlos. The only main road stretched straight and long, with crowded buses speeding along, swaying past slower vehicles and memorial markers, indicating the spots where previous travellers and migrants had died.

Sarah chatted easily about her deceased parents and her sister in the Bahamas. Living alone had given her an air of crusty suspiciousness, which was simply a defence against the world. Beneath she was soft, generous, kind and well read. Enjoyed opera as well as country and the finer side of dining. Like me, fate had dealt us a hand we had no choice but to play, without complaint.

We landed at Guaymas, completed the Customs formalities, refuelled and were cleared to a private helipad on the outskirts of San Carlos. Sarah laughed and joked with the officials, as I sat quietly waiting, like a bored tourist.

The flight to San Carlos was less than five minutes, Sarah flying this time, making my landing look amateurish as she settled the helicopter on the pad and shut down.

"I'll stay in town until you call and tell me where to pick you up. Any trouble, call. You get bored, call. Okay?"

"Yes ma'am."

"Don't get too cute, Thomas. Julie will kill me if anything happens to you."

SEVEN

Sea of Cortez – Baja – July 30th 2013

Reality returned slowly, my brain beginning to work beyond survival mode. I threw up again, coughing out the last of the seawater becoming aware of the wind rising, the motion of the boat more pronounced.

It was a Chubasco. A wild squall that could hit without warning during the summer months in the Sea of Cortez.

Staggering up to the pilothouse, I slammed the throttles fully forward. To starboard I could make out the outline of an island looming and knew I had to get off the lee shore or be smashed to pieces. Checking with the chart plotter I saw that it was Isla Espiritu Santo. I spun the wheel and headed out into open water. Turning I struggled to open the hatch to the flybridge. Searing hot pains shot through my chest and I knew I'd broken at least two ribs. Well maybe cracked, not broken, but it didn't matter which because they still hurt like hell.

The four steps to the flybridge would be easy under normal conditions, but in my state in a rough sea it was an agony that seemed to last forever, until I could see aft. The first thought was that the dinghy was missing and the second that the line of black clouds advancing rapidly towards the boat from the south-east was indeed a chubasco, the wind speed climbing rapidly.

There was no time to think, so I staggered back inside the pilothouse and spun the wheel hard to starboard, bringing the bow up towards the advancing storm. There was nothing else I could do except sit and wait. To try running for the other side of the island would be courting disaster, as I knew the wind and seas would be upon me before I made it a quarter the distance, where the boat would be smashed against the rocky headland.

The chubasco hit with furious sixty knot winds that churned the sea into a maelstrom of white flying spray howling over the Bay-Cruiser and it was all I could do to hold her steady and on course, keeping the throttles fully open to keep from being pushed backwards. The engines strained at full revs and I prayed they would survive the punishment. A wave tore across the foredeck and thundered against the pilothouse, shaking the boat until it sluiced away and we slammed down into the trough and I wondered how much of this the boat could take before the fibreglass cracked and splintered under the onslaught.

For an hour the chubasco raged, pelting horizontal rain, with howling winds, huge seas thrashing at the boat trying to turn it sideways so it would be rolled and devoured by the waiting ocean, but somehow I managed to maintain direction and the engines never missed a beat. Not for the first time did I thank God I'd cleaned the raw water filters yesterday.

Then it was over.

The seas remained big but gradually subsided, and as dawn broke were small enough for me to spin the wheel to port and turn the Bay-Cruiser around the cape and head for La Paz. There, four hours later, I thankfully dropped anchor and shut off the engines.

The first aid box was in the forward head and contained some hefty painkillers. I figured three washed down with a large slug of tequila would do the trick, before I could begin to make sense of the last twenty-four hours. It took fifteen minutes for the painkillers to kick in, so I spent the time searching the yacht for any clues as to what had happened.

Moresby's papers were nowhere in sight, nor was his laptop, so I set about cracking the safe I'd spotted earlier. Inside, neatly stacked, were ten bundles of crisp new one hundred dollar bills. Each bundle contained two thousand dollars. The precision with which the bundles had been placed seemed odd to me, so I went to my cabin and returned with my iPhone and photographed the cash. The rest of the safe contained the normal dross of contracts and personal documents. Most people searching for anything, whether it be in a safe, a closet or desk, always concentrate on what they think is the most least likely place to look, when actually the best place to conceal anything is in plain sight. So I shut the safe and turned my attention to the saloon, remembering that the last time I had seen Moresby he was sitting on the aft deck sipping Courvoisier L'Esprit Decanter Cognac. Why he should have such a ridiculously expensive brandy on this tub was beyond me.

A cursory look in the drinks cabinet produced nothing. I took out the bottle of Cognac, opened it and poured myself a generous shot. The brandy was smoky strong with a slight apricot flavour. It was interesting, but to me it didn't seem worth $5,000 a bottle.

The rest of the yacht was clear. Nothing in the staterooms. No sign of Chaz Duprés, and I wondered how the hell he'd managed to get off the boat in the middle of the night after knocking me unconscious. Moresby had said he had a jet waiting in Cabo, which meant that I was going to have to tell the authorities what I thought had happened. The bodies would never be found, the hammerheads that swarmed through the Sea of Cortez would make quick work of them, and I was left with even more unanswered questions.

I don't like confusion.

I like to know what's going on. To be able to know my enemy and go after him, but as with any form of terrorism, you never know who your enemy really is.

Capitan Ernesto Rodriguez watched me from over his reading glasses as he laid down my written statement. It was cool in his office but I felt a trickle of sweat gather in the small of my back and run down the waistband of my pants. Waves of pain washed through me as the drugs wore off and my ribs throbbed with every movement and intake of breath. Immaculately dressed as always, his small, slim, well-muscled body was deceptively relaxed under his crisp uniform.

"That is all, Tomas? Nothing else?" His voice tipped with just the right amount of scepticism and query.

"I received a package by courier a week ago, a cash advance and ferry ticket to Guaymas," I lied easily. "A car was waiting to take me to San Carlos and the boat. Mr Moresby arrived the following day. I was satisfied there were no drugs, weapons, or illegal immigrants and that the ship's papers were in order. As you can see."

He leaned forward and peered at the documents on his desk, nodded, sat back.

"Please forgive my questions, Tomas. I know you for one week only. I do not see you as a delivery skipper. So..." He let his voice trail off as if further explanation was required.

"Sometimes I get asked to do high end sailing jobs. It's a hobby that keeps me busy." I knew Ernesto wasn't as laid back as he seemed. I picked up the kitbag and placed it carefully on his desk. He watched the zip slide back and looked up questioningly. "I found this in the safe. Twenty thousand very crisp, very new dollars."

He let his eyes drift down to the open bag and the neat stack of bills.

"This wasn't murder for gain, Ernesto. Somebody wanted Moresby dead and didn't care about anything else."

"You have a theory, Tomas?"

"No. Except Moresby told me he owned electronics companies that built guidance systems for NASA rockets."

Capitan Ernesto Rodriguez sat back in his chair and studied me carefully, his perfectly manicured fingertips together forming a pyramid as he closed his eyes and pursed his lips, deep in thought.

"This could be embarrassing for us, Tomas. Two US Citizens vanish without trace in of the Sea of Cortez. I can see the headlines, now. *'Pirates roam Baja Sud'*. It is not something I look forward to explaining. In ten minutes I shall have to call the American Consul. What shall I tell him?"

"The truth, Ernesto. The truth."

"I have not seen the bag. It is of no consequence anyway and there is an orphanage of which I am a trustee that is in need of new equipment. Besides, I have not heard of this man Moresby."

"That sounds like a good idea," I said carefully, wondering whether the money would really go to the orphanage.

"I shall take care of the Consul, but I'm sure he will need to talk to you, Tomas," he continued smoothly as he zipped the bag. "There is more to this than either of us need to know."

The phone on his desk rang crisply, startling me. It seemed an odd noise in this quiet office. Ernesto leaned forward and picked the receiver from the cradle.

"Ola. Si. Si. Gracias." He replaced the receiver slowly and turned to stare out across La Paz harbour towards El Mogote, an incongruous sand spit that separated the city from the Sea of Cortez beyond, sprinkled with the empty condos of an abandoned resort.

"There was no private jet waiting at Cabo San Lucas airport for Mr Randolph Byron Moresby and so far no information as to the existence of him at all. Immigration at Guyamas, Nogales or any of the International airports do not have any record of Mr Randolph Byron Moresby, or Mr Chaz Duprés," he said slowly before turning to watch me carefully. "If I did not know you Tomas, I would think this a practical joke or an illusion on your part."

I could see his point. No passports, no identification papers, nothing to show that either man had ever been on the boat. Just me, a 47 foot Bay-Cruiser, and twenty thousand dollars in cash.

After a quick medical check up at the clinic, a stop at the Bay-Cruiser to retrieve my possessions and the bottle of water that I drank before I passed out, I drove my rented Volkswagen beetle convertible back towards Loreto where *KOLOHE* was moored, with the unnerving feeling that Capitan Ernesto Rodriguez had not been entirely forthcoming. Something about the almost casual way he dismissed the incident and suggested a home for the money, was almost as if he already knew the story even before I'd appeared in his office. But then again it may have been my raging paranoia, because it's not every day that I nearly drown and two men - one of them my client - disappear into the ocean.

It was a long drive from La Paz to Morgan's ranch. Perhaps it was a stupid idea to return to the scene of my crime, but something niggled at a memory somewhere in my confused mind. It was the anomaly of Moresby's expensive cognac that set my mind on edge. A memory from six months ago that insinuated into my thoughts. A guilty memory perhaps. But it had finally dawned on me what she had been trying to tell me as she died.

We sat on the beach one last time in her favourite spot the night before I left for the Irish Republic a changed man. But instead of an ice-cold cocktail shaker of vodka and a jar of small onions, she had a bottle of Baron de Lustrac 1947 Armagnac, two crystal goblets and plate of goat cheese with crackers.

"What's the celebration?" I said sensing her bleak mood and trying to lighten the occasion.

"Celebration?"

"Have you forgiven me for leaving? Expensive Armagnac, Capricho de Cabra and black pepper crackers. A meal fit for a King."

"Don't play with me Thomas," she said softly, tears in her eyes, staring at the calm waters of the Sea of Cortez like a lonely lost little girl.

"I can't give you what you want, Morgan."

"I know. But it doesn't stop it from hurting."

"Perhaps in another life it might have been different."

"We only get one chance."

"I don't believe that."

She shrugged and brushed the tears from her eyes. Poured two very large measures into the goblets and handed me one. "Come back safely. You are always welcome here."

"Once again, thank you for all you have done for me. For saving my life."

We touched glasses and drank carefully, savouring the strong yet smooth Armagnac and plummy aftertaste. Perhaps I could fall in love with her. God knows my body wanted her but I still had the memory of Julie in my heart. And I could not be unfaithful to that.

"I bought a horse this morning," she said brightly, changing the subject, spreading a generous portion of cheese on a cracker and handing it to me.

"Really."

"An Arab stallion called Roshan. I've been wanting him for a long time and finally the owner agreed to sell. He's very handsome."

"Lucky horse."

"Not so lucky. He's a gelding, and that's why they sold him to me. He can't breed."

We laughed, she relaxed and the mood lightened, as two friends sat enjoying an early evening digestif, as the last of the sun's rays flickered across the Sea of Cortez. A slight warm breeze rustled through the brush, sending the smell of wild Baja blue sage across the beach in the balmy January night air.

The dirt road approach to Morgan's ranch was hidden from neighbouring ranches by a small bluff. For the past ten miles I had checked to see if I was being followed, circling back on several occasions until I was sure there was nobody on my tail. I turned off the headlights before driving slowly down the meandering track until I could see the outline of the ranch house, turned off the engine and quietly left the car to walk to the house.

There was no real reason to think that anyone would be here, but I was taking no chances. Too much had happened, in too short a space of time, to be sure of anything.

Fifty metres from the house I stopped by a torote tree and sank down on one knee, watching for any signs of movement. Eliseo had told me his men had 'cleaned' the ranch and I wondered if he had left anyone behind to see if I returned. Cicadas chirruped continuously and Baja night creatures rustled through the dry undergrowth.

After thirty minutes I crept to the house and climbed in through the newly replaced bedroom window having jimmied the latch. As Eliseo had said, the room was spotlessly clean with no sign anything had happened. Satisfied the ranch was empty, I went into the living room and opened the drinks cabinet.

What had been niggling in the back of my mind were Morgan's last words. *'Lost... Track...'* was what I thought she said, but that wasn't it. She was so impossibly injured she could barely speak, slurring her words in a last effort to tell me where to look for her files. Actually what she had said was *'Lustrac'*, the name of the Armagnac we had shared on the beach.

The bottle was in the cabinet. I pulled it out and examined it closely. There was nothing on the label, but I noticed something strange about the base. Then I remembered the other thing Morgan had said before she died. *'Bottom'*.

The bottom of the bottle, that should have been a deep concave shape, was covered in the same cream coloured wax seal that covered the top. Using my knife I prised the wax off and felt inside the concave base, finding a small flash drive. No wonder nobody could find her files. She had hidden them where nobody would think to look. Etched onto the side of the concave base of the bottle were two letters and a number DC 243-8-110-2, the same as on the drive. I put the drive in my pocket, typed the letters and numbers into my encrypted phone's notepad, then opened the bottle, poured a generous amount into one of the crystal goblets, and drank a toast to my friend.

"Maybe in another life, Morgan," I said softly, feeling her loss more than I wanted. I carefully replaced the wax seal on the bottle, so even I couldn't see it had been tampered with, washed and dried the goblet and put it back in the cabinet. Then walked away quietly, leaving melancholy behind and an uncertain future ahead.

Usually returning to *KOLOHE* gave me a sense of peace and security. An oasis of calm away from the noise and bustle of a life controlled by economics and petty laws designed to further reduce my bank account and restrict my freedom. But I was still troubled by my meeting with Ernesto and the old me, the suspicious killer that existed in the shadows, had taken a firm hold and I didn't like the feeling.

Once back on familiar ground, I carefully put the cans and bottle I'd taken from the powerboat into a plastic garbage bag and stowed it in a cockpit locker until I had the chance to have the contents analysed. But it didn't take a brain surgeon to tell me I'd been drugged.

Then I went over *KOLOHE* very carefully, looking for any signs that anyone had been on the yacht while I was away. When trying to search a boat without leaving a trace, it is difficult to remember exact patterns. There was nothing major that gave away the intruders, just the odd cushion slightly out of place. Clothes in the lockers not quite right and items in the drawers back to front. Patterns that people just didn't recognise. Eliseo had told me that someone had tried to get on the boat, and now I knew that he'd had his men search it as well. But they had missed the safe behind its false wall in the locker.

Trust is an uncomfortable concept in an untrustworthy business.

Sitting in the cockpit with a well earned ice-cold Baja Blond spiked with a slice of lime and shot of tequila, letting the thoughts organize themselves into some semblance of reason should have been easy enough, but there were pieces of the puzzle that ought to have slotted into place and just didn't.

Capitan Ernesto Rodriguez seemed casually uninterested in my adventure and the money I'd placed on his desk.

It was pretty clear that Eliseo had a tight hold on some aspects of the Provincial Government, but he didn't know Morgan as well as he thought. Or maybe he did, which was why he needed me to gather intelligence for him. Everyone was after the information I now had in my possession.

I was about to insert the flash drive into my laptop when the thought occurred to me that perhaps just about every electronic device I had, except for the encrypted phone, was bugged.

So far we had been pre-empted every step of the way. I needed to know from where this leak of information was coming. Not that I mistrusted Oldfield, I didn't, but Radley knew of him and no doubt so did Sutherland. And with their assets, at some stage, they'd crack Oldfield's communications encryption.

Julie wasn't expecting me to call for another day, so I opened another beer and sat thinking. We had been reactive and not proactive and it didn't sit well with me. I felt like an avatar in a video game, with the main players moving the pieces and changing the rules at will. Somehow I needed to be the one manipulating those rules and leading instead of being led.

Be the hunter not the hunted.

To pursue the computer analogy, I needed a disruptive algorithm of my own. But I knew I needed a little more information first.

I had to know just which side Sutherland was on. And that meant baiting a trap with him as the goat.

Surprisingly I slept well, perhaps secure in the knowledge that Eliseo had two of his men watching *KOLOHE* at all times. He didn't want me killed before I had given him what he wanted. I awoke with the rising sun, just before six, feeling refreshed although aching from my sore ribs. Just as I finished a light breakfast of coffee and honey melon my mobile rang. It was Julie.

"Why didn't you call?" she asked anxiously.

"I needed a good night's rest."

"Everything okay?"

"Not quite."

"Are you going to tell me or not?"

I took a deep breath, wondering just how much I should say, considering my suspicions about Sutherland and Radley somehow being able to access our calls. Maybe I'd put too much reliance on Oldfield's abilities.

"Moresby disappeared off the boat in the middle of the night."

"What?"

"Vanished without trace. I'll fill you in when I see you."

"When will that be?" Julie sounded tense, distracted and I noticed I really had to raise my voice for her to hear me.

"In forty-eight hours. I have a meeting with Sutherland late tonight."

"Say that again."

I repeated myself then asked, "...did the Professor get the information off the laptop?"

"Yes. He's sending the decrypt key."

"Okay. See you soon."

"What?"

Again I repeated myself then hung up wondering if I should have insisted she have the operation instead of acquiescing to her obstinacy. Annoyance crept over my mind and I shook the irritation away. I couldn't afford distractions.

The next call was to Sutherland.

"Took your time reporting in," he said tersely. He sounded none too pleased hearing from me, especially when I told him Moresby was dead.

"How did you let that happen?"

"Believe me it wasn't by choice. I have a headache and cracked ribs that attest to it."

"What did you find?"

"Meet me at the Healing Spirit Hot Springs Resort in Murrieta tonight at 22:30hrs."

I hung up on him and called Sarah and told her I was in Loreto. The town was - at a heading of 189.9° - almost due south one hundred and fifteen nautical miles across the Sea of Cortez from San Carlos. An easy hop for the Explorer and she'd be at Loreto Airport to pick me up in just over an hour.

Then I called Eliseo.

"Tomas, I hear you have been busy."

"I trust the money was useful for the orphanage Eliseo."

"Indeed. Santa Maria Theresa in Loreto. You should visit sometime, it was Morgan's favourite charity."

"I'm glad it's doing some good."

"Did you find what you were looking for?"

"No. I thought I may have missed something at the ranch but it was clean." I figured he'd know I'd been there, even though I was sure I was not being followed. And I felt that lying to Eliseo about something he would already know was not something worth doing.

"Are we any closer?"

"Maybe."

"I hope you are not playing with us, Tomas."

"You need me to keep the focus off you, Eliseo. A leash on me is a rope around your neck."

"I will remain true to Morgan's memory, Tomas. She was a friend to us both and we both have a debt to pay."

"Indeed. I will tell you that I plan to rattle Sutherland's cage tonight."

"Be careful. My sources tell me he is not what he seems."

"Would you care to elaborate?"

"If I could, I would. We have to move carefully. As you just said, we do not need scrutiny."

"I'll be in touch."

"Tenga cuidado mi amigo," he said softly.

In the port side cockpit locker I located three items of equipment I needed. The first was a Böker Plus Ginger Fighter Tactical knife with 6.25 inch blade, the second a Boye Cobalt Basic 3 sailing knife with 4 inch blade, and the third a small Night Owl Explorer infrared monocular night vision scope. The Böker might raise an eyebrow at San Diego customs, but together with the other items like sailing gloves, jacket and tatty deck shoes in a Ronstan dry sailing bag, they should pass as yachting equipment.

Sarah was waiting at the airport when I arrived and when I explained where we were going, plotted the route to San Diego and then to the French Valley Airport near Murrieta.

"We'll need to refuel at Bahia de Los Angeles. They have jet fuel for helicopters there. God only knows why, it's such a funky little strip, but it does. Then clear customs at San Diego." She finished laying the course into the flight computer and looked me over. "You wanna tell me what happened?"

When I'd finished she just shook her head and stared at an AeroMéxico jet landing in front of us.

"Ever felt like you have a ring in your nose and someone's tugging it real hard?" she said quietly.

"I do and it's time to start changing the game. That's why we're flying to Murrieta. Did you find out about the Resort?"

"I did. Used to be owned by the mob back in the 1950s and 60s. They laundered their money through it and entertained all the Hollywood celebrities. Then some pseudo religious new age spiritual 'blah blah' outfit got their hands on it. Nobody really knows whose money's behind it, but some suspect it's another money laundering operation."

"Sounds like a set-up to me."

"Oh good. Just when I thought I'd left all that crap behind."

"You're staying with the helicopter."

"Damn right I am. With this leg I'd be a liability."

"You remember the unofficial codex system we used in Afghanistan?" I asked suddenly.

"You mean between certain SEAL, DELTA and SAS teams on joint operations?"

"Yeah."

"I do."

I wrote out a simple code and handed it to her. "Just in case somebody's monitoring our communications."

"That's the problem with modern technology. There's always some bright hacker up to no good who can crack anything."

EIGHT

Surprisingly, at this time of year the resort was pretty empty, so I had a fair chance of spotting anyone who seemed out-of-place. It had the air of a nineteen fifties Spanish style ranch that had been turned into a rambling hotel. A seedy rundown reminder of a Hitchcock movie set.

The main reception, restaurants, hot spring pools, mud baths and massage rooms were concentrated in one area, a hundred yards from euphemistically named 'lodges', which were the accommodation buildings. They looked more like barracks.

It was dark by the time the taxi dropped me off on a quiet side road half a mile from the resort, out of sight of the highway. I walked across freshly cleared land made ready for a new housing tract. Little boxes all looking the same, built in a mock Spanish style. Dozers and graders stood abandoned for the day, strange metal monsters in the night. I kept to the trees as I neared the accommodation blocks, staying out of sight of the occasional car that drove slowly down the road.

There were two blocks, virtually side by side, Harmony Lodge and Lakeside Lodge, both with reasonable views. I chose Lakeside. Now all I needed was a room that gave me unrestricted view of the pool area. The side entrance was lit, the door hidden in a short porch in the side of the building.

It took a full minute to get the door open and I was beginning to think I'd lost my touch, but then I was through and into the hallway. The only sound was the humming of the air conditioning. The main stairway was at the front of the building by the entrance. Beside it a soft drink machine in brightly lit garish colours, waiting to be fed quarters before it released cold cans of Coke, 7-Up, or Fanta. The machine seemed a strange anomaly at a 'spiritual' health spa. I chose the second floor rooms facing the lake. As there were no lights on in the Lodge, I guessed it was nearly empty.

Inside it was dusty. Builder's tools and materials lay in disorder among sheets of drywall as if it had just been abandoned. I found a room upstairs which was clean, tidy, smelling of fresh paint and waiting for a new resident. I left the lights off, closed the door and walked straight through to the French window that led onto the veranda, opened it slightly, dragged a chair over, set my sailing bag down, then crossed to the bathroom where I found a boxer's style terrycloth robe with hood, and a big beach towel. I brought them back into the room and sat down looking across the half-acre lake to the hot spring pools beyond.

It was 21:45hrs.

Small low wattage lights glowed eerily through the steam coming off the bubbling water.

There was movement to my left, up by the main building, and I saw young two men in white terry towelling robes with towels draped around their necks, step out and sit down at a table on the patio by the main swimming pool. They seemed uneasy and I guessed they were Sutherland's advance party. Focusing my small monocular night scope, I could pick out their ear mikes.

I swung the scope back to the pools. There were three people, two men and a woman, all in their mid-thirties. The woman stood between the men, breasts taut against the material of her swimsuit. She looked at Sutherland's men and put her arms over the shoulder of her companions, then turned and kissed each one long and passionately.

Sutherland's men sat quietly at a darkened table watching.

The woman giggled and broke away from the men. She said something and they laughed. One of the men, tall, slim, well-defined muscles, climbed up the steps of the pool and onto the side. He stood facing the men on the patio, dried himself and wrapped a robe around his body then walked away to the main building. The other man left the pool with the woman, but instead of following the first man, they went off toward detached villa-style lodges on the far side. I swung my scope back to Sutherland's men who still sat staring at the hot springs.

Something was wrong.

I couldn't put my finger on it. But something was wrong.

I scanned the far buildings and the walkways. A light flickered on in one of the small villas.

I switched my attention back to the men on the patio.

They still hadn't moved.

It was 22:30 hrs.

There was movement and I saw Sutherland walking from the direction of Harmony Lodge down to the hot springs. He was dressed in a tracksuit top and Hawaiian pattern swimming shorts.

His men still hadn't moved.

I pulled my jean legs up to my knees and put on the terrycloth robe, positioning the hood over my head, then slipped the knives into the pocket. Nobody was about as I left the building, and keeping to the shadows headed up the path towards the main pool, carrying the bag with the towel draped over. The odour of sulphur hung in the air, smelling faintly like rotten eggs.

I deliberately walked slowly, slightly bent over. Not as a caricature, but as one might expect an old man to walk. The steps led down to the right, the swimming pool steaming slightly in the moonlight, surface a flat calm, but I wasn't interested in the beauty, just the silhouetted figures on the patio before me.

I knew what was wrong, what had been bothering me, before I got to them. They were too still. Both men had been killed by a single bullet to the side of the head. A small calibre, low velocity round, that penetrated the brain without blowing the entire side of the skull off. They sat pinioned by the arms of the chairs.

And I'd missed it.

It took me five minutes to manoeuvre around to the villa-style lodge. The door opened and the woman came out. She was still in her swimsuit, with a towel over her shoulder. I waited until she'd walked around the corner towards the hot springs area, pulled out the knives then moved quickly up the steps to the villa. There was the sound of movement and low voices. I'd have one chance that was all.

The door opened to my knock and the first young man died without making a sound. Still standing, the Böker buried deep in his chest, thrust up underneath the rib cage into the heart. I pushed him backwards and caught the second man, before he had a chance to bring the automatic he'd picked up, into a firing position.

He gurgled as the keen edge of the Boye knife found his windpipe and blood sprayed across the wall. He collapsed instantly, feet drumming momentarily on the floor and then he was still. I closed the door behind me.

The whole episode had taken no more than seven seconds. My Special Force's instructor would have been pleased.

Quickly I rifled through their belongings, although God knows what I thought I'd find. The silenced automatic was a special design, carrying a magazine of .22 calibre rounds. Each round was flattened on top with a file. No wonder there wasn't an exit wound. The small bullet would have fragmented inside the brain. Neat, clean, deadly. Someone was very professional. It seemed to me too professional for a Government Agency. These guys were hit-men. Paid assassins who took a great deal of care about the equipment they used. I found a towel and wiped some of the blood off my hands and face.

It was 22:35 hrs.

Sutherland was still in the pool, the woman on the other side her back to me as I approached. Neither of them paid any attention to this old man as he shuffled towards them.

A few people walked past on their way to the swimming pool, but far enough away not to see what was going on.

Sutherland looked up as I got nearer. The girl turned her head just as I reached the edge of the pool. She must have seen the blood spatter on the robe because there was a moment of surprise, then fear. I had the knife out and against her throat before she could do anything. Sutherland froze in horror. On the side of her neck I noticed a small tattoo of a butterfly.

"Who do you work for?"

"I don't know what you're talking about. Let me go."

"You work for Marika Keskküla don't you? I've seen the butterfly tattoo before."

She smiled visibly, even in this light. "Mariposa de la muerte. But it's a moth not a butterfly."

"Very dramatic. Your two boyfriends are dead."

"What the hell's going on Mr Gunn?" Sutherland started across the pool.

"Stay there." The menace and command in my voice stopped him dead in his tracks.

"Gunn? You are dead." Fear started in her eyes and she raked her long nails down my arm.

I yanked back on her hair, bending her neck over the bar, knife tight against her throat. "Marika Keskküla. Tell me where she is."

The knife cut into her skin and blood flowed down her neck across her breasts, spreading pink across the water.

She started to whimper. "We don't know. Just get instructions and money. Nothing else. She is Mariposa de la muerte."

"Yeah yeah. I've heard that story before." I was becoming a very mean son-of-a-bitch.

"It's true." She smiled, a beautiful, sensuous, erotic, poisonous, evil assassin.

Then she started to fight. Kicking. Jerking one way and then the other. My grip tightened involuntarily and the knife slid easily through her windpipe and arteries, blood bursting in a crimson fountain. Her eyes widened as the awful truth hit her, then she died and floated away across the pool.

Sutherland stood mouth open, looking ridiculous in the spreading red water.

"Get out of there, Sutherland."

As he clambered out of the pool, I quickly went through the girl's bag. I found what I was looking for. One of those deadly syringes. I showed it to him.

"This was meant for you. It's what they used to kill Hal."

Sutherland glanced back at the pool. "Jesus," he breathed.

"Where's your car, Sutherland?"

"In the parking lot."

"Where's your phone?"

"In my pocket."

"Show me."

He dug into the pocket of the tracksuit top and pulled out the phone, handing it to me. I opened it, dropped the battery in the pool along with the body and chopped up the SIM card with my knife, scattering the pieces in the flowerbed.

"What are you doing? What have you done to my men?"

"Your men are dead. Jesus Christ, Sutherland. This woman's friends killed them. What made you think these people wouldn't be onto you?"

He shook his head, still in shock at seeing the woman die. I guess he hadn't been involved in fieldwork. Just a desk jockey.

One thing I did know was that Sutherland wasn't the leak. It didn't make anything any clearer.

I pushed him ahead of me to the patio, where I stopped by his men and quickly retrieved the car keys, ear mikes and weapons, making sure there was nothing to identify them as Feds. Sutherland turned away until I had finished, then led me to the parking lot and the new black Chevrolet Suburban, by way of his room to collect his clothes. What is it about Federal Agencies that they choose big black SUV's?

Once inside the SUV I called Julie. There was no answer and my blood turned cold.

I tried Paul's phone. After five rings there was a crackle and I could hear his garbled voice.

"Thomas... you..?"

"Where are you Paul?"

"Seventy-four... Idyllwild... Crash..." Then the phone went dead.

'Idyllwild? What the hell are they doing there?' I thought, my mind racing again. Seventy-four, although a well travelled road, had hidden curves and at a couple of points, steep drops on either side of the road. What on earth would have made them travel to California, after I told Julie to stay in Tombstone?

The French Valley Airport was on our way and I found Sarah resting on the comfortable seats in the back of the Explorer.

"No way I can get this baby in there at night," she said, after I explained where Julie and Paul had crashed. "Nowhere to land, but my uncle's ranch is near Indio." She showed me exactly where on the Suburban's navigator and marked the route. "I'll meet you there. His

104

name's Jake. Be careful, he's one of those pack-rat recluse types who lives alone and doesn't like strangers. Actually he pretty much doesn't like anyone."

Ignoring the traffic coming up behind me I drove slowly along Highway 74. The moon was our ally, helping us find what we were looking for just a few miles before reaching Idyllwild. It was nothing much, just a faint imprint of tyre tracks leading off the side of the road, down a steep slope that disappeared out of sight within twenty feet of the highway.

I stopped the Suburban and crossed to the edge of the slope. There at the bottom, another fifty feet down amongst the boulders, scrub brush and trees was the Porsche. Dented and buckled from the fall, windscreen shattered. There was no sign of life.

Sutherland stood beside me, pale and angry. "Murderous bastards." He started forward.

"See if you can find some rope in the Suburban. I'm sure you Feds carry all sorts of shit in there," I said quietly.

He looked at me, anger burning in his eyes, then turned and went back to the SUV. Within a few moments he was back, with a brand new length of climbing rope. I tied one end around my waist, the other to the front axle of the truck, and started down the steep slope, sliding on the sandy surface, scraping elbows and knees on the jagged rock as I went, finally reaching the car.

There is a moment of revulsion whenever you approach the scene of either an accident or an ambush, when you just don't want to be faced with the awful truth of death. It was strong at that moment, lasting a few seconds before I peered in through the broken windscreen.

The Porsche was empty. Airbags on the driver's and passenger side deployed looking like flaccid dead white fish.

"Anything?" Sutherland shouted. I swear if I'd had a gun I would have shot him there and then.

Off to my left I heard a rock slide down the hillside.

"Paul? Julie?" I whispered.

"Thomas?" came the reply out of the darkness.

"Yes."

More rock slid down the hillside and Paul appeared. "Thank God it's you. Julie's hurt. She has a broken arm."

He led me back to where she lay.

She smiled weakly. "Took your time, Gunn."

"Got a bit tied up back there."

"I bet it was a bitch with a tattoo on her neck."

"It was and she won't be any more trouble."

"Good," she sighed and closed her eyes, drifting in and out of consciousness. Beside her was a black kitbag.

It took a half-hour to get her to the Suburban with Sutherland standing wringing his hands in what I hoped was genuine distress. Paul and I laid her on the back seat.

Sutherland climbed in beside her and cradled her head in his arms, then looked up at me, pleadingly. "We've got to get her to a hospital."

"We can't afford to do that. She'll be okay."

Paul looked at me questioningly. He had a nasty gash on his forehead that would need stitches.

Sutherland grabbed my arm, fingers digging into my flesh. There was a cold ferocity in his voice. "Anything happens to Julie, you're a dead man."

"Really," I replied calmly and prised his hand off my shoulder.

For a moment the anger boiled in his eyes, then he deflated like an old balloon and sighed heavily.

I turned to Paul. "What happened? What the hell are you doing here?"

"We got a call from Sutherland, who said to meet you both at an address just off Highway 74. I should have known it was a set-up. It didn't feel right from the start. Came around the corner and there was a truck stalled across the road. We had no time to stop, sideswiped it and ended up against the barrier. Then it backed into us and we went over the edge. I got Julie out just before they came looking for us. They searched the wreck took the laptop, then left."

"I never made that call," Sutherland said, sounding bewildered.

"Why didn't you verify with me, Paul?" I asked.

"Heard your voice in the background. He said you were busy on the other line. Then I heard you say *'tell them listening watch only'*."

"Somebody's playing us for fun."

"Who?" Sutherland asked.

It was a rhetorical question, as none of us had the answer.

From this side of the mountain it was a straightforward drive down to the desert plain and Sarah's uncle's ranch, hidden away in the foothills of the mountains, seven miles east of Indio. I kept the speed down, so as not to attract attention from the Highway Patrol and Riverside Sheriff's Department cars that we occasionally saw passing us by. And by the time we turned off the I-10 Freeway towards the ranch, it was three in the morning. It was another three miles up a dirt road, the only indicator there was a ranch here at all was a dot on the GPS navigator. I didn't know whether Sarah was going to try a night landing or wait for dawn to break, so after driving through the dilapidated main gate to the ranch, we stopped about a mile up the dirt road in the shade of a cluster of sorry looking palm trees, that had been imported to add colour to the place.

Paul and I walked up the track towards the run-down ranch house and stopped fifty yards from it, as a man's voice whispered from the shadows.

"I guess you must be my niece's friends."

There was the sound of footsteps behind us and a bow legged African American walked towards us, a menacing looking Magnum revolver in his hand. He may have been in his late seventies and walking awkwardly, but the hand that held the Magnum was rock steady and beside him loped a very large dog.

"Thomas and Paul. Sarah said to be careful."

The man chuckled softly. "She did, did she? Name's Jake. Get your vehicle and bring it on up. Dog's name's Frankie. Catahoula Dane mix so she don't stand no nonsense." He walked past us towards the ranch house. The dog walked up to me, sniffed and then licked my hand before walking ahead. I followed as Paul went back for the Suburban.

We carried Julie carefully into the house where Jake had prepared a bed, and laid her on it. He examined her carefully.

"She's got a concussion and her arm's broke. Needs setting. I'll get my bag," he said and started towards the door.

"You a doctor?"

"Nope. Medical corpsman back in Vietnam days. It won't be pretty but she'll be better off if I set it."

"Okay."

He returned a moment later with a battered red Paramedic bag that had seen better times, gave Julie a pain killing injection and went about setting her arm. "Feels like a clean break. Hold the top of her arm still for me." I did as I was told while he manipulated the bones of her forearm into place. When he was satisfied, he carefully laid her arm on a pillow.

"That's pretty good," He sounded surprised he still knew how to set a broken arm, then looked at Sutherland who was standing in the doorway. Frankie watched him carefully. "There's a glass bowl next to the sink in the kitchen. Put some warm water in it and bring it here."

Jake took out a cotton bandage and two rolls of lime green coloured plaster cast material.

"Lime green?" I exclaimed.

"I get what I can. Ain't much call for lime green so I can pick it up real cheap." He winked at me. I guess when he said 'real cheap' he meant free.

"You live alone up here?"

"Past twenty years, since my wife died. No kids. Sarah looks in every once in a while. Spread's been in the family for a hundred years."

"That's unusual."

"Sure is. Nobody wants this place. Nothing here anyway 'cept buzzards, rattlers, rabbits and coyotes. San Andreas Fault's about four miles north. Some day this'll be beach front property."

He gently wrapped her arm with the cotton bandage, making sure it was wrinkle free and then unrolled the plaster as Sutherland arrived back with the water, edging past the big dog who growled softly but didn't move. Jake dipped the plaster in it, squeezed out the excess water and starting from above the break, rolled the first roll around her arm and down and around her hand and thumb; folded over the ends of the cotton bandage and did the same with the second roll. He smoothed the plaster and studied the results.

"Not bad." He turned to me. "Make sure she stays still until that hardens. Shouldn't take long. I'll check out your buddy."

"You're pretty handy with this stuff."

"You live out here, you better know how to fix things. Doctors don't make house calls, and the ambulance fellers these days know nothing."

NINE

Sarah arrived just as dawn was breaking over the desert mountains to the east. Little dust devils spiralled in the occasional gusts that blew down the canyons onto the flat plain, and the air smelled of dried sage and mesquite. Julie was sleeping with Sutherland at her side, Frankie keeping guard over them, while Paul, Jake and I sat drinking rotgut black coffee on the stoep, watching Sarah set the Explorer down gently close to the ranch house.

"She's not going anywhere just yet," Sarah said emphatically, after I told her what had happened.

Jake nodded in agreement. "Couple of days. Make sure the concussion ain't causing any troubles." He took Sarah to see Julie.

Paul sipped the scalding coffee and stared into the distance as the sun rose above the mountains. "Another fine mess you got me into, Thomas," he said with a wry smile.

"What else would you be doing?"

He shrugged. "Do we need the rest of the team?"

"If we had a defined mission, I'd say yes. But we're fighting shadows. I'm still no closer to finding out where Marika Keskküla's operating from and who she's working for or with."

Paul was interrupted by Sutherland joining us. "I need a phone to call my men."

"You do that and we're all dead. Whoever you're protecting wants you dead too," I ventured, to see what reaction I'd get.

"There are some things that not even your security is high enough to know, and your capabilities only go so far," he responded hotly.

Paul looked up slowly his eyes stone cold. "You have no idea what our capabilities are. Neither does Radley. You tell that bastard when I've finished with you, I'm coming after him. Bureaucrats," he said disgustedly. "You're all so full of shit and secrets."

Paul's quiet outburst surprised me and I wondered what he knew that

I didn't. We hadn't had time for an *'in depth'* conversation since he'd arrived in the States.

"We need a 'come-to-Jesus' meeting. All three of us. Now," I said, growing angrier by the second. "What are you two not telling me?"

Paul stood. "Let's take a walk." He led the way behind the ranch house where a trail led up towards a canyon, found a quiet spot and sat down. He looked at Sutherland. Then at me. "After you left, Radley had me arrested. Threatened thirty years in Wormwood Scrubs if I didn't cooperate. My job was to track down Marika Keskküla, she's still got her hand in the nuclear cookie jar." Paul sighed heavily. "I should have told you earlier but..."

"Yes you should."

"You weren't involved. Radley didn't want you to shoot off his other ear. Anyway, you were in the middle of the ocean." He grinned sheepishly and carried on when he saw I wasn't smiling. "We suspected Keskküla was still operating for the ISEC members who remained part of the old Order of the Orange Moon. She's a sociopath with a ton of money. Everything went pear shaped when Morgan was killed."

"You knew about that?"

"That's where Sutherland comes in. We were pretty sure Morgan had information on the Order of the Orange Moon people through this guy Ted Lieberman of the Griffin Trust." Paul looked up at me again. "You should know. You were the one who sent her looking."

"I did, but I expected her to call me if she found anything." It was my turn to look away. "She did call, but too late."

Each of us had pieces of the puzzle, but none of us really trusted each other and what little trust there was, was being sorely tested now. I didn't want to share my connection with Eliseo, but now that Paul had confessed to being in Radley's employ, I didn't know how much he'd shared with me and how much he still kept to himself. I didn't expect Paul to apologise. It's not what you do in this business.

Sutherland stood a few metres away, staring back at the ranch, seemingly in his own world. He spoke without looking at either of us, still staring at the horizon.

"You were on the high seas, Mr Gunn. I sent an agent to interview

Morgan Alvarez in Baja. He never came back. Then three days later, you showed up in East LA." He turned his head slowly and looked at me accusingly. "So you see, trust is not an easy commodity when we don't know who is an ally and who isn't."

"Are you an ally Sutherland?"

"The only one you have this side of the pond."

"So what do you know?"

"I did a little digging about this Dean Stockton guy. Seems he's pretty heavily involved."

"So tell me something I don't know."

"What you don't know, is that he has links to Bank Unione d'Italia, Credit Suisse and Schloss Fürnsberg Bank of Austria as well as the Futures markets in London and Wall Street."

"You're telling me a radio talk show host is involved in the giddy heights of international high finance?"

He shrugged. "There's no solid evidence, just hearsay from my informants on Wall Street. I don't know how you can get it, but we need that evidence. Maybe then we'll know who's pulling the strings."

"If he's involved as you say, what the hell's he doing messing around with a small fry like Hal?"

"Like I say, I don't know. That's up to you to find out."

"Where is he?"

"I don't know. Yet."

"Anything else you know about him?"

"Not a lot. Apart from being an obnoxious radio host, he's squeaky clean."

"That it? Nothing else?"

He shook his head. "Nothing Stockton was involved in seems worth the deaths of five people."

"You want to get to the bottom of this Sutherland, you do things my way from now on. You're on their list, so just like me you're going to back off. Officially that is."

"I can't do that."

"Are you a field agent, Sutherland?" I asked and he reluctantly shook his head. "So just how long do you think you are going to last out there? You planning on going back to work? Just breeze into the office as if nothing had happened? If so, you're even more naive than I thought."

"You need someone on the inside Mr Gunn."

"For Christ's sake, Sutherland. There is no 'inside'. Don't you understand? We're all on the outside. We're all on a list that makes America's Most Wanted look like a church committee. They will kill us no questions asked. It'll be like we never existed."

He was silent again, staring out across the desert. It was only a matter of time before somebody found us. Either Keskküla's killers, or Eliseo looking for answers. Julie had the code key for Dean's laptop files and I noticed that Paul stayed silent. He knew, but he wasn't telling Sutherland.

"The Hollywood Hills house is safe. Not even the department knows about it," Sutherland said eventually. More as if he were talking to himself than us.

"Not a good idea. There are people watching it. Friends of mine."

"You have friends?" he growled sarcastically.

"None that you would want to know. And the less people that know about your involvement the better."

"It figures."

"I'll figure out a way for you to disappear," I said as confidently as I could.

Sutherland didn't like me much and the feeling was mutual. I didn't know whether that came from my living with his daughter, or that he now saw me as a real threat to whatever it was he was hiding. And I was sure he was hiding something.

Paul and I walked back to the ranch house, leaving Sutherland alone with his thoughts.

"Any other secrets Paul?"

"There never were any secrets. Like I told you, I just didn't have a chance to explain before now."

"What about Radley? Is he expecting a report?"

"Every week."

"What are you going to say?"

"That we know very little, except that we have confirmation that the Keskküla woman is running a contract assassination team. I'll give him the grisly details and he can track her down."

Sarah and Jake sat on the front veranda watching the gathering clouds on the peaks, sipping bourbon-laced coffee and picking at maple syrup covered waffles.

"Want some?"

"Sure," Paul said quickly and went inside.

"Not for me."

"Should eat something."

"Can't. Too early."

"Do you have a computer Jake?" I asked, wondering if that was even a possibility.

"Yup. Ain't used it. Got a phone too," he said witheringly.

Sarah laughed. "My sister Leila thought he needed to get into the modern world."

"It's sitting on the desk in the office. Makes a good paper weight," Jake muttered, stuffing another forkful of pancakes into his mouth with relish.

"Mind if I take a look?"

"Help yourself."

Jake's office was surprisingly neat and tidy, and the laptop, a brand new MacBook Pro, sat on the side of the desk on top of a pile of receipts. Next to it was a wireless modem that was switched off.

The computer started immediately and I could see that Jake had not used it at all. It was as if it came straight out of the box, except that his niece had set it up for him so he could access the Internet and create files in Word and Excel.

"That's my job," Julie's voice startled me and I turned to see her leaning against the doorjamb, smiling.

"You should be in bed."

"I'm hungry. Beside, it's lonely in there."

"How're you feeling?"

"How do you think?" she laughed. "Like I was in a car wreck.

Nothing breakfast won't fix."

"That's if Paul left anything to eat. How's the arm?"

She lifted it showing off the lime green colour. "Painful and not exactly the colour I would have chosen."

After a solid meal of bacon and eggs, fresh orange juice and coffee, the colour was back in Julie's face and her eyes brighter. I was sure that she didn't have a concussion, just some facial scrapes and bruising. After examining her Jake agreed, but still suggested we stay another couple of days just to make sure. While we were discussing her health, she went into the office and sat down at the computer with the flash drive I'd taken from Morgan's ranch. Armed with another cup of coffee and a bacon sandwich I'd made for myself, I followed her and sat down in one of the old but comfortable armchairs in the corner of the office.

After a few minutes typing with one hand, she turned to me with a smile.

"This is the story she was working on. And it's not what you think. Take a look."

I leaned over her shoulder and stared at the screen.

JT Purdue – The Man, the Money and the Politics

"I've heard of this guy," Julie said as I read the first page. "Caroline talked about him. Something about his company funding movies."

"And I saw posters of him. He's running for Mayor of Los Angeles. Can you print this?"

Julie looked around and spotted a printer beside the desk under a box file. There was dusty paper in the tray.

"Turn that on for me."

I found the power switch and the printer hummed. Within a minute it buzzed and rattled out three pages of text. I took the pages and sat down. "There's a bunch more."

"Great."

She smiled, turned and went back to work. I watched her for a few moments as she slowly typed and moved the mouse with her left hand, then turned back to read the freshly printed pages.

<u>*The Jonas Trust Deception*</u>

No article on the business life of Los Angeles, or the inhabitants of Beverly Hills, would be complete without an in depth study of the man the Beverly Hills Chamber of Commerce calls "The Businessman of the Decade." He is JT Purdue, entrepreneur extraordinaire, financial genius and manager of the affairs of numerous famous stars of the entertainment industry.

So just how does a son of a poor dirt farmer from Oklahoma and mediocre student, rise to the top level of society and business in the entertainment capital of the world? How does a complete unknown with little talent, no charm, and the manners of a goat become the Chamber of Commerce's Businessman of the Decade?

By graft, corruption, blackmail and extortion.

By gathering information on people in places of power, and utilizing the information to build his own inviolate power base.

By becoming indispensable to those whose dreams of success can only be accomplished with the help of men like JT Purdue. What is being written here will be scoffed at, disbelieved and I will no doubt be castigated for levelling such accusations at the man some consider to be a pillar of the community and the next Mayor of Los Angeles. Those people are liars and cheats, who would say anything to ensure that their part in this saga of robbery and murder does not come to light.

I have spent the last four months gathering enough evidence to show that JT Purdue is a pariah.

A leech on society.

A vampire tearing at the very soul of American ethics. American principles. American values.

Tearing at the very fabric of our freedom.

For JT Purdue, the road to power and wealth began early in 2003. As a minor executive of Trans-Oceanic Mutual Assurance, he was assigned to cover insurance losses in Iraq and Afghanistan. This of course covered the Persian Gulf and the vessel losses claimed by international shipping lines flying flags of convenience.

He was able to put together a complete dossier of several of our nations most trusted servants, who are suspected of being involved in a variety of activities from drug smuggling to heavy equipment sales, uranium yellow cake sales, and the granting of contracts of everything from oil exploration to massive infrastructure construction in South American countries. It was the intention of these trusted servants of democracy to utilize the money to build a firm political power base back home.

JT Purdue utilized this information to secure for himself a position with one of Wall Street's biggest investment brokers and learned the trade for which the Beverly Hills Chamber of Commerce awarded him their highest honour.

During the next seven years, he worked behind the scenes through his brokerage house, THE JONAS TRUST, to orchestrate some of the most spectacular financial coups in the history of Wall Street. His financial dealings, using what he euphemistically called 'The Green Light Investment Algorithm', were at best, a deception, and at worst, wholesale theft.

By then JT Purdue had pocketed a tidy fortune, and increased his portfolio considerably. For a man of infinite arrogance and vanity, Hollywood became a goal. The ultimate manipulation of people and their lives. But there was more. Much more. This wasn't just a move for the sake of vanity. This was a carefully calculated move in association with...

That was it. Just at the point names should have started tumbling out of the computer, it stopped.

Julie was still hunched over the computer, brow furrowed. Through the window I could see Sutherland beyond the barn, walking further up the trail into the canyon, disappearing into the distance. The rusty cogs in my brain started ticking over. Slowly.

Purdue was the key.

Julie sat in her own world, head rattling with numbers, letters, codes, bytes, entry systems, data bases, menus and God knows what else. I seemed superfluous.

Sarah was checking the Explorer while Jake sat in the living room, reading glasses perched on the end of his nose. Paul stood on the veranda, watching the sun climb higher and sipping another cup of coffee. We seemed to be a house under siege, waiting for the attack, never knowing when it was coming, or from where.

"What's in the barn Jake?" I asked.

He looked up. "My truck. Equipment. Other stuff," he said taking his glasses off. "Wanna look?"

"Sure."

The old barn doors creaked open and we walked inside where a large sand coloured truck sat on oversized wheels and tyres. It had a custom built RV-style back with jerry can holders, off-road sand ladders, shovel on the side, spare wheels, solar panels and spotlights facing forward and back on the roof. On the front it had a big 'bull-bar' protecting the radiator and a snorkel for fording deep streams. It sprouted two CB radio antennas.

Jake opened the rear door and climbed inside, sitting down on the fore-and-aft settee on the right. There was a small boat-style galley with two burner stove, sink and fridge at the rear on the right and an enclosed 'head' on the left.

"Underneath it's a 1990 Jeep Grand Wagoneer 4X4. Had this camper back custom built by a friend of mine. Rebuilt the suspension myself to take the desert tyres, heavy duty springs and shocks and put in a 5.2 litre turbocharged diesel engine which runs on standard or B100 biodiesel. Seventy gallons of fuel in two tanks; forty gallons of pressurised water in a single tank; two five-gallon jerry jugs of biodiesel and four 12-volt deep cycle batteries and a small generator. Used to spend two weeks out there roaming around prospecting."

"Impressive."

"Like bein' on my own sometimes, away from all the bullshit."

He reached up and opened a hatch in the false roof. Inside were an AR-15 assault rifle, Glock 9mm handgun and Remington Pump action shotgun. He grinned at me.

"Never can be too careful. They're loaded ready to go and spare ammo's under the seat. Usually carry a few pounds of Semtex and detonators for blasting as well."

"Find anything?"

His grin grew wider. "Now that would be telling wouldn't it? Let's just say I don't need to work." He pointed to the instrument panel. "Leila installed one of them GPS things so's I don't get lost. Like that's gonna happen. Told her it needed a password so nobody can check my route."

I nodded smiling. Prospectors are a cagey bunch and no wonder, with the insane greed that the thought of a gold strike imbues in people.

Jake clambered out of the truck and explained every nuance of his prized possession. He was convinced it could go anywhere a Humvee or Land Rover could, and I had to agree. The Jeep pedigree was solid, uncompromising and rugged. Jake carried spares for the engine, suspension and transmission and enough tools to rebuild the entire vehicle. Under the settees were his prospecting tools and a small bucket sluice concentrator was stored on the heavy-duty roof rack.

The rest of the barn consisted of a woodwork bench, routers, table and band saws, and a storage room piled high with all sorts of junk collected over the years. Some from military surplus stores and other equipment from auctions or salvage yards. A couple of old dusty armchairs sat near the workbench where an old fridge rattled noisily.

Jake opened the fridge, rescued two bottles of cold beer, tossed me one and flopped down in a battered armchair. We sat drinking, with me listening, while he talked at length about the intricacies of prospecting for gold. Whether to go for alluvial placer gold as opposed to lode gold, and the best techniques for finding either. It was a pleasant way to pass the time. A brief respite in the insanity of our lives.

Julie sat back tiredly as the printer whirred, churning out more pages from Morgan's files.

"She was going to '*try*' this JT Purdue character in the press," I said incredulously. "Somewhere there must be a connection between him and Ted Lieberman."

"Why would she do that?"

"It was her job as an investigative journalist. She believed that the press was the weapon of the people against oppression. Pure. Inviolate."

"And you don't believe that?" she asked enquiringly.

"No. I'm too cynical. I've seen the press simply create situations they think the public will want to read. Sometimes I think that the only true journalism comes from rags like the National Inquirer. At least everyone knows they're absurd and the ridiculous stories total invention. There's a warped kind of honesty in that."

"Strange logic, but I see your point."

I settled down with the latest printed papers and began to read.

JT PURDUE
File 2
Investment Portfolio and Client List

I ran down through the listings, none of which seemed out of place. The clients were those you would expect of a major entertainment figure. Littered amongst the names of big movie stars, producers and directors, I noticed there were very few writers on the list, but there were senators, congressmen, the Governor, council members, bankers, lawyers and accountancy businesses. Purdue had his finger in every conceivable pie. What was strange, though, was that neither Dean's nor Hal's names were on the list.

Why?

But there was one name that jumped off the page at me. Randolph Byron Moresby. It seemed everywhere I turned that man was there. First in life, and now in death.

What the hell was his connection with Purdue?

Questions, questions. If I was a financial wizard perhaps I'd understand all this, but what I did know was that when people started creating complicated financial schemes, they were trying to hide something. I just needed to be able to see the trees instead of the forest.

It seemed that perhaps one man had the answers and his business biography was in my hands. But none of the information was of any use at all. Nothing here demonstrated any criminal intent or act whatsoever. It was interesting; it was detailed, but said nothing.

Surely Morgan had not been killed for information that was unusable. It may have been confidential, but the journalist's job is to break confidences. They do it all the time. The other sheets consisted of boring details of loan packages, arbitrages, CDs and prime bank notes. Again, nothing illegal. Just a complex system of structured international money deals, running into billions of dollars at a time.

JT Purdue was a broker. And the purpose of a broker is to put together a portfolio of clients and invest on their behalf, or to arrange arbitrage deals. That much I already knew. I was rehashing old information in an effort to make some sense here.

I skipped through the remaining pages and stared at the ceiling, listening to the soft drone of voices in the living room. Outside the Santa Ana winds began blowing down the canyons and around the ranch, finding holes in the walls to blow in sand and dust. Julie closed the office window and sat down, swivelling the chair to look at me.

The longer I waited to get into action, the more time the forces of darkness had to arm themselves and venture forth from their fortress to destroy us. The analogy was a little over-the-top, I know, but that's how I felt.

When I was researching everything there was to know about the Gunn Group last year, I studied various financial schemes and scams that cost governments and individuals billions of dollars.

"What if the money deals are not actually illegal. Unethical maybe. Bordering on fraudulent, but not actually illegal," I muttered, thinking aloud.

"You mean that it's not the way the money is generated but where it goes and what it does?"

"Something like that. Also, if it is unethical and perhaps fraudulent, maybe the people who have been defrauded don't want anyone to know. For example the Mexican Mafia. They invested to launder their dirty money and have been ripped off, so they want their pound of flesh."

"And perhaps some government agencies, like the black ops part of the CIA for instance, got stung the same way," Julie added.

"That goes some way to explaining why they want everything kept quiet. If the general public were to find out, there'd be hell to pay."

"Especially if there are political hopefuls like JT Purdue involved."

"Exactly."

"You've got a plan cooking, haven't you?" Julie asked cautiously.

"Maybe. But I need another conversation with Sutherland."

Julie turned back to the computer. "Just a minute. Something's been bothering me. The flash drive is 8GB and though we've only got a few megabytes of data, it says the drive is full. There are some hidden files that I missed." She concentrated on the screen scrolling through the pages trying to glean a clue as to the missing files.

"I'm an idiot," I exclaimed, showing Julie the letters and numbers etched onto the drive.

Julie stared at the innocuous looking reference number and then back at the screen, deep in thought. She moved her finger on the trackpad down to where the last sentence on the last page ended '...all proceeds were sent to lobbyists Lerner's & Associates in DC'. She hovered the cursor over the letters 'DC' then clicked.

The screen went blank.

"Shit. Did I just erase everything?" she exclaimed, but a few seconds later a small white box appeared on the black screen and the cursor blinked, waiting for a password. Julie typed '243-8-110-2' and again the screen went blank. This time a box emerged with the word 'IDENTIFY'. Next to it was a timer set for thirty seconds, counting down as we stared at the screen. "What on earth could that mean?"

I wracked my brain as the seconds ticked away. "Roshan," I said quickly. "Upper case R and N."

Julie typed 'RoshaN' quickly as the seconds ticked down.

Again the screen went blank.

Then a list of file names appeared. The first was entitled 'National Bank of America – Transaction #87'. Julie opened it.

"How did you know the password?"

"It just seemed odd that she'd spelled Roshan's name on his stall with two upper case letters. You'd only do that for a password."

The file was a detailed account of an arbitrage using a small obscure Fiduciary Bank in Phoenix Arizona. Apparently a subsidiary of the National Bank of America. On the surface the conduct of the loan transaction seemed above board. The lending bank was Schloss Fürnsberg Bank of Austria.

The purpose of the loan package was to supply five billion dollars worth of funding for power plants in Bolivia. All the documentation seemed to be in order. Engineering reports, design drawings, extensive inventory of machine parts, generators, switching gear and computers. On the surface it could be seen to be a noble enterprise because the money was a self-liquidating loan operating on the fall-out from the arbitrage transaction, which meant that the receivers of the loan didn't have to pay it back. The total was underwritten by a Jonas Trust Synthetic CDO (Collateralised Debt Obligation), valued at two hundred and fifty billion dollars.

Julie sat back and stared at the screen in total disbelief.

"Two hundred and fifty billion dollars? Who the hell has that sort of money?"

Hal's words sprang into my mind. *'We can finance our own movies this way.'*

"It's financial gobbledegook for manipulating loans, selling debt and making a fortune. That's how the Global Financial Crisis occurred. Banks passing on debt, until someone is left holding a worthless piece of paper. Hell, I don't understand any of it and neither do the people who invented the whole mess. It's a smoke screen. An illusion. A magic trick."

Then my eyes shifted back onto the screen. Bolivia? Who the hell had dealings with Bolivia? It was a country almost under permanent siege. Generals becoming Dictators, being killed to be succeeded by another General who became a Dictator, who was ousted by yet another General. I read on.

Manuel Rives de Cordoba, a Junior Minister of the Bolivian Government concerned about the obvious corruption of the regime, communicated details of an arrangement made between Savings and Loan Bank of Beverly Hills, the Jonas Trust, the Bolivian Department of Energy, and Sanchez Rivero, the Minister of the Interior and Colonel in the Bolivian Army. The agreement was that Sanchez would provide phoney documentation for the proposed power plant in return for funds into his own personal account. Funding for the phoney power plant was a cover for financing US covert operations in Latin America.

At the same time, Sanchez provided a conduit through the Mexican drug cartels for opium trading with Afghanistan. The profits would go back to the Savings and Loan Bank and the Jonas Trust, as repayment of the loan for the 'notional' power plant investment.

Savings and Loan Bank of Beverly Hills concurred with the arrangement and set up the necessary paper work to cover their tracks.

The broker in the centre of the deal was JT Purdue. Cordoba was brutally tortured, then killed, several months after he began his investigation. The Bolivian Government blamed terrorists and gave Cordoba a hero's funeral.

Julie turned and looked up at me, her eyes filled with fear. "The US government must be involved in this in some way. You can't fight a country, Thomas."

I knew what she meant. It seemed that the further we went with this, the bigger the problem became.

In order to carry out this little deception, JT Purdue had to have some pretty heavy artillery on his side. Now things were beginning to slot into place.

I picked up the printouts and leafed through them. The listing of Purdue's clients was conspicuous by its absence of names. Excitement was building inside me, and Morgan's face leapt into my mind's eye with all the clarity as if she'd just stepped into the room. Julie watched me as I walked back to her.

"You're enjoying this, aren't you?"

"Morgan wanted me to figure this out. She knew she had limited time."

"And now she's dead, Thomas." The flat simple statement, spelled out slowly with her slender beautifully shaped fingers, was more devastating than any spoken word.

"Yes. She's dead and we are going to find out why."

"Okay." She turned back to the computer and began to print out all the information from the drive.

My problem was how to use all this. I could communicate to the Press but I didn't know how far Purdue's talons stretched. Morgan was the Press and she was dead. And yet the only way to keep ourselves safe was to expose what was happening. The plan that had been forming in my mind suddenly seemed, to me at least, more feasible than ever.

"Listen Julie, the how doesn't matter. All this stuff about Banks and dubious loans and theft and how Purdue and his bosses do it doesn't matter. What matters is why they are doing it. What is the reason everyone who gets close to this, dies? Hell, the Banks caused the Global Financial Crisis everyone knows that, so what's different about Jonas and his cartel, cabal, syndicate whatever they call themselves? Everyone in the entire world knows that most banks, trust funds, savings and loans and other variously-named and so-called secure financial instruments are all managed by crooks with a licence to defraud, but what makes these guys different? We don't need to understand the financial shit, just who's running it and why."

"And you know how to find out who and why?"

"I'm working on it."

Sutherland was quite far up the canyon trail, walking slowly, breathing hard. He sat down on a large rock, leaning forward, face pale. He looked up slowly at the sound of my footsteps. Frankie loped beside me and growled at Sutherland. I thrust the papers into his hand.

"What's this?" he grunted, just wanting to be left alone.

"Read it."

He raised an eyebrow but didn't comment, then looked down and started to read. Gradually the colour returned to his cheeks. The sweat dried on his forehead and he shivered in the keen wind. When he was through he looked up once more.

"You must have known all this. Why didn't you share?" I challenged.

"It's hearsay. If we listened to everything that was said about people, especially successful people, we'd have no time to catch the real criminals."

"You don't think he's a real criminal?"

"Like I said, it's hearsay. No evidence. Can't do anything without evidence."

"Or don't want to. Just who is pulling your strings Sutherland?"

He stood angrily, the colour seeping up his neck and into his face, a vein throbbing at his temple. "You think I'm setting you up?"

"It had occurred to me."

"You think I set my daughter up too?"

"Possibly. But I think the truth is you miscalculated, just like Radley did. Just like all you people do. You think you have the power, but you don't. You have no idea the degree to which these people will go. You're out of your depth Sutherland. In way over your head. I don't know whether you still believe in principles and morality, rules and regulations, but they don't exist in the real world. Rules and regulations are for idealists and dreamers. Money and power know no rules. Haven't you learned anything in all these years?"

Then he took a swing at me, a lazy curling right hand that I easily stopped, catching his fist in my hand. Frankie barked and was about to lunge at him. For some reason the dog had appointed herself my guardian.

"Down girl," I said and she backed off, still growling. "You wanted me in this, Sutherland. You thought you had conned me into working for you. But you are wrong. I only care about the people I love. I don't give a crap about you."

"What about your own life?"

My laugh must have sounded like the screeching of a madman. "My life? That's the least important thing to me. My life? I died once already, now I'm simply working to live again." I left him there, staring after me, as I continued up the trail.

Suddenly I was done with people. I wanted to be alone without responsibilities. And I yearned for *KOLOHE*. For the peace and serenity that enveloped me every time I stepped aboard her. I was finished with death, murder, killing, lying, cheating and the mistrust that came with this world.

The trail petered out so I found a convenient rock and sat down. Frankie lay down in the shade of a boulder, panting, watching me. The sun shone warmly, the canyon breeze drying the sweat, cooling my body. It was peaceful here away from the ranch.

Honest.

Real.

We were but fleeting specks on the surface of the desert mountain.

126

Minuscule barely visible dots on its slumbering mass.

I could spend weeks, maybe months thinking about everything, but the truth was something had to be done, and whether I liked it or not, I was the designated one. My plan was insane within the parameters of normal life, but we didn't live normal lives.

Light bulbs really don't go off in your head, but there are moments of clarity and usually the simplest solution was the best.

JT Purdue was the key.

I needed to cut out the complex crap, the false trails, the misdirections, and focus on reality.

Finally I stood. I knew what I wanted to do. Frankie looked at me questioningly.

"Come on, let's go back." She gratefully walked by my side as I headed back down the trail.

"Purdue is the key and I'm going to going after him," I told everyone as we assembled in the living room.

"Just what do you mean by 'going after'?" Paul said carefully.

"Kidnap him."

"What the hell? Are you insane?" Sarah exclaimed.

Jake smiled and giggled softly. "You sure know how to make friends son."

Julie's eyes narrowed. "Explain."

"As far as I can tell from these papers, JT Purdue and his Trust are the centre of a huge deception that makes Madoff look positively insignificant. But money on this scale needs Government backing because they have to secure the financial arrangements. No individual or corporation can cover multi-billions of dollars. You need the Federal Reserve for shit like that. Purdue knows where inside the Government the trail leads."

"How do you know that?" Sutherland asked.

"He's running for Mayor of Los Angeles. Maybe that's his payoff. Money isn't everything to these people. Power is. We need to know why these people are killing our friends and trying to kill us, and who the hell they are. Purdue is the key."

"Why not present him with the facts and tell him to come clean or we go to the media?" Julie said quietly. I could see in her eyes she knew the answer, but she wanted me to explain to everyone else.

"You know that will never happen. He'll laugh in our faces and kill us," I said a little cruelly, but there wasn't time to be nice, even to Julie.

"So you're going to put him under protective custody?" Paul said wryly, a slight grin on his face. I could see he was warming to the idea.

"Something like that. Nobody will be expecting us to do anything this nuts. That's our advantage."

Jake pulled a cigar tube out of his top shirt pocket, opened it, drew out a Hoyo de Monterrey Short Corona and studied it carefully. I watched as he lit it slowly, circling it in his fingers as he warmed the end, before putting it in his mouth and drawing fully. Another crazy idea came into my head.

"Do you have anymore of those tubes, Jake?" I asked.

TEN

Paul slowly drove the rental car Jake had acquired for us along the palm tree lined street, past the quiet graceful homes of the Beverly Hills rich. Manicured lawns where sprinklers, unaware of water shortages in this desert land, sprayed happily all day long, while bored migrant Mexicans walked the gardens with noisy blowers attached to their backs, blasting leaves, grass cuttings, dirt and dust from one part of the yard to another. Metal stakes with yellow coloured boards proclaimed the area was patrolled by PacWest Security - *'Armed Response'*.

Black and yellow patrol cars cruised the streets, while the guards sat immobile in their starched uniforms and mirror sunglasses hiding listless eyes. Staccato radio messages, brief and indecipherable, barked instructions to them as they listened but did not hear.

Ragtop Mercedes and Targa top Porsches vied for prominence, paintwork gleaming from their daily wash and wax, tyres shiny black from tyre paint. Chrome dazzling to hurt the eyes, as painted ladies maintained their mask-like features sporting Rodeo Drive suits, diamonds sparkling in the continuous daily sunshine.

Scrubbed garbage cans stood in clean back alleys where even dogs and cats feared to tread.

This is where JT Purdue lived in luxurious security. Glamour and wealth side-by-side with corruption.

Julie and I knew this world. Once it had felt comforting and secure, but now it felt suffocating to be driving down these wealthy streets.

Purdue's house was hidden behind high walls and trees, large black double steel gates, spiked at the top, closed off the entrance to the driveway. Inset into the left hand, five-foot square, twelve-foot tall pillar was an intercom grill. Neatly hidden above it, was a fish-eye closed circuit TV lens.

Paul's eyes flickered over the walls and the gate posts as we drove past an intruder alarm system and armed guards discreetly hidden in the grounds.

"So how do you propose to get in, Thomas?" he asked quietly.

"Through the front gate, by invitation of course," I tried to sound as matter of fact as possible.

Paul rarely showed emotion, but this time he turned and gaped at me in disbelief, then almost as quickly his face became expressionless again, his tone terse and unemotional. "You're either a clever bastard or just plain crazy. You think he's going to let you out alive?"

"No. That's what I'm banking on."

Paul shook his head, kept his eyes on the road, turned the corner and continued slowly along the street. "So what do you want me to do?"

"Just be here when I call."

"What now?"

"Let's take a drive to Malibu."

Paul drove to Sunset Boulevard and we spent the next half hour meandering through Bel Air and the Pacific Palisades, to where Sunset emptied out onto Pacific Coast Highway. It was another half hour drive to Caroline's beach house.

The Friday afternoon traffic was as bad as ever, cars crawling two abreast at a snail's pace, snaking along the coast, drivers impatient to get to the beach and spend as much time as possible, before having to drive the thirty miles back on Monday morning to begin a new week.

The sea looked warm, inviting, mysterious and exciting, making me homesick for the open ocean with *KOLOHE* slashing through the water on a beam reach in a stiff breeze. I longed to hear the slap of the sails and the wind humming through the rigging once again. God how I missed the heaving deck and the thud of waves against the hull.

Paul drove with one arm on the window's edge, the other resting on the steering wheel.

"You'll find an Omega 10mm automatic in the kit bag in the back seat with two clips." Paul said. "The ammunition is Norma 170 grain JHP. Gives you 618ft/lbs, that's 20ft/lbs more than a Magnum's best ammo. Maybe slower but hits much harder and you get three more rounds in a magazine." He was comfortable talking about something he was very familiar with, back to a trade he knew well.

I knew what he meant. Visions of the enemy still charging, after being hit five times with a high velocity M-16 round, until they were chopped down by bigger, heavier, slower machine gun rounds. The M-16 round was only effective when it started tumbling after 100 meters, then it would rip off an arm or a leg.

Christ, here we were driving along a beautiful stretch of coastline talking about the merits and demerits of bullets and guns. Worse, it didn't bother me at all.

"It's a nice gun, the Omega. You'll like it."

Reaching into the bag I pulled out the box, opened it, and looked at the black, five inch barrelled automatic. I picked it up and held it firmly, feeling the stippled grip fit snugly into my hand, fingers falling naturally on the trigger and guard, thumb within easy reach of the safety and magazine release. I pressed the release button and the magazine slid into my left hand. The flat-nosed rounds sat neatly in the magazine, looking harmless enough, shiny and smooth.

"There's a shoulder holster as well, spring clip, slot the gun in upside down. Has a safety clip on it which will rip off if you're in a hurry."

I opened the other box, took out the shoulder holster. The fit was snug and the action smooth. The gun was a lot bigger than the small 9mm Beretta I used in Baja. This Omega was a beautifully crafted piece of engineering, designed for the express purpose of hurting someone or something very much indeed.

"I like it."

"Thought you would. Made by the Springfield Armory, this one has a Peters-Stahl barrel and slide unit. Helps hold the breech closed a little longer." He carried on about calculated energies, velocities, group sizes and the different grains of ammunitions. My concern was that the weapon fired without stoppages, was accurate and caused maximum damage to whomever I was shooting.

The morality of taking life just did not enter into the argument. That was a luxury afforded to those who lived the average life of a citizen, in our so-called civilized society. To outsiders like us, it did not apply.

"No problem with leading, either. In fact, the paper polishes the barrel. Do it properly, you get a great bullet." Paul started to sing softly.

"Hi ho, Hi ho,
It's off to war we go,
With a bucket and spade
And a hand grenade
Hi ho, Hi ho."

A stupid song we'd all sung back in the base camp near the Afghan/Iran border, waiting for another two week operation deep behind Taliban lines, polishing our black bladed knives, filling magazines, checking grenades, but always waiting for that moment when the helicopters dropped us off and we disappeared into another world. A world of no rules. No laws except those of survive and kill.

And we were very good at that, people like Paul and me.

"Shitty song. It was shitty then, it's still shitty now," Paul laughed.

"Kind of catchy, though, isn't it?"

He shrugged and turned his gaze back on the road. "Do you remember the combined operation in Nimruz?"

"I do."

"Lost a lot of good people there." He lapsed into silence.

It was an understatement. The whole operation had been a disaster based upon unreliable intelligence. The purpose had been to destroy a large ordinance supply depot the Taliban had set up on the Iranian border. Problem was, we had been fed intelligence by a double agent and ended up walking straight into a trap. Soon as we knew it was a trap, we had 'Starburst', split up, every man for himself. As a combined operation it was a fiasco.

Everybody blamed everybody else, but somebody found out the Intelligence Officer was deep in with some Afghan drug traffickers, who in turn were playing 'footsie' with the Taliban. The officer was found with his head neatly tucked beneath his spread thighs, teeth clamped onto his penis.

Paul was looking at me again and the smell and fury of Nimruz crashed banged and exploded in the silence between us.

"No secrets Thomas."

"No secrets Paul."

"Radley told me that Marika Keskküla set us up in Nimruz."

"Why?"

"Rumour has it she was importing yellow cake for the Iranian nuclear program."

"Things just got a whole lot more complicated."

We parked the car west of Caroline's house and sat on the beach, watching the pelicans, gulls and the sunset. A few hardy surfers were out testing the four-foot swell, well clothed in multi-coloured wet suits. A woman walked along the surf line with four dogs of various shapes and sizes, who ran in excited circles and chased each other into the waves crashing onto the beach.

The breeze and smell of the ocean was so good and yet again I felt my legs turn rubbery and a flutter in my stomach at the very thought of long a passage down to the South Pacific, where the wind and the waves were immune from ethics or morality. Where the laws were laws of nature, and there was no way to trick the elements.

"After all the years, I still don't understand it," Paul was saying. "As a soldier, I served my country without question, as every loyal Brit should. I believed in my duty. Yet it all got twisted around. We ended up hated in our own country, for serving it, dying for it. We're outsiders." He fell silent.

As the sun set, the surfers packed up in the twilight and headed home, and the last flock of pelicans skimmed low across waves flying to their roosting spot on the Marina del Rey breakwater. The lights were on in Caroline's beach house and the sound of music drifted across from the open window. I could see a shadow moving about in the house. Paul followed my gaze.

"Want to tell me what's going on?"

"She's a very powerful and persuasive agent. She knows studio heads, owners of TV and radio stations personally. And her name was on Purdue's list of clients."

"Okay," he said slowly. "So what?"

"I need studio time somewhere for my plan. Caroline can arrange that for me when the time comes."

"Studio time?"

"We live in a digital YouTube age Paul. What better way to get the message out there?"

"Sarah was right. You are definitely deranged."

"Maybe."

He shrugged, took out an identical Omega automatic to the one he'd given me, and checked the magazine before replacing it in the shoulder holster. Then he looked at me and there was a plea deep within his eyes. "Don't get me killed, Thomas. I'm just beginning to get back. I have a purpose again. Know what I mean?"

I nodded. There was no need for words. His eyes stayed on me for a moment, and then gave one of those rare smiles before returning his gaze to the ocean.

The floodlight from the house lit the beach and a short way out across the ocean, reflecting off the waves like the incandescence I yearned to see again out in deep water.

Then we moved closer to the house. The deck was twelve feet from the ground, so Paul and I employed a method we had used before in the army. I stood on his shoulders, grasped the railings and when I had a good tight grip, Paul used my body as a rope, to pull himself up and onto the deck. Then he pulled me up after him. We sat a moment catching our breath then went into the house.

"What the hell are you doing here?" Caroline shouted, not recognising me.

"Thomas Gunn. Julie's friend. We met a week ago."

"What do you want?"

"A couple of things."

"What are you talking about? Does Julie know you're here?" She watched me carefully.

"She does."

"I don't understand."

"You thought we were dead. That's why you're so shocked at seeing me. Now you're scared."

"But..."

"But nothing. I know you're linked to JT Purdue, Dean and Hal in an investment scam." I took out copies of the papers I had printed and handed them to her.

She took them and read slowly, turning a deathly shade of pale and sank down onto the settee.

"How did you get this?"

"A friend. She was killed because she found out what's happening."

"I just got paid to keep quiet. I'm useful to them. I'm an agent. It's what I do. Put deals together."

"Who are they?"

"Financiers, bankers, businessmen. I don't know. Purdue is the money. We can make the films we want without going to the majors. Be in control. Who wouldn't want to do that? In this business, you don't ask where the money's coming from, you just take it."

"Who else is in on this?"

"I don't know much. Just do as I'm told. Persuade my clients and friends to invest and stay out of the way."

"Your friends killed my friend. They also killed Hal, his wife Marie and Julie's sister. You know that don't you?"

She turned away guiltily. "Yes."

"They will kill you too," I said roughly. She gasped, her hand to her mouth. Then I relented slightly and sat down beside her, taking her shaking hand. "We can protect you Caroline, but we need your help."

"What's all this about?"

"I will need you to arrange some film production facilities."

"What?"

"Julie will contact you with the details later. If you want to stay alive, wait for Julie's call. Don't talk to anyone. Don't tell anyone about us being here."

She nodded without enthusiasm. We left her beached, bleached and helpless, staring blankly at the ocean as she saw her world collapse in the scattered tinsel of an illusion that no longer existed. Within a few minutes we were back in the car and driving to Beverly Hills.

Paul dropped me off three blocks from JT Purdue's house with instructions to stay close, out of sight of the circulating PacWest Security cars. I was dressed in jeans and T-shirt and carried a ring file I'd specially prepared, gambling on the guards fear of their boss. The grounds and gated entrance were lit by 1,000-watt spotlights, which penetrated every shadow for a good distance from the walls.

I took a deep breath and pressed the button on the gate intercom.

There was a short delay, then a tinny voice echoed through the machine. "Yeah."

"Thomas Gunn to see Mr Purdue."

"Do you have an appointment sir?" The voice sounded efficient, if disinterested.

"No, but he will want to see me."

"Just a minute sir." The intercom clicked off, but I knew the camera was scrutinizing me closely.

Two minutes later, the gate opened and a smartly dressed twenty-five year old man beckoned me inside. I noticed the bulge underneath the expensively tailored lightweight grey silk suit. He wore a military style crew cut and his blue eyes studied me coldly, without a hint of emotion. He glanced at the file and held his hand out, waiting for me to hand it over.

I smiled pleasantly. "Mr Purdue won't appreciate you looking through confidential papers." I lifted the file box and leafed through the first half for him to see. There was a moment of hesitation before he turned and led the way to a small golf cart, gesturing to the passenger seat. I climbed on and we drove the short distance to the house, parking by a side entrance where another equally well dressed young man stood by, watching.

If I was expecting giant, broken nosed, chisel jawed bodyguards I was disappointed. But I was sure these young men were well trained and totally ruthless. The difference was they were presentable and lent a professionally efficient business-like air to personal protection.

I was led into the house, which exuded an atmosphere of calm and order. The hallway gleamed with a beautiful polished redwood floor and original Norman Rockwell paintings lined the white washed walls. I glanced into a couple of rooms as we passed and saw heavy wooden desks, highly polished, and big overstuffed easy chairs. Whatever else JT Purdue may be, he was at least a man of subtle taste. The house was modelled on a Mexican hacienda of the nineteenth century.

The young bodyguard stopped outside a door and motioned me inside, then stationed himself outside in the hallway, closing the door behind him. I walked in, still clutching the file box and found myself in a large library with a huge open fireplace covering one wall, brown leather settees and armchairs close by, with big, solid oak rough-hewn coffee tables separating them. Purdue's English oak 'Partners' desk stood at the far end. Campaign posters were stacked neatly in one corner, near wall photographs of Purdue with various senators, congressmen, the Attorney General and even the President.

The man himself watched me enter with an air of amusement dancing in his piggy eyes. He was bigger than his photographs made him appear. A tall, thickset man, with heavy paunch and thick neck supporting a fat, heavily jowled face. He was dressed in a white shirt, sleeves caught by those flexible armbands always seen in old forties gangster movies that made him look like a malicious Sydney Greenstreet caricature. The waistcoat was unbuttoned and of the same thick pin stripe as the suit pants. There was a fresh cigar clamped in his fleshy mouth.

"Mr Thomas Gunn?" The question tinged with benign amusement, as if I had no right being here with this great and powerful man, but that he would allow it for a moment or two until I started to bore him. I inclined my head a little but said nothing, waiting for him to make the conversation. "What can I do for you, Mr Thomas Gunn?"

Still I said nothing, just let my eyes wander around the room.

"I know who you are, of course, but I confess I'm at a loss as to why you should want to see me." He sounded East Coast, the accent had a touch of wealthy New York, and his coolness was unnerving.

He moved away from the mantelpiece where he'd been leaning, the irritation more obvious now, the piggy eyes losing their amused look.

"Okay. Let's get down to it. You got something on your mind, boy?" his cultured tone disappeared into the Southern drawl of his youth. Still I kept calm; just let him sweat for a little longer. He knew I had something by the way his eyes kept flickering to the file in my hand.

"You had my friend Morgan Alvarez killed," I said softly, conversationally. Purdue's eyes slid up to my face and for the first time showed a touch of fear.

"What you talking about? You know who I am? I'm gonna be Mayor of this city. You read the newspapers?"

"You killed Hal Gordon and his wife Marie and God knows how many others."

Purdue's expression had solidified into one of sheer venom, anger and hate pulsating from him, like a dark evil suffocating cloud.

"I hope for your sake you don't know what you're saying, boy. Because if you do, you're gonna be in deep shit. You got that boy?"

He reminded me of the other corrupt American businessman I'd met in San Francisco, Samuel De Costas, who had tried to kill Julie and me last year. They could almost be related.

I raised the file box and tapped a couple of times with my forefinger.

"My friend Morgan left all the evidence on a flash drive. You don't believe me, take a look at this." I opened the file and took out several sheets, passing them across to him, continuing as he read. "You thought with her out of the way the problem would be solved, but you didn't count on me. That was a mistake. I'm surprised. Your file says you don't make mistakes."

He read quickly and paled visibly. Then looked up. "You're a dead man, Mr Gunn. You know that don't you."

"I don't think so. Take a look at this sheet." I moved closer, rifling through the papers, taking my time until I was close enough to him. I handed over a sheet then slipped the Omega automatic from its concealed place at the back of the box. He saw the gun and started to call for help. I jammed the barrel into his crotch hard and saw the tears come to his eyes with the pain. "Do anything, I'll blow your goddam balls off."

It is amazing how, if you threaten a man's testicles, he becomes a pussycat, amenable to any suggestion. All the blood drained from his face as he stared at the gun.

"Anything you want. You got it. There's plenty for everyone. One, two, three, ten, fifteen, twenty million. Thirty, fifty million. Anything you want. I can make you rich Mr Gunn, very, very rich." It was almost too much to curb the overwhelming desire to pull the trigger.

"I'm already rich, more than you can ever imagine. This is about honesty and decency, not money." I was having difficulty keeping my voice down, so as not to alert the bodyguard outside the door.

Purdue had started to sweat, his eyes still riveted on the gun. "What d'you want?"

"I want you, Jonas. I want you."

He risked a glance up at my face. "I don't understand."

"I think you do. But right now, I want you to get that bodyguard of yours to go bring the limo around to the front entrance. I remind you that this little weapon has soft flat-nosed bullets. They'll rip your balls off and tear half your pelvis out. It's a long and painful death and in the event you do survive, you'll never sing bass at Christmas again."

He turned his head and called to the bodyguard. "Randy!"

"Yes sir."

"Get the car, bring it out front."

"Yes sir." Randy's footsteps faded along the hall and we heard the front door open and shut again.

Purdue watched me carefully. "You'll never get out of this house."

I took the small device I had made at Jake's, out of the file. It was the small cigar tube, which I had cut down to half a thumb length and filled with Semtex industrial explosive. Jake had brazed a small loop, to which was attached a nylon self-locking tie. We'd used them in Afghanistan as very efficient handcuffs. The only way to remove them was cut them off. I showed the device to Purdue.

"There's a little radio receiver in the end, the type used by model aircraft. I have a transmitter in my pocket. Drop your pants."

He did so and stood ridiculously naked in front of me. I handed him the device.

"Now slip this over your dick and balls. You have three seconds." The fear was back in his eyes and he quickly did as I said. "Now tighten it." He did so. "More, we don't want it slipping off now do we?" He pulled the tie tighter. Now there was no way he could get it off by himself without a knife. "Okay, pull your pants up."

His face was grey with pain and fear, but underneath was hatred, pure and evil. The bulk of the cigar tube was barely visible under his suit pants. I put the Omega back out of sight.

"Now what?"

"Now I take you out of here."

"You're crazy, boy. You know that? You don't think the LAPD, FBI and every other Federal Agency aren't gonna be all over this town looking for me? You think there's any place you can hide?"

"I'm counting on it. It's what will keep you alive. Now that I have the evidence, your puppet masters are going to be very keen to see you in a coffin. Marika Keskküla works for the highest bidder."

At the mention of her name, he started to sweat.

But I was too confident, hearing the slight sound behind me at the last moment, the bullet catching my left shoulder muscle just as I started to spin out of the way. It went straight through the muscle, missing the bone. As I fell, I pulled out the Omega and fired. Randy toppled through blood soaked drapes, half his head missing, and crashed to the floor.

Purdue was halfway across the room.

"Stay where you are, or I press this button."

He stopped dead in his tracks.

"Now we get out of here. Tell your other goons to keep away. Any dumb moves and you're a dead man."

It had all happened so quickly. I'd forgotten that Purdue probably had a CCTV camera in the room. My shoulder hurt like hell. I backed up to Randy's body, ripped pieces off his cotton shirt and quickly stuffed my wound. I used small pieces to plug both entry and exit to staunch the flow of blood. Purdue watched, never taking his eyes off the transmitter I had on my right.

I called Paul and told him to be ready.

Wound bandaged, I walked across the room and pushed him forward. Three bodyguards stood in the hallway, guns in their hands. I showed them the transmitter.

"Drop the guns and slide them over."

They shifted their eyes to Purdue. He nodded and they carefully placed their guns on the floor then slid them over. I picked them up, one by one and stuck them in my belt, then nudged Purdue forward.

Anyone who thinks you can get shot in the shoulder and carry on smiling, as if nothing had happened, should be shot themselves. The pain made waves of nausea flood through my body. I blocked out the pain and shook the nausea away. Shock would set in later, but for now I had a job to do.

The car was a black stretch limousine. The chauffeur sat behind the wheel waiting. When he saw Purdue he got out of the car. When he saw me, he started to pull his gun.

Purdue held up his hands. "Drop it. Don't do anything." Sweat poured down his fat face. The chauffeur dropped the gun and slowly backed away, cold eyes watching me, waiting for an opening.

I shoved Purdue in front of me then slid into the car, moving over to the passenger seat, pulling Purdue after me.

"Drive."

The other two bodyguards had appeared at the door. I raised the transmitter for them to see and they stopped, tensed.

As soon as we were out of sight, all hell would break loose, that was guaranteed. My shoulder felt as if someone had thrown a brick at me, then an elephant had kicked me, then somebody had stuck a poker through my flesh. I felt sick and wanted to vomit. Purdue glanced at me every now and then, as we drove down the drive.

"Turn left," I commanded.

Paul had parked the car one hundred metres around the corner in a darkened deserted driveway. It would take our hunters a few hours before they located the car and by that time, we'd be long gone.

Purdue pulled to a stop behind the car as I commanded. Paul had the trunk open and stuck Purdue in the neck with a needle, the fat man collapsed and we bundled him inside and slammed the lid shut, I climbed into the back seat and lay down out-of-sight, then we casually drove away.

"What happened?" Paul asked.

"Shoulder. Through and through."

It took thirty-five minutes to reach Sutherland's safe house in the Hollywood Hills. Paul drove calmly as police sirens blared, the news of Purdue's kidnapping already spreading through the city like wildfire. The road to Sutherland's safe house was quiet. We stopped a hundred metres away and checked the area on foot. There was no sign of Eliseo's men. We went back to the car and continued to the gate, which opened as we approached when I pressed the button on the remote. Paul turned into the driveway, flicked off the lights, and drew the car into the garage.

I was fast approaching collapse from blood loss, but helped Paul drag Purdue out of the trunk and bundle him into the house. He would be unconscious for a while.

"Is there a first aid kit in this house?"

"Earthquake survival kit in the bathroom off the hall."

Paul returned with the first aid kit, broke open the seals and took out what he needed. Swabs, disinfectant and morphine, curette, and sutures. The tissue surrounding the wound cavity made by the passage of the bullet was dead, and if left would turn gangrenous. It needed cauterising. He drew morphine into a syringe, tapped the end and then injected me.

He eyed the curette he'd just slipped out of its sterile container and grinned. "Takes me back," he said calmly.

The pain was easing and I knew he had shot me with a big dose. I could feel the effects of the drug coursing through my body, soon to hit my brain and send me into a state of semi-consciousness, enough for Paul to work without having me crawl the walls in agony.

"Ready, Thomas?"

I nodded, fixing my gaze on Purdue's large comatose frame, while Paul probed the wound. Even with the morphine the pain was exhausting, forcing grunts through gritted teeth.

"Doing well, mate. Nearly finished. Got to make sure this bugger's clean." He worked steadily, scraping, swabbing, cleaning out with disinfectant, then packed the ends of the wound and bound the shoulder. "Maybe our friend Jake can do a better job when we get back there."

ELEVEN

For two days I crept through the hours of darkness and sunlight in a pain filled haze as helicopters and police cars scoured Los Angeles for Purdue. Paul entertained our captive with his own particular brand of homespun philosophy, a pastime guaranteed to turn even the most hardened stoic into a gibbering idiot. Purdue was on the verge of a breakdown when I decided it was time to stop feeling sorry for myself and get on with the next part of my insanity.

The newspaper, radio and television had been full of Purdue's disappearance, especially as no ransom note had been received, nor any statement given out by what the authorities had concluded, must be a new and very militant terrorist organization. Amazing what bullshit they give out, when they don't want the truth to emerge. I was sure they knew that I was behind this little caper, and would be pissing in their pants wondering what the hell was going to happen next. The thought helped ease the pain and brighten up my day.

I was the only one who knew what needed to happen next, the other players had no idea at all. I was just hoping they would play along. If not, then I may as well open an artery and end it all.

Sutherland, Morgan and Sarah must be wondering what the hell was going on. *'Don't worry if you don't hear from me for a few days,'* I'd told them. I got through on the second ring, thankful that Sarah answered the phone.

"Been causing quite a stir, Thomas. Got any other surprises for us?" Sarah's tone was mildly rebuking, but there was also a sense of excitement and suppressed joy.

"I might. You'll get a message in a few days. How's Julie?"

"Misses you and worries like hell. She got more stuff out of the computer."

"Put Sutherland on."

"He's not here."

"What? Where the hell is he?"

"Search me. Just took off saying he'd be back tomorrow, 'bout noon."

"Shit. Next time, tie him down, I don't want him sticking his nose in anywhere."

"Here's Julie."

"How bad?" she asked.

"What?"

"How bad are you hurt?"

"Just a flesh wound. Paul fixed me up."

"So what's next?"

Maybe Purdue was right. I might just be the biggest idiot in creation, but it was the only way I knew of getting out of this alive. All that was left was to convince Purdue, because sure as hell he was not going to do anything to help me. He was still asleep when I walked into the living room, his fat bulk spread out over the settee, engulfing what was really quite a sizeable piece of furniture.

I tipped him onto the floor. He rolled over, grunted, shook his head and stared at me with those little piggy eyes trying to focus in his sleepy state. Sleep drool ran down his heavily jowled chin, he wiped it away with the back of his hand in an unconscious move.

"What d'you want?"

"I'm going to make you a reality star, Jonas."

He looked at me completely incredulously. "What you talking about? My face is already spread all over the television and newspapers. You're an idiot, boy, and that's a fact."

I moved a little closer to him and held the small transmitter in my hand. Purdue glanced down at it and paled visibly, but in spite of his fear he kept control.

"You use that thing, I ain't gonna be any use to you at all."

I grinned what I hoped was my most malicious grin. "Jonas. I don't give a shit whether you're alive or dead. But for the moment, you're more use to me alive. Either way, I'll get the job done."

I could see his mind ticking over like a jet engine, figuring the odds, trying to come up with a deal. He could not and he knew it. I was too far gone.

"Now as I was saying, I'm going to make you a movie star, and you're going to do it, because you have no choice. Either way, by the time I've published just a little of what I know, there's going to be a lot of people who will want you dead. Your only choice is to go along with me. Do what I say and you may just get out alive. Don't, and you're a dead man."

He was going to have one last try, anyway. I knew. It was there in his eyes, the disbelief that he couldn't buy me.

"I can make you richer than your wildest dreams, Gunn. You never have to work again. Never have to do anything you don't want to. Think about it. You can have it all. Everything."

My hand flashed out, grabbed his shirt and dragged his body over so his face was a few inches from mine.

"You don't listen do you Jonas? I could press this little switch right now and your balls would be spread all over this room and you'd die slowly Jonas, screaming all the while. I've seen it before and you'll be begging for me to put a bullet in that fat head of yours. Begging, Jonas, do you know what I mean?"

Now he was looking scared and he had nowhere to run. He was not quite where I wanted him, but pretty soon he would be begging me to save his miserable hide. At least that's what I thought then.

Paul had slipped back into the room without me seeing, but Purdue's piggy little eyes slid up to him and gazed pleadingly.

"No good looking at me, fat man. I got everything I need. What I don't have, you could never give me anyway," Paul said.

Purdue crumpled and for a moment I thought he was going to cry. He looked up once more, this time there was a resignation to his eyes.

"I got to hand it to you boy, you're something else. Maybe different circumstances we could have been partners."

My shoulder was beginning to ache, but there was too much to do and so little time, the aches and pains had to take a back seat.

We drove out of the gate with JT Purdue sedated once more in the trunk and me lying on the floor of the back seat. Paul drove slowly, obeying all the traffic laws. Los Angeles traffic fumed its way along in the heat; music from stressed stereos mixing with exhaust gases as harassed businessmen driving alone sucked hungrily on surreptitious roaches, hoping the drug would heal the tensions of the day and make going home to kid-crazed households more bearable.

Paul kept the radio tuned to the news channel, but there was nothing. After two days, Jonas was no longer headline news, as another national security analyst leaked military secrets, embarrassing the Government further. The air-conditioner cut in and the stifling heat in the car began to dissipate. If he was lucky, Purdue may get some slight benefit, but I doubted that. The heat in the trunk must be unbearable, not enough to suffocate him, but enough to make life very unpleasant.

The drive was uneventful and long, but finally we arrived at Jake's ranch. Paul drove into the barn at the rear, parking beside Jake's Jeep Grand Wagoneer. I was glad to get out and stretch as Sarah, Jake and Julie closed the barn doors, and stood watching as we hauled Jonas out of the trunk. He was starting to regain consciousness. Jake unceremoniously splashed a bucket of cold water over him.

"Fuck you, Gunn. I'm gonna crucify you," Purdue spluttered, his eyes rolling in his head as he tried to shake off the effects of the sedative. Then noticed everyone else. "Who the hell are you people?"

Sarah shook her head. "Pleasant feller ain't he?"

Jake walked across to him and pulled down his eyelids. Purdue moved his head away, but Jake grasped his chin and finished his examination.

"He'll live."

I shoved Purdue down into a dusty old armchair Jake had left in the barn. Purdue tried to stand up again.

"Sit down," I said quietly, with enough menace in my voice and the transmitter in my hand to convince him. He sat down, the anger becoming a look of bewilderment.

"This man is obviously in need of psychiatric care," Jonas said, looking from Jake to Julie. "I'll make sure he gets the proper treatment when we get back to civilisation. If you'll just call my office, we'll get this straightened out. There is a reward for my safe return and you

146

won't find me ungenerous." He smiled what he thought was a generous, sympathetic smile.

Jake eyed Purdue, looking down into his eyes as he offered him a bottle of water. Purdue took it and drank greedily, tossed the empty bottle on the floor and offered up his bound hands. Jake looked at them, then leaned down and stared JT Purdue firmly in those piggy eyes.

"If there's one thing I know, this man is not the lying son-of-a-bitch you are. I've seen your commercials. You may not have killed anyone personally, but there's sure as hell blood on those hands."

Purdue stared unbelieving. "You help him, you're in big trouble, Pop."

"You call me 'Pop' once more, I'm gonna bust you right in the mouth. Jeez, some motherfuckers gotta talk all the time. Never know when to shut-the-fuck-up."

Purdue slumped down in the armchair, defeated. "Listen, we can strike a deal here. I mean, there's no need for all this. Think, for Christ's sake. What you're doing is a capital offence. They'll stick a needle in your arm for this."

Jake closed his eyes for a second before speaking. "Sounds to me like the Feds don't want this to get out. The way I figure it, you're as good as dead anyway. You got too much information, Purdue, and now they know that Thomas here has access to that information, whoever's pulling the strings don't want no word getting out. Besides, what you've done are crimes against humanity."

Purdue stared impotently.

So far I'd been lucky. Luckier than I could ever dream. The script was marching on slowly, but perfectly. Nothing untoward so far, except for the wound, which was making itself felt again, the arm and shoulder stiffening, the ache penetrating through to my already laden brain cells. I still held the transmitter in my hand and when a sudden wave of tiredness swept over me, the device slipped from my grasp and fell onto the floor.

JT Purdue squealed in terror, the sound snapping my eyes open. He was staring at the small black box.

Jake look at it inquisitively.

Julie bent down and picked it up. "What the hell's this?"

I explained and her face cracked into a wide smile.

Sarah started laughing until the tears ran down her cheeks. "Oh boy. You know where to hit where it hurts most and that's a fact."

Purdue was not enjoying the moment at all. His face was grey and there was a sheen of sweat on his skin, giving it the texture of a dull fish just plucked from the ocean.

"Take this thing off, for Christ's sake. Listen. You got me, okay. There's no need for this. I'm not going anywhere. For Christ's sake, all it would take is another box on the same frequency."

I have to confess to enjoying the fear in his voice. I was now the most basic of human animals that had discarded all the appearance and values of normal society, even of good human living. This was a dirty, filthy business and I didn't care at all. But he was right. It wasn't needed anymore and a freak transmission could activate the device.

Purdue showed no modesty in struggling to take off his pants. Julie turned away laughing. I took out my knife and cut the plastic tie, catching the device in my hand. Jonas heaved a sigh of relief and relaxed back into the armchair once more.

"Any screwing around and it goes right back on. Understand?"

He didn't answer. Didn't even look at me. Just closed his eyes.

Paul looped a length of chain around Purdue's ankle and padlocked it to one of the barn posts. Frankie stationed herself in front of him and growled, showing her teeth.

JT Purdue wasn't going anywhere.

"Where did Sutherland go?" I asked Julie.

"He didn't say."

"Idiot. He'll get us all killed."

Paul must have been thinking the same thing. "Can't stay here too long, Thomas."

"I know."

I felt very, very tired all of a sudden. The pain in my shoulder was like a knife slicing slowly through my flesh, stopping to twist every now and then just for good measure. I knew the wound was bleeding again as I felt the trickle of blood just before Julie spotted the stain seeping through my shirt. She moved forward, startled and carefully took my arm. Jake gently examined the wound. I was on the point of collapse from blood loss and Jake and Julie helped me back to the ranch. Sarah had gone ahead and prepared the first aid kit and plenty of hot water. She and Julie cut off my shirt as Jake washed his hands. Frankie lay down at my feet and whined softly.

I slept fitfully that night, trying to isolate myself for a short time, and forget. I had backed myself into a corner and was searching for a way out. Flying by the seat of my pants, not knowing where the hell I was going. Dreams filled with visions of Julie fluttered in my semi-consciousness just out of reach. She was caught in the jaws of a giant butterfly that beat its wings quietly, and slowly devoured her.

I half woke, but knew I had to go back to sleep in order to save her. So in the half sleep of semi-conscious reality, I drifted back to the world of make-believe and changed the scene. Julie was no longer caught by a giant butterfly, but was swimming in the azure blue of a sun drenched Caribbean afternoon. In the background, *KOLOHE* swung gently at anchor and Morgan lazed naked on the foredeck. I felt myself being drawn by the silent beauty of Morgan. Her nakedness stirring the passion long denied, long buried. But that was betrayal. I shouldn't be feeling those things. And as I stared at her, her smiling image was replaced by the image of maggots. Fat, white wriggling obscenities crawling through her face.

I woke in a cold sweat, shivering in the rising heat of the early morning. There was a cold beer in the fridge, which I took, and went outside to sit on the stoep and listen to the dawn calls of the desert animals as they headed back to their lairs after a night of foraging.

So far I had relied purely upon instinct. Moving as my subconscious directed as if to a predestined set of orders, set down and immobilized generations previously, activated now when I was ready and able to carry out the commands.

Was I simply a puppet of my own imaginings?

Were our lives like the pages of a book? Existing complete, yet unfolding page by solitary page?

Why didn't I just open the last page and see how it all ended?

The quiet of the early morning always brought out the brooding melancholy of my Celtic background. I was still a juvenile idealist determined to tilt at the windmill one last time, and return successfully to my home so that *KOLOHE*, my Rocinante, and I could once more ride out and face the honest elements and cleanse ourselves of the layers of death and deceit that were accumulating like a thick grey cloak, threatening to devour, just as the beautiful butterfly threatened to devour Julie in my dream.

I swore a curse upon my Celtic ancestry, drained the beer, swallowed four Tylenol and went back to bed.

It was early evening when I finally awoke, refreshed after the sleep but with a stiff arm. Julie was talking outside with Sarah, as she carried out an inspection of the Explorer, and Jake sat on the stoep smoking one of his cigars. Frankie lay by his side and lazily thumped her tail a couple of times.

"Good sleep?" he said, as I stepped outside.

"Pretty good."

He stood and walked over to look at my wound. "Got to watch for infection. Your buddy did a good job gettin' out all the dead tissue, but in this heat you gotta be careful."

"Where's Paul?"

"Entertaining your prisoner." He stepped back from examining my wound. "I got one thing I want you to do Thomas Gunn," he said, eyes unfathomable dark pools. I'd seen the look before and it was unsettling.

"If I can I'll do it."

"You'll do it alright. You'll take care of my Sarah. Whatever happens, make sure she's okay."

"I will. You have my word."

He nodded and sat back down on the stoep. Frankie laid her head on Jake's lap.

I thought of checking on Purdue, but decided to grab some cheese and crackers and a couple of beers from the fridge instead. Jake and I sat together, watching as the sun slowly sank across the desert plain, eating, drinking and talking about nothing in particular, while a crazy scheme unfolded in my mind.

"We are going to make a documentary. An exposé, and Mr JT Purdue is the star. He has enough information to blow the lid off just about every corrupt deal ever perpetrated in this great country, and none of us have anything to lose," I said as we ate a communal dinner of barbecued chicken, baked potatoes, yams, whole zucchini baked in butter, black pepper and garlic, and plenty of ice cold beer. Purdue ate his meal in the barn.

Sarah raised an eyebrow. "Got a title?" she said sarcastically, continuing before I could reply. "Jesus Christ Almighty Thomas, half the Federal Agencies, NSA, Police, Secret Service, and God knows who else is out there looking for you and you're gonna make a movie?"

"You got a better way?"

"Yeah. Leave him on the side of the road and I'll fly us out of here until the heat dies away."

"Come on Sarah. That's impossible and you know it. I know too much and by implication, so do you. They're not going to stop until we're dead and buried."

"What really sucks is that I do know that." She tipped back her beer.

Julie watched the exchange. "This affects us all. Every one of us sitting here. We have to do something outrageous, otherwise Morgan died for nothing. Besides, as Thomas said, we're all a part of it now, whether we like it or not."

Paul was leaning against the doorjamb eating an apple, crunching slowly and deliberately. He stopped mid-bite, staring me. "A documentary."

"A documentary," I repeated watching Paul's expression turn to incredulity.

"Any particular type?"

"Well more like reality TV and Purdue's the star."

"Are you serious?"

"Never been more serious in my life. Where's the biggest audience in the world? The YouTube generation. Stick it in a newspaper who gives a shit. Put it on film, now that's a different ballgame. This can go viral in no time."

"Guess there's some logic there somewhere if I could find it." He finished the apple and tossed it into the garbage bin, then started to laugh. "You have to be the craziest son-of-a-bitch in creation."

"No crazier than you. We dropped in from 30,000ft and blew up an Estonian island facility in the middle of the night, remember?"

"You've a point there, but we did have British Government sanction," he said grudgingly. "Sort of."

"How much help can Radley give us?"

"Not much."

"Can he get Sutherland to shut down the NSA satellite surveillance feed for a few hours?"

"Maybe. But he can't go through normal channels."

"But he might get the necessary coding for Oldfield to do it."

"Maybe. But I don't see where you're going with this."

"We have to buy ourselves some time. Disappear. I just haven't figured out how yet."

"And just how does a public figure disappear? They will find him before you can get your movie out," Julie asked, but I could see by the look in her eyes that she already knew how.

"He dies."

"What the...?" Sarah exclaimed. "That's murder."

"Metaphorically."

"How's that in people talk?" Jake said slowly.

"We make everybody think he's dead until we're ready."

"Kill him, metaphorically, on TV?" Jake asked cynically. "The viewing public would see through that in a second. Even an old ignorant black bastard like me knows that."

I went to the window and looked at the helicopter sitting behind the ranch.

"Paul, can you contact the ATC guy Danny used last year?"

"Just what do you have in mind?" he said, eyes narrowed.

"I don't know. Just thinking out loud. Julie, get your Dad on the phone. Paul, wake up Radley."

"What's the plan?" Julie asked.

"You, Sarah and Jake will drive out of here in Jake's truck. We'll figure out a rendezvous. Paul, Purdue and I will take a one way trip in the Explorer."

"I still don't get it." Sarah shook her head, brow furrowed.

"We need the NSA surveillance satellite shut down for thirty minutes so I can get the helicopter in position. It needs to crash somewhere in a remote part of the San Bernardino Mountains, but not too remote. We need the search teams to reach the wreck in a day."

"Yup, just as I thought, completely deranged. But every Special Forces guy I ever met was the same," Jake muttered. "What the hell. Guess it beats the hell out of staring at my navel until I die."

Paul handed me his encrypted phone. "Radley."

"This better be good, Gunn," Radley growled, sounding pissed off at being woken at four in the morning London time.

"I told you that if you screw with me, I'll screw with you."

"What are you talking about?"

"Sutherland."

There was silence on the other end of the phone for ten seconds. "What's your point," he said at last.

"He's gone missing. What didn't you tell Paul?"

"Missing?"

"Marika Keskküla's assassins tried to kill him the other day, now he's vanished and I need some technical assistance."

"What sort of technical assistance?"

"Block the NSA satellite feed for two hours, starting at three o'clock tomorrow morning, LA time."

"And just how do you expect me to do that?"

"You'll get a call from Professor Oldfield. He'll walk your lab rats through the procedures you need to implement. The rest is up to you and your secret friends this side of the pond."

"What if I can't?"

"Your mission will be dead in the water, and you'll be up-the-creek without a paddle while the crap hits the fan in a very big way."

"What's this all about?"

"You don't need to know. Plausible deniability if my plan goes pear-shaped. Besides, I'm sure you read your intelligence briefs."

"That was you?" he exploded.

"Now you see why you need to shut down the NSA satellite like I said, or you'll be neck deep in the shit with the rest of us."

"Put Paul on."

I looked at Paul and he shook his head.

"He's taking a leak."

"Tell him I meant what I said."

"You'll get the pleasure of doing that in person, Radley. And I wouldn't want to be you. And just remember, I still have the video tapes." I cut him off before he could reply.

"How do you know he'll do it?" Paul asked.

"Because he has no choice. An international incident on this scale would be very difficult to explain."

The next call was to Oldfield who, unlike Radley, didn't mind being woken up and was eager to crack the NSA's satellite coding.

"What next?" Sarah asked.

"You guys need to get going asap." I turned to Jake. "Is there a back road out of here?"

"Not a road, a trail. Took Sarah and Leila a few times when they was kids."

TWELVE

If you have ever been in combat, you understand the sixth sense that warns of an impending attack. Neither Paul nor I had to tell each other that the 'forces rallied against us' would soon be on the march. I worried that Sutherland had perhaps tried to make a deal, given them all the information they wanted and was probably dead. He hadn't contacted us, and of course I had destroyed his mobile in Murrieta, so I had no way of calling him and all I had were concerns in my head based on nothing. Perhaps he'd simply dropped out-of-sight just to stay alive.

It was a strange war, this. Battling an invisible enemy that only showed itself through acts of extreme brutality. But Purdue was my key. He could unlock the identities and then I would be able to put names and faces to these violent sociopaths.

Frankie padded up to me, sat and looked inquiringly into my face as I sat on the stoep in the moonlight. She whined gently to catch my attention, raised a giant paw and dropped it on my knee. I ruffled her ears and she closed her eyes, enjoying the attention.

She turned her head, dropped her paw and stiffened at a slight noise, uttering a low growl, ears pricked, the hair standing up along the back of her neck. In the distance Paul walked slowly, carefully covering his tracks with long sweeps of a mesquite branch until he reached the driveway, then he walked along the wheel tracks in a circular route until he reached the deck. Frankie calmed down, stood and wagged her tail gently. Paul climbed the steps to the deck and softly stroked Frankie's head, then sat down next to me.

"I planted some UGS (Unattended Ground Sensors) out there. Give us a little warning."

"Where the hell did you get those?"

He shrugged nonchalantly. "Jake's got all sorts of shit in the barn that he got from military surplus stores. This is a Vietnam era system. Bit clunky but it'll work. Receiver's in the house."

UGS are radio-transmitting devices used to detect the approach of people or vehicles. We had used more sophisticated versions in Afghanistan on the perimeter of our forward bases, to pick up the sound of metal usually associated with the placement of mortar base plates. The Vietnam era systems were big, unwieldy and difficult to place as the transmitter had to be dug vertically into the ground, leaving only the antenna, thin as a hair, invisible amongst the wispy dry grasses.

Paul pulled the Omega from his belt and checked the magazine, replaced it, cocked the weapon then let the hammer off gently. He applied the safety catch, removed the magazine once again and replaced the round that was now in the chamber. Then once more slid the magazine back into the handle. He hefted the gun a few times and stared out at the snowy landscape.

"I have a bad feeling Thomas."

"Are you thinking what I'm thinking?" I said.

"Get the others out tonight. Before you do your stunt. We can't wait."

"You go with the others. Purdue stays with me. If this goes wrong, at least they'll have a real body and real culprit."

Paul did not like the idea, it was obvious from his expression, but he didn't say anything, just nodded.

Jake had a map of the Mojave/Sonoran desert to the east of the San Bernardino Mountains in his office. Paul and I spread it on the floor in the living room. The desert covered an enormous area, most of it barren sand and scrub with burnt blistered rock, some volcanic, other alluvial, creating a landscape more suitable to a lunar or Martian surface than planet Earth. Highways crisscrossed the open expanse, major interstate freeways lay like static black ribbon snakes burned into the earth, whilst a myriad of metal insects skittered along the surface, the occupants sealed in air-conditioned comfort, oblivious of the prehistoric countryside and the swarming life that teemed in the seemingly sterile, lifeless desert-scape.

The map was large scale, 1:25,000 and showed small trails, contours and local features. To say map in the singular was wrong, for in reality there were several of them taped together, which when unfolded, covered most of the floor. The 10 Freeway slashed across the lower right hand corner while the edge of the San Bernardino Mountains crept along the bottom, with flat occasionally mountainous desert covering the remainder of the map. Marked in pencil were many camp locations, deep in the heart of the Mojave.

We didn't hear Jake enter the living room.

"Spent a lot of time out there prospecting in the truck," he said softly, not wanting to wake the others. He pointed to a spot located about ten miles from the freeway. "That's a good place to get lost." From the map there looked to be no way to get to it. "Found it by accident. Small ghost town I call Louisville, snugged in against a canyon wall close to a dried riverbed. Nobody goes there. Hell nobody knows it exists besides rattlers, rabbits and mangy coyotes." The total distance to Louisville from the ranch was one hundred miles.

"Louisville?"

"I was a Joe Louis fan as a kid. It's a good hide out."

Purdue sat uncomfortably looking sullen, a stubble of beard like a smear of greasepaint on his jowled face, piggy eyes watching me closely as I came into the barn. Jake dug out some old clothes and boots suitable for hiking from his military surplus stash and big enough for even Purdue's bloated frame. Purdue struggled into them.

Sarah, Jake and Julie loaded their gear into the Jeep with enough food for a week. Paul checked the fuel and water levels and fired up the engine. It started first time and ran smoothly. He turned it off.

Jake went to the back of the barn and returned with an AK-47 assault rifle. He checked the magazine and looked at me. "I'm staying. Make sure you and the fat man get away clean."

"That's not a good idea Jake."

"I'm too old and this is the only place I know. One way or the other, I'm gonna die here."

Sarah watched him, walked over and hugged him closely. "We'll see you in about a week when all this has blown over," she said, but I could see in his eyes he didn't believe her.

"Just don't bust up the Jeep. It's the only one I got."

"Better give Julie the password to the GPS and show her the route then," I said, knowing that Jake wasn't going to change his mind about staying.

"Got some of them night vision things too," Jake said digging around in his store. He pulled out a box containing four and handed it to Paul. "Think the batteries are still good. Used them a coupla times, just so I don't have to use the lights. Didn't want anyone seeing where I was going." He grinned mischievously. Sarah rolled her eyes. Paul handed one each to Sarah and Julie.

"You're a regular pack rat Jake."

"Ain't that the truth."

All the while JT Purdue sat watching us and I could see his mind working overtime figuring all the angles and the odds, while knowing nothing about my plan. Perhaps somewhere in his mind he had realised that he was trapped. Or perhaps that was just my hope. It didn't matter anyway. What I knew for certain was that he was going to have apoplexy when he understood just what was going to happen.

It was 00:30hrs.

Hopefully Radley and Oldfield would succeed in tampering with the NSA satellite system. In these modern times of shared intelligence, super computer spying and global hackers, nothing was impossible. All it took was a disenfranchised and disillusioned intelligence contractor in the right place and everything was available. Radley was unscrupulous enough to have his mole wherever he thought was most valuable. One thing I knew about British Intelligence was that they were totally ruthless, even with their own people if they perceived they were a threat or if they thought that person needed to be taught a lesson. And there were no limits to what they would do to achieve their aims.

I was counting on it.

It was the art of boxing. Use your opponent's own weight against them.

Jake went back to the house to collect some warm clothing. The high desert can get cold at night. Julie climbed into the Jeep and stowed the rest of the cans of food into the galley locker. Paul took off Purdue's chain. For a moment I could see him thinking he could just run, then he sat back down in the armchair and watched us sullenly.

Away to the west I thought I heard the sound of a helicopter approaching, landing about half a mile away. Frankie's ears pricked up and Sarah glanced across at me. "You heard that?"

"Yup. We've got company."

"Sounds like a Huey. UH-1Y."

To Purdue the realization was a comforting thrilling moment that made him smile, the taste of victory and escape a tantalizing step away. For me, it was a moment of confusion and déjà vu, the emotional feeling so exactly corresponding to the minutes before the dawn attacks that came in the damp, mist filled mornings of Nimruz province.

Every particle of hair on my body stood up, quivering, sending shivers of fear down my spine. Jonas sat listless and sullen, bravado and defiance gone. He still had no idea what I had planned, but sensed that this was now a life or death situation.

I felt a sense of quiet joy. A revengeful glee at his predicament. It was an unholy, mean, primitively satisfying feeling, that at the same time left a sense of deprivation and distaste as an after thought.

"Looks like someone's changed our plans for us," Paul said quietly, heading for the barn door.

"Julie stay here, cover the back with Sarah."

Paul and I ran to the house.

Several minutes passed and then I heard the UGS receiver Paul had set up in the office click three times.

The indicator showed that number four UGS had picked up humans approaching. Paul had drawn a rough map of the location of the six UGS. Number four was on the east corner of the ranch, hidden amongst the palm trees beside a large group of boulders.

Paul glanced through the window, scanning the dirt road leading up to the ranch. "What d'you think?"

Jake was standing in the centre of the living room, but something was not right. He turned to me and I saw the small bloody hole in his chest and the shattered window behind him. The next shot blew him off his feet, the back of his head exploding in a sheet of blood and brain.

They were using silenced weapons.

My emotions clicked off. All I saw was a body. Another body to add to the growing list. One more vivid image to march through my nightmares and fill the dark hours of my life. But I wasn't thinking about that either. I had the Omega in my hand and was crawling out of the back door.

I signalled to Paul that I was going to outflank them. He understood and fired a few rounds from the window as I slipped out of the back door and ran quickly to the boulders behind the barn, then slipped around to the back of the advancing men under cover of the rocks. Satisfied I was in the right position, I peered from cover.

My brain turned over quickly and smoothly, calculating the possible approaches, thinking as my enemy would be thinking, all the training efficiently working together as if it were only yesterday. A shadow looked out of place behind one of the palms. The lines not as they should be in nature. The barrel of the MAC-10 straight, wavering slightly as the gunman moved, adjusting position.

That was one.

I stayed where I was, low, lying behind a boulder, only my eyes moving. The second man moved and I watched as he crawled across a short piece of open ground towards the ranch house. He reached the deck and crouched underneath, looking back to his companion. He motioned them to stay still.

Them?

Yes. Two separate signals. Where was the third man?

Think. The UGS showed movement on the east corner.

North. South. East. West.

East.

Over there.

I spotted his position with the night vision goggles.

They were in too much of a hurry and I could sense the thrill of the adrenalin coursing through their young bodies, as they felt the surging power of victory well up inside them. That feeling that made you think you were invincible, able to walk into the very jaws of death and return without a scratch.

The quiet was shattered by the hoarse scream from the barn door.

"Over here. Over here."

Jonas had decided that his best bet was to shout for help. He took a step forward and tripped over a fallen log near a woodpile by the barn door, falling flat on his face just as the rounds from the silenced MAC-10 scythed across the walls and door where he had been standing a moment before.

The three men were moving forward now, purposefully, calmly, firing at where Purdue had fallen. He was saved only by the woodpile, the rounds bouncing off the logs. He was screaming. Fear had found life in the terrified, shrill, formless sound that burst from his throat.

The men came on.

I calculated the distance.

Allowed them a few more moments.

Then fired two carefully aimed shots that felled them in the dirt, blood mingling with the sand. Dying limbs jerking unconsciously, eyes wide in surprise, fear and realisation.

Paul took out the third man.

I got up slowly, ignoring Purdue lying face down, shaking with fear, as I walked carefully across to the men. Two had died instantly, eyes still open, staring up accusingly at me, their young faces barely used to the scrape of a razor.

The last man was older. My age. The boss. Still alive, if barely.

The bullet had hit him in the stomach as he'd tried to take cover. In a cold analysis, it was a good shot, considering a target moving away from me as I rolled, but there was little time to reflect on the skill of my shooting.

I knelt beside him and pulled his head up so that he was looking at me.

I recognised him.

He was one of Eliseo's men I'd seen in East LA. When I first saw him I thought I'd recognised him from somewhere. I was sure he was a contractor. The puzzle got more complicated.

There was a deep scar on his forehead and what looked like an old bullet wound on the side of his neck. He nodded and smiled. Coughed up some blood and spoke raspingly.

"They said you used to be good. Said you'd lost it though. Guess they were wrong." He coughed up more blood and winced in pain. He was dying and he knew it. "I should have known." He smiled again, closed his eyes for a second and looked at me once more. I could see the light was fading from his eyes.

"Who're they?" I asked.

He coughed again, laid his head back and looked at me a little more clearly. "They're gonna have a hard time with you. Man are they gonna have a problem." He laughed. Softly, then put up his hand and gripped my neck tightly. "Don't let them get you, man. Do it for me, yeah?"

"What's Eliseo got to do with this?"

"Everything. Nothing is what it seems. They had this planned from the beginning. Years ago. 'The Devil's Cauldron' they call it. That's when there's no other way. They call us in. We're the cleaners. Nobody survives. Guess they didn't figure on you." His eyes brightened once more. The last fanatic gleam of life and his grip lessened. "I heard about you in Nimruz. I told them you were good. It was nothing personal. Okay?"

"Nothing personal," I said quietly, cradling his head. "Why does Eliseo want Purdue dead?"

"It's a bonus. That way Carlos Santos is a shoe-in for Mayor. Hell, the cartel will run the city." He smiled. "Go get the bastards."

"One last thing you can do," I said handing him his radio. "Call the chopper and tell them we've escaped, headed to Lake Arrowhead in a 4x4. Tell them you found a map and are following."

It was a lot to ask a dying man, but he did it, the effort taking the last of his strength. And then he died, his life evaporating into the atmosphere, leaving a cold empty corpse that stiffened slowly. The helicopter took off and veered away to the north-west, headed for the San Bernardino Mountains and the direct route to Lake Arrowhead.

Paul carried Jake's body from the ranch house and laid him gently on the floor in the barn. Sarah knelt down beside him and touched his face gently, tears coursing down her cheeks. As I looked down at Jake, I too felt the sadness well up inside me, wash through my body and settle in my soul in selfish grief.

I had no right to feel this way.

No right to mourn and feel loss and grief.

I only had the right to feel anger at his death and guilt for causing it.

But that would not bring him back.

I also had no right to wallow in self-pity. He would not have liked that.

Paul and I left her alone for a while to mourn her loss.

"What are you thinking?" Paul asked.

"How the hell did they find us?"

"Maybe Sutherland made a call on Jake's phone before he disappeared. Called his office maybe and that was traced. Jake's phone isn't encrypted."

"Could be. When I find the son-of-a-bitch I'll be sure and ask him."

"What now?"

"We have to go after them. Take them out. Can you get your friendly ATC on the phone and see if he can track the chopper?" I spread the map out on the ground and searched for a suitable ambush point. I stabbed my finger on the map.

"Here near Belleville. We'll make that the ambush, and the RV for Julie and Sarah over here at the Belleville parking lot."

Julie walked towards me, tears in her eyes and I took her in my arms, wondering if I would ever see her again. Wordless because words couldn't express how we felt. We knew each other too well now. Or thought we did. But how much do we even know ourselves.

I held her tightly, not wanting the moment to end and fearing more the loss of her than my own life.

"Julie, take Sarah and the Jeep and we'll meet you in the Holcomb Valley. Here at Belleville. There's nowhere they can land the Huey in Arrowhead, so once we're on the ground near Bertha's Peak, I'll give Eliseo a call. A plea for help. I think there's another way we can still *'kill off'* Purdue and get back on track."

Paul took out his phone and walked away a few paces to make the call to his ATC friend.

It was 00:00hrs.

"You be there at Belleville or so help me I'll kill you myself," she signed as she pulled away from me.

"I'll be there. I love you," I signed back in our own silent language that everyone watching guessed anyway. She climbed into the truck.

Sarah limped over to me, put her arms around me and kissed my cheek. "It's not your fault, Thomas," she said softly through her tears. "Take care you son-of-a-bitch. I'll watch her, don't worry."

"Travel safely."

Frankie climbed into the Jeep on Sarah's command, his eyes deep dark pools of sorrow.

Then they were gone, driving slowly up the canyon, following Jake's secret route out of the plain through the mountains to the high desert beyond. Paul and I watched them go and went back to get Jonas. It was time to start up the Explorer and begin the next part of the plan.

Julie and Sarah were headed north-east and wouldn't be spotted.

Jonas raised himself to his knees with difficulty. "They tried to kill me."

He sounded surprised, like a school kid who had suddenly learned that the other kids in the playground didn't want him on their team.

"They tried to kill me."

He was shaking as shock took hold of his body.

There was little time. We had to go. Now.

Purdue was staring at the corpses, shivering although it was a comfortable seventy-five degrees Fahrenheit.

"Help me dress this guy," I told him, dragging one of the corpses closer. He was slightly smaller than Purdue, but I figured after a good fire, he'd be pretty unrecognisable.

"What?" He looked at me blankly.

"Your suit."

There was a spark of understanding in his eyes.

"Jonas you need to understand these guys were out to kill you, not rescue you. If you want to live, do as I say. Now help me dress him and

164

I need your wallet, credit cards, anything that's going to say this heap of shit is JT Purdue."

Survival instinct is a wonderful thing, especially when you know that someone is really trying to kill you. There's a sudden realisation that makes your whole body tingle with fear, anticipation, excitement as the adrenaline courses through your veins.

It's not abstract anymore, it's real.

Purdue now knew what it was like to be hunted to death. It wasn't a game anymore. We dressed the corpse and I made sure that Purdue's wallet was in the pocket, and his watch on the dead man's wrist. Then I tied his hands together with zip ties. We then loaded the corpse into the Explorer as Paul went back for Jake. I figured the least I could do for him was a Viking funeral. Perhaps Sarah would appreciate the gesture, or perhaps she'd just shoot me. I didn't know which, but I thought it might have made Jake smile.

"Time to go Jonas," I said. He nodded and climbed into the passenger compartment with the corpses.

"You need me in the back with him?" Paul asked.

"No. I think he's realised that without us, he's a dead man."

I went through the pre-flight checks, made sure the cyclic and collective were locked, turned on the fuel boost switches, flipped the left engine switch and held it for two seconds until it spooled to idle, did the same with the right engine, then selected 'FLY'. The two Pratt & Whitney 207E engines came up to flight mode and the FADEC (Full Authority Digital Electronic Control) system managed the smooth wind up. The temperatures were all in the green.

With the route programmed into the EFIS (Electronic Flight Information System), I unlocked the flight controls and made sure the cyclic was functioning, then called ATC telling them we were a medical emergency flight headed for a ridge between San Bernardino Mountain and Mount San Gorgonio, at an elevation of nearly nine thousand five hundred feet (2,895m). I figured I could work my way through the passes and over the ridges around the peaks surrounding Big Bear Lake, and slip into Holcomb Valley unseen.

At least that was the plan.

The Explorer, with its NOTAR tail system and five carbon fibre rotor blades, was very quiet compared to something like the Huey. The 'medical emergency flight' was the same ruse we used in England and it seemed to work as we were cleared en route. The MD-902 Explorer was recognised as a Police or Medical Flight helicopter, so there were no questions asked.

THIRTEEN

Flying was a return to some semblance of normality for me. Not withstanding we had a prisoner and two corpses in the passenger compartment. Low level up the mountains, from the Palm Springs plain at an elevation of 466ft (142m) to the Mount San Gorgonio ridge overlooking Big Bear at 9,500ft (2,895m), meant a steady climb while still only remaining several hundred feet above the terrain. The night vision goggles worked perfectly for the view outside, but didn't work too well on the instrument panel. Fortunately, I could still see the terrain mapping on the EFIS. I calculated it would take us about half an hour as we doglegged through the mountain passes. Longer if I flew a little slower around the mountain peaks.

"This is getting weirder by the minute," Paul said, putting down his phone.

"What is?"

"You're right, that's a Huey up ahead according to my man. What the hell is the Mexican Mafia doing with a Huey?"

"They can afford several. Maybe they've become the NSA's newest contractor."

"The deeper we get the more insane this becomes."

"The guys who came for us at the ranch were a probing party. We've got a black ops team on our arses, Paul. This goes all the way to the top."

"Time to play, Thomas. We need one of these buggers alive."

"I told you they'd come for me," Jonas said. He'd found a headset and had been listening to our conversation.

"You did, but you thought it was a rescue operation. They want you dead Jonas. Maybe they'll give you a posthumous medal and a hero's burial."

"Now you're taking the piss."

"I am, but I guarantee I'm not far wrong."

"So what now?"

"Your political ambitions are dead so we're still going to metaphorically kill you, but first we need to neutralise the guys up ahead."

"Perhaps when this is all over you can rise like a phoenix and still be Mayor," Paul added, with more than just a hint of sarcasm.

"You're a regular comedian," Jonas muttered.

ATC called as we neared Los Angeles International eastern approach corridor, clearing us through below the lower flight path altitude. Paul was talking on the phone again.

"Huey's taken the bait and is searching the Lake Arrowhead approaches."

I hoped Radley and Professor Oldfield had managed to disable the NSA satellite. There were so many USAF bases around Southern California, not to mention International airports, but at least we could 'hide' as I flew low level through the canyons to the north facing side of the San Bernardino Mountains. That's when I wanted Paul's ATC friend to blind the radar at the Yuma Marine Corps Air Station that covered the airspace over the Twentynine Palms Air/Ground Training Area.

We were playing a high-risk game of cat and mouse with a military always on edge and paranoid about an imminent attack. The Explorer responded easily to my touch as we skimmed over the San Bernardino ridge and down through the pass towards the next peak, Grinnell Mountain. From there I was going to fly north-east, skirt Onyx Peak, and then east of the dry bed of Baldwin Lake, before turning at Gold Mountain and making the approach into the Holcomb Valley. I was sweating with the concentration of keeping the helicopter low and banking through the steep passes, although the air at this altitude was quite cold. I was sure Purdue wasn't having much fun in the back, but I didn't care.

At Gold Mountain, I banked hard to port and dropped the helicopter down towards the ground, straightening and slowing as we crept forward, heading towards Bertha's Peak. Ponderosa pines dotted the valley making choosing a landing site particularly difficult. My eyes strained through the night vision goggles and then I spotted exactly what I wanted.

A small clearing probably with a diameter of about sixty feet in a break in the trees, surrounded by ridges and out of view of the dirt road that ran on the north side of Bertha's Peak. I'd only get one chance at this, so I settled into a hover and gently brought the Explorer down between the trees. At just over forty feet total length and a thirty-three foot rotor diameter, the helicopter nestled neatly into the clearing.

My instructor would have been impressed.

I centred the cyclic, pushed the collective fully down and locked the controls, then shut down the engines, waiting until the main rotor slowed before applying the rotor brake.

The silence was eerie.

In the distance was the low roar of a jet on approach to LAX, strobes flashing in the clear night sky.

"Nice flying," Paul said at last, as we all breathed a sigh of relief.

"Now what?" Purdue asked quietly.

"We set the ambush and you're the bait."

"I hope you guys know what the hell you're doing."

"We do," I replied looking at Paul, who grinned wryly.

Next job was to call Eliseo. He answered immediately, as if he was waiting for the call.

"Tomas, my friend. I hear you have been busy."

"Got to keep this short, Eliseo," I whispered. "Keskküla's people are after us. Managed to escape into the mountains and am on my way to Big Bear Lake. I need help. Can you get your men up here in the next two or three hours?"

"Of course. Where exactly are you?"

I gave him coordinates of the location I'd picked as the ambush, about a mile east of where we actually were.

"Stay there, I'll have my men meet you in two and a half hours."

"Thanks Eliseo, I owe you."

"Indeed you do."

If I had him figured out correctly, we had perhaps fifteen minutes to get in position.

It was 00:45hrs.

In the distance I could hear the sound of a helicopter approaching along the lake from the west. The Huey is a big helicopter capable of carrying up to a dozen soldiers. I calculated that they still had five or six men on board and would land at Big Bear Airport, dropping off half their number to approach the fake RV coordinates I'd given Eliseo on Van Dusen Canyon Road, which wound into the Holcomb Valley. At least that's what I was counting on. We could ambush Eliseo's men on the ground of my choosing.

I could see the Huey approaching Big Bear Airport, disappearing down behind the ridge.

A black bear appeared from the trees fifty yards to my right, sniffed the air, then started to amble across the road, large feet flapping silently on tarmac, head swinging from side to side. I watched, fascinated, all thoughts of ambush, killing, JT Purdue, forgotten in the beauty of the bear, until it stopped suddenly and reared up onto its hind legs, sniffing the air. Then it turned in my direction and cantered towards me, before suddenly veering off and diving down the mountainside out of my sight.

Ten minutes passed and then I heard an approaching vehicle.

Then Jonas appeared. He stood in the middle of the road, waiting for Eliseo's men to arrive. It was my cue.

I slid off the bank and crossed the road, keeping low, crawling along on my belly, waiting for the bullet to tear into my flesh, knowing what it felt like and reliving every moment, almost wishing that it would happen and end my fear and torment. I made it into the trees, rolled behind a large stump and waited for a few moments for my heart to calm down, before taking a peek.

Jonas was still in the middle of the road, gesticulating, looking around, to see where the men were. Then they appeared, stopped the vehicle they must have stolen from the airport and stepped out. I flicked the switch on the transmitter just as the lead man was lifting the radio to his ear. He pulled it away in disgust.

There wasn't much time now. The men had MAC-10s lined up on

Jonas who was grinning and walking towards them with open arms, as if he'd suddenly happened upon friends after an eternity in the wilderness.

There were three of them spread out across the road, the lead man watching Jonas carefully, the others walking in a semi-crouch, eyes scanning the trees above the road. I slipped the Omega from my shoulder holster, kept low and moved fast, reducing the distance between us as quickly and quietly as possible. Jonas did not have long to live. The closer I got, the clearer the voices became.

"Boy, am I glad to see you guys," Jonas was saying. "Never thought I'd see the day. He's up there in the trees. Go get him, boys."

They ignored him, as I knew they would. They were going to kill him. Execute him quickly, efficiently. They would get close, then finish him with a bullet in the head.

Surprise was total. The lead man collapsed in a heap as Paul fired from his position behind them, while the other two scattered, diving for cover. I got one before he made it, but the third found the rocks and disappeared from view, until he reappeared again firing burst after burst from the MAC-10.

Time was running out. The sound of the echoing gunfire bouncing off the mountainside, ricocheting back and forth. Jonas still stood in the middle of the dirt road, watching in astonishment as the bullets marched across the ground towards him.

"Get the hell down," I shouted across the gulf of his panic, jarring something loose in his frozen brain that had him running across the road towards me, meaningless sounds bubbling from his mouth as fear loosened his bladder, leaving a spreading stain at his crotch as he ran.

The bullets followed him across the road, kicking up flying shards of rock and dust, missing him by inches as some instinct within him made him jump sideways, trip and fall, rolling down the bank to fetch up hard against a tree trunk, the wind knocked out of him.

I took a deep breath, then stood up in full view of the gunman. It took him by surprise. Just the fraction I needed for Paul to see exactly where the gunman was before the killer lifted the MAC-10 for what would be the final devastating burst. The 10mm round caught him in the chest and flung him backwards against the rock, held there for a moment, spread eagled before sliding down, surprise in his dead eyes.

Purdue lay wide-eyed, still uncomprehending. I could hear the helicopter in the distance, rising above the ridge behind us. Dragging Jonas by the lapels, I recrossed the road and slipped back up the bank, retracing our steps, until I found Paul half hidden by a tangle of dead tree trunks and fallen pine needles, the ground soft, mushy and smelling of damp earth and rotting vegetation from a recent summer rain storm. Paul was already digging shallow 'graves'. I made Purdue lie down then covered him completely, leaving a gap for his face that I covered with a fallen pine branch.

I cleaned up the area of our footprints, then dug myself a shallow grave and covered myself, leaving enough room for the Omega to nestle in my hand ready. The helicopter flashed across the sky moments after I had finished, then wheeled in a tight torque turn and settled into a hover above the ridge. By the sound of it, it was hovering within a few feet of the ground, then moments later the pitch changed and it rose and banked away back to Big Bear Airport, having dropped off the sweeper group.

Worms, beetles and other crawling things began to investigate the warm human bodies that lay under the layers of humus.

Purdue squirmed and moaned.

"Shut up, for Christ's sake, unless you want to die," I whispered harshly. The squirming and moaning stopped.

I could feel something about three inches long crawling on my face, the hundreds of legs scraping across my skin. For a moment my imagination went wild, as I pictured the furry undulating centipede that wandered slowly over my flesh, then brought the picture under control, forcing myself to concentrate on the helicopter and what was happening down on the road. Other insects tested the flesh with tiny mosquito-like bites. The larvae of hundreds of different insects crawled, scratched, dug and bit in places that seemed impossible to imagine. A worm wriggled across my lips, head burrowing trying to force its way into my mouth, before giving up and slithering across my closed eyes and into my hair, struggling for a half hour to get through the matted mess and continue on its way.

Purdue could not keep totally silent, and had succumbed to tiny barely audible whimpering sounds, that were lost in the sound of the rotors and the heavy tread of approaching feet.

The three-man sweeper patrol was now moving fast down the mountainside towards the road. The lead man was close. So close that his first step slid off my shin, taking the flesh with it as his heel caught the bone, the second step glancing off the side of my face, exposing it to view and I found myself staring up at a middle aged man, an Ingram MAC-10 in his hand, who had stopped for a moment, looking from side to side. But he never looked down.

I could smell the odour of wet boot leather and sweaty feet, and felt the blood trickling across my cheek where the sole of his boot had scraped harshly across my forehead and down the side of my face.

Within seconds the whole raw bleeding mess was covered in hungry insects, all vying for position to feast on fresh blood and exposed tissue. The pain and irritation was enormous, but I hardly noticed, holding my breath and praying that the man would not look down. He dug in his pocket, pulled out a small pouch and opening it, tore off a plug of tobacco, spat out the old plug in a long dark brown dribble that clung to his chin, then tucked the new piece into his mouth, making his cheek bulge obscenely. He chewed for a moment then spat out another long dribble of dark brown juice.

Paul rose from his cover and the man died without making a sound, as Paul's knife found his throat.

"Jonas."

"What?"

"Stay here until we come for you," I whispered, and followed Paul down towards the road. The other two men didn't see us until it was too late and we dragged their bodies off into the undergrowth, out of sight of the road. Paul and I retrieved the MAC-10s and headed back for Purdue.

It was 01:15hrs.

As we sat, shaking in the cold, someone, somewhere, was calmly ordering a new strategy for our deaths. An as yet faceless, nameless person, who knew every intimate detail of our lives, was closeted in luxurious comfort, abstractly figuring the next move as if he was choosing a tie to wear to the next meeting of the Rotarians.

Trees shivered and moaned in sympathy as the wind rose a knot or two, shaking loose pine needles that showered down on us, scattered on the water and washed down the stream. Somewhere, just out of sight, the bear moved, keeping clear. Jonas looked around warily, the fat on his white body quivering as he shivered. I could see the bites, big red welts all over his chest and face, some bleeding where he scratched unmercifully.

"What do we do now?" Purdue flickered his haunted eyes to me, searching for an answer.

"We get the bodies from the Explorer and then go steal ourselves a Huey." I studied Purdue, seeing as if for the first time the furtive deceitful eyes shifting side to side, the puckered lips wet every now and then by his pink tongue as it flickered out.

"Tell me, Jonas. What is it that you know that makes these people want you dead?"

He looked at me nervously, then shifted his eyes down to the pants he had turned inside out, busy picking bugs out of the seams.

"Later. When you get me out of this place." He looked up. "You keep me alive, I tell you everything you want to know. Deal?"

"Deal."

Jonas watched me from lowered lids, staring for quite a while, until I could no longer ignore him.

"What's on your mind, Jonas?"

"I was just wondering what kind of pious bullshit makes you the conscience of the world?"

"Do you want to explain yourself?"

"You've committed just about every crime in the book, and probably some that haven't been invented yet. Yet you preach and posture like some demented born-again Baptist TV evangelist."

"Good, Jonas. For a while I didn't think you capable of even stringing one sentence together without an obscenity."

"Judge, jury and executioner, hey?"

"You think you have no responsibility for the death of Morgan Alvarez?"

"I don't even know who she is."

"Really? She was investigating you when she died, Jonas. Digging out all the filth of your past, enough to prevent any notions of Mayor of LA."

"Can we do this shit some other time?" Paul cut in urgently.

We spent the next ten minutes loading the bodies into the F150 pick-up Eliseo's men had undoubtedly stolen, drove back to the Explorer for the other corpses, then headed for the rendezvous with Sarah and Julie at the Belleville site.

It was 01:35hrs.

Sunrise was in three and a half hours, but it would start getting light in about two hours and I wanted to get away from here before then.

It was just a few minutes drive down the dirt road to Belleville, in an open area of the Holcomb Valley. It was the site of an old gold mining town in the years before and during the Civil War. Now there were just plaques with the history of the area and the addition of a replica log cabin. Close by was the entrance to an old mine.

Paul parked the F150 in the trees on the other side of the road so we could be hidden and yet see the RV. Then we settled down to wait.

"I never seen a man killed before. Never in my life," Purdue muttered.

"Politicians never do. We're the guys who do the dirty work. Clean up the mess you guys create," Paul said roughly. He wasn't feeling very magnanimous. Neither was I. We didn't enjoy killing. We did it, but we didn't enjoy it.

Purdue lapsed into silence. He was trying to get to grips with his new reality. I could see that one side of him was still the arrogant mean and nasty manipulator, but the other side was a frightened man stripped of the illusion of his psychological protection. Instinct told him he was safer with us.

Not 'safe', but 'safer'.

But that was cold comfort with several bodies lying behind us in the flat bed of the truck. I heard the sound of the Jeep Wagoneer a while before it turned the corner and drove into the parking lot. I waited a minute or two to see if anyone was following, before getting out and walking over.

"I thought something had happened when I didn't see you," Julie said, after throwing her arms around my neck and kissing me.

"We took care of it."

Sarah, Paul and Purdue joined us.

"Okay, let's have it," Sarah demanded.

I explained my plan in detail after which there was silence for a moment.

"Got it all figured out then?" she said slowly.

"As best I can. I need a quick run-down on Huey start-up procedures and whatever quirks it has and how to take the front doors off."

Sarah went through the procedures with me slowly, as Paul helped Julie load the Louisville coordinates into the Jeep's navigation system. Purdue sat on a rock and watched, sunk in his own thoughts. Right now he was just baggage and he knew it.

"Paul will show you where the Explorer is. You need to get going as soon as the Yuma radar is down. Keep as low as possible to keep out of sight of LA centre and you'll be fine."

Sarah looked at me in disgust. "Did this stuff for real with rockets and bullets coming at me. Remember?"

"Just be careful. I promised Jake..." I let the sentence hang in the air.

She nodded. "You too."

"No phone calls in the desert, it's too close to Twentynine Palms and China Lake. They could get a fix on the signal," I told Paul, who nodded in agreement.

The Huey sat on the south side of the Big Bear Airport runway near the eastern threshold. An emergency access gate was open, so I drove through and backed up to the open rear door. The pilot walked towards me carrying a Glock 9mm.

I stepped from the truck and went to meet him.

He must have sensed something was not quite right and started to bring up the Glock, but I was on him before he had time to fire and the knife did the work.

So far I'd managed to leave bodies littered over Southern California and as far as I could tell it wasn't going to stop anytime soon. At some point there was going to be a nationwide hunt when Sutherland could no longer keep a lid on our activities, if he was still alive. That's if he wasn't in the process of outing us to every agency anyway. I was pretty sure he'd given our position away at Jake's ranch.

Rigour mortis was just starting to set in on the bodies as I loaded them into the back of the Huey and strapped them in. Then I strapped the dead pilot in his seat. I was going to fly from the left seat. Then I took the front doors off as instructed by Sarah and stowed them in the rear compartment too. Next I made sure the body I'd dressed in Purdue's clothes was secure. The illusion would only work for a while before DNA tests showed that the body wasn't Purdue's, but it would buy us extra time.

The exertion opened my shoulder wound. It hurt like hell and I could feel blood seeping through the bandage as I got into my black jump suit and pulled on the parachute I'd taken from the Explorer.

If, according to the proverb, 'Necessity is the Mother of Invention' I reasoned that 'Insanity is the Offspring of Desperation'. If I died I was obviously nuts. If I survived I would still be nuts, but lucky.

Julie knew that when she'd kissed me goodbye, with a lost expression I couldn't fathom, and I hoped I'd see her once my daredevil act was over.

So far I'd been lucky, with the residents of Big Bear remaining sound asleep as I climbed into the co-pilot's seat and familiarised myself with the controls and switches. All I needed to do was start the beast, take off, fly south to the high mountains of the San Gorgonio wilderness range, and crash the helicopter.

The Huey is a bigger heavier helicopter than I was used to flying. The starting procedure was pretty simple. I made sure the twist throttle was set to idle start, flipped on the master switch, the fuel switch, and the DC generator to start, then pressed the engine start button on the collective. The main rotor began turning as the engine ran up. Sarah told me to watch the engine instruments until it reached 40% of N1. I did so, before releasing the starter button. Then I turned on the avionics, flipped the generator switch to standby, set the altimeter to the runway altitude, brought the engine up to 6600 RPM and pulled the night vision goggles over my helmet.

At 6,752ft (2058m) elevation the Huey required a handful of collective to raise it off the ground. I steadied the heading with left pedal and left cyclic, pulling back slightly as the nose dipped. I bumped back down and raised even more collective until the big blades dug into the thin air. Finally I was climbing out, turning to the right, which allowed a little more power from the engine to the main rotor. It was like a lazy upward spiral until I had completed 360° and climbed away towards the south-west and the San Gorgonio range, keeping fairly low as the first very faint glimmers of dawn began to lighten the sky to the east.

It was 02:15hrs.

Mount San Gorgonio peaked at 11,502ft (3505m). A few hundred feet below the peak would be a good place to crash the Huey, in a canyon on the north facing slope I had picked out earlier on the flight to Big Bear. At this height I needed a minimum of about eight hundred feet for my jump, to make sure I could 'fly' away from the crash site in the thin air.

The plan was simple. Fly over the ridge between Lake Peak and Ten Thousand Foot Ridge into the valley below the north face, set the Huey for the mountain, and jump.

With the doors open it was cold at this time of the morning and at this altitude I shivered even in the jump suit.

Distances and heights are deceptive in the twilight hours before dawn, especially when you're wearing night vision goggles. The ridge was rapidly approaching and the Huey was beginning to feel the height, even though its service ceiling was several thousand feet higher. At 120kts I didn't have much time to turn to starboard, line up on a spot below the peak of Mount San Gorgonio, engage the autopilot and jump. Steady and level at 10,200ft (3108m) I took off the night vision goggles, tossed them on the pilot's lap, undid my seat belt, switched on the autopilot and carefully swung my right leg past the cyclic, clambering out onto the skid.

Danger always heightens the senses, and the feeling of the rotor downdraft and noise of the engine beat at my mind.

One last look at the rapidly approaching mountain and I jumped, made sure I was clear of the tail rotor, reached for the drogue and pulled it out of its pouch.

The ground seemed way too close, like a low BASE jump.

It felt like an eternity, but was only two seconds before the parachute banged open above me and I was swinging below it, turning to see where the Huey was as it headed for destruction, then I searched the approaching ground for a landing spot clear of trees. Before I was ready I hit the rough ground between two large boulders, falling to my knees unceremoniously and rolling onto my bad shoulder. Luckily I missed the jagged pine trees and hit a reasonably soft spot just below the start of a boulder field. Pain jangled my nerves, but I needed to get moving and back over the ridge towards the north, headed for Highway 38, skirting to the east of Grinnell Mountain. I roughly packed up the chute and strapped it to my back, then headed north up to the ridgeline above me. A minute later the Huey impacted the mountain in a loud explosion and sheet of flame. I knew I only had about five or six minutes before emergency helicopters would be en route, alerted by the jet flying overhead towards Los Angeles Airport.

Climbing mountains as fast as possible was not unknown to me, as our training in the Parachute Regiment and Special Forces Support Group required a punishing selection process that included just this sort of thing. The only difference was that here I was at 10,000ft (3048m) and not acclimatised to the altitude, so I had to be very careful. Only the urgency to beat the searching helicopters propelled me upward, scrambling over the rough rocky scrub-bush terrain. It was hands and knees stuff up the steep slope to the ridge, over the top and then sliding dangerously down the other side, almost out-of-control as I heard the sound of helicopters in the distance. Jagged rocks tore through my clothing, slashed my hands and grazed my knees. Nothing that rest and antiseptic cream wouldn't fix, but it smarted like hell.

I slammed into a pine tree and held on tightly, crouching low as the first search helicopters flew up the valley, on the Mount San Gorgonio side of the ridge. They wouldn't be looking in my direction and I carried on down the slope to a dried streambed where I sat and pulled out my phone. My shoulder had taken the brunt of the collision with the tree and my arm was weak and virtually useless.

I got a strong satellite signal and checked my position with the GPS on Google Earth. Well what else would you do?

A mile or so down this gulley was Fish Creek Trail, which was where I was headed, and from there it was just a few miles to the trailhead where Julie should be waiting. Just above the ridge, I could see the glow of the police helicopter searchlights as they arrived at the scene of the crash and circled slowly. I had chosen that site because it was quite tricky to reach, with no 4X4 trails nearby. The search and rescue team would have to land in the valley I'd parachuted into and climb up to the site. They'd wait until daylight to begin the operation, after reaching the conclusion that such was the impact there would be no survivors.

It was 03:45hrs.

In just over two hours the sun would be up and the world waking to a new day. But I had to find the Fish Creek Trailhead in the dark, relying on my phone. The lower I got the more 'spotty' the signal would become, but at least I was still at nearly 8,800ft (2590m). It was another 2.5 miles (4km) to the trailhead; the going was easier if I avoided fallen logs and ankle turning rocks. My shoulder throbbed unmercifully and I thought that perhaps it was well-deserved pain. I was alive and shouldn't be complaining.

We needed to be gone from the Wilderness Area before 05:30hrs and from the trailhead back to the highway was at least seven miles. I didn't want any Forest Rangers stumbling upon us and asking awkward questions, such as *'where is your Wilderness permit?'*

I started jogging, mindful of the terrain and wishing I'd kept the damn night vision goggles, but it was getting a little lighter. A creature I took to be a small black bear crossed my path, pausing to look at me, then I saw its longer tail and white streak before it disappeared into the trees. With those markings it could have been a wolverine, but it was way too far south. I cautiously made my way along the trail, looking behind and to the side. If it was a wolverine it was much more dangerous than a black bear. But somehow I doubted it was, and after five minutes I resumed jogging along the trail.

At 04:45hrs I reached the Fish Creek Trailhead and was more than happy to see the Jeep with Julie and Frankie standing anxiously beside it. Thankfully there were no other vehicles or campers there. Later in the morning, those backpackers and hikers who had stayed at the Heart Bar campsite would be venturing down the trail, but now we had it all to ourselves.

"What kept you soldier?" she whispered, as if that would make a difference out here alone in the wilderness.

I kissed her, patted Frankie, threw my kit into the Jeep, climbed into the back and lay down, hurting and exhausted. Frankie lay down on the floor. Julie started the Jeep and without lights, drove carefully back the seven miles of undulating winding dirt road to the highway intersection.

"Sarah suggested we take highway thirty-eight to the ten and go east to the sixty-two. It's a circuitous route but we don't want to be driving through Big Bear again."

"Sounds good to me."

"I saw the explosion. Lit up the sky."

"Let's hope it does the job," I said, but she couldn't hear me over the sound of the engine and I was too tired and hurt to shout. Right now I was just a passenger.

So far we had accomplished the impossible, now we just had to get to Louisville and disappear for a few days while we reassessed the situation and started the next phase. Hopefully our antics over the last seventy-two hours had caused confusion and had everyone looking in the wrong place.

After tonight, I hoped they wouldn't be looking at all.

FOURTEEN

Louisville was indeed every bit the ghost town Jake said it was. Abandoned long ago and forgotten in the mists of time, no longer a tourist attraction, it was just a small group of dusty dilapidated worthless wooden buildings hidden from the rest of the world in a dead end canyon. The water had dried up nearly a century ago about the time the minimal amounts of gold had been exhausted. The only tracks that led down to what used to be the main street were those that we were now making, soon to be cleaned by the tidy desert winds.

"Stop here, let's just check the place out first," I asked Julie and she pulled into the cover of a rocky outcrop at the entrance to the canyon.

There were no signs of life and I couldn't see the Explorer anywhere.

Julie, Frankie and I walked slowly along the main street, if that's what it could be called. It was now a dried streambed that during winter would become a raging torrent, and during summer thunderstorms, a flash flood. Most of the buildings were completely beyond repair, gaping holes in the walls and most of the roofs gone. The roof of the only slightly worthwhile building had fallen through onto the second floor. It was the old Hotel, recognisable only because of its sign hanging forlornly chipped, cracked, warped and in desperation trying to relive the proud days of its youth, creaking in the slight breeze.

Sarah, Paul and Purdue stepped out of the battered door, relief on their faces. Frankie bounded forward to greet Julie.

"Finally. We thought something had gone wrong. The news is full of the crash," Sarah said. "Where's the Jeep?"

"Back there. We wanted to make sure you were here. It looked so deserted. Where's the Explorer?"

Sarah grinned and Paul shook his head. "Sarah decided to outdo you and park it in the tiniest helipad I've ever seen. It's back there."

Purdue stepped forward his hand outstretched, which seemed odd to say the least. "Glad you made it," he said, sounding sincere.

I shook his hand. Which was a mistake because of the lacerations on my palm and fingers. "Glad we did too."

"Apparently the Mayor elect is going to give me a big funeral." He smiled tiredly and I could see that he had lost weight, the clothes hanging loosely on his frame, cheeks sunken and eyes haunted.

"Well, he's going to get a hell of a surprise very shortly, isn't he?"

Paul stepped up and took my arm leading me into the hotel out of the heat of the day, sat me down on a rickety chair and carefully cut off the sleeve of my torn and filthy jump suit. My shoulder was bleeding, the wound looking inflamed and possibly infected, not to mention the scrapes on my face and leg.

"Julie, can you bring up the Jeep? Jake kept a pretty comprehensive first aid kit stowed in the back," he said, probing the edges of the wound with his fingers. "You can park it in the barn at the back."

Sarah went with Julie and I sat back, eyes closed, gritting my teeth.

"Never thought you'd make it Thomas."

"Thanks for the vote of confidence."

"Guess there's a first time for everything and maybe just for once the Gods are on our side." He cleaned the wounds and redressed my shoulder.

"Danny would have said we're just good at this stuff."

"Would rather have been a rock star personally. If only I could sing I would have been great," he said laughing, and even Purdue broke into a grin, breaking his defeated melancholy.

Tiredness swept over me in waves, seeping up my legs and washing through my head and all I wanted to do was lie down and sleep. To forget all my troubles for a few hours and let the world of the unconscious take me and carry me away to a place where trouble and death and destruction did not exist.

Instead, Paul, Jonas and I climbed the nearest hill and scanned the land all around for as far as we could see, not knowing what we were looking for, but desperately feeling the need to see something. Empty desolation stretched to the horizon, beyond which lay the biggest military training area in the world at Twentynine Palms. We could have been in the middle of the Sahara, or the desert of Saudi Arabia, or the Jebel of Iraq or Afghanistan, waiting for an attack by the Taliban.

But we were here. In America. The USA. Half-a-day's drive from one of the biggest metropolitan areas in the world. The centre of sun, sea, sand and sin.

I looked back at the tiny forgotten ghost town of Louisville and for a moment of rising panic, could not find it, so completely did the buildings blend into the landscape. There were no trees here, only mesquite brush scattered across the sand and rock, with tumbleweed balls sitting like strange hay bales, some as big as a small car.

What folly had tempted a group of people to build a town here?

Someone had struck a gold vein and the town grew into a brief melange of greedy-eyed hopefuls intent on following the American dream and striking the mother lode. But the vein that promised so much had turned into false hope, and shattered dreams blazed bitter trails back to the city, where empty lives struggled through their last days in disillusion and despair.

And now I was here, driven out of the city to the town of broken dreams in an attempt to make mine come true. Perhaps in some odd way, there was a poetic justice. The possibility of setting free the spirits that still haunted the hotel, the saloon, the livery stable and the last remaining small house, still clinging stubbornly to its identity on the very edge of town, nestled up against the hillside.

In the fullness of time, did anything really matter, except for that one moment in time we called the present, which was forever an illusion?

It mattered to me. Now.

In the futility of my present, it mattered a lot.

That evening, Julie and I sat close together for a long while, silently enjoying each other's company. Paul lay down and slept, curled up like a little child, head pillowed on his arm, legs pulled up, blanket dragged up to his chin. By ten o'clock the moon had risen, bright, full, in the clear desert night and the coyotes howled in the distance as rock fragments cracked and exploded like tiny pistol shots. Once again the strange tormented spirituality of the town grew in strength, as if night gave freedom to the trapped souls that roamed the old dilapidated buildings.

Julie turned her face up to mine, large, blue, unfathomable eyes studying every contour of my face, fingers lightly caressing the length of my now shaggy beard and my heart ached with an intensity I hadn't known since I first met her a lifetime ago. I leaned down and tasted her lips with mine, feeling their soft fullness and her tongue as it entwined with mine and we both intuitively knew that we would be together, but not now, later, when this mess was cleaned up and we could lead our lives in peace and comfort.

Slowly we moved apart, she smiled, gently mouthed the words 'I love you', lay down, closed her eyes and slept.

I couldn't sleep and saw Jonas slip quietly out of the building and followed after a minute.

He was sitting on a rock, halfway up the hillside, staring out across the desert, lit by the moon reflecting off the stark grey rocks and sand that spread to the horizon in a ghostly re-incarnation of moonscape photographs. I sat down beside him, knowing that he was at a watershed, and for all the dislike I felt I could not help also feeling pity for the man. We sat for a long while, absorbing the tragic beauty laid out before us, witness to an unchanged scene, a vista that had been enjoyed by the inhabitants of Louisville some hundred years ago.

"How d'you know this is going to make any difference?" He didn't look at me as he spoke, just continued to stare blankly ahead.

"Nobody can ignore a testament on film. And you know as well as I do, that people believe what they see."

"And how the hell are you going to make sure people see this film?"

For the first time he turned and looked at me, doubt written in the folds of flesh on his face. "You sure as hell fly on the edge, don't you?"

The question was rhetorical and he turned to stare once more at the images in his own mind.

"You'll get more than you ever dreamed Mr Gunn. But you'll have to go places. Places you don't want to go. It's the only way. If you do, you'll get everything. If you don't you'll have nothing, just a dead guy talking."

"You just give me the information and I'll worry about putting it all

185

together."

He smiled and shook his head, as if a little boy had just asked a dumb question and he would have to laboriously reply.

"I'm gonna give you places and times and names of people that will make your eyes pop. You have to get them on film. Right when they're doing their stuff. And let me tell you. If they catch you, they'll take a long time killing you and they'll enjoy every moment."

"And who's behind all this?"

Again he shook his head and smiled, wearily this time. "When the time comes, you'll find out. I don't even know. I could make a guess but I'm not sure that it's right. That's why I now know we need each other. Kinda like an arranged marriage."

I held out my hand and he took it firmly.

"We have a deal?" I asked, as sincerely as I could.

"We have a deal," he concurred.

It's not everyday a kidnapper and his victim agree on the future course of action. One thing I did know was that Purdue was not suffering from Stockholm Syndrome.

Now all I had to do was convince Paul, Sarah and Julie of the next phase of the operation.

"I swear to God, all I wanted was a nice, little, luxury airport vacation resort for like-minded pilots. And what do I get? A lunatic with the Federal Government on his ass and price on his head bigger than the damn deficit," Sarah exploded after I finished explaining how we needed to now co-opt Caroline for the next part of the plan. "You ever hear of the Lindbergh Law? I've had enough needles in my arm, I don't want the last one to be fatal."

"I'll go with Paul," Julie said quietly, placing a hand on Sarah's arm. "Caroline will come if I ask her. We have no other option."

"Sure we do. Get the hell outta here." Sarah stomped outside. I followed her. She turned as I walked up beside her. "Goddam you Thomas Gunn," she cried, tears running down her cheeks. I took her in my arms and let her cry out her pain, knowing that this wasn't about me, Caroline or Jonas, but about Jake.

After a minute she took a deep breath and looked up at my face.

"That wasn't very professional of me, was it?"

"You're the most professional person I've ever met."

"You don't get off that easy," she said gruffly, but smiled. "Hell, Jake wouldn't have wanted it any other way. He could be an ornery bastard when he wanted."

We walked on and she talked, telling me stories of her childhood and her family, now only consisting of her sister Leila in the Bahamas.

By the time we returned to the Hotel, Paul and Julie were ready. Frankie padded up to Sarah and licked her hand.

"Go with them girl," Sarah urged and Frankie climbed into the Jeep.

We watched the slowly settling dust, kicked up by the Jeep's tyres as if the last stagecoach had passed us by. The only sound in the still air, was the sonic boom of a high flying jet from China Lake Air Force Base, as a lonely pilot rode the screaming cylinder up in the stratosphere on the edge of space. Where the sky turned deep blue and layers of colour from white through azure, red and green, melted in a surrealistic brushstroke with deep black space beyond. And the emptiness seemed all the more tangible with the sound and the distant vapour trail.

Behind shadowed hills, a perfectly spherical light yellow sun rose majestically claiming the earth with its rays. At this distance, the cataclysmic ear shattering roar of thousands of explosions that shot billions of flames and gases hundreds of thousands of miles towards earth was unheard, just a silent, shimmering heat, growing to blast furnace temperature.

Jonas opened one of the water jerry cans and drank carelessly, spilling valuable water onto the ground, where it pooled for a second or two before vanishing into the starved sand.

"Hey," Sarah shouted angrily.

Turning slowly he looked at her.

"This is a desert, Jonas. You don't just turn on the tap. Watch what you're doing."

"You're right," he said contritely and took more care drinking. Next, he broke open a packet of dry crackers, tore the wrapper off a hunk of cheese and settling down on the broken boardwalk ate the snack, eyes staring into the far distance.

Wiping his lips with the back of his hand, leaving cracker crumbs smeared across his chin, he nodded towards the distant horizon.

"This is the first time I've been out here. I mean, first time I wasn't in the air-conditioned office or hotel. Never realised how big the state really is. It's the emptiness that makes you realise."

"For a potential Mayor, you don't know very much do you?"

Turning he looked at me without malice, but with a thoughtful expression. "Maybe. Politics happens on the TV and in the newspapers. Most of the time people don't want to see you for real. They want an illusion. Hell, isn't that what your whole premise is based on?" He turned back to stare at the vastness of the desert and the utter desolation.

"You think that's acceptable, Jonas?"

The question caught him as he was about to bite into another cracker with a large lump of cheese.

"No, and that's the truth." He sipped a little more water. "Shit, we all use labour saving devices. In the old days, hardly anyone even knew what the President looked like. Then came photography. The world series of 1919. When the White Sox threw the Championship. Hell, those guys were banned from baseball, so they changed their names and still played. Not in the majors, maybe, but they still played. Why? Because hardly anyone knew what they looked like. Couldn't happen now. Christ, everyone knows what everybody looks like. But the question is, do they really care?"

He had a point, but I really didn't need to listen to baseball analogies.

"You're going to Atlanta," he said slowly. "Just as soon as your buddy and your girlfriend get back."

"What the hell's in Atlanta?"

"The beginning," he said softly. He lapsed into silence watching a small dust devil spiral across the flat desert. After a while he spoke again, causing me to look at him sharply for there was no malice in his tone, just quiet inquiry.

"Tell me about this Morgan woman. Why do you seem to think I killed her?"

I studied him looking for the cynicism I thought was there, but it wasn't.

"She was investigating you. Had your whole life story and every corrupt scheme you ever created on a flash drive."

Slowly he shook his head, still without malice. Thoughtfully, as if trying to work something out in his mind. "If she had everything, we'd all be dead, would have been a long time ago. No. She didn't have everything, she had an idea and she found a weak link which led her to me and which then led you to me."

Now my mind was racing. Throwing off the dust of inaction, and grating into gear.

"Weak link?" Then my dusty mind cleared and I looked at him for confirmation. "Dean Stockton?"

He nodded. "Trouble is, with a big mouth they never know when to keep quiet. My fault. My obsession with the entertainment business. Always wanted to be in movies. Guess I'll get my chance after all," he said without glee and looked at me with a hint of sadness. "He'll be dead, of course. You know that don't you? Guess you saved my life after all. If you hadn't kidnapped me, I'd be dead too."

"You're just another pawn. Like Dean, Hal, and Morgan. You're a puppet being groomed. An office boy they were going to dress for the occasion."

"Almost. But I kept records. Not just written ones either, that would have been foolish." He tapped his head. "Up here, where nobody else can see. I have a photographic memory, anything I see or hear gets stored away for the future. Just never told anyone. Figured someday I'd be able to use it. Looks like that day has come."

"And they never thought some dumb idiot with a grudge, like me, would come hunting and take the only living evidence and disappear. No wonder they want us dead."

"That's why I didn't know about your friend Morgan. Wasn't me. You went after the wrong guy and struck gold." The analogy to our surroundings made him laugh. A short soft sound that died in the hot air, leaving the hint of an echo drifting in the breeze that vanished in the swirling dust as another gust blew in from the north.

Watching him eat made me hungry, so I helped myself to cheese and crackers. Sarah joined me and sat down on the broken down veranda, massaging her thigh where the prosthetic attached.

"You okay?" I asked.

"Get's a little sore every now and then. Nothing a few days rest in my own bed wouldn't fix."

"We'll be out of here in a couple of days, as soon as Julie and Paul get back."

That night I dreamt of Morgan, Julie and Morgan, all in the same person, parts of each blended to make the whole. A frighteningly beautiful erotic mix, that tantalized, soothed, frightened and frustrated me at one and the same time. Dancing out of reach on the edge of consciousness and then just when I thought I had hold of the reality, she, they, the amalgam, drifted apart. Silent Morgan, and Julie battered and bleeding, and behind them a monstrous indescribable beast rearing up to claim them and wrench them from my grasp forever. The scream died in my throat as I woke, sweating and shivering at the same time.

Jonas lay snoring softly. I wrapped the sleeping bag around myself, and stared out through the hole in the roof at the stars, clear and bright, turning slowly around the Pole Star, as seemingly we lay immobile beneath this great spectrum.

A shooting star flashed across the sky in a glorious arching blaze, before extinguishing itself in the pinpricked blackness.

For two more days, we waited, sleeping through the long hot days, looking mistrustfully at each other during the cool nights, listening to the distant coyotes and the scurrying of small nocturnal rodents that lived amongst the derelict buildings, gradually becoming more accepting of our presence.

I had rationed the water and food, much to Jonas's disgust, but even though he moaned and complained incessantly, he never drank or ate more than his allotted amount, much to my surprise.

But then he was a survivor.

I was getting worried. Paul and Julie should have been back by now. And my imagination began to work in fantastically irrational ways, more akin to writing a horror screenplay than dealing with reality, but then hadn't everything that had occurred seemed to be out of a blockbuster thriller?

On the third day I could not sleep, just sat watching the distant horizon hoping for the telltale cloud of dust that would signal the approach of the Jeep. Instead I caught the ominous sound of an approaching Blackhawk helicopter, the sound taking me back to the mountains of Afghanistan and the chatter of machine guns and ground shaking explosions from shells and IEDs.

For one moment the smell of battle was strong in my nostrils and then it had gone, and low in the sky the black dot was moving in a direct line for Louisville. I reached for the Omega and watched, heart pounding as the Blackhawk drew closer and with an ear shattering roar swept overhead, continuing on its way to Twentynine Palms, the Marine Corps markings clearly visible. Gradually the sound diminished and the aircraft disappeared into the heat haze.

Suddenly the vastness of the desert did not seem so enormous. We were still within easy flying time of central LA, a short hop by helicopter, and all our pursuers had to do was look in the right place.

There was nothing for the rest of the day, except the far distant vapour trails as test pilots practiced their craft way up in the atmosphere. In the evening I dozed fitfully, starting at every slight sound. Evening stretched into night and lengthened into early morning and still I could not sleep, feeling lightheaded now, with eyes red and sore and a tongue that felt swollen, filling my dry mouth, the urge to drink more water tempting, but I resisted.

Then, just when I had succumbed to blessed sleep, lights momentarily flickered across the building and the Jeep pulled up outside, Julie at the wheel, Paul beside her. Caroline lay unconscious, wrapped in a blanket on the back seat. It took several minutes for Paul and I to manhandle her out of the Jeep and into the building where we laid her on the floor. Frankie flopped onto the floor panting.

Julie touched my arm. She looked pale, tired and she seemed to have aged. There were two deep vertical furrows between her eyebrows and blue circles beneath her eyes, which had lost their lustre. She moved her hands slowly and mouthed the words. "She went crazy. Hysterical. Paul gave her something to knock her out." There were tears in her eyes.

I put my finger to her lips and pulled her to me, letting the silent sobs break over me in waves of fear and loneliness. Why had I brought her into this world of violence, terror and death?

Paul checked Caroline, then sat and looked across at us, knowing what was going on, the compassion obvious in his face.

He spoke softly. "Julie's a remarkable woman, Thomas. She shouldn't be doing this."

I could not answer. I did not trust my voice. I just held her tight in my arms.

Caroline woke later that day, with a headache. She looked at me uncomprehendingly.

"You're dead. They told me you were dead."

"Who did?"

She wrinkled her brow, thinking, trying to clear her head. "Some men. They said they were from the police. That they were trying to find next-of-kin for you and Julie. I didn't know." She stopped and stared at me for a long time, trying to understand what was happening.

She noticed Purdue sitting close by and put her hand to her mouth, the shock of seeing another dead man very much alive, almost too much. When she did speak, she sounded like a little girl who had been caught out and did not understand what wrong she had committed.

"But I watched the funeral. On the news. They said you died in a helicopter crash. What's going on?" The tears fell down her puffy pale cheeks and Julie crossed the floor, put her arms around Caroline and silently comforted her.

Purdue sighed heavily. "Now I know how Mark Twain felt," he said, with faint flicker of humour.

Once more I felt a sense of total worthlessness, at having caused so much misery to so many people in an effort to complete a task I had decided was more important than any one person's comfort and happiness. I had chosen to be an outcast. Embraced the role of avenger and burned all my bridges, venturing forth with every passing minute into the wilderness of loneliness and desperation, revelling in my pain and humiliation.

Paul brought me back to the immediate present and the practicality of the situation. "There's no sign of this Dean feller. Caroline still insists he's taking a vacation."

"A wonderful euphemism for murder."

Paul pursed his lips and closed his eyes. "I don't think so. Doesn't feel right. Somebody needs him alive." He paused and cracked a smile. "Don't the talent agents say 'taken an extended vacation' meaning their clients are either in the nuthouse or at the Betty Ford Centre?"

Maybe he was right, but I was not smiling, there was too much teeming through my mind. "So if that's the case, then Purdue's buddies don't have him. So he's either gone to ground, or..." I let the sentence hang, thinking hard.

"Or what?"

I lifted my hand, thinking hard, concentrating. Paul fell silent and waited. Julie held Caroline's hand and they all watched me. Jonas lay snoring gently.

"Or Sutherland has him."

Paul stared at me in disbelief. "What?"

"Think about it. Who else knew?"

He shook his head. "Speculation. You're assuming too damn much."

"Give me a better scenario."

The challenge was left lying in the static air between us. Then he shook his head again, watching his own finger draw meaningless doodles in the dirt.

Caroline turned to Julie, eyes wide. She had recovered her composure and stared at me intently. "I don't understand. What's it all mean? What's going on?" Her voice trembled a little. I got up and moved towards her.

"You're safe here. Safer than you would be at home."

Looking at Julie for confirmation, she found it in the gentle smile. Then she turned back to me. "What's it all about?"

I told her, leaving nothing out and when I had finished, her face was ashen and hand trembled. "It seems so improbable, like I'm living a screenplay."

Smiling, I laid a reassuring hand on hers, all the time knowing that I was acting, drawing myself into her confidence before I used her like I would use a milk carton. "Tell me about it."

Paul pointed to Jonas. "He told you anything yet?"

"Just that I'd be going to Atlanta."

"Atlanta? What's in Atlanta other than peaches?"

"That's something I'll find out, but first I've got to find Sutherland. Then I'll have Dean. I need him just as I need Caroline. Links in the chain."

Paul looked at me questioningly.

"If I'm going to make Jonas a national star, I've got to have access to air-time. Only Caroline and or Dean can get us that air-time without someone pulling the plug."

"How do you figure that?"

Julie answered the question. "Caroline's got more contacts and more dirt on more people in the entertainment business than anyone I know. Dean? Well, he supplies the link between us, and the outside world. Adds credibility and respectability to the program."

"Program?"

Julie grinned. "Fifteen minutes on nationwide TV, once a day for a month."

Paul's mouth fell open and he gaped at her. "We've spent our lives being anonymous, now you want us on national television?"

"What have we got to lose?" I said. "Listen. YouTube is one thing, and it will get a huge audience. But it's still YouTube. Now, national television is a whole different ballgame. Nobody's going to question Dean, everyone's lovable loudmouth, doing a daytime TV slot. Shit, the executives'll think it's a great idea. And when Caroline's through with them, they'll sign Dean and Jonas up for next season."

Everyone, with the exception of Purdue, regarded me as one might regard a good friend suffering from the final stages of Alzheimer's disease.

Quiet pity.

He, on the other hand, seemed to embrace the idea.

"You'll see. Thomas here's got something you're all missing." They waited in silence for the explanation, but he took his time. "Surprise. And the public's insatiable desire to watch some poor bastard get shot down in flames, with all the gory details on film. Especially over breakfast. Think about it."

"Morgan already had the title. *'The Jonas Trust Deception'*."

"Paul, we have to get into LA tonight."

He looked up sharply. "Why?"

"Just a feeling. I don't think we've much time to find Sutherland. I think he started to figure things out at the same time I did. Maybe he got there a little quicker. There's only one way to find out."

Paul let a handful of sand trickle through his fingers. "Where is he?"

"At the safe house in the Hollywood Hills. Eliseo won't be looking there because I think that maybe his men followed us to Jake's ranch after we picked up Jonas. I thought it might have been Sutherland that tipped him off, but now I'm not so sure."

He stood, brushed off his jeans and nodded. "Great. Could have saved a trip if you'd worked this out sooner." He walked off towards the Jeep, unstrapped one of the Jerry cans from the side and began to fill the gas tank.

Julie watched him, then turned and touched my arm. Everything was in her eyes. The fear. The hope. The love. And something else. A sadness? A longing?

And all I could do was touch her face gently and kiss her full lips, in the lie that all would be fine and the day would come when we would step from the nightmare into the light of happiness and peace forever.

"I'll be back."

She nodded and smiled.

"Jonas. Look after the ladies or they'll look after you. Know what I mean?"

He glanced at the Omega in Sarah's hand and smiled ruefully.

FIFTEEN

Paul and I drove in the gathering darkness, weapons taped to every conceivable space in the Jeep, hidden from view but quickly accessible. Dust and sand swirled in a cloud behind as we sped across the open desert towards the distant lights that glowed against the night sky. He was quiet and I deserved the silent treatment. It could have been my stupidity that got Jake killed, but I had been sure that Eliseo's men hadn't been at the house when we'd arrived with Purdue. I would have known if they were there and they would have taken us down then, wouldn't they? The questions kept coming.

The trip was uneventful, although I spent the entire time watching every fleeting shadow, every glaring light in the totality of my paranoia. A strange feeling came over me as we approached the roaring crash of civilisation, an adrenalin rush in preparation for entering the jungle once more. When we reached the Hollywood Hills, we took a circuitous route, stopping in the shadows of overhanging trees while I doubled back to see whether we had been followed.

The city mocked me with its total indifference as eclectic music drifted from open windows, mingling with the balmy air in seeming multi-racial harmony, so soon forgotten when the light of day struck gold on the hills. Gradually we made our way to the walled and gated house standing in solitary anonymity, silhouetted against the lights of the city spread out below, twinkling through the smog.

The Jeep coasted to a stop and we sat for twenty minutes watching the house before I slipped out, Omega clenched firmly in my fist, and doubled back once more to check the road.

It was empty. Asleep.

Back at the Jeep, Paul was lounging nonchalantly against the fender. As I walked up to the front gate, I turned to see his shadow disappearing around the wall towards the back of the house. The gate silently swung open on its well-greased hinges. Sutherland had

196

reinstalled the CCTV cameras.

This was one of those times when instinct was the prime mover. The sole reason for continuing, when logic, rationale and common sense take a back seat. All my senses were alive and pulsating, the adrenalin released into my blood stream sending my heart rate up a few notches, and I could feel my muscles pumped up with energy, ready for action. The door opened quietly and I slipped through into the hallway and down towards the office. A faint perfume of gardenia tinged the air. It wasn't what Julie wore.

Sutherland sat at the desk, crumpled and old. "I knew you'd come Thomas. Eventually."

I shrugged and sat down in a worn leather armchair that reminded me so much of the many army officer's mess chairs in which I'd sat in my previous life.

"It's what you wanted," I said. He nodded tiredly. I continued, my voice sounding a harsh echo in the room. "I know Dean's here."

Sutherland studied me for a moment or two before speaking. "You don't trust anybody, do you?"

"Give me a good reason why I should. You made a phone call from Jake's ranch didn't you?" I asked with conviction. His answer would prove to me if I was responsible for Jake's death.

"I had to. We're in over our heads. We need each other."

His admission didn't make me feel any better. I knew I was still ultimately responsible.

Sutherland sighed heavily and passed a weary hand over his face before continuing. "There's a lot of stuff I've found out, but it just makes the problem bigger."

"Now you're talking in riddles. This stunt of yours got Jake killed. Do you know that?"

He flushed angrily, but quickly recovered himself. "No, I don't. What happened?"

"We were attacked at the ranch. The gunman tracked your phone call."

He sat silently, staring at me trying to decide if I was telling the truth or not. "I'm sorry. He was a good man."

"Save it Sutherland. You don't give a crap."

"Blame me if you like when this is over, but in the meantime let me give you a little theory to play around with. It's not new; it's been around for some time. It's a tale of two worlds that we can call the Overworld and the Underworld."

I smiled incredulously. "The Overworld and The Underworld? Sounds like an MMORPG computer game to me."

"Hear me out. I'm not talking about fantasy. Think 'Top Down Globalisation'. The Overworld are those who control everything. The Underworld is us. We the people. The great unwashed. The toilers. The worker bees. The Overworld are the people who control our lives, our religion, our politics, our living and our dying. They are the people who have most to lose as the New Technological World takes over. When knowledge becomes power and everyone acquires that power, then the Overworld no longer has the monopoly."

"You're talking gibberish."

He closed his eyes. "Look, you have to think Wikileaks. Think Julian Assange. Think little people doing things the Overworld never imagined could happen. Morgan Alvarez stumbled onto something far bigger than even she anticipated. She thought she was uncovering a nasty little plot that had its beginnings in the banking crash. But what she actually found was a hornet's nest that has ramifications far beyond our simple everyday lives. In the past, there has never been a connection between the Overworld and the Underworld. That is, the only connection has been through our power politicians and the major religious orders. But recently, because of the banking scandal, financial crisis, and wars in the Middle East, a window opened that allowed certain people to glimpse into the Overworld. The world of the International Mega Rich, Mega Powerful and, ultimately, not so smart. And I'm not talking about the jet-setters who appear in the society pages and the gossip columns, they are like us, they are part of the Underworld."

I was getting lost fast. Suddenly he seemed to be talking about aliens from outer space. Underworld? Overworld? He must have seen the disbelief in my face.

"There are a group of people who control International Finance, Politics and Religion. A group who use presidents, prime ministers and religious leaders to control the very countries we live in, and have the power of life or death at their finger tips. Not just one or two people, but thousands, millions can die at the stroke of a pen. Glasnost didn't happen by accident. The allying of the Soviet States and the Western Democratic States wasn't a sudden move by heads of countries in the interests of humanity. Hell, there's money to be made. There's power to be harnessed, and the Overworld know that the best way to get the Underworld subservient, is to give them what they think they want, as long as it's controllable."

I held up my hand to stop this flow. "Are you trying to tell me that there is a Government above the Government? One that has no boundaries? No country ties? No loyalties except to themselves?"

"That's about it."

"So that's what Radley has been investigating. And one of those people who stumbled into the Overworld is Jonas T Purdue? Right?"

Sutherland nodded slowly. The extraordinary thing was, it made sense. It gave a logic to everything that had happened. To the complete lawlessness of it all. "But how does Dean fit into all this?"

Sutherland looked over my shoulder. "Ask him yourself."

Dean stood in the doorway. He looked thin, gaunt, emaciated, his skin grey with fatigue, eyes red and haunted.

When he spoke his voice was a whisper. "Hello, Mr Gunn. I've heard a lot about you."

He sat down in the armchair next to mine and for a moment I felt I was a fly on the wall, observing these slowly moving characters as if a stage play rehearsal was in progress and not going very well.

Sutherland leaned back in his chair, elbows on the leather arms, fingertips together, watching me whilst his mind was a thousand miles away.

Dean looked at Sutherland, who nodded, then at me. This wasn't the King of the Airwaves. This was a broken shell of a man.

"I'm not who you think I am." His voice was no stronger than before, but so quiet was the room that it sounded loud and echoing. "I was once, but not now. Not for a long time. Not since I fell in love."

Pain flickered across his face, like a moth across a light bulb.

"That was a mistake. Falling in love. I didn't mean to. I meant to use her. Use her connections, just as I'd done so many times before. But it happened."

"Who is this 'she'?" My tone was harsh, unforgiving.

"Her name is Natasha Gregory." Something clicked and whirred at the back of my mind, but failed to engage. "Her family owns publishing houses, newspapers, radio and satellite TV providers in Europe, the USA, Australia and New Zealand."

Of course, now I had it. I'd met her father, Simon Gregory, at a fundraising event my father had organised years ago before I joined the Army.

Dean slumped back in the chair and closed his eyes. "To me it seemed a good way to advance my career. Up until then I only had small spots, mostly late night graveyard shifts making two hundred bucks a week, with little thanks. I was going nowhere in a hurry."

"What's this got to do with anything?"

Dean smiled thinly at my impatience. "I got my opportunity when Natasha's father pulled some strings and had me assigned to a plumb spot on KZP. But there was a condition. I was never to see Natasha again."

I rolled my eyes heavenward and sighed. If I'd hoped for some explanation, it wasn't here. Or so I thought.

"By then I'd fallen in love with Natasha and she with me and it seemed absurd to stop seeing each other. She was scared. God was she scared and I didn't understand why. A motel here, a hotel there. By this time I was a pretty good asset to KZP. Good ratings and a minor celebrity. That made her even more frightened. I tried to get her to tell me why, but she wouldn't. Kept saying that we were in different worlds. Hell, I said, I'm making a million a year now, shit, that puts me in your world. She laughed at me. Then she gave me a few business tips. Said I could figure it out for myself, but I'd have to be real careful. Cover my tracks."

"The investments? Arbitrages? Purdue's investment trust fund?"

He nodded, breathed a deep sigh and squeezed his eyes with thumb and forefinger as if trying to force the images from his mind.

"I already had some money invested with Purdue so we talked, and he saw an opportunity, how I don't know. I knew of an investigative journalist who had been digging into another investment bank, so I contacted her to see if she could find out anything before I really got dragged into investing more." He paused and closed his eyes again.

"Morgan Alvarez," I said softly.

"Yes. That was when the lid came off. She must have found out something, or triggered a response. All I know is Natasha disappeared. Morgan was killed and some thug smelling of cheap Eau Sauvage started putting the squeeze on me." He turned to me, his eyes pleading. "I'm a coward. I've no courage. They said they'd kill me too if I didn't cooperate."

"They would have done if Sutherland hadn't got you out first." I turned to Sutherland. "Which brings me to you. Who the hell tipped you off? Who's pulling your strings?"

Sutherland pulled the pipe out of his pocket and stuck it in the corner of his mouth, eying me the whole time, but not saying anything.

"You lied your arse off the last time we met in this room, didn't you? You're not some bumbling old fart close to retirement trying to piece together the puzzle. You pretty much know what's going on and somebody's feeding you the information. The why, the how, the where. Somebody from the 'Overworld'? Isn't that what you said 'They' were? And me? I'm just the stupid shit with his head up his arse risking everything to keep the heat away from you."

Sutherland stood wearily and puffed on his pipe. "Let Dean continue."

"The investment deal tips Natasha had given me were huge. Over three and a half trillion dollars of assets under management."

"What? Who the hell has that sort of money?"

Dean looked bleakly at me. "The people of the Overworld do. That's why they can make or break anyone. Any corporation. Any government. Any country. To be a multi-billionaire is nothing. Peanuts to these people. They don't even use money in their everyday lives; hell they own the global financial institutions. How do you think a black lawyer from Chicago gets to be President unless someone wants him there?"

The fairy-tale was getting too much, even for my very vivid imagination. "So what happened to you?"

Dean dropped his eyes from mine. "I made ten million dollars hush money. Purdue handled it, but I knew I was a dead man and I knew Natasha was as good as dead."

The silence in the room was a tangible item that could have been plucked from the air and stored as a precious jewel, but now it was a painful knife in the minds of everyone in the room.

"You're telling me we're all being controlled by a bunch of guys with so much money, they can buy and sell governments at the drop of a hat and they don't care which way it goes? Correct?"

Sutherland stared out of the window. "Not all the Overworld are bad. There's a status quo. An understanding like a benevolent dictatorship. At least there was a status quo, until somebody started rocking the boat. Dismantling it piece by piece. The GFC (Global Financial Crisis) didn't happen by accident, it was deliberate. We have to find out who those people are."

"Why don't the people of the Overworld do it themselves if they are so all powerful?" My sarcasm fell on deaf ears.

"Has it ever occurred to you that a professional ball player would probably make a bad lawyer or nuclear scientist? That a nuclear scientist might make a bad professional ball player? These people are the planners and the strategists. The global accountants and bankers. We are the ones who are involved in the filth of corruption and crime. To them, trust and confidence is everything. But somewhere along the line that trust got broken."

I shook my head. "I know something about corporate finance, but I'm not in their league."

"And they're not in yours. "

I guess once you grasped the concept it wasn't too difficult to follow. Hell the stories and rumours had been around a long time. This was nothing new as I said before. Isn't that what I dealt with back in

England with Hamish and the Orange Moon debacle?

"So you're saying that as a world community we are living under a benevolent dictatorship, but there's a rogue on the loose with the power to destroy a carefully controlled status-quo?"

"Is that too hard to believe?"

"And the others are running scared, so they drop down to the proletariat for help? Come on now. This sounds like a movie plot."

"Think what you will. Just look at the facts. If they don't convince you, then just think of it as revenge. That's something you can understand, isn't it? How do you think you've been able to stay under the radar after kidnapping Purdue and scattering bodies all over Southern California?"

Why was it that I found the notion so absurd?

Because I thought myself too important to be controlled by anyone?

Hell, I had thought that when I was in the army only to realise too late that I was a pawn then. So what had changed?

"Okay. Say, for argument's sake, I accept your explanation, but that doesn't change anything. Jonas is still the vital link. And if you're right, with what he knows we can blow the lid right off this pile of shit." I paused and neither of them said anything. "Do you have anywhere else you can stay? This house isn't safe anymore."

"I have a place up in the mountains, near Three Rivers."

"I'm familiar with the general area."

"I'll draw a map before you leave."

"Fine. Take Dean with you."

"What are you planning?"

"Later. What communications do you have up there?"

"Satellite phone and an old SSB (single-side-band), sort of thing you should be used to on your boat."

"Okay. Listen out on the eight-megahertz channel. If you get nothing then try six and then four. We can switch once we've established a link. Do you know the Codex system?"

He screwed his eyes and shook his head. "No."

"Okay. I'll write out a simple one for now. Next time we meet I'll give you a complete set. Basically, it uses a four-letter code for a word or a phrase or a number. You just match up the grids and you've got your message."

So while Sutherland drew a map of Three Rivers and the route to his cabin, I devised a simple Codex system with enough letters, phrases and numbers to last a short time. Then I showed him how it worked, and made a copy. By using this system, we could communicate on any well-used channel without being compromised. For a short time anyway. Any code can be broken, it's just a matter of time, but this was old school and hopefully would confuse the ultra smart cryptographers who relied on computers, long enough.

Before I left I turned to Dean. "Your girlfriend Natasha needs to change her perfume. Gardenia is a dead giveaway."

Paul was waiting by the Jeep, looking bored. "Find your boy?"

I nodded. "He's there."

"Now what?"

I climbed into the Jeep and gently shut the door. "We get ourselves a decent video camera."

"Where from?"

"From a camera store."

"Of course, why didn't I think of that?"

He started the engine and we drove off into the dawn as I told him what went on in the house.

As an exercise in story telling it was very simple. All you had to do was look at nature. Everything has its order. A structure for survival. Why were we any different? Why should we, the human animal, not have a pyramid structure too? In our minds our President, or Prime Minister, or King, or Queen, or God was the big chief. If so, then why not take it a stage further and have a superstructure above that, to control and run the entire human animal kingdom.

There had been times when we as a species had come pretty close to global war. Was it too difficult to conceive, that from the aftermath of the Second World War and the increase of wealth, a group of powerful business people had created a situation where they could control government policies the world over?

It was here. We could see it.

Didn't several owners of multinational companies have homes in both the East and the West, and weren't they personal friends of the leaders of the Super Powers, and didn't they intervene when communications between countries broke down? We had seen it on several occasions, but only paid it fleeing attention before getting on with our mundane lives.

I could list some of them off the top of my head. Armin Assante, Owner and Head of Amerasian Oil. Paul Gladstone, Chief Executive and Chairman of Oki-Cola Corporation, and of course Australian born Simon Gregory of Global News International Media Group. There were more, I couldn't recall them off hand, but a quote from Paul Gladstone stuck in my mind. In an off camera reference to the power of his company in global politics he said *'Hell, when the President wakes up in the morning, he has his dick in one hand and a bottle of Oki-Cola in the other.'*

Yet, somehow I couldn't see any of these people as benevolent dictators. Who was kidding whom? After all, they were human too and greed still had a place in their world as well.

The parameters had changed once more and my mind had to shift to accommodate the new situation. But it was difficult. I could accept the basic principles, but the reality was another ball game. My mind couldn't comprehend the trillions of dollars Sutherland and Dean had talked about. But I didn't need to think about that; all I needed to think about was revenge. After all, wasn't that why I was doing this in the first place? Revenge for my father. Revenge for Danny. Revenge for Morgan.

I told Paul all this, while we were parked up, waiting for the store to open. He didn't seem at all surprised.

"I always thought there was more going on than I knew about. Throw in the Mafia and we have a real crock-pot of nastiness. Think about Kennedy and Sam Giancana fixing the votes. They even had the same mistress. What does that tell you?" He stuffed the last quarter of a donut into his mouth, washing it down with bad watery coffee we'd picked up at the small hole-in-the-wall cafe that supplied the early shift for a local Hollywood studio. The electricians and carpenters slowly made their sleepy way to the gate with their waxed paper coffee cups, rubbing their eyes, before beginning another day in Fantasyland.

This was the real Hollywood, where in days gone by the grunt and sweat of the industry worked in small houses in quiet streets.

Now condos had sprung up where quaint California craftsmen houses used to be, and at night police helicopters circled endlessly, picking out drug deals on the street with their stabbing searchlights. Where gangs roamed the darkness in sinister looking cars, killing each other in an orgy of violence. Where once sleepy neighbourhoods now rocked to the sound of Rap and Mariachi music.

This was the real Hollywood.

The Hollywood of the pulp soft-porn novelists who had yet to learn to write, but who stashed millions in the bank every year by catering to an uneducated taste for a world far removed from everyday life.

This was the breeding ground for the numerous badly written, badly acted daytime soaps that filled the airwaves with endless inane utterings in the excuse for entertainment. The twentieth-first century opiate of the masses, where thought and knowledge were kept to a minimum.

Was this how the Overworld exerted a control over the Underworld, by bombarding the people with enough crap to atrophy any living brain cells? Monopolising the media with brainless content?

Was Big Brother a fact, far more sinister and subtle than George Orwell had anticipated? At least the 'They' of my daymares now had an identity, still formless, but an identity nonetheless.

Within half an hour, armed with a Sony HXR-NX30 camcorder, wireless mikes; a small GoPro simple lighting set-up, and a tiny camera where the lens looked like a Phillips head screw, all purchased on my aircraft charter company's credit card, we were on our way back to Louisville after filling up with fuel. We had explained we were filming wildlife in the Sierras, which caused no interest at all.

This time our route was circuitous, driving out to the town of Mojave, and then circling around half way to Las Vegas and back to Louisville, late at night. Taking off across the trackless desert for the last fifty miles using the last set of night vision goggles. Any lesser vehicle than Jake's custom Jeep trying to follow us would have fallen by the wayside many miles ago.

When we arrived at one thirty in the morning, Julie was sitting on the veranda with Sarah drinking coffee. Jonas sat in a sleeping bag, back against the wall.

Sarah held up the coffee pot, Paul picked up the two extra mugs that sat beside them and Julie poured. It was surprisingly good after the long drive.

"Where's Dean?" Julie asked.

"Safe."

I recounted the meeting with Dean and Sutherland.

When I finished Purdue nodded. "Things are starting to make sense," Purdue said sombrely. "My backers assigned me a new security detail two weeks ago. Maybe that's why you got in so easily. Question is are my backers the good guys or the bad guys?"

"Are there any good guys?" Sarah offered. "Sounds like this 'Overworld' bunch are just as bad as the guys who are trying to take over."

It was at that moment that I fully realised that I wasn't as in control as I thought. We were being manipulated, and those that ran Radley, Sutherland and their organisations, counted on my irrational behaviour.

"Logic can't win this war, Mr Gunn. That's why they sent you after me. They knew you'd do something absurd," Purdue said pointedly, but without accusation echoing my own thoughts. "We're all pawns in one way or another."

"I guess we just keep on doing then. But just what is it we're doing?" Sarah asked.

"We fly back to Tombstone leaving in two hours, Julie and I have an appointment in Atlanta, which Jonas is going to explain."

"The first link is Senator Jackson Doleman," Purdue began. "He's one of those that set me up with an injection of foreign investment for the hedge fund. He has an office in Atlanta and a country house on Lake Sydney Lanier where he does most of his deals. He's charming and sincere. When he kills you, you'll enjoy the experience and thank him with your last breath. That's what you'll be dealing with."

"When did you last see him?"

"Six months ago, he wanted me to run an arbitrage on a deal in Bolivia."

"Power plants," Julie said quietly. She had been sitting quietly beside me, listening.

"Lot more than that. Pure opium from Afghanistan shipped through Bolivia, then flown to Mexico for processing, then distributed by Mexican cartels into the USA."

"I still don't get the connection with the financial and political structure in the USA. What's it to do with the global economy?" Julie questioned.

"Liquid assets give investment trust funds like mine unlimited collateral."

"And opens the door to every sleazy criminal in the world."

"Organised crime will do anything for a big payday. They don't discriminate as long as they get paid. My Trust was just one of many that laundered their money."

"Why didn't you just come clean?" Paul asked frowning.

"Seven billion dollars is why."

"Oh boy. Ask a stupid question and..." Paul muttered.

"That's the amount Eliseo said was taken from his cartel," I interrupted.

Purdue looked taken aback. "Eliseo Martinez?"

"The same."

"Just when you think you have it figured, something else jumbles it all up again," Purdue said shaking his head.

"Paul we need your friend to deal with the Yuma radar again and your ATC guy in Phoenix, Sarah." They both nodded.

"Why Atlanta now, Jonas?" I asked.

"I was supposed to attended a meeting with Jackson's investors. I'm now thinking it may have been an invitation to my own funeral."

"When's the meeting?"

"Four days from now."

"Then we better get going."

Much to Sarah's annoyance, I decided to leave the Jeep in the ramshackle barn at Louisville until we could retrieve it later. It seemed to me to make sense for all of us to leave in the Explorer and get to Sarah's base in Tombstone as soon as possible. Paul could secure the surroundings, and Julie and I would take the Mustang to Atlanta.

SIXTEEN

We sat in the almost absurdly comic book opulence of the Peachtree Plaza Hotel, staring at the unnecessary insanity of the towering foyer with a ceiling that stretched seven stories and a bar that floated on the connected islands of a half acre 'lake'. Where rich young Georgia rednecks, drunk and out-of-control, ogled even younger brassy barmaids with obscene promises they couldn't keep.

Green plant tendrils drooped over surrounding balconies on each level to the seventh floor, and the constant hum of voices together with canned Musak, gave the hotel an impression of a modern Tower of Babel.

The cylinder that speared the sky with steel and glass, swayed and creaked in an alarmingly lifelike fashion while couples copulated in segmented rooms, their groans mixing with the whirling 'thwack thwack' of circling tourist helicopters that swarmed around the technological wonder gracing the downtown Atlanta skyline.

In one of the two dining rooms we sat beside a hundred-foot wide, thirty-foot high waterfall, eating gourmet food served by waiters with fixed smiles and exaggerated concern. Watching the parade of uniformed business executives flow backwards and forwards with manicured, made-up, hair-sprayed colleagues, whose final act for the day would be to spread their thighs and ride the adrenalin rush of taboo sex, before returning to humdrum husband/lovers and the myriad problems of everyday home life.

It was all encapsulated in the crass, ugly, coldly designed banal testament to Man's bad taste.

Julie sat opposite me, sipping a cocktail from an oversized glass, watching the carnival, eyes mirroring the comic parade with a seeming innocence that made my heart falter and beat an irregular tattoo, causing a lump to form in my throat.

Even dressed in a simple twenties style 'Flapper' outfit, she stood out from the crowd, making heads turn and even curbing the intoxicated adolescent tongues of the young Southern Aristocrats. Only I knew that beneath the seeming fragility of her physical appearance lay strength. Deep. Firm. Formed in the maturity of self-knowledge. And the more time I spent in her company, the more secure I felt and the stronger my love grew.

We sat quietly, each with our own thoughts, communicating in silence with just small movements. Watching as we might watch a play, where the audience could freely wander from room-to-room with the players. Involved, yet voyeurs, and when our thirst was assuaged, we could retire to our separate segments on the sixty-fifth floor and listen to the creaking of the structure as the floor-to-ceiling, wall-to-wall glass moved within its steel frame, as strong winds blowing from the flatlands buffeted the Hotel in protest.

Somewhere here, amongst the crass, the beautiful, the bold and the deceitful, was Jackson Doleman. He had a permanent suite at the Peachtree and it was a good place to catch sight of the man and get a measure of him.

On our first night there was no sign of him, so Julie and I relaxed, ate well, then retired to our suite and made love slowly and gently for what seemed the first time in months. The following evening we sat in the oyster bar, eating a dozen each on ice, sprinkled with Tabasco and accompanied by a large frosted glass of cold Chablis.

The first sight of Doleman was a surprise. Instead of the tyrant, we saw a mild mannered, immaculately dressed, short, slim man with a ready smile. He sat at a corner table talking quietly with an aide and two colleagues, while close by, but unobtrusive, two bodyguards lounged, professional enough to melt into the crowd, yet attentive enough to always know exactly what was going on.

On several occasions, their gaze turned in our direction, but we behaved like star-crossed lovers, who only had eyes for each other. Julie was facing Doleman and talking to me through her fingers in my hand, telling me of the conversation as she read his lips. I felt a vicarious pleasure at this simple ploy that enabled us to eavesdrop in complete safety.

"Not so much a conversation, more Doleman holding court," Julie signed. "Talking about education funding cuts to finance infrastructure spending. Now he's telling them he's taking a few days vacation with his family at his holiday house on Lake Sydney Lanier in two or three days time."

"Jonas was right about the date. Question is was he right about this supposed meeting?"

"I guess we'll find out," Julie said quietly, smiling sweetly.

We finished our meal and left without fuss, returning to our suite, planning to checkout early the next morning for the journey to the lake house.

I closed my eyes and slept to the swaying creaking of the hotel, with disturbing dreams of Julie and Morgan flitting through my erotic sub-conscious, mixed with the screaming thump of high explosive shells and the staccato stutter of machine guns.

Now in the half sleep of night the memories were a symphonic disharmony, a discordant backbeat to my thoughts.

We rose early, breakfasted lightly, turning away the constant flow of orange juice and coffee that threatened to drown us in equal doses of Vitamin C and caffeine, and within an hour left the fractured turmoil of the awakening city behind, driving between the peach orchards heading north east for the forty minute drive to Lake Sydney Lanier, stopping on the way to buy easily consumable food to last us up to four days. That meant canned fruit, canned tuna, ham and salmon, crackers and bottled water.

This was my first visit to the South and although the city of Atlanta bore little resemblance to '*Gone With The Wind*', glimpses of white mansions with long sweeping driveways leading to colonnade entrances, told me that the spirit of the Confederacy was still alive and well and prospering.

It seemed an anomaly that Jackson Doleman, a black politician, should figure so prominently. But whoever said greed and corruption were restricted to certain cultures or ethnic groups. Hell, that was one equality nobody could deny.

Julie echoed my thoughts. "Surely he wouldn't have that power? Not here?"

"He's a pawn. I was thinking last night that he is the perfect go-between in any dealings with South America."

"Bolivia?"

"And Mexico. That's what Purdue said."

After the conversation with Sutherland, I was now thinking of Global Politics, as if trying to come to terms with billions and trillions of dollars wasn't enough.

The deeper we plumbed the depths, the less we knew.

Was there really such a thing as an Overworld and an Underworld?

It began to rain. A steady summer downpour that we knew would turn off as soon as it had started. For a moment or two my mind turned from current affairs, as I watched the windscreen wipers slash the drops away, enjoying the sound of the tyres on the wet road. I opened the window a crack and let the fresh sweet smell of rain tease my senses in the knowledge that soon, back in Southern California, the rain would be just a distant pleasant memory.

But for now, the drops that flickered through the window and fell on my face were cool trickling reminders of a youth spent in England, tracing drops down the window and staring out at the grey rain-lashed countryside, while crumpets toasted on long forks in front of a roaring log fire.

We were headed up the 85, past DeKalb Peachtree Airport where the Mustang was parked, and on to Lake Sydney Lanier with its thousands of inlets and coves, and a shoreline that stretched for hundreds of miles. Purdue had given me detailed instructions on how to get to the lake house on the Doleman's private estate.

"Most of the year it's deserted. An old holiday house for some rich Southern family. Doleman bought it twenty years ago. Some say he wanted it because his Grandfather had been a slave there," Purdue cackled meanly. "Maybe he likes to walk around the grounds barefoot, in chains, just to get the atmosphere right." He broke off, laughing quietly at his own bad joke, before continuing. "Get there two days before the meeting. You can set

everything up and nobody will bother you."

"What about bodyguards?"

"They get there about a day before everybody arrives, to check the place out. Hell, these guys feel very comfortable. They don't think there's a problem. He has a remote camera security system that monitors the gates and immediate grounds."

"How do you know all this?"

"He showed me. He's an arrogant son-of-a-bitch and as I said, thinks he's completely secure."

Purdue drew a map from memory of the camera locations and the security room that operated remotely when there wasn't a physical presence. Julie called Oldfield and gave him as much information as we had, which included the satellite security system Doleman used. If we could hack into the system, we could cover our tracks and get in unseen. The rest would be relatively easy. I had done it many times in my old life.

Purdue's photographic memory was superb. Every detail, every bend in the road, even the shapes of the trees and the glimpses of the lake from certain turns in the road, exact.

The estate was nearly two hundred acres and we were at the very extreme southern end. The road swung away to the right and continued on down to the lake about two miles distant.

I pulled in to the side of the road and looked at the fencing. It was old post and rail that had been patched roughly in places. The rain slowed. I sat for a moment, thinking, then got out of the car, retrieved the wheel brace from the trunk and walked across to the fence. The distance between the posts was just wide enough for the car, so I set to work prizing off the old timbers, being careful not to split the wood, until I had cleared an opening.

Julie reversed the car slowly through the gap, trying not to disturb the wet ground too much, then replaced the timbers, hammering them roughly into place. She drove a little way into the cover of the trees and switched off the engine while I covered the tracks and hid the car from view. While I was busying myself, Julie sat back against a tree trunk, hair plastered down around her face, which was dirty from tree bark and mud. We were both sweating in the humid heat.

"What now?"

The one thing about having your own aircraft is that you can carry weapons coast-to-coast. I took two small silenced Beretta 9mm from their cases in the trunk that Sarah had given me from her armoury, and handed one to Julie. In my sailing bag I also had the knives and the 'screw' camera equipment, the food and a double sleeping bag.

"Now we take a look at the house."

The two hundred acres were not flat. There were hundreds of small rises, deep steep gullies with small streams trickling beneath scrub grass and twisted tree roots. The wet foliage and sodden ground smelled musty and dank. In places steam rose in a thin mist, dissipating a few feet above the earth, and as the rain stopped altogether, shafts of sunlight pierced the trees, sparkling off the raindrop laden leaves, shimmering and dancing to the ground below. We sweltered in the heat and humidity and wondered if a tornado was long overdue.

Over the lake, a rainbow hovered, fading and brightening with the cloud shadows shifting across the sun. We were not dressed for scrambling around in the wet woods, water seeped into our sneakers, soaking socks and squeezing between toes.

I carried the camera equipment, taking care to keep the case out of the streams, an almost impossible task as we slipped and slid off barely exposed tree roots and dead leaves. Then the ground flattened and there, two hundred feet beyond a lawn of long uncut grass stood the solitary house.

Fading white clapboard, water and sun stained, still supporting its former glory proudly, even as the years creased, warped and cracked its lined exterior. There was a homely warmth that radiated from the house, an old fashioned hospitality that refused to remember the Civil War carnage, that once had turned formal flower beds into gruesome headstones as a testament to a long forgotten, ill-formed ideal. All the house saw and remembered was the gentility, the almost European attention to manners and propriety, and a drooping sadness mourned its passing.

And while the atmosphere of the house seeped through the pores of my skin, we circled the grounds in cover of the bushes, stopping every twenty yards to look and listen. The only sounds were the rustle of leaves and the drip of water.

We stayed in cover and Julie spread out the drawings of the CCTV camera positions Purdue had indicated that were linked to the security surveillance system.

"I hope the Professor managed to hack into the system."

Julie sent a text message on her secure phone and we waited.

"Another five minutes," she said and closed her eyes and rubbed her forehead while we waited.

"You look tired," I said, stating the obvious. The stress of the last few weeks was beginning to tell on her.

"I need a vacation. Somewhere nobody can reach us."

"I've got a nice little South Pacific atoll picked out. We could stock the boat up and stay there for months."

"Sounds perfect. When do we leave?"

"Right now if you want." I was serious. It would be easy just to fly to Baja, get on the boat and disappear.

"Keep dreaming soldier," she retorted, holding the back of her hand to her forehead.

"Headache?"

"A little. The humidity always does it to me."

"This better be worth the discomfort, otherwise Jonas is going to suffer."

"We'll see." She sighed and again brushed the back of her hand across her forehead. "It all seems unreal. Overworld and Underworld. Drug cartels doing business with banks and the CIA. People killing each other over religion. It's insane."

"Been going on for thousands of years. Can't see it ending anytime soon." Her phone beeped softly. "Okay. We have thirty minutes."

An expensive antique Persian Bakhtiari carpet covered half the wooden floor of the entrance hallway. The carpet was probably worth more than all the simple furnishings of the house, but hid its value behind a worn appearance and only a diligent, educated eye would spot the telltale weaver's name woven into the pattern in the bottom corner. My scant knowledge put the age at somewhere in the region of a hundred and fifty years, and the value in the tens of thousands of dollars.

In some strange way, the carpet seemed to fit with the image of the man I saw at the Peachtree, and the subtle humour of placing this antique for unknowing guests to walk over, was not lost on me.

Purdue had told me the meetings usually took place in the formal living room, the only room not covered by cameras.

I sat in the middle of the floor of the living room and looked around. It measured thirty feet by eighteen. Set into the west wall was the doorway to the hall. The entire south wall was a French window leading to the patio, with the lawn beyond.

Julie lay down on the overstuffed settee and closed her eyes. "Wake me when you're done."

"Yes ma'am."

A stone fireplace, that must have been an addition at a later date as it did not seem in keeping with the design of the house, lay on the north wall. Above it was a 52" Plasma TV and on the east wall built into a wall cupboard was a professional looking video and Hi-Fi bank for a cinema experience. Large Bose speakers in the corners and sides of the room provided total surround sound. I stared at the equipment rack and spotted what I was looking for. The perfect sized Phillips screw. If there was enough room behind it I could place the hidden 'screw' camera in the enclosure and wire it to the tiny wireless transmitter/receiver. I could activate it once the bodyguards had cleared the house.

Five minutes later, I had opened the equalizer and had the small camera and transmitter/receiver secured inside. It operated from its own AAA battery and transmitted to an app on Julie's iPad mini that her father had developed. From the front, there was no difference to the casual observer. I sat for some time staring into the lens, trying to tell whether it could be spotted or not.

I didn't think so.

Julie still lay sleeping on the settee. Hair tangled, spread over her shoulders and out in a fan shape across the settee cushion. Her breathing light, child-like, eyes flickering beneath lids as dream images flashed across the rich landscape of her mind.

It always amazed me. The astonishingly beautiful, porcelain fragility of soft smooth almost translucent skin, sculptured in gentle sweeping contours that simply by existing created such strong emotions within me.

Our car was too far away for the transmit range of the camera, so I had to find somewhere close by where we could hide. I had fifteen minutes before Oldfield had to switch off his system hack. Outside I searched the gardens and then the immediate wooded area within line of sight of the house.

I stumbled upon it by accident. A tumbled down, dilapidated, overgrown groundsman's shed, that had long fallen into disuse. So much so that it was invisible from even a couple of paces away. The only way I found it was to fall through the rotting sidewall that had sagged with the weight of the creepers and fallen tree branches.

Inside it was small, filled with the odour of rotting vegetation that had seeped in through the walls, but it was surprisingly dry. The floor, hard packed earth.

Julie was awake waiting for me in the hallway. "I didn't know where you went."

"I'm sorry." I kissed her softly, holding her hands in mine.

"Find anything?"

"Come I'll show you. I found a little place where we can monitor the meeting."

"Oh?"

"You don't belong in this mess."

She still watched me, silently.

"I've asked myself the same question but I don't know the answer. It was so simple. Help you find out what happened to Morgan. Now?" She spread her hands and shrugged, waiting as if to try and pluck the reason from the air. "It's out of control. You're driving and I can't get out of the car."

"You can. Anytime you want."

"But I don't want to. My other life seems so far behind."

We made sure that we left no sign of our presence in the house and moved to our hideout in the woods.

It was a circuitous route, walking down the driveway then stepping into the trees closest to the drive where our footprints wouldn't be seen in the wet grass.

Julie had recovered and looked rested and calm. The morning shafts of light penetrating through the broken walls of the dilapidated shed reflected a warm glow off her skin. There was a slight contented smile on her face as she took my hand and gently pressed my palm to her breast.

"My love."

It seemed this shed was a womb, holding our love and letting it grow safely, even though we both knew it was false.

So I stopped trying to understand anything that was happening and gently made love to her on the hard packed dirt, as if we were in our own private paradise, instead of the musty rotting womb of the abandoned and forgotten shed.

We were in another world that had somehow side slipped into a temporary transcendental dimension. Even I didn't know what that meant, and at this moment I didn't care.

The heat of the day barely lessened as sunlight faded to dusk and into a clear starry night. Rain came again and we held each other closely as night moved to dawn and the new day broke quietly with blue skies, sunshine and the arrival of Jackson Doleman's men.

Julie slept on as I watched the men moving around the grounds checking for tell tale signs of intruders.

They were thorough, but not thorough enough. Coming to within a few feet of the hidden shed, yet not discovering it. I should not have been surprised, for how many times had they done this? And how many times had they seen the same sights?

One of them, a short, stocky man with ebony skin and slightly slanting eyes, unzipped his fly and relieved himself close-by. The stream of urine playing against the tree trunk, steam rising and the acrid smell drifting into the shed, hanging in the still air.

He finished, and tucking himself away in his pants snorted like a pig, and spat into the bushes.

Julie stirred, pulled her knees up a little closer to her chest, but did not wake.

I turned my attention back to the man, to see him walk away, farting as he went. He did not seem too concerned about anything.

The day was long. Julie and I talked with our hands. Slept. Held each other and ate survival chocolate, drank bottled water and sweated in the humid heat.

The bodyguards had turned on the TV and were watching a movie, the sound turned up echoing across the lawn and insinuating itself through the trees to where we lay. Every now and then, I caught a glimpse of one of them, walking casually around the house as if on a low level patrol. The only sign that he had a weapon, the lump beneath his jacket.

As the hours grew longer, the tension in my body eased with the knowledge that they suspected nothing. They were safe here and had been for some considerable time. So there was no need to be concerned. They had checked out the house and the grounds, found nothing amiss, so settled down to enjoy themselves until the Boss arrived, when once more they would be relegated to the servant's quarters.

The house lights finally went out at two in the morning. I waited another hour before unfolding my stiff legs and crawling out of the shed. The moon was up, but not high enough to cast light deep into the woods. I needed to stretch and I was bored, covert OPs were not my favourite, never had been, and I wanted another look at the house. Albeit from the cover of the trees. Everything was taking far too long to unfold and I was getting impatient. I felt that I needed to jump start the action and surprise Doleman and his cohorts. But I knew that all impatience did, was get people killed. So I settled down at the treeline and watched the house in the moonlight.

SEVENTEEN

A small dormouse scurried across the dirt floor, stopped to stare at me, twitched its nose and, feeling no danger, ran away to reappear with a morsel of food. It made ten trips, backwards and forwards, carrying small pieces of food on each return trip and each time it would stop for a moment or two, watching me closely to see whether the status quo had changed.

My concentration on the little mouse was broken by the sound of a car in the driveway, followed by a slamming of doors and faint voices.

I untangled myself from Julie and reached for the iPad, put in earbuds and stared at the small screen.

The bodyguards had been busy in the early morning, laying out presents and setting up an animated film on the Blue-ray.

The living room door opened and a middle-aged woman entered, followed by preadolescent twins who clapped their hands and shrieked with delight. One of the bodyguards stood behind, laden with gaudily wrapped presents of varying shapes and sizes, whilst the woman decided where they should be placed.

"I think we'll have them over there Herman. Mildred has the cake and I think it should be on the table by the window."

"Yes Mrs Doleman." Herman did not look happy with his task as he tried to arrange the presents 'artistically' while the children fought to see whose name was on what package.

Doleman appeared in the doorway and watched with a slight smile on his face.

"Well Anthea? What do you think?" He spoke so softly I had to turn the volume up to hear.

Anthea Doleman stood with her hands on her hips looking around the room, frowning.

"They never do it right. Never."

Herman paused in arranging the presents and watched Doleman with trepidation. The kids raced out of the room and Anthea spotted something beyond her husband in the hallway and pushed past him.

Doleman looked down at Herman and smiled.

"Relax Herman. Don't forget I have visitors. I want you to take Mrs Doleman and the children out on the lake for a couple of hours."

Herman looked crestfallen. Doleman smiled and left the room. Herman finished arranging the presents and set about changing the other items, muttering to himself as he worked.

"Damn kids. Damn woman. Nothin' but trouble. Always complainin'. Always whinin' 'bout somethin'. Never satisfied."

I took out the earbuds and sat back. Julie stifled a giggle.

"You were watching?"

She nodded. "How would you like to be married to that?"

"It takes all types."

She grimaced. "Yeah. Right."

Shivering suddenly she pulled the coat around her shoulders, signing quickly. "Things better shape up. I'm not sitting here making a home video of a family birthday party."

"Patience. Patience."

She grimaced.

I turned back to the iPad and watched Herman rearrange the furniture in the room. He brought ladder-backed chairs from the dining room and set them side-by-side close to the coffee table, then pushed the two settees so their backs were to the window.

It was as if he was arranging the room purely for my benefit, ensuring that everyone would be right in front of the camera. Then he walked over to the TV set, knelt down and stared at the Hi-Fi deck. Literally straight into the lens. It was creepy.

"It's all set up on the lower DVD recorder Herman. Did it myself." The voice, harsh and loud, came from the French windows. The bodyguard who had peed by the shed, walked across the room. "Okay?"

Herman nodded into the camera lens.

"Sure." He stood, shrugged and left the room. The other man stayed, scratching his crutch and snorting, looking around for somewhere to spit and finding nowhere, swallowed whatever was in his mouth.

I almost felt sorry for Herman. He was just a big dumb gopher, with scarcely enough brains to pull his pants on in the morning and who had to suffer his indignities in silence. He frowned at the machines, thinking hard, then shook his head and walked slowly to the door. He stopped, turned, looked back at the machines again, then once again shook his head and left the room.

For the rest of the morning, there were just general comings and goings. The kids playing havoc with everyone and everything, and Anthea Doleman alternating between fits of depression and anger, mostly aimed at the hapless Herman.

Jackson Doleman remained quietly enigmatic. A paradox. Mild mannered and quiet, never losing his temper no matter how provoked by his wife and children. His men treated him with deference, respect, and obviously commanded instant obedience.

I must have dropped off to sleep for a short time, for I found Julie shaking me and pointing to the iPad. Jackson Doleman, with two of his bodyguards, was in the room. One of them set up a video camera unobtrusively against the wall pointed at the ladder-backed chairs, then positioned himself next to the other bodyguard, his back to the bookcase facing Doleman, who sat in the corner of one of the settees.

Two well-dressed people were shown into the room. A man and a woman. The woman was in her thirties, medium height, good figure, black hair and porcelain-white skin that made the red sweep of her full lips all the more startling. She wore a black two-piece suit, white blouse and single string of pearls. I was willing to bet they were not cultured.

The man wore a grey suit, tinted horn rim glasses and looked to be in his early sixties. He was tanned and looked faintly South American. It was difficult to tell, but I had the feeling I had seen him somewhere before.

Following them was Marika Keskküla.

Jackson smiled and gestured to the two ladder-backed chairs. In the distance, on the lake, I caught the sound of a motorboat engine starting up, and guessed that Herman was carrying out his task of taking Mrs Doleman and her odious children on a boat ride.

Doleman sat very still, smile on his face. "Welcome to my house."

"It's always a privilege." To my surprise the man spoke with a New York accent. Where had I seen him?

"Do you care for coffee? A glass of wine perhaps?"

The woman nodded. "Do you have 2008 Didier Dagueneau Silex? It's the only wine I drink." Her tone was perfunctory, business-like and challenging. It was obvious she did not like Doleman, and by her demeanour did not consider him her equal. I didn't know if it was racism or simply a class thing.

Jackson raised an eyebrow, the other visitor looked sharply at the woman. Jackson nodded to the servant standing in the doorway. "A glass of the Dagueneau for Miss Gregory."

The name jumped out at me. Jangled my brain and in my memory I saw Dean sitting crumpled in his chair telling me about Natasha.

"And I think a bourbon for Senator Travis. A large one."

The servant nodded and slid quietly away.

Senator Travis. Now I could place him. He was on the Senate Defence Budget Committee. A strong supporter of the Strategic Defence Initiative Program that was so hotly debated. He had been at Purdue's 'funeral', captured in a photograph standing beside the Vice President.

Miss Gregory shifted impatiently in her chair. "Can we get on with this. I have an engagement to attend in Washington tonight."

Doleman smiled. "All in good time, Anna. All in good time."

Not Natasha. This was her sister. It was getting weird.

Anna Gregory looked up sharply at the sound of her name. Her voice was cold as ice. "Miss Gregory if you please, Senator."

Jackson Doleman stood up slowly and paced backwards and forwards while he talked.

"It has been brought to my attention that certain events have occurred which are not at all conducive to the success of our enterprises. I refer of course to the loss of several billions of dollars in the Saudi Bank Note deal and the unfortunate interception of the freighter *GEORGIA BELLE* in the Gulf last month. The Consortium, which I represent, finds that there has been a disturbing leak in our operations. Or should I say that certain more 'Official' elements are trying to prevent our success. I think you know what I mean."

Anna Gregory shrugged impatiently. "So what has this got to do with us? If you can't manage your affairs, that is your problem, not ours. We expect you to do your job."

Senator Travis coughed nervously and smiled. "I think you are being a little hasty, Anna. Please Jackson. Go on."

Marika Keskküla positioned herself behind them as the window drapes closed automatically.

"When my Consortium first advocated the redistribution of power and wealth and laid the foundations for the execution of the plan, it was made quite clear where the responsibilities of each of the participating parties lay. But alas we have already seen in the Bank crisis, excessive greed has made a severe dent in our long-term aims. My Consortium cannot allow further problems to arise." He paused and returned to his seat.

Anna Gregory had grown very quiet and was watching Doleman closely.

"That brings me back to the Saudi Bank Note Deal. Essentially a very simple transaction. My Consortium arranged for the supply of the necessary notes at generously discounted prices, in order that the net profit be enough to satisfy all our needs and enable my Consortium to finance the acquisition of RBM Defence Electronics Corporation, of which your companies would own a percentage."

Small red anger spots had appeared on Anna Gregory's cheeks.

"What are you suggesting?"

Doleman remained calm and quiet. He motioned to the taller of the two bodyguards who crossed the room to the table, picked up the video remote and pointed it at the DVD player.

The film that appeared on the screen was not of the highest quality, but it was clearly a film of Anna Gregory and two other men deep in conversation on the aft deck of a luxury motor yacht, which, by the look of the background, was moored off a private island in the Bahamas. One of the men was clearly an Arab.

There was no sound.

Doleman spoke over the film. "You visited Prince Abdul Bin Fahad of the House of Saud. I believe to negotiate different terms."

Anna Gregory stared at the screen, open-mouthed, face ashen.

"Terms beneficial to you and your father I believe. Terms that you no doubt hoped would put myself and those I represent out of business."

The film cut to black and then opened up again. This time the scene was a dirty courtyard in a large house that looked to be Italian or Spanish architecture. There were armed guards around the walls and in the centre stood a hooded man. There was something familiar about him. He held a wickedly curved sword. Prince Abdul Bin Fahad was escorted to the centre by two men, who forced him to his knees, his arms twisted up high behind his back so that his head was forced down.

As Anna Gregory screamed the swordsman quickly and efficiently severed the luckless Prince's head from his body.

Julie clutched my arm and turned away.

The film stopped and all attention in the room was focused on Anna Gregory.

Doleman was watching her carefully, the smile still on his lips, his eyes cold, voice quiet.

"The House of Saud was not happy, but we did dispatch the Prince in a manner they could appreciate. They considered the mating of one of their Princes with an Infidel unacceptable, so did not make a fuss. The deal went ahead as arranged. After all, business is business." Doleman turned and looked out across the lawn, his tone almost dreamy. "We of course have to take care of our own. It's only fair."

Anna Gregory's cry was cut off as Marika Keskküla stepped forward and wrapped a steel garrotte around her neck and snapped the noose tight with two wooden handles.

Senator Travis stared, pale faced and sweating as Anna Gregory's feet drummed a tattoo on the floor, her eyes and tongue bulging, face turning purple. Then with a quick flick, Marika Keskküla broke the unfortunate woman's neck. Anna Gregory's body sagged into the chair, a stain appearing as her bladder relaxed in death.

The two bodyguards unemotionally carried the corpse from the room, while a servant entered, removed the chair and checked to see if there were any stains on the floor.

Only Doleman, Keskküla and Senator Travis remained in the room. The drapes slid open and Doleman crossed to the windows, he stared across to the lake and smiled, turned back from the window, voice calm and quiet.

"Well, Senator, I see you haven't touched your drink. No matter. I think you understand the importance the Consortium places on securing control of RBM Defence Electronics Corporation. There can be no interference."

The Senator was trembling. "Is this what you did to Purdue and Moresby?"

A flicker of annoyance crossed Doleman's otherwise calm features.

"They are gone. What does it matter who was responsible? It's the Devil's Cauldron, Travis. Time to clean house." It was the second time I had heard that expression.

Travis shook his head and reached a trembling hand for the glass of bourbon, downing the contents in one draught. "Did she have to die?"

Doleman laughed quietly. "You will take a message to Simon Gregory. And you will deliver it in person." He smiled and spread his arms, beckoning Travis. "Come, it's time you were on your way. I promised my wife that I would not spoil the twins' birthday with business."

In a moment the room was empty. A bodyguard appeared, removed the DVD disc and left the room.

Morgan and I sat staring at the iPad, wondering if we really did see what we thought we'd witnessed. We could hear the distant laughter of the children on the lake and the gentle 'putter' of the motorboat's outboard.

Reality crashed in on us, reminding us why we were here.

One thing I knew instantly.

I was going to kill Marika Keskküla.

Today. No matter what.

"Can you send the video file to your father?"

"Of course."

"Do it."

Julie heard the edge in my voice and glanced at me as she typed rapidly on the iPad. "What are you thinking Thomas?"

"Keskküla. I can't let her get away again."

"Because of Danny?"

"Because of Morgan, Danny, Anna Gregory and God knows how many others."

"Oh boy. Here we go again."

I'd heard that refrain before.

Only then it had been me saying it.

"It's a pub near Tufnell Park. The boyos go there," Danny said mischievously, as he drove ridiculously fast through the late night London traffic.

"Oh great, here we go again."

"Where's your sense of humour and adventure for God's sake."

"If I had any brains I'd lock myself up for the night," I said resignedly, and went along anyway.

Hell what else was there to do on a boring Friday night?

We'd just returned from our foray into Sligo and been threatened with almost immediate extinction if we didn't get the hell out of Ireland, and here we were heading into the viper's nest again.

We'd already drunk way too many Jameson whiskeys and were buoyed by rousing operatic arias that had our testosterone flowing in copious amounts. Now we wanted a fight, to release the pent up emotions and energy of the last few weeks. It was stupid, reckless and oh so needed.

They knew who we were as soon as we stepped through the door. And within a minute after ordering two pints of Guinness, the head of the local Sinn Fein approached us and in a quiet friendly way asked us what the hell we thought we were doing coming here, and perhaps we'd think about leaving as soon as possible if we wanted to stay alive.

Danny turned and leaned back against the bar, smiling at the faces watching us over the rims of their glasses. He smiled and said very quietly to the Sinn Fein representative. "If any fucking idiot tries anything, there's going to be a lot of dead Irish in this bar tonight. Including me and him," he said pointing his thumb at me. "So tell your people to have a drink on us and we'll all be happy. Your boys had their fun in Sligo, they'll not screw with me in my town."

We finished our drinks and left, but that wasn't enough for Danny. He knew of a club that was frequented by even more radical Irish, and was determined to see this night through to his satisfaction.

It was the sound of the door being locked behind us, that gave us a clue as to what the local patrons of this seedy single-room club off the main road had in store for us. I don't know if it was the drink, but from that moment on everything was a blur of action and then we were outside headed for the car.

The next morning I awoke in my own bed covered in blood. Stripping off my clothes I checked myself in the mirror but found no signs of physical damage, just bruised knuckles. I called Danny.

"What the hell happened?"

He laughed. "They got more than they bargained for."

"I don't remember."

"You were a bloody madman mate. Yelling, slicing with the bottle."

It had happened before. It was as if a switch flipped in my head and I literally saw red. Instinct and training took over at that point and everything else was a blur.

The memory had me in a cold sweat, which I shrugged off quickly. Marika Keskküla was responsible for the deaths of my friends. That's all I wanted in my head.

"Get hold of the Professor. We need to tap into their security system and have the feed directed to the iPad." I didn't mean it to sound like the command that it was. Perhaps I did mean it to sound that way. All I knew was that there was a job to be done.

Julie quietly typed into the iPad and waited.

"Do you want to think about this first?" she asked quietly.

"If I think about it, I'll never do it."

"That's what I meant."

"I know," I said roughly. I didn't want to hear another opinion. It was an unwanted distraction, no matter how sensible.

The next few hours were going to be messy. There was no time to meticulously plan anything. Marika Keskküla would no doubt be gone very soon and so would Senator Travis. I needed to move now and take it as it came. I just didn't want the children anywhere near the action.

Perhaps I should do what I did best and get them out of the way first.

"Okay. The system is ours for the next thirty minutes," Julie relayed the Professor's message. I had this bizarre fleeting image of him sitting in his pyjamas working at the computer with a glass of his favourite 30-year-old Talisker single malt at his side.

"Where are the wife and kids?"

"Still out on the lake."

"Doleman and Keskküla?"

"At the front door. Senator Travis is leaving."

I heard the sound of a car door closing, an engine starting and a car accelerating down the driveway. No doubt the Senator was eager to get away as fast as possible.

"The bodyguards?"

"Two of them just stepped outside, heading this way, I guess for a break."

"We'll take them first. Then we'll go in through the kitchen."

We checked our weapons and crept out of the shed.

The first bodyguard died without uttering a sound, the 9mm round catching him in the temple. The second turned in surprise and dropped beside his partner as Julie felled him before he had time to draw his weapon, surprise still showing in his open dead eyes.

Julie was at the back door to the kitchen within fifteen seconds ready to enter, as I pulled the bodies into cover and ran quickly across the lawn.

The door opened easily and we slipped into the house, with Julie watching the security feed on the iPad. Doleman way too confident in the belief that he was secure in his own house. But it was my sense of righteous confidence that was almost our undoing.

As I slipped into the kitchen I almost missed the woman who was standing at the island kitchen unit cutting slices of ham for a sandwich, the butterfly tattoo clearly visible on her neck.

She turned and threw the knife in one movement at the same time I fired. The knife thudded into the doorframe and my bullet caught her in the chest, throwing her back against the double door fridge. She lay half conscious, gasping for air, staring up at me as I quickly crossed the kitchen and checked to see if anyone had heard.

I recognised her as Camilla who had tried to kill me at Richard Stacy's office in London months ago, and again was amazed at the reach of Marika Keskküla's organisation. Also at my stupidity of thinking that she would have come to Doleman's house alone.

Camilla tried to call out, but instead blood bubbled from her mouth and she lay still. Julie was already at the door to the hallway listening for movement.

We had no time to waste and crept through into the hall just as the door to the living room opened. Julie fired one round without waiting to see who it might be and one of the servants fell into view. The thud as his body hit the floor was enough to shake the hornet's nest and in moments all hell broke loose.

Three rounds thudded into the wall beside my head as I turned and fired at one of the bodyguards who appeared on the stairs, and I caught the fleeting sight of Marika Keskküla heading for the front door. Two rounds from my Beretta missed, breaking the glass in the window beside the door and I heard her laugh as she fled out of the house. Julie was a better shot and her round caught Keskküla in her right hip, stifling the laugh and throwing her onto the ground but she managed to crawl toward the car.

Julie's gun fired again near my right ear almost deafening me, in spite of the silencer, as she took out another bodyguard.

"Get her," she shouted.

I sprinted for the door and met a hail of rounds from a MAC-10 as Keskküla's chauffeur opened fire, covering his boss as she struggled into the car. By the time I poked my head up the car was accelerating down the driveway.

Keskküla stared at me through the back window and smiled painfully as she sped away.

"Mr Thomas Gunn," Doleman said softly behind me. "I thought you were dead."

I turned slowly and looked into the barrel of a very big Magnum. "A lot of people have said that lately."

"Well it ends here."

"Maybe. Maybe not. We have you on film killing Anna Gregory."

The momentary flicker in his eyes was all I needed. That instant of uncertainty. I rolled to the right just as he fired and heard the crack of Julie's Beretta.

Doleman folded slowly like a marionette at the end of the show. Crumpling onto the Bakhtiari carpet, the spreading blood stain mingling with the deep reds and blacks of the design. It was the shock of being shot that immobilised him, not a fatal wound as he stared at the hole in his lower left abdomen.

Julie stepped forward and aimed at Doleman's head.

"No sweetheart. You don't need to do that."

"He killed Morgan."

Doleman watched her in horror as her finger tightened on the trigger. The hammer slammed against my thumb as I took hold of the Beretta.

Julie looked at me with blank expressionless eyes. "He deserves to die."

"Probably. But you don't have to be the one. He's not worth it." I turned to Doleman. "You and your buddies have nowhere to hide Senator. You think you're safe, but you're not. We can get to you anytime, anywhere, when you least expect it. And next time I won't stop her from killing you."

Outside the sound of the outboard grew louder and the children's screams of delight more shrill, as Herman brought the motorboat back to the dock.

Doleman moved suddenly, scrabbling across the floor in search of the Magnum. His fingers closed on the grip and I put one bullet through the back of his hand.

He squealed and writhed in agony.

"I'll leave you for your masters. I'm sure they have many more creative ideas as to how to deal with you now that you're a liability."

I took Julie's hand. "Let's go."

EIGHTEEN

The flight was uneventful. Julie lay back in the sheepskin covered seat and was so emotionally and physically drained, that she slept the whole way from DeKalb airport until I started the descent into Sarah's Tombstone airfield.

Paul was sitting outside the hangar as I taxied from the runway, shut off the engines and coasted to a halt with the front wheels just inside the hangar.

"Thought you'd got lost," Paul said half in jest, his face appearing as I opened the door and let the cool desert night air into the Mustang. The Omega hung loosely in his right hand. He grinned and tucked the gun in his belt.

"Everything okay here?"

"Sweet as a nut." He grinned, took Julie's arm and led the way to the building. "Sheets aren't back from the laundry yet and the chef's buggered off with the boy from the livery stable, but otherwise can't complain."

I still needed a moment or two by myself, to let the jangled nerves in my body settle back down. I was not twenty years old anymore. Now, staying alive mattered more than thrills. I followed slowly, feeling the tight muscles in the back of my neck and across my shoulders like steel rods, unbending and painful. Frankie bounded down the stairs to greet us and pranced about me, which was something for a dog that, if she stood on her hind legs, would be taller than me. I petted her and she whined gently and knocked my hand, wanting more before loping away.

Julie worried me. She was distant, in another world as if she didn't care anymore. She went straight to the bedroom, lay down and was soon fast asleep.

"Do you want to talk about it?" Sarah asked.

"It was messy. She was there."

"The Keskküla woman?" Paul joined us on the deck, followed by Jonas. I nodded.

"Marika Keskküla?" Jonas asked.

I glanced at him to make sure he wasn't being obtuse. "The same. You know her?"

"The Consortium's very own arms dealer. At least she was. Had some problems a few months ago and went to ground."

Paul glanced at me quickly and I knew he was wondering just how much Purdue knew about our Estonian adventure.

"We know," I said watching his face. "We were there."

Purdue nodded. "Pieces of the jigsaw," he muttered.

"Meaning?"

"The Consortium has been trying to gain control of the new laser nuclear re-enrichment technology. This Keskküla woman brought us her version for the production of small calibre DU ammunition, but her plant was destroyed before she could fulfil the contract." He looked at Paul and me. "That was you?"

"It was," Paul said quietly.

"No wonder they want you dead."

"What does the Consortium want with the technology?" I asked.

"Control. Power. Another weapon in their arsenal." He shrugged. "I don't really think they care that much. We can do more with a stroke of the pen and a bank instrument, than a DU round."

"Then why do they keep her around?"

"She has diplomatic immunity, an ability to move anywhere at anytime and essentially is the Consortium's enforcer. I've never met her but I'm told she enjoys her work. She certainly doesn't need the money."

Something was ticking over in the back of my mind. Obviously the purpose of this game was to win, but still I wondered just who the other players really were. We were being guided and protected to a degree, but just where did that come from, and how quickly could that change if the players changed their minds?

It was all about power and control. Not morality, values or decency. And we were the pieces. Is that what Purdue meant when he said 'pieces of the jigsaw'? That we were the pieces in a dangerous game of global three-dimensional chess, in which there were no rules. Only survival. But it was not only the players who had control. The pieces did too, which made the game even more unpredictable and dangerous.

"Did you see Doleman?" Purdue asked.

"Personally. He has two bullet wounds. One from Julie and one from me. He'll live, but for how much longer is anyone's guess." I paused and looked at Purdue. "He had Anna Gregory executed in the house. We have it on video."

"Dear God," Purdue exclaimed, the blood draining from his face.

"Senator Travis was there as well."

Well before dawn, I was up walking the property in the neutral early morning light, as the last vestiges of distant stars gradually faded with the rising sun. Black brooding hills slowly took on lighter colours and rugged textures, and the ridges, cracks and folds in the terrain became visible as another brilliant cloudless day was born.

We were about to break new ground in investigative reporting. To challenge the might of the Overworld, the Club of Rome, the Illuminati, or whatever other name anyone cared to use for the Consortium that presumed to control the lives of everyone on the planet.

As the sun peeked over the horizon and began its steady march up the sky, signs of life began to appear. Paul wandered out of the hangar door.

Julie was sitting with Caroline on the deck, sipping coffee and talking softly. They were relaxed, and Caroline looked as if at last she was beginning to accept the situation. At least she looked more secure with Julie at her side.

It all looked so peaceful. So pleasant. Another day, another story.

Paul spotted me on the hillside and climbed up to where I sat. His hair was still wet from an early morning shower after his usual run.

"What's the plan for today?"

"We'll get started on the film. Caroline needs to make a phone call to Simon Gregory and arrange a meet."

"She can do that?"

"She can get to just about anybody if she wants to. That's why I brought her here."

He shrugged and pulled a face. "The way she's been behaving, I wouldn't trust her to make a cup of tea."

"Paul, you wouldn't trust anyone unless they had an affidavit from the Lord God Almighty, and even then you'd question it."

He laughed. "You're right."

Paul fixed up the tripod and the camera where I had indicated and Jonas stood watching, waiting, brooding as I checked the rest of the equipment. The sun provided enough light for the purpose, and the hillside a background that couldn't be traced.

Caroline sat with Julie, wide-eyed and pale, but in control.

I walked across to Jonas. "I'm going to film you first talking over in general terms what has happened and then we'll move into specifics, particularly Jackson Doleman. I can cut in that piece of footage later. Then we'll move on to the next piece."

Jonas had a serious expression. "Okay. Just allow me little leeway. This is complicated stuff."

"Sure. But just remember we can't spend days doing this."

His expression didn't change. "We want the same result. Maybe for different reasons, but we want the same result. I do my thing, you do yours. Agreed?"

I looked at him for a long moment, searching for any signs of the slick, sly schemer I knew him to be, but there was nothing. "Agreed."

"Good. Let's get started."

Paul had the camera set up and was waiting for me. I went over and looked through the viewfinder, then looked around at everyone.

"No noise while we're doing this. You don't want to watch, take a walk."

Nobody moved.

I turned to Jonas. "Ready?"

He nodded, cleared his throat, and for the first time looked a little nervous. I pressed the start button, waited a few moments then looked at him.

Jonas looked directly into the camera and he seemed to change. He straightened, and although his face was thinner and paler with a few days' beard growth, gradually became the Politician. It was an extraordinary transformation. A change that took place mentally within him that shone through.

"My name is Jonas T Purdue. I am a businessman and candidate for Mayor of Los Angeles and contrary to popular belief, I am very much alive as you can see from this electronic newspaper article with today's date." He held up the iPad for the camera. "Two weeks ago the State of California claimed to have cremated my body at Forest Lawn Crematorium. I have here a copy of the Los Angeles Times Magazine, which relates specifically to my death. I believe some kind things were said at the ceremony. As Mark Twain once said, 'Reports of my death have been greatly exaggerated', but in the near future it may be a reality. What I am about to tell you may well tax the imagination and indeed may stretch my own credibility. However you will see that every statement I make, can and will be substantiated."

He allowed himself a wintry smile, but his eyes never left the camera.

"I was kidnapped by a man who claimed I was involved in the death of Morgan Alvarez, an investigative journalist. Indirectly I was, but didn't know it, and it was not until he gave me further information that I began to understand what was happening. Indeed what is happening in this country of ours. A few weeks ago, I would never have made the confession I am now about to make. I was a corrupt businessman looking for ways to line his own pockets at the expense of everyone else. I made seven billion dollars from illegal activities and in the process collected information that will destroy many men and women who enjoy a rich and secure life both in the public and private sector. Why am I doing this? Simple. Because my life is at risk."

Again Jonas paused to let his words sink in.

"There are Government agencies and private consortiums who want to see me dead because of the information I have. Before I die, I want to see these agencies, these cartels and consortiums, these individuals who control the very existence of everyone in this country, and indeed many other countries throughout the world, destroyed. Forever. It will not absolve me, but maybe I shall be able to rectify some of the damage I have done."

Jonas spoke for an hour in front of the camera, leading up to the first exposé, that of Jackson Doleman. And for an hour, Paul, Julie, Caroline and myself sat spellbound, watching and listening. I was going to cut in the video we took at Doleman's later. But I knew that in spite of this seeming reversal of character, I would still not be able to trust this man, even if he took to religion and became a born-again Christian.

When he finished he looked exhausted, took the glass of water Julie offered him and moved away to sit on his own. I led Caroline to one side. She looked back at Julie as if her lifeline was being stretched, before turning to me. "What do you want?"

I sat down and gently pulled her down beside me. "This is where I need your help, Caroline."

She paled and began to shake. "I can't do anything."

"Yes you can."

"What is it?"

"I need to get this on the air. I need to get it to Simon Gregory and I need you to make the appointment. But it's got to be confidential. I need to see him alone, without anyone else knowing."

She shook her head violently from side-to-side. "No. No. I can't. I can't. It's impossible."

"Caroline, listen to me. Listen carefully. Unless you do this we are all dead. Do you understand what I'm saying? We are all dead. This is all I'm asking you to do. Nothing else. Do this and you're out of it. Do you understand?"

She nodded. "I'll do what I can."

"I know you will. Paul and I will be with you. You'll be safe. I promise." And once again I felt the cold wings of a lie brush across my conscience.

She looked into my eyes. "Is this the only way?"

I nodded.

She looked across at where Purdue sat, then to where Julie was helping Sarah prepare lunch. Then to where Paul sat polishing the Omega and checking the magazines. She shivered then looked back at me.

"Okay. I'll do it. I know Simon will meet with me." She stared past me, drifting back to another world, another time. "We go back a long way."

"It has to be somewhere no one knows about. Is that possible?"

"Yes. I'm sure he remembers," she smiled tiredly. "I wasn't always a tired fat old bitch. There was a time..." She drifted off into her own world for a moment. "Give me your phone."

I handed it to her and she dialled. "Hank, it's Phoebe, long time no see." She paused listening. "Oh, I'm so sorry, I must have dialled the wrong number. That's the third time this week." She hung up and laid the phone down and sighed heavily. "Done."

"Done what?"

"We had a code for when and where we wanted to meet. It was a long time ago but I'm sure he's not forgotten."

"So when and where?"

"Little house in Aspen, three days from now. I bought it under the name Phoebe Riggs about ten years ago."

"Okay, we'll finish up with Purdue and then go see Gregory."

"Randolph Byron Moresby. Chairman and CEO of RBM Defence Electronics Corporation is the key. He's the way into the Consortium." Jonas said sipping his coffee.

"How did you meet him?" I said, trying to keep my tone as normal as possible.

"Back about ten years ago we had a thing going. A little scam. He was the business front of the CIA in Baghdad..."

"You were CIA?"

"No. Just a banker. That's how I got into this stuff in the first place..."

Julie interrupted. "Anna Gregory talked about Moresby on the film."

Jonas looked puzzled. "What film?"

"The one Doleman showed her. She was with the Prince on the yacht. No one heard it because there was no sound on that part."

"Shit. Maybe there's more," I said leaning forward and picked up Julie's iPad. I handed it to her.

My brain was racing, trying to fit the pieces together. Such as what the hell did Moresby want with me in Mexico? Was he just checking me out? Or did he need a witness for whoever was pulling my strings?

Julie stationed herself close in front of the monitor and concentrated.

"Anna says: *'Moresby asked me to put the proposition to you, Abdul. He thinks we can keep Doleman out of this. He's getting too powerful'*. Prince: *'My country will not deal with corruption. Business is one thing, but we are concerned about the balance of Power in the Middle East'*. Anna: *'I don't know about that. I know that Doleman is dangerous. Moresby says my father and he are convinced that Doleman is behind the latest arms shipments to the Taliban in return for control of the opium trade through Bolivia.'* The Prince: *'I heard about the Bolivian affair and there are elements in my country who would gladly see our King replaced'*. Anna: *'Moresby wants me to go to a meeting with Dolem...'*" The film ended and Julie turned off the video.

Jonas sat for sometime staring at the screen, without moving, his brain clicking over fast, analysing everything he'd heard in context with what he already knew. He took another sip of coffee, sat back and sighed heavily.

"Seems to me Moresby set her up. Sent her to meet Doleman, knowing she'd be killed. Gregory's in this somewhere, but I don't know how he fits in. I never had dealings with him."

"What about Moresby, Jonas? Where does he come from?" I wasn't going to say anything about his death, until I knew more.

"Let me start from the beginning." Jonas T Purdue settled himself a little more comfortably. "See if we can't make some sense out of this. Back before the start of the Iraq conflict, there was a brilliant young electronics engineer drafted to work with Harris Engineering, of which Moresby was the CEO at the time. The company was building military camps, refitting the damaged oil pipelines and a ton of other stuff to do with rebuilding the country's infrastructure. They were also developing lots of ingenious weapons systems and surveillance devices. The forerunner of the 'smart' systems we now have. There was one particular mission in Afghanistan that Moresby sent the engineer out on, flying to a forward base to work with the SEAL Teams on some magic gadget he designed to use for their deep penetration patrolling. He never got there."

I felt very cold all of a sudden. I was back. Back in the deafening crash of high explosives, the stench of blood and screams of the dying. "Nimruz?"

Jonas looked across sharply. Frowning. "How did you know about Nimruz? It was buried. Nobody knows."

"I was there. I was with a British Special Forces unit attached to an American SEAL Team. It was a joint operation." My voice was so quiet I could barely hear it amongst the exploding shells and screams of dying men.

"It was a set up."

"How?"

"The engineer was killed by Moresby's men."

"Why?"

"Moresby told me the man was a double agent, supplying information to the Taliban. Nimruz was his proof. I didn't question it, but after the war Moresby started an electronics corporation with big Pentagon orders, supplying 'smart' weapons. RBM Defence Electronics Corporation is a market leader in space defence technologies. Hell, Moresby cornered the market."

Jonas closed his eyes and shook his head. He looked tired and old.

"What you don't know, is that Nimruz was the recovery point for $6 billion dollars in shrink-wrapped $100 bills that was part of $8 billion sent by the Federal Reserve, no questions asked. It was the same as the $20 billion to Iraq in 2004. The money disappeared. You must remember. Pallets of money flown over on C130 aircraft over about a year?"

"I heard something about it. I thought it was bullshit, just another conspiracy theory. And how the hell do billions of dollars that weigh a hundred tonnes or more, go from Iraq and Afghanistan back to the

USA, without anyone knowing?"

Purdue laughed without humour. "Money buys a lot of co-operation. It took two years and $1 billion but it was worth it. Hell, it wasn't US taxpayers' money we took and nobody gave a damn. It was all frozen Iraq and Afghan assets from foreign banks transferred to American Banks and then cashed by the Federal Reserve. You think the Government is going to tell you the whole truth? My job in Iraq was to launder fifty percent of the cash out in containers they called 'the Diplomatic Bag' and the rest in oil drums via freighters from Basra."

"And Nimruz?"

"The same sort of deal with the Kabul government in the early days, somebody cottoned on and was about to blow the whistle. That was the Nimruz operation. Shipped about $6 billion through Chābahār on the Gulf of Oman and into various banks in Dubai, Kuwait and Dhofar, then into the Jonas Trust as liquid investment assets for the newly formed RBM Defence Electronics Corporation."

"And you didn't think that was treasonous?"

"Hell no. Everyone had their sticky fingers in the pie. Senators, Congressmen, the Coalition Provisional Authority in Baghdad and the Karzai Government in Afghanistan. It was easy. It was a licence to print money, or steal it. One thing is for sure, none of the ordinary people of Iraq or Afghanistan saw a penny. Government Ministers, US defence contractors, security contractors, they were the ones who benefited. All sorts of people were doing a ton of illegal things out there. Phoney contracts. Cash disappearing with no accountability into black hole bank accounts. You name it, it happened. You want to get rich, start a war."

Again Purdue paused, looking at me trying to see whether I was faking my surprise.

"Have you any idea how many bureaucrats in the Foreign Service have retired multi-millionaires?" It was a rhetorical question.

"Where is Moresby now?"

"About two years ago he went undercover. I haven't met with him since. Talked on the phone and by email, but never seen him. Guess he got paranoid."

My head was pounding. Sutherland. Radley. Moresby. Nimruz. Now the botched mission made sense. We were supposed to die as part of a diversion while the money was spirited away.

"Moresby's dead, Jonas."

Jonas paused, picked up another pebble and missed the can by a couple of inches. "No he's not. He's somewhere out there still controlling everything. Got an email from him the day before you took me."

"I saw him drown in the Sea of Cortez the week before."

"No you didn't. Moresby wouldn't go near a boat."

"Then who the hell drowned in the Sea of Cortez? I spent two days with the man."

"Maybe nobody drowned. Maybe Moresby wanted to disappear. Like I said, he doesn't like publicity. No photographs. Nothing."

"Would you recognise him if you saw him again?"

He shook his head. "Probably not. Plastic surgery can make anybody disappear."

"So what do we have?"

"Senator Travis. He's on the Senate Banking Investigation Committee amongst other things. Hell, I introduced him to Moresby when the Senator took a trip to Kabul. Once a month he meets with a group of bankers. It's very private. He supposedly takes a fishing trip. Regular as clockwork. He's been siphoning money from the Treasury for years, ostensibly for covert operations. That's how we funded some of our deals. Laundered through arbitrages, Prime Bank notes, zeros, anything he can lay his hands on. I set up a company in La Jolla called South Seas Consulting that supervised the money into blind trusts offshore. Last I heard he'd just made a deal to sell $2.25 billion dollars worth at eighty cents on the dollar. Before that I fixed up a deal with a consortium of European Bankers. Thirty billion."

"Where does Travis go for his meeting?"

"Lake Powell."

"Could you be more specific, the Lake's got nearly two thousand miles of coastline and a hundred canyons. He gets in there, we wouldn't find him for a year."

"Picks his boat up at the Wahweap Marina."

"Name of the boat?"

"WANDERLUST."

"Very creative."

"It's always the last weekend of every month. Parks up in the same canyon every time."

"And you know where that is?"

"Sure do. I got a..."

"I know," I interrupted. "Photographic memory."

There was silence as we digested the information and wondered what the hell to do. It seemed straightforward. Meet Gregory. Get Jonas on the air and nail Doleman and Travis. Then Moresby. I had to find out more about him, because nothing was fitting into place. It was all too easy.

I found myself starting to respect the new Jonas, and it worried me.

"Do you have proof of these deals?"

He didn't say anything, just tossed another pebble at the can as if considering whether to tell me or not. "I've a safety deposit box in La Jolla. Nobody knows about it except me. Under the name Patrick Cleary. There's a bunch of photographs and documents relating to Moresby and the operation in Nimruz. Thought I'd better keep something aside for a rainy day."

He paused, was about to toss another pebble but instead threw it up catching it in his hand absentmindedly.

"First Trust Bank of San Diego in La Jolla. You have to get me there."

I raised my eyebrows.

He nodded. "I know. How can you trust me? You've got no choice Thomas. You need to know what this guy Moresby looks like, and the information is vital if we're going to nail him and the people he represents. I'm the only one can get it."

"Sutherland can get it. I'm sure he'll have some pull with the Law Enforcement Agencies and the DA's office in San Diego."

Jonas shook his head vehemently.

"No way. You bring anyone else into this we're as good as dead. You know that. There's no telling who's on Moresby's payroll."

"I'll think about it."

"Don't take too long."

NINETEEN

Aspen is one of those mountain airports that is always a challenge. I'd flown in twice before and the approach was between the mountain peaks, down low over a ridgeline onto the single runway at an elevation of over seven thousand feet.

There is little room for error.

Caroline sat quietly in the cabin with Paul, as I concentrated on the approach. The weather was clear, a little breezy, the wind rolling off the peaks down into the valley, the little jet bucking in the thermals as I carefully corrected, keeping the runway lined up and the glide-slope indicator on the numbers. Then in a moment we were on the ground, airbrakes deployed and braking before turning off onto the ramp.

Simon Gregory was already at the cabin near Snowmass Village, pacing the floor like a caged lion. He was tall, slim with a leonine head, thick grey curly hair and a trim moustache above a full mouth. He was immaculately dressed in a dark blue suit, with red handkerchief poking neatly from the breast pocket of his jacket. But for all the outer appearance of calm, his eyes betrayed him. They were fearful and his face was gaunt.

When I walked in beside Caroline, with Paul following behind, he stopped pacing and looked shocked. "Caroline. What's going on?"

Caroline moved towards Gregory, pecked him on the cheek and went over to the wet bar.

"Anyone care for a drink?" She poured herself a shot of vodka, filled it with tomato juice and dosed it liberally with Worcestershire sauce. Then sank the Bloody Mary in one gulp before pouring herself another.

Gregory looked at me more carefully. "Do I know you? Have we met before?"

"Thomas Gunn. Sir Ivan was my father."

He sank down into a big soft brown leather Chesterfield style armchair. Caroline selected a 14 year old Wild Turkey Rare Breed bourbon from the bar fridge, filled a glass and set it on the table beside him.

"I'm sorry for what happened to him. We were working together. He thought I was someone he could trust." Gregory's hand shook as he picked up the glass and sipped. "I know why you're here."

"Senator Travis has been in contact?"

"Yes. This morning."

"He told you about Anna?"

Gregory seemed to crumple even further into the armchair, tears in his eyes. "Yes."

Caroline put her hand on his shoulder, squeezing gently.

I didn't feel that generous. "What did he want from you?"

"The Consortium wants control of all global media companies. My companies own majority market share in east and west Europe, Australia, New Zealand and here in the USA. They want illicit wiretapping, online eavesdropping, financial markets information manipulation, political party polling manipulation. Pretty much everything." He took another sip. "Power is a disease. And these people are addicted."

"Who?"

"Faceless people. Your father wanted to identify them."

"And the Consortium had him killed, but then you knew about that didn't you?"

He paled, looked away and drank the rest of the bourbon as if it would somehow make his life easier. "Why should I answer your questions?"

"Because you don't want your other daughter, Natasha, to end up on a mortuary slab."

He winced but took it, his eyes never leaving my face. "What do you want from me?"

"I need a studio and editing suite in San Diego. You have a station there. Then I want you to broadcast a segment every morning on your national, cable and satellite networks. An exposé."

Gregory nodded. "I can arrange that."

Caroline was gradually drinking herself into a stupor and I motioned to Paul, who roughly took the bottle and glass from her grip and made her sit down. Gregory watched then turned back to me.

"You seem to know quite a lot of what's going on, don't you, Mr Gunn?" he said quietly. He was under control now and the bourbon seemed to have helped.

"The name's Thomas. And yes. Some."

"Do you believe in a New World Order?"

"If I knew what that really meant, I could make a judgment."

"I take that to mean you don't believe in it."

I shrugged. "Just sounds like political word games to me. At the end of the day, it makes no difference."

He shook his head. "You're wrong. It means Government by Law. International Law. It means all the countries of the world agreeing and being signatories to that agreement. It means arbitration instead of war. It means an end to famine and disease and poverty."

"Isn't that what the United Nations was supposed to do? Isn't that the guiding principle behind the formation of the World Bank?"

"They are two different things."

"Not really. It's about business. Money. Not Politics. Government by blackmail. Foreign Policy using the mighty dollar instead of a gunboat. And with the new smart weapons, any country could be wiped off the face of the earth if it refused to comply. Zap. They're gone."

"Simplistic and naive."

"Then tell me why Anna was involved with Doleman?"

"He was a rotten apple. We were trying to infiltrate his organization."

I stared at him aghast. "So you used your own daughter?"

"You don't understand. How can you?"

"I understand because my father was killed by people like you. I understand that your daughter was killed because you're busy trying to play Emperor."

He opened his mouth and closed it again. The pain was back in his eyes. I didn't want to let him off the hook.

"Do you know Randolph Byron Moresby?"

Gregory did not want to talk to me, I could see it in his eyes, but he was smart enough to see where this conversation was going.

"He was one of Doleman's mentors. Ran RBM Defence Electronics. Died several years ago. At least that's what I heard. He was trying to take over. We heard he was the head of a Consortium, but then he disappeared."

"Who're we?"

"We are a group of businessmen dedicated to the New World Order. Moresby tried to join us. But his ideas were too radical. Too greedy. He had Doleman infiltrated into our ranks. We found out too late."

"And Moresby's dead?"

"Yes." He paused looking at me, eyes narrowed. "How do I know you are who you say you are?"

I took out my wallet and removed an old photograph from a concealed pocket. It was the last time my father and I were photographed together by the lake at Calder Hall before I joined the army.

"Does that answer your question?"

He stared at it for a long time before handing it back to me.

"Those were happier times. We were in control then, before the radicals took over. How do I know you can stop this madness?"

"You don't, but you want to save Natasha's life and I'm her only chance."

"Do you know where she is?"

"Maybe."

"Where?"

"I'm not saying. For all I know, you want her dead just like you sent Anna to her death."

He ran at me with a yell that sounded part lion and part hyena.

I was ready and tossed him easily to one side. He landed with a thud on the settee, my knee on his throat.

"Easy. Breathe."

"You bastard."

"I've been called worse," I released the pressure on his throat and stood aside. "I need to know just where your loyalties lie Mr Gregory. This isn't a game we're playing. Whatever we do from now on cannot be undone."

Caroline sat down beside him caressing his face and making soft soothing sounds. There were tears in Gregory's eyes. He looked small and defeated.

"Find her Thomas. Please. You have my entire company at your disposal. I'll make the arrangements. Just find her and bring her back safely." He took a silver business card holder from his pocket, selected one, quickly wrote on the back and handed it to me. "My private number."

We left Gregory in Caroline's care and headed back to the Mustang and the flight to Tombstone.

"Somebody's lying," I said to Julie, as we sat looking out over the airfield.

"Explain."

"Gregory says Moresby's been dead for several years."

"And Jonas said Moresby went underground several years ago. Only contactable by email."

"Well?"

"Well what?"

"Somebody's lying."

She looked at me as if I was really stupid. "Why? Both say that Moresby went missing five years ago. Jonas says he was in contact with him by phone. But he never saw him at all. Gregory was never in contact with him. Seems you've got to get that stuff out of Purdue's safety deposit box in La Jolla. It's the only way we're going to get to the bottom of this."

The confusion noose around my neck was getting tighter and the only person who had any way of breaking this open was still JT Purdue. He'd become more valuable than gold dust.

Purdue joined us on the deck. "Made up your mind yet?"

"According to Simon Gregory, Moresby's dead."

"We've already been through that."

"He says several years ago, about the time you said he went underground."

Jonas laughed and shook his head. "Impossible."

"How do you know?"

"Because all our communications by email and fax use a code that only he and I know. I told you I was in contact with him the day before you kidnapped me."

I watched him a little while longer. "You get your trip to La Jolla."

I went back inside and found Sarah talking to her sister on Skype. They didn't look anything alike. Leila had a narrower face and lighter skin colour.

"Leila, meet Thomas Gunn. Thomas meet Leila."

"I've heard a lot about you, Mr Gunn," Leila smiled, her voice soft as honey, expression open and innocent.

"You too. And it's Thomas. Can I steal your sister for a minute."

"Of course, Thomas. I can catch up with her later."

Sarah spun her chair to face me. "What's on your mind?"

"While I take Jonas to San Diego tomorrow, I need you to reposition the Explorer in Page, near Lake Powell."

"What about Julie and me," Paul interrupted.

"Yeah what about us?" Julie chimed in, flopping down onto the settee.

"You both go with Sarah. We need to vacate the premises here."

"You expecting trouble?" Sarah asked, her eyebrows raised in concern.

"At some point somebody's going to wonder about the comings and goings into this airstrip. So we'll leave. Lock up and go."

"And my dream? What about that?"

"You'll have it, just as soon as we've finished this."

"I'm holding you to that, Thomas Gunn. Don't think I won't."

"The papers are sitting in a bank in New York, ready for you to sign. You've been a co-owner of Solent Jet Services for the last week. I had Julie's father transfer funds into the account."

"Now I just have to survive to enjoy it all. Guess that calls for a drink."

It was a light moment that broke the tension and even Purdue relaxed and joined us, toasting Sarah's new enterprise.

Leaving Julie behind was the hardest thing I've ever done. And Jonas wisely kept his mouth shut during the flight.

One of Gregory's men was at the airport to meet us, with a limousine for the short ride downtown to the office. He was a young, studious looking pleasant man, who went by the name of Terry. Which seemed to fit his short fat frame and fresh scrubbed tanned face. His dark eyes peered fashionably through colourful spectacle frames, giving him a somewhat owlish appearance. He was polite, circumspect and efficient.

Jonas's eyes flickered about from one side of the car to the other, expecting any moment a bullet or bomb to come crashing through the glass. He hurried into the elevator in the underground car park of the office building and stood pale and frightened as the doors hissed shut.

By midnight, we had the first three days of tapes complete, and on their way to the studio for airing on the morning show. I sat back in the chair, staring at the bank of monitors and the face of Jonas T Purdue frozen on the screens. Terry was quick and knowledgeable and had allowed himself only the occasional glance at Jonas as we'd edited the video.

America would wake up to breakfast with Jonas T Purdue, and the nation would have another scandal to gorge itself on for the next few weeks. In the meantime, Terry showed us a suite consisting of a small living room, bedroom, bathroom and kitchen. He bade us good night, promising to return in the morning and take us to the airport via the bank.

"Do you have a short wave radio by any chance Terry?"

"We do. Not sure why but it's still here. I think from the old days. Mr Gregory likes to keep the old equipment, to remind us what it was like way back when. Follow me, I'll show you." He led the way along the corridor to another room and unlocked the door. "There. Mr Gregory told me to let you have anything you want."

"Thanks."

"You're welcome. See you in the morning." And he was gone.

I went back to the suite. Jonas was lying on the bed watching TV with a can of beer in his hand. He grinned tiredly. "Guess I'll watch some TV and then get some sleep."

"Good idea."

I grabbed a beer too and went back to the radio room, sat down at the desk and switched on the set. Waiting a moment while the transistors, diodes and whatever other electronic wizardry that was encased in the black anodized metal container warmed up. Then I dialled eight megahertz and tried the call sign.

"Golf Foxtrot Alpha Romeo One Zero Four Niner calling Alpha Lima Echo Two Three, over." There was just the buzz of static. I tried again, then a third time. On the fourth attempt I raised him.

"Alpha Lima Echo Two Three, roger. That you Thomas?"

"Roger. Switch to Codex Delta Oscar. Over."

"Roger. Out."

I checked with my codex grid and dialled the new frequency and called again. Sutherland was there loud and clear.

"Thomas? Can you hear me?"

"I hear you."

"Where the hell are you?"

"Come on Sutherland, this is an insecure net. Use the codex."

I told him briefly in code and then we got back to voice.

"Watch your TV tomorrow morning. Everything we could want."

"Great."

I shut down, sat back and let the tension ease from my body.

My next job was a call to Eliseo.

"Eliseo, it's Thomas Gunn."

There was a momentary silence at the other end of the line. "You are full of surprises my friend."

"I like to be prepared. You killed a friend of mine, I don't forget things like that."

"You are in no position to make threats."

"I don't make threats, Eliseo, I make promises. Tell Marika Keskküla that she will not escape next time."

"She wants to meet you again too."

"Watch your television tomorrow morning, Eliseo. You are a feature. I'm sure your employers will be more than upset when the pipeline from Bolivia dries up."

"You play a dangerous game Tomas."

"Is there any other?"

I hung up feeling less than happy with what I had just done. A niggling feeling that poking the cobra at this stage was probably a bad idea. I lay down on the settee and drifted off to sleep. But my dreams were filled with horrors. Julie was drowning and I could not reach her. A huge sea monster that looked like Purdue, smiling, with Paul riding on his back Omega in hand loomed up, jaws open wide, ready to engulf Julie. She looked serene, unaware of what was about to happen. My legs were encased in thick gluttonous mud and every step was a nightmare.

I woke sweating, made myself a cup of coffee and fifteen minutes later, fell into a dreamless sleep.

The first segment of *The Jonas Trust Deception*, was broadcast at fifteen minutes to eight o'clock in the morning on Gregory's network breakfast show and syndicated all across America, running for an hour and five minutes.

Coast-to-coast, Jackson Doleman's face was spread across the land.

Purdue watched himself without comment. The film was received with stunned silence in the studio, the program presenters unable to say a word for a few moments, until they had recovered their composure. There of course followed a retraction by the station to say they were not responsible for the content, and it did not necessarily reflect the views of the station or the staff, they were simply reporting. They also asked the public not to phone the station, as all the lines were jammed.

When Terry arrived an hour after the show had aired, I could see he was bursting to say something, but protocol and the fact he valued his job kept his curiosity confined to the occasional glance at Jonas.

We needed to get to the Bank in La Jolla as soon as possible. Terry had the limousine ready in the loading bay.

Twenty-five minutes later we pulled up outside the front door of the bank. Jonas and I exited the limo quickly and slipped inside while Terry waited for us outside. There were no pieces of paper to sign, or special codes for access to safety deposit boxes in this bank. An optical scan allowed us access to the boxes in the secure room, and then Jonas held up three fingers of his right hand in front of the optical biometric keypad on his box. It clicked open. Inside was a single three-inch-thick red plastic filing box and nothing else. He removed it, closed the safety deposit box and together we walked out of the bank. It had taken less than twenty minutes.

As we stepped towards the limousine, the first burst of machine gun fire ripped across the walls of the bank. The crowd first froze, then scattered in confusion as the dead and injured fell in the hail of bullets. I pulled Jonas down and ran in a crouch for the corner. We nearly didn't make it, the bullets following us across the sidewalk. We ducked behind the car then saw Terry climb out of the driver's side. My screamed warning too late as his head exploded in a crimson spray.

It was over as quickly as it began, with a number of dead and injured lying on the sidewalk and Terry's lifeless body sliding off the door onto the road.

All I knew was that I had to get Jonas out of here. Already police sirens were blaring. Luckily nobody was paying any attention to us.

Four blocks away from the bank I found a cab, the driver completely oblivious to what had happened, half asleep, eating a donut and sipping black coffee from a paper cup. He grumbled at having to drive to the airport, but faced with a fifty-dollar tip, shut his mouth and drove.

Soon the incident would be all over the news and on everyone's lips. We had no time to lose. At the airport, I paid the driver and walked Jonas to the Mustang. It took a further hour for the refuelling to be completed, as the ground crew had failed to do it on time and no amount of threats made them speed up.

Finally refuelled for the flight, and with clearance routing overhead Salt Lake City, the Mustang climbed up into the clear blue sky, heading towards Lake Powell.

It was 15:30hrs.

Jonas was ashen faced, hands clenched tight around the documents, sweat beading his forehead.

"This is what it's all about, Jonas. People die because of what you did." I didn't mean to sound flippant.

He gave me a quick glance then closed his eyes briefly. "Poor kid."

I was still trying to figure out what had happened. How had they known where we were?

The answer was simple. Moresby knew of the sham consulting firm Purdue had organised, and all his men had to do was wait for him to turn up, however long that was. It also tied Eliseo directly to Moresby and the Consortium.

"Still want to carry on Jonas?"

"Until it's finished." There was resolve in his voice. A determination I hadn't heard before.

"There's a leak."

"You tell anyone, Thomas?"

"Sutherland," I said reluctantly, knowing what was coming.

"Why?"

"He's one of us and we need all the help we can get."

"You sure?"

I wasn't. But I could not see why he would want to kill us. Paul there was a question over, but nothing made sense.

The Mustang was equipped with a short wave radio, a necessity for Trans Atlantic flights. I got through to Sutherland on the third attempt.

He sounded tired. "I heard what happened. You okay?"

"Yes. Did you tell anyone where the hell we were?"

"No. Course not."

"I'll call you again tomorrow." I switched off the set.

To the left was the sprawling plateau of the Grand Canyon at seven thousand feet. To the right the Hopi Indian Reservation, that encompassed Monument Valley up to Lake Powell and over to Four Corners. That sacred Indian area that had been desecrated by open cast mining, where Arizona, Utah, Colorado and New Mexico meet.

I began to feel the awesome atmosphere of the area as the plains stretched away, interrupted by the Buttes and Stacks that jutted skywards. Tall stark and beautiful.

Before Columbus ever reached America and before Cortez brought the first horses to the continent, the native Indians were wandering these ancient plains and mountains on foot. Worshiping the sun, the sky, the land, living pure and simple lives at one with the earth. Now roads and townships scarred the landscape, all in the name of 'progress'.

Purdue seemed to have forgotten his troubles as he stared out of the windshield at the passing panorama. "This country is so beautiful. Until now I never took the time to appreciate it." He glanced across at me. "Thank you for opening my eyes."

"I hope they stay that way. Maybe there's hope for you yet."

"Maybe," he said wistfully, turning to stare down at the desert. "Just maybe."

"What do you know about Lake Powell?" I asked, tired of sitting in silence and needing to talk.

"Not much."

So I told him the history as we flew.

The lake was man-made, caused by the construction of the Glen Canyon Dam at Page and the trickle of the Colorado River backing up and spreading into the surrounding canyons to form the Lake, all two hundred and fifty-two square miles of it.

But long before the White Man came, the Anasazi Indians roamed the land, living in Pueblos cut into the canyon walls, in houses constructed of mud, shaded from the devastating heat of the summer sun. Now, in the off season, there were only a few house-boats on the water, moving slowly up the still calm, spreading their wakes across the glassy surface as we winged along, causing the holiday makers to look up in annoyance.

I recounted to Purdue everything I could remember from my wanderings as a young man.

Of the Rainbow Bridge, the largest natural arch in the world at nearly three hundred feet high.

Of the Defiance House ruins in the Forgotten Canyon that dated back to between 1250-1285 AD. But those were the areas reserved for the tourists. There were still many more canyons accessible only to those willing to hike in with a guide.

Those with hardy constitutions and a love for the preservation of the country. For those were the areas where litter was non-existent and the true spirituality of the area enveloped everyone who set foot on its sacred soil.

This was the conscience and the spiritual centre of the continent.

The forgotten and ignored living essence of America, that existed in spite of modern man's attempts to destroy it.

TWENTY

It was late afternoon when I contacted Page ATC ten minutes from landing and was routed over Lake Powell for the ILS approach to Runway 15. It looked so serene from our lofty perch, the wakes from tourist houseboats clearly visible on the sparkling water of a beautiful summer day. There was a slight buffet from the hot air rising off the desert, contrasting with the cooler air from the water, but the little Mustang loved to feel the air and turned in a lazy arc onto finals. All the violence of the past weeks left behind as I concentrated on making a precision approach and landing. As far as ATC was concerned this was a 'normal' VIP flight.

I could see the Explorer parked on the furthest of six helicopter pads to the west of the runway as we landed and turned off to our allotted parking bay.

Sarah limped over from the restaurant to meet us, with Frankie on a leash. "Made quite an impression on the TV this morning."

Jonas just nodded without speaking, his eyes wandering over the airport looking for likely snipers, drops of sweat running down his cheek.

"Where are Julie and Paul?"

"Went on ahead to Wahweap Marina, about eight miles down the road to rent a boat. She said it would save time. I don't like boats so I stayed here. Figured I'm better suited to looking after the aircraft. Julie said she'd call you."

Alarm bells sounded silently in my head and every fibre of my being jangled. "How long ago?"

"Couple of hours. Soon as we arrived."

"God damn it, she never called. What the hell do they think they're doing?"

I made a quick call to the marina to be told that nobody matching Julie or Paul's description had rented a boat.

"Sarah, get the Explorer fired up. Jonas, help me get the bags from the Mustang," I shouted my heart pounding, fearing the worst.

Sarah stomped away to the helicopter with Frankie, while Purdue and I collected my sailing bag and his box file from the Mustang, then ran across as the engines of the Explorer wound up and the main rotor started to turn.

"Where to?" Sarah asked as we strapped in and settled the headsets over our ears.

"About twenty miles up the canyon. Jonas tells me the Senator usually anchors his houseboat in the same place. I know an inlet close by, but hidden from view. Jonas and I will camp there tonight and move on the houseboat at first light. Keep low and they won't know we're coming."

It was 18:30 hrs.

As we headed out over the lake I tried to put thoughts of what Julie was going through out of my mind. I was convinced she'd been taken, because when I tried to get her on the phone it was dead. Ahead of us the awesome sight of the red/yellow rocks and the blue sky dotted with small white clouds reflecting off the lake.

We left the holidaymakers behind and headed up one of the many canyons I had explored with a girlfriend many years ago. A canyon where my need for isolation had been gratified and we had stayed for two weeks without seeing another living soul. At the sheer face at the end of the canyon, twenty miles in, the water stopped in a natural round lagoon and off to the side was a ledge big enough to take the Explorer.

"There." I pointed. "I'll call you on the phone when we're ready for pick up."

"Bring them back safe Thomas. And be careful."

Sarah set the Explorer down, waited until we had climbed out and struggled to get our bags to the canyon wall before lifting off, backing out over the water, executing a 360° and flying off low and fast. Purdue and I sat for a long time until the echoes had faded and the silence, deeper than the deepest ocean, descended upon us.

Jonas lay back against the rock wall, closed his eyes and let out a deep sigh. The skin on his face seemed to hang loosely, as if all the weight had fallen off him, leaving the skin as a sad reminder of what once was.

As the sun set I found the path that led up to the tiny dwellings half way up the rock face, hidden from view unless you knew where they were and how to get to them. What they were I had no idea. Maybe a meditation site far from the village, where young boys fasted and prayed to the sun and the moon, and eventually became men. Or perhaps where the elders came to die, away from the village.

Each small 'house' was accessed through a wooden trapdoor in the roof and a ladder descending five feet down into the confined interior. A small window looked out down the length of the canyon. There was straw on the floor and the remnants of clay pots on the narrow shelves.

I lay down on the hard packed earth and stared up at the mud ceiling in the gathering darkness, seeing Julie's face and wondering in my desolation what had become of her.

Celtic melancholy wasn't going to solve anything so I returned to the campsite.

"We'll stay here overnight and start for the boat at first light."

Jonas had set up a small camping stove and boiled water for coffee. He handed me a cup.

"Guess you've been thinking about your girl." It was a statement, not a question. He sat down on a small boulder, cupping the coffee mug in his hand as the chill of the desert night started to creep into the canyon with the disappearance of the sun. "I'm sorry."

I risked a look in his direction. "Why should you be sorry?"

"It's because of me. All this."

"You're right."

"I've been doing a lot of thinking over the past few days. My conclusion is there are just three people that control the Consortium. Moresby is one. Maybe he's the head but there are two others." He was quiet again. Reflective. Delving into his memory to see what else was lurking there.

"Do you have names?"

"Ted Lieberman and Charles Delgado."

"Morgan was checking Lieberman out for me. He is on the Board of ISEC (International Security & Economic Council) and on the Board of the US Federal Reserve."

"He founded the Griffin Trust. The 'clean' end of the money trail. It's where a lot of my laundered funds ended up. Keeps a very low profile, nobody knows much about him."

"And Delgado? I've never heard the name."

"On the Board of the World Bank and tipped to be its next Chairman. Very low key guy."

"Not for much longer if he gets the position. But why did they decide to kill us in broad daylight on a public street? Unless Moresby was just waiting to find out where you kept your information." I glanced across at him. "There's something in your files that scares the hell out of Moresby. This whole exercise was a set up to get you to retrieve the documents. Me. Sutherland. Julie. Hal. We were all set up. Fed just a little piece of information at a time, pointing the finger at you. Moresby knew my background. He knew I'd go after you. He knew I'd get the documents." Then I told him about the Baja fiasco.

"Why you?"

That was a question I had no answer to. Or did I?

"Maybe he thought Morgan had told me something. He couldn't find it in her files. She didn't tell him. So maybe he thought I had it. He knew I wouldn't talk because he knew my training. I was the perfect tool."

"But Gregory says Moresby's dead. And you say you saw him drown."

"Yes."

"So if everyone else thinks that he's dead, why the hell should he care what's in the documents? What the hell's so important to a dead man?" Jonas opened the file box and took out the contents, spreading papers and photographs on a flat bare rock. I found the flashlight in my bag and shone it on the documents.

They all related to covert operations in Iraq and Afghanistan during 2003/5. Several photographs showed Moresby and Purdue together, dressed in white short sleeved shirts, lightweight pants with revolvers strapped around their waists like a couple of teenage gunslingers.

Moresby was slim, tall, with fairly long hair and a Zapata style moustache, giving him an altogether cavalier look. To them the war was a candy store full of opportunities to plunder, of which they took full advantage. Amongst the photographs was one taken at an Air Force Base, with Huey's in the background. Next to Moresby was a younger looking Sutherland dressed in combat fatigues, helmet and flak jacket. Beside them a scholarly looking man the same height and build as Moresby but younger. All had nametags on their combat jackets but I couldn't read them in the slightly out-of-focus black and white photograph. Not that I needed to, I could see who they were.

"Who's he?" I asked pointing to the scholarly looking man.

"That's the scientist I was telling you about. The one Moresby killed."

Then something else caught my eye. It was in the background. A man climbing into a Blackhawk, his face was turned towards the camera and I could have sworn I'd seen him before. I pointed him out to Jonas.

"And this guy?"

"Just a grunt assigned as protection I guess. The photo was taken around the time of Nimruz. I guess all the guys in the chopper died. I don't remember seeing any of them again."

I wasn't listening, I was staring again at the photograph and remembered Eliseo's killer at Jake's. Just inside the door of the Huey, was a fresh faced looking young man. Eager. The prospect of combat shining in his eyes.

It was Paul.

I sat back, my mind a jumble of thoughts, all of them echoing with the rattle of gunfire and the screams of dying men.

Jonas stared at the photograph.

"You sure nobody got out of the helicopter alive?"

"Not anymore. A Special Forces rescue team was sent in, following one of those beacons. They picked up some alive, the rest dead."

Something was bothering the hell out of me. Something that Paul had said when all this began. 'Were you part of the Nimruz operation?' He had known I was because he'd seen my file. But who had given it to him? Then he'd said, *'A lot of good people died there.'*

There were suddenly more questions than answers. We were all at

Nimruz. Before the operation we had studied satellite photographs, read the intelligence reports, but what was it that lurked somewhere in the back of my subconscious? Snapshot images flashed across my mind.

Sealed oil drums stacked in neat rows but no oil refinery in sight.

Purdue said they were shipping out cash in oil drums, but supposing it wasn't just cash. Supposing it was raw opium from the poppy fields of Afghanistan as well? No, Paul said there was a rumour that Marika Keskküla was selling yellow cake to the Iranians. That's why we were sent in, to stop that from happening.

Or was it?

As soldiers, Paul, me and countless others were just pawns in a conspiracy, a deception that we didn't even know was happening. We trusted our Government and those that worked for it, so we were all looking in the wrong direction as these men carried out their corrupt magic trick under our noses.

But Sutherland, Paul and I had seen something we were not supposed to see. It was in the photograph. I just had to figure out what that was.

It was simple. All the players, all the bank accounts, and all the unfathomable international financial manipulations were sleights of hand that simply protected the identities of the crooks. They had stolen ten of billions of dollars to finance their own power base. And it started in Nimruz where Paul and I and a few dozen others, who subsequently died, were unwitting pawns.

We woke, cold and stiff. Jonas had taken it upon himself to be chief cook and soon had the stove going and water boiling for coffee. The sun was beginning to reach into the canyon, creeping across the still water and splashing across the mountains in a golden glow.

I was stretching, trying to ease my cramped muscles when the first rounds ricocheted off the bare rock.

Instinctively dropping to the ground I saw Jonas hit by a round, knocking him down behind a rock. I crawled across to him and turned him over.

He grimaced in pain as I quickly tore his shirt off, rounds continuing to pepper the rocks around us, and bound the wound in his right thigh.

The round hit his leg, breaking it and exiting above his knee. He wouldn't be running any marathons even if he wanted to. Luckily there were no arteries severed and I staunched the bleeding as best I could.

"Shit it hurts."

"Lie still. Hold your hand here and don't let go. I've got to find out what the hell's going on here." I peeked around the side of the boulder to see where the shots had come from. Nothing. No telltale glint of sun off a rifle barrel. No strange lumps on the horizon. Nothing.

Pulling back into cover, I checked the magazine in the Omega and thought hard. Jonas looked grey with pain, but his eyes were open and focused.

"Jonas. Don't move. Just stay here. Whatever happens, stay here."

His eyes watched me and nodded his head very slightly in acknowledgement.

From my previous weeks spent in this canyon, I knew just about every nook and cranny. Even underwater, down at what had been the original canyon floor when the Indians lived here and before the dam was built. To get to the plateau and the dwellings in the cliff face, the Indians had had to carve a tunnel through a projecting rock slab, in order to climb to the shelf where Sarah had dropped us off. Now that tunnel was underwater and it was my only way to get around the gunmen.

Before I could change my mind I started running, bullets following me, catching up fast. Then I launched myself into the air and plummeted thirty feet to the water below.

The water was cold, clear, refreshing, knocking the wind out of me, but I carried on down to the bottom and swam until I found the tunnel, swimming into it with my lungs already bursting as I swam around two 'S' bends before daylight showed above and I shot to the surface in a tiny pool, breaking the surface and drawing in a great lungful of clean air.

I scrambled up the side of the pool and rested a few moments on the edge, my head pounding, gasping for breath. From where I was I could get around the back of the gunmen before they had the chance to figure out where I'd gone. The path wound up and around through narrow crevices in the rock, towards the far end of the rock shelf where Jonas lay.

I worked my way to the shelf and then scrambled along to the cliff face, finding the path that wound up to the top and climbed as fast as I could. There was no sign of Jonas and no sign of the gunmen, except for sporadic firing from the plateau above me. They would be moving soon, I knew that, so speed was essential.

It took me three minutes of backbreaking exertion to scramble to the top and start to ease my way towards where I thought the gunmen were.

Then there was a noise to my left.

"Thomas," a voice whispered. I turned slowly and saw Paul crouched against a rock, M16 pointed at my belly. "Move over here."

He still whispered. I didn't know why. He had me cold and the rifle never wavered. I held my hands up and stood.

"Why the whispering Paul? You've got me. Finish this."

The rifle barked and rounds whipped past my head and I heard a scream from behind. Instincts took over and I dove into cover as a vicious firefight broke out. I rolled, came up and fired towards a couple of gunmen who had appeared over the ridge twenty yards away. They fell soundlessly and I spun to face Paul.

He was lying against the rock, chest red with blood, the rifle slipping from his hands. Beside him lay one of Eliseo's assassins with Paul's combat knife sticking from his chest. I scanned the rest of the rocks for any signs of gunmen, then climbed across to where their position had been.

Their view was perfect. The whole of the end of the canyon, plus the ledge was visible and I could see their semi rigid inflatable tucked away out of sight.

Returning to Paul I found that he was barely conscious, with an upper chest wound which looked worse than it was. From what I could tell it had missed his lungs, but had broken the left collarbone and exited just to the right of his spine at the base of his neck and he'd lost a lot of blood.

He looked up at me, pain fogged his eyes. "You're a real asshole sometimes Thomas. Why the fuck did you think I was whispering?"

"You tell me. You're one of them, aren't you?"

He moaned and pulled a package out of his pocket. "No, I'm not. Shit I've been trying to figure this crap out just like you. Julie and I got jumped; they knew we'd go to the marina. They thought I was dead and took her. I followed them." He groaned in pain and squeezed his eyes shut gritting his teeth. "Christ, didn't you think they'd know a helicopter landed here last night? What happened to you, you dumb ass? Morphine. Give me a shot, then help me down there." He nodded to the ledge. "Then go get Julie. She's on the houseboat in the next canyon north. Use the inflatable."

After I administered the morphine I half carried, half dragged him down to the ledge where he passed out with the pain. I laid him down, rebound the wound and then crossed to Purdue, who was still sitting behind the boulder.

He looked at me weakly. "It's over?"

"No, it's not over."

I checked Purdue's wound and saw that the bleeding had stopped. It was a clean wound, but the bone would need splinting. I injected him with the rest of the morphine Paul was carrying and searched for something to make a splint. There were several straight pieces of wood in the caves, which would work. They didn't look like artefacts to me, so I took them. Jonas stood up well to my rough first aid; sweat pouring down his face, slumping back against the rock when I was through.

"Jeez. Glad you're not a doctor. I'd be in real trouble then." Smiling weakly he nodded across at Paul. "You got him then?"

I shook my head. "Not me. Eliseo's men. They have Julie."

Jonas frowned. "What?"

"They took her."

Jonas closed his eyes and gently moved his leg to a more comfortable position. "This is getting weirder by the minute."

Leaving him I went back to Paul, who had lapsed into unconsciousness.

Once again we had been set up. They had known that Purdue would tell me of the monthly meetings. How perfect. There was not a soul within ten miles and even if they left our bodies, by the time we were found, we would be bleached bones.

The gas tank in the inflatable was half full and the engine started first time, then I was skimming across the flat water towards the entrance to the canyon. There was a handheld radio in the boat which wouldn't be much use to me this far from Page and hidden behind the canyon walls. Still, one thing at a time. First, I had to find out who this mysterious Moresby was and end his little game for good.

Half an hour later I cut the engine and let the craft drift into the shore, grinding on the pebbles that formed the beach. I pulled it up as far as possible and then headed off on foot to the end of the canyon. It took a further twenty minutes and then I caught sight of the houseboat, *WANDERLUST*.

It was about seventy feet long with a small helicopter pad built into an awning over the aft lounging deck. She swung gently to a single anchor about one hundred yards offshore in the lee of a narrow headland, a jet ski hanging on a davit on the stern.

From where I was, I could see no signs of life. There were two decks, with what I thought was a raised saloon and cockpit on the upper level and the sleeping quarters on the lower deck. I would be exposed as soon as I stepped aboard, but there was no other way.

Slipping into the water I swam slowly out to the boat until I was within thirty yards, then dipped down and swam underwater until I came up against the hull by the rudder. I held onto the rudderstock for five minutes, just listening. But there was no sound that I could hear, so I slowly climbed up the aft swim ladder and onto the deck, crouching, with my heart beating a thundering tattoo.

Now I could hear a sound. The sound of a radio or record player turned real low and if I strained I could make out the South American Bossa Nova sounds of Astrud Gilberto and Antonio Carlos Jobim softly seeping from the upper saloon/cockpit.

A cursory examination of the sleeping quarters revealed nothing. So I started up the stairs, Omega gripped tightly in my hand as my feet left wet trails up the steps.

The door was shut, so I steeled myself and quickly wrenched it open, rolling through the gap, coming up on my knees and staring wide eyed into the saloon/cockpit.

Senator Travis lay sprawled on the settee. Naked. Eyes wide. Staring. Hypodermic sticking out of his arm.

On the floor beside him lay Julie.

She looked dead.

Pale, twisted.

Then I saw the slight flutter of her chest rising and falling and quickly knelt down. There was a large bruise on the side of her head, behind her right ear where she had been hit, and the signs of a puncture wound in her right arm. Whoever had tried to kill her, had not finished the job.

I covered her with a blanket and ran to the lower deck in search of the medical chest. It was in the master cabin for some unknown reason, buried in the bottom of a locker. I was frantic, tearing open the lid and rummaging through the contents, trying to find anything with which to stem the narcotic in her system. A small bottle caught my eye. I grabbed it and read the label.

IPECAC.

It might work.

I raced back, cradled Julie's head in my arms and forced some of the liquid between her lips, trying to make her swallow. She gagged momentarily then it slipped down her throat. A few moments later she started to vomit. She brought up her breakfast until her stomach was empty and dry retched for another minute.

I had no idea whether it would do any good. She was semi-conscious, but stable and needed an intravenous flush. And that meant a hospital.

There was nothing I could do for Senator Travis.

Then the lights went out.

My lights that is.

Someone hit me from behind, a sharp blow to the side of the head. Not an expert blow, as it wasn't quite hard enough to knock me out, just render me groggy for about ten seconds.

"Adios amigo," a voice said close to my ear. I lashed out at the sound and connected with something that broke under my fist. Then I felt for the man's throat and dug my fingers into his trachea until I felt the cartilage crush and my fingers break the skin. There was a momentary struggle as my fingers and thumb met behind the throat and choked the life out of the man.

My head hurt like hell, but somehow I struggled back from the brink of unconsciousness and forced my body to co-operate. I sat up and my blurred vision cleared. Beside me, eyes wide open in horror, his throat torn open by my hands, was one of Eliseo's killers.

Something was running through my mind. Something telling me I had to get out of here and take Julie with me and I didn't know why, until the flames started to flicker, reflecting off the shiny varnish on the underside of the cockpit table and the thick smoke crawled across the roof, descending towards us in a billowing cloud.

Somehow I made it out of the saloon and down the steps to the aft lounging deck, carrying Julie over my shoulder like a sack of potatoes. I knew that it would be impossible to swim with her. So I wrapped her in a lifejacket and tipped her over the edge into the water. She hit face down, but the jacket turned her over and she floated away from the houseboat.

Just as I fell overboard an explosion ripped through the houseboat.

The concussion threw me twenty feet into the water, just beyond Julie, and when I surfaced I swam over and pulled her with me, heading for the shore.

The boat erupted in a sheet of flame and burned merrily until the automatic fire extinguishing system took hold and doused the flames leaving a blackened smouldering hulk. The upper deck was a twisted mess and black smoke still poured from the shattered windows.

Having made the shore and dragged the limp form of Julie up the beach, I turned to look once more at the boat.

The would-be assassin Eliseo had sent made sure that the boat would not burn completely. It had to look like a murder and suicide. Again questions pounded through my aching head as I carried Julie back to the inflatable, pushed off and drove back to the lagoon at the end of the canyon.

Paul was supposed to kill me.

No. Wait. That's not right.

Paul was a dead man. They were aiming to kill Jonas and to capture me. Then take me to the boat, knock me out and then carry out the rest.

No.

Kill Jonas and Paul, then melt away. Leave the inflatable and I would find the houseboat. That made more sense. Because I sure as hell would not have been taken alive. And Moresby knew that. He had seen my file.

Which meant that Moresby was still alive.

The Baja incident had been a set up just like everything else. He must have escaped in the tender, before the chubasco hit.

And I was the only witness. I had seen him die.

But what he did not know was that both Paul and Jonas were alive.

Slowly through the pain filled haze in my head, I was beginning to figure this out.

Or was I?

Everything stemmed back to Nimruz.

Somehow we had seen something we were not supposed to see during the operation.

Or was it that we were simply not supposed to survive?

But why try and kill us now and not years ago after the operation?

None of it made any sense. Perhaps it only made sense after my father started investigating and opened the can of worms. Then I became a liability and so did anyone else involved in the operation.

Then I began to have a glimmer of understanding.

Moresby had lots to hide. That much I knew. But it wasn't just corruption we were dealing with. Murder was something else. That had to be kept hidden. But why the photographs and the documents? It was still Purdue's word against his and there was enough on Jonas to discredit him and let Moresby walk. After all, wasn't Moresby a captain of industry, the pride of American scientific discovery and free enterprise?

All these thoughts teemed through my mind as I made the trip back to the lagoon to pick up Paul and Jonas.

I glanced down at Julie and saw that at least a little colour had returned to her cheeks, but she would be sleeping for sometime yet. At least she was alive. But I had three people who needed medical attention and fast.

TWENTY-ONE

With Jonas, Paul, Julie and myself on-board, the little inflatable was overloaded, but the water was flat calm with no wind, which did not help abate the searing heat of the sun as it beat down mercilessly. It would take at least an hour to motor to the nearest marina and call for an ambulance.

Julie was unconscious. Paul had lost a lot of blood and looked pale, his breathing light. He swam in and out of consciousness.

Jonas did what he could to make them comfortable while I steered the boat, but he was in agony from his leg wound, although he never complained once. The morphine was wearing off and his face was grey with pain, sweat dripping down his forehead whenever he moved.

I rescued my phone from my pocket but it was wet, despite having been in a waterproof pouch. I stripped out the battery and dried the internals as best I could, but I needed an oven and a bowl of dried rice.

The outboard motor spluttered a few times, ran for a minute then coughed to a stop, the sudden silence deafening.

Jonas looked at me questioningly. "Out of gas?"

I nodded.

He sighed and shrugged. "This just isn't our lucky day, is it?"

"No."

"Now what?"

"The houseboat. I'm pretty sure I saw the automatic fire extinguishers go off."

"Let's hope it's still floating."

It took half an hour for us to paddle the mile out of the canyon to the blackened hull of the houseboat, still lying to anchor on the glassy water of the still lake. The fire extinguishers had done their work and stopped the fire before it had a chance to destroy the boat. I tied up alongside the aft deck and Jonas slumped back against the side of the inflatable, eyes closed, face grey with pain.

In the pilothouse the medical chest was where I'd left it, lying on the floor, lid closed. The contents intact and untouched by the water or fire because the chest was almost indestructible metal, made for emergencies at sea. Indeed this particular chest would have been more suited to a blue water cruiser than a houseboat on a lake.

The radio was useless and all the engine controls were damaged beyond repair.

Below, the guest cabins were undamaged as was the galley, but the master cabin situated below the wheelhouse was wrecked. The water tanks were half full and there was food in the lockers and refrigerator.

Returning to the aft deck, I rigged up a couple of bosun's chairs on the davits, lashed one of the inflatable's floorboards between them to make a stretcher and one at a time, hauled Jonas, Julie and Paul on board, then carried Paul and Julie to the guest cabins.

Jonas crawled after me and lay propped up against the wall, watching as I checked Paul's vital signs. He was still holding his own. I crossed to Jonas and took off the dressing, cleaned the wound with disinfectant and rebound it with a fresh dressing. Sweat poured off his face.

"Thanks. Got anything for pain?"

"I think so. Just let me check the medical chest." I glanced across at Paul. I was more worried about him than anyone. Without a transfusion, he wasn't going to last. Then a thought occurred to me. I reached out and pulled the dog tags out from beneath Paul's shirt. Inscribed on the flat metal rectangles was his name, rank, serial number and blood group 'A' Positive. I looked at Jonas.

"What's your blood group?"

He looked up at me suspiciously and answered slowly. "O positive. I think. O or A. Why?"

I didn't answer immediately. I was thinking back to my lectures on emergency medical procedures when I was in Special Forces.

"Paul's going to die without a transfusion. O positive blood to A positive can work. There's a chance of an allergic reaction but he'll die anyway unless we do something."

Jonas looked at me sideways. "Wait a minute. Am I thinking what you're thinking?"

There was nothing I needed to say because he read it in my eyes.

"Oh shit."

Just then I heard a groan from the other cabin. Julie was regaining consciousness. Her eyes blinked open, glassy and unfocused and wandered around the cabin before finally resting on my face. Slowly her eyes cleared, she recognized me, and tears began to run down her cheeks. "Thomas?"

I took her in my arms as gently as I could. "It's okay. You're safe now. Safe."

She sobbed quietly until the fear passed. Jonas handed me a cup of water, which I pressed to her lips.

"Drink slowly. Small sips."

Having finished drinking, she lay back down.

"I can't remember much... Don't know what happened to Paul... Maybe he's dead... Don't know... All so hazy... Stupid mistake... Paul tried to talk me out of it... Didn't listen." Her eyes glazed over and she slipped back into unconsciousness.

Paul was fading fast and needed blood urgently. Another couple of hours would be too late.

The medical chest yielded a couple of nasal gastric catheters, small size probably for children. In fact it seemed that this particular medical chest was stocked more for a young family setting off around the world than a houseboat on Lake Powell. There were several syringes and four Heploc sets for starting up IVs. There was also an ampule of heparin and several of ampicillin, adrenaline, atropine sulphate and an ampule of Demerol. Many different types of salves and creams, plus the usual bandages and splints.

The engine room revealed an extensive tool kit with just the thing I was looking for. A rubber bulb with a one-way valve commonly used in the fuel line of outboard motors to prime the engine. This one was still in its wrapping.

There was a large soup saucepan in the galley which I filled with water and set on the stove, found a packet of dried rice which I emptied into another bowl, buried my phone's SIM card and battery in it, then returned to the cabin. Jonas sat on the floor, eyes closed, holding his leg. I knelt down beside him.

"There's Demerol in the medical kit, but I can't give you any until we've finished the transfusion. Just hang in there, okay?"

He managed a smile. "Just don't take too much. I'm bigger than he is. I need more."

I helped him onto the berth beside Paul and set up a table between them. Then checked on the water in the galley. It was boiling, so I put in the rubber bulb and checked my watch. I would give it twenty minutes. When I returned to the cabin with the Heploc sets the catheters and the Heparin syringes, Jonas eyed me with trepidation.

"You ever done this sort of thing before?"

"Sure. When I was in the army. Everyone in the patrol had to be familiar with setting up an IV."

"What about transfusions?"

"First time this way. It's an old fashioned method, before they knew how to store the stuff. Don't worry. Relax."

"Relax the man says. Jesus. Think I'd prefer to take a shit in a cage full of man eating tigers."

"Think of it as paying your dues."

Jonas gave me a very nasty look.

"I think I'm in credit."

He watched as I swabbed down his arm, attached a tourniquet, and searched for a good vein. He turned away and closed his eyes.

"Shit. I can't watch. Just tell me when you're finished. Got a bullet I can bite on?"

"You might need it. This is going to hurt. Let's hope I only have to do it once."

He groaned and gripped the side of the berth with his free hand. Luckily he had good veins and I hit the spot in spite of his groans of pain, taped the Heploc in place and shot Heparin in to keep the line open. Then I moved over to Paul and repeated the procedure. He wasn't so lucky. I had to use the remaining three sets before I managed to get in a vein. I just hoped to God I was doing it right.

I calculated the amount of fluid each tube and the rubber bulb would carry, then how much would be transfused with each pump of the bulb. It would take about an hour to transfuse half a pint, providing that my math was reasonably close. It only remained to connect the tube to Purdue's Heploc set and pump the blood through to the end of the other tube, before connecting that to Paul's set.

It was working and I sat down to pump for the next half hour, hoping that the Gods would be on our side this time.

After I'd finished I left the sets in place, shot Heparin into them to keep the lines open and checked Paul's vital signs. The colour had returned to his face. Jonas fell asleep after I shot him with Demerol. Having looked in on Julie, I helped myself to a beer from the fridge before having a look at the engine and establishing the fuel level. All the electrics for the remote starter in the upper cockpit were shot and the cables had melted, so I spent the next three hours well into the night, rigging up an alternative system. When I got through, the engine started on a hand crank and I could select the gears and apply the throttle from the engine room before going up to the cockpit to steer the boat.

There was no way of getting lost on the main lake. It was simply a question of chugging along to the southern end, and docking near Page. But that wasn't such a good idea. The authorities weren't likely to look the other way if I deposited my patients at the local hospital then flew away.

There was a steep, narrow canyon several miles upstream that wound down to an open area with a beach I had found years ago. I hoped it was empty and nobody had decided to camp for the night. So I turned the houseboat around and chugged slowly along the shoreline, searching for the hidden entrance. I almost missed it, but saw it just in time, threaded the houseboat slowly down the narrow channel, reversing on occasion to turn the corners, until it opened out into a spoon-shaped dead end. There was enough room for Sarah to land the Explorer on the beach if I could get the phone working.

The first try was unsuccessful. I found a hair dryer, plugged it in, and spent the next half hour drying every conceivable part of the phone.

It worked. Just. The beauty of satellite phones is that they just need to see the sky, and providing a satellite was in sight, everything worked.

Sarah answered, her voice faint and crackly.

"Thomas? That you?"

"Yes."

"Do you have Paul and Julie?"

"Yes. Julie's in a bad way and Paul's been hit. We have to get to a hospital. I've moved the houseboat upstream." I gave her the coordinates and then dialled the secure number Simon Gregory had given me. I told him I needed a private hospital close to Page, no questions asked.

"I'll make some calls and get back to you in five minutes," he said, sounding relieved to be doing something useful.

Julie worried the hell out of me as she lay unconscious, breathing shallowly. There was nothing more I could do for her.

Paul had stabilised and was regaining consciousness. Apart from his broken collarbone and the obvious wound, he was in reasonable shape. He'd need surgery to clean the wound and probably pins in his collarbone, but he'd be up and about in a day.

"Nimruz," I said as I checked his wound to make sure there was no infection.

"Everything started there. Trouble is, I still don't know what it was that started," Paul replied.

"You sure?"

"Still don't trust me?"

"You keep information from me. I want to know why? You told me that Radley told you that Marika Keskküla was selling yellow cake to the Iranians. How did we not know that at the time?" I reached for Purdue's file and pulled out the photographs. The one I wanted was the one with Paul in the background inside a Blackhawk. I thrust it in front of him.

"Moresby, Sutherland, the guy who tried to kill us at Jake's ranch and there in the background. Recognise this guy, Paul?"

He took the photograph and studied it carefully.

"That's not Nimruz. The photo was taken a few days before the operation at the assembly point. We'd escorted civilian contractors in to consult on a new forward base they were planning to build. There

278

was nothing there, just concrete pads and building materials."

"Civilian contractors? For a forward base?"

I turned to Purdue who shrugged.

"I wasn't in country at the time, so I don't know when that was taken. I told you, I was the banker. Had nothing to do with military operations."

"How did you get the photograph?"

"It came in the mail."

Both Paul and I looked at him in disbelief.

"Oh please," I said mockingly. "It came in the mail?"

"I swear to God. It came in the mail. I recognised the faces and thought someone was helping me out."

Every time we thought we had this worked out, something happened to add another wrinkle.

In the distance I heard the clatter of the Explorer above the canyon walls and went out onto the beach with a flashlight. Sarah could put her landing lights on once she had dropped below the lip. Slowly she descended down onto the beach and shut down.

My phone rang. Surprisingly it was still working.

"I have arranged a suite in a private clinic in Page. It has a heliport on the roof," Gregory informed me crisply, and gave me the coordinates, which I in turn passed to Sarah.

"I need transport tomorrow morning in the San Joaquin Valley. I'll let you know where later."

"Natasha's with Dean, Thomas. I don't know where they are but they're in danger. Find them. Please."

"I know where they are. I told you that in Aspen."

When I'd met Dean and Sutherland at the safe house in Hollywood, I had noticed a slight perfume in the air. And it wasn't anything Julie wore. It hadn't taken a rocket scientist to work out to whom it belonged.

"I'll have one of my personal bodyguards meet you wherever you need him. His name is John Shand, he's in Santa Barbara right now."

"Okay."

I helped Paul and Purdue into the Explorer then ran back for Julie.

The fifteen-minute flight was the longest of my life as I held Julie close to my chest, speaking softly, telling her that I loved her and that we were done with this life. I'd never take another mission because all I wanted to do was to spend the rest of my life with her.

Sarah settled the Explorer on the hospital helipad. The doctors and nursing staff were ready and waiting, whisking Jonas, Paul and Julie away as Sarah and I followed slowly. One of the staff took Frankie, promising to take care of her.

"Can you call Page ground services and ask them to refuel the Mustang. Three quarter tanks only," I asked Sarah.

"Sure no problem."

I went inside as Sarah made the call. Julie and Jonas were taken straight into surgery and Paul made comfortable in a private room. I waited until they had checked him over before going into his room. His was sitting up in bed, satellite phone in hand waiting to be taken in for X-rays on his collarbone. He held the phone out to me. "Radley."

I took the phone and put it to my ear, while Paul and I stared at each other. "What is it Radley?"

"I've arranged for Professor Oldfield to arrive in Page tomorrow. I thought he should be there."

"Why?"

"He'll tell you when he gets there."

"Tell me about Marika Keskküla, Nimruz and yellow cake to Iran."

"Ask Robert Sutherland. He was there," Radley said and hung up.

"What the hell is this, Paul?"

"You tell me. I just follow orders. Sometimes."

"How's the arm?"

"Not as bad as they thought. Bullet missed anything major and the X-rays will tell them if they need to pin the collarbone. They said I can get out of here in a couple of days." He paused. "You know Radley plays both sides don't you? That's his job. We're expendable."

"I know that, that's why I'm going to get Sutherland and Dean before Eliseo's men get to them."

"Eliseo's men?"

"Yup. They are cleaning up everything and everybody. Then we'll go after Moresby."

"You know where he is?"

"I've a pretty good idea."

"Take care." He held out his right hand. "Thanks. The doc said you saved my life with that blood transfusion stunt."

I shook his hand. "See you in a few days."

Purdue was in surgery having his broken leg repaired, and the doctors had put Julie in an induced coma. The blow to her head had caused complications to the previous injury last year which caused her hearing loss. I felt there was something they weren't telling me, but I knew she was being well taken care of and reluctantly let go of her hand, bent down and kissed her forehead.

Sarah flew me to the airport after collecting Frankie, and together we walked across to the Mustang. I settled myself in the cockpit, turned on the power, and flipped the switch on the short wave radio.

"Sierra Uniform this is Tango Golf over."

Sarah looked at me questioningly. I answered her question before she asked. "Sutherland is Sierra Uniform..."

"...I got it," she said shaking her head. "Keep it simple."

I nodded, waited for thirty seconds and tried again.

"This is Sierra Uniform."

"Send your location codex five."

There was silence for another thirty seconds.

"Alpha X-ray Echo Lima 73 over."

"Roger. Codex two four zero alpha."

"Roger that."

I switched off the radio and turned on the Multi Function Display on the panel and transcribed the codex into co-ordinates.

"Very cryptic."

"Got to keep it short. No doubt somebody will be listening in on all the frequencies."

"They'll break your codex. You know that don't you?"

"But hopefully not before I get there."

We studied the MFD, which showed the location Sutherland had given me. It was deep in the Sierras near Mineral King on a private road that led to a cliff face, and what didn't show on the MFD Sutherland had drawn on the rough map he'd given me.

"How does a guy manage to build a cabin in the National Forest?"

"Because he's not your ordinary citizen. It's a safe house."

"Oh." Sarah turned to me. "I think I'm beginning to see."

"Really?"

"Our Government's not telling us the truth is it?"

"Not the entire truth. What happened all those years ago in Nimruz set the stage for a silent coup. It provided the financial foundation."

"Holy crap."

"That's why Moresby wants everyone who was there wiped off the planet."

"Who the hell is this Moresby guy?"

"That, my dear, is the question. Who indeed?" Then something crossed my mind as I looked at Sarah. I reached for Purdue's file I was still carrying, opened it and found the photograph I was looking for. I showed it to Sarah. "You told me your sister Leila was a computer graphics geek?"

"That's right. Digitally restores old photos amongst other things."

"Can she do something to find out what the names are on those badges?" I pointed to the photo.

"If she can't nobody can. I'll ask her."

"Better still, FedEx it to her overnight."

"Okay. I'll make a copy first. Why?"

"Then perhaps we'll find out who Moresby really is."

We turned back to the MFD and I showed her where I was going to land the Mustang.

"There." I jabbed my finger on the screen. "It's a bit short, but with the displaced threshold on the east end of the runway I'll be fine."

I'd selected a little airfield called Woodlake, east of Fresno, near Visalia in the foothills of the Sierra Nevada Mountains.

"That runway has an eight thousand pound weight limit and it's only fifty feet wide. You sure you can do that?" Sarah read the airport details.

"I know this aircraft, she's nimble and I'll be light, about six and a half thousand pounds. Anyway maximum landing weight is eight thousand pounds on this baby. You can fly into the mountains once I've located the cabin and picked up Sutherland."

"How do we know it's not just another trap?"

"Moresby probably thinks we're out of action right now, which is why they're going after Sutherland. He's the last link in the chain. And that's why I've got to get to him first. He has Simon Gregory's daughter and Dean with him."

"Gregory's daughter?"

"Leverage. That was one piece of the puzzle I couldn't connect earlier. Controlling the media has always been the number one priority of any would-be dictator. Control of information is paramount, especially with Twitter, Facebook and every other social media site. Then there are satellite communications. Gregory's vital to the Consortium's media control."

"Somebody's going to be pissed with you fighting a private war on US soil."

"I think that 'somebody' already knows. It's unofficially an official unofficially sanctioned operation."

"How do you figure that?"

"British Military Intelligence isn't going to get involved with anything that doesn't have White House backing. Unofficially of course. I'll tell you all about it when I get back."

She climbed out of the plane, then turned and kissed my cheek.

"Take care soldier. Call me when you need me to come and get you. It's what I do. Remember?"

TWENTY-TWO

The little Cessna Citation Mustang climbed rapidly with a three quarter fuel load and no passengers, and I felt comfortable at the controls banking towards California at full throttle. I reached cruising altitude of 31,000ft in about fifteen minutes and having set course, switched on the autopilot and sat back thinking of what lay ahead. It was only 368 nautical miles to Woodlake but with take off, climb to altitude, and the approach to landing I was looking at about one hour and forty-five minutes before I was in the car on my way to Mineral King. I'd be lucky to get anywhere near Sutherland's hide out before late afternoon.

Should I have waited? No. My instincts told me to get moving and so far they hadn't let me down. The only time I'd been in big trouble was when I didn't listen.

So I turned my mind to the situation in which we found ourselves. At least now I had a pretty clear idea of what was happening. Not happy about being kept in the dark by Sutherland and Radley for so long, but at least I felt I now had a purpose beyond just survival. Once again it astounded me how greed, immoral ambition and absolute power could sabotage even the most stable of Democracies.

In the distance, the Sierra Nevada Mountains rose up above the desert floor beyond Death Valley that lay sweltering in the summer heat. Mount Whitney, the highest point in the contiguous USA at 14,505ft above sea level, would pass to starboard as I crossed the mountains before letting down rapidly into Woodlake, which nestled in the flat plain of the San Joaquin Valley below the foothills of the mountains.

Yet again I was a *'mercy flight with urgent medical supplies'* according to the flight plan I had filed with Page ATC over the radio, then contacted San Francisco who had control over the Visalia area once I was at cruising altitude. Initially they questioned the suitability of the Mustang for such a short strip and suggested Visalia airport, but I argued that the extra twenty-five minutes it would take to drive could be critical as this was a medical emergency, besides I was a former military pilot who was well used to short field landings and take-offs.

That seemed to do the trick and they briskly told me that the wind at Woodlake was zero knots, but there was another storm front moving in with a change in wind direction increasing to thirty knots. I had a two hour window with the current conditions so I requested runway 07, which meant an approach from Visalia to the west of the Woodlake runway, as it would give me a flatter, slower landing.

Beyond the mountains I could see the front still out over the Pacific and increased speed as much as I could, nudging the maximum allowable for the Mustang at this altitude. There was a moment of déjà-vu as I passed to the north of Desert Rock airfield, where Julie and I had crashed last year.

What had I done to her?

I shook the thoughts away, because as callous as it may seem, they were a distraction that could get me killed, but the feeling lingered until I brought my mind back to flying the aircraft.

Mount Whitney stood clearly on the starboard side, but even though I flew close to the coordinates of Sutherland's hide-out on the port side, there was no way of spotting it from this altitude.

Visalia ATC called and I started a rapid descent towards Woodlake as instructed. I looked down at the runway as it passed below me on the starboard side, before following vectors via the Visalia VOR beacon, turning onto final approach and slowing the jet to one hundred knots. I was aiming for about seventy-five knots when I touched down on the numbers, with full flap and speed brakes deployed. The Mustang was sluggish at this speed wanting more power, so I dribbled on a little thrust and she settled down, resigned to the slow speed.

The runway looked like a narrow postage stamp, which didn't seem to grow any bigger the closer I got, but now was not the time to have second thoughts. Right in my path were fifty-foot trees, which I knew I was going to touch with the main wheels. Just how hard was the question. As soon as they flashed beneath I pulled back the throttles to idle, nudged back the yoke a touch and hit the speed brakes. The

Mustang slowed rapidly and I needed more back pressure so I didn't hit too hard, then I kissed the numbers and stamped hard on the brakes. The nose wheel banged down and I kept the speed brakes on as the end of the runway rapidly sped towards me. And just when I thought I'd screwed up, the little jet slowed, and I turned right onto the tiny apron by the car park and the airport building, stopping in front of an SUV where a young man in jeans and T-shirt stood waiting.

He looked fit with big shoulders, deep chest, bulging biceps and a slim waist. With his short hair and direct gaze he oozed ex-military. I slowly breathed out, ran through the shut down procedures and grabbed my sailing bag, now sporting a big red cross courtesy of Sarah, which was supposedly full of medical supplies, and went to meet him.

"Mr Gunn," the young man said crisply. "Mr Gregory said I was to take you wherever you want to go."

"What's your name?"

"John Shand," he confirmed.

"Thomas."

I shook his hand and climbed into the passenger seat of the Audi Q5 Quattro.

If there was ever a time to trust, now was the time. Either Gregory was on our side or he wasn't, I'd find out very quickly.

"Army Ranger?" I asked.

He stiffened and looked at me quickly. "How did you know?"

"Lucky guess."

Actually I had done a little research on Simon Gregory. He had been an Army Ranger during the Vietnam War, so it would make sense that he would recruit from his own kind.

"Where are we going?"

"Three Rivers first, there's a store where I can buy hiking boots some rope and a good jacket."

"I've got hiking and climbing gear in the back."

"What else have you got in the back?" I asked pointedly.

"Remington pump action 12 gauge short barrel. AR-15, C4, dets, timers and a Glock in the glove box. Mr Gregory says his daughter's life is at stake."

"Natasha?"

"Yes. He says you know where she's being held."

"I do."

"You want to fill me in?"

"Drive and we'll talk."

Rain started to fall as the next front moved in, an unseasonably cold snap, while north in Yosemite National Park wild fires raged.

Even the weather didn't make sense.

We parked in the Mineral King Trailhead parking lot. There were only three other cars there. John showed me his climbing gear and we filled backpacks with ammunition, guns, water and some energy bars. Then he dug out a bag full of mothballs and scattered them beneath and around the car while I laced up my newly acquired lightweight hiking boots.

"Keeps the yellow bellied marmots away," he said as I watched. "They just love to gnaw on car tyres, hoses, insulation. You name it they'll eat it."

"I know," I said unnecessarily. "I've been hiking here before. Long time ago."

John looked a little crestfallen, finished scattering the mothballs and then we shouldered our backpacks and laid a backcountry hiking map out on the hood of the Audi, alongside Sutherland's rough drawing. I had already marked the coordinates of the hideout so we chose our route carefully. I had no idea where Eliseo's men might be, but they may well be watching the car park, so we headed off in the opposite direction, having plotted a meandering route that would take us out and then back to our destination with a few peaks thrown in.

John and I spotted the two 'look-outs' in the first five minutes. Swarthy Mexicans who just did not seem to fit the backpacker type, studiously avoiding looking at us as they fiddled with their backpacks at a makeshift camp off to one side of the trail.

It started to rain and John smiled. "Guess they won't be enjoying the hike."

I knew what he meant. As Special Forces we only ever seemed to train or carry out missions in the worst weather. It was comforting in a strange way, and the men following us would be hard pressed when it came to clambering over the huge boulders in the rock falls I was planning on traversing. In the dark it would be treacherous for them. As we hiked, the only sounds beyond our footfalls were a steady wind in the trees and the rain building to an icy intensity as the temperature decreased with altitude and dusk fell.

After two hours we stopped to rest, eat energy bars, and check to see where our followers were. John saw them struggling through the boulder field about a half mile behind us. We hiked until night fell and turned towards what I euphemistically dubbed 'Sutherland's Mountain'.

Rain continued to fall and we slowed our pace, making sure our followers stayed in touch, then stopped in the cover of massive boulders to see where they were. I caught sight of them several hundred feet below us, heads down, toiling through the rocks.

"We'll set up a camp here. Make sure they see us."

"Then what are we going to do?" John asked, working the slide on his Glock then slipping the magazine back in.

"They'll be glad to hunker down in this weather, especially if they think we're here for the night. We wait an hour and then take them out."

"Sounds like a plan."

"There will be others, probably up ahead and they may have figured out where Sutherland's hiding."

"How?"

"Sutherland sent me the coordinates by radio. In simple code, but they could have broken it."

"Wouldn't these guys have tried to take us out if that had happened?"

"Probably," I conceded. "But if they haven't, we need to get rid of these guys. Besides, they're irritating."

An hour after darkness settled in we left the comparative warmth of our nine thousand foot high bivouac and quietly made our way back down towards the last sighting we'd had of Eliseo's men as they set up their camp for the night.

As we approached we could see flashlights moving in the small dome tent they had erected. They obviously didn't expect us to be wandering around in this weather. Rain spattered off the rocks and ran in rivulets down the cracks and crevices between the boulders as we quietly approached.

John circled away from me to the down slope side of the tent.

We could hear them talking in hushed tones and then one of them crawled out of the tent and walked a few paces away to relieve himself. John slipped up behind him and the man died silently.

I opened the tent flap and shot the second man with the silenced Beretta.

A quick search through their clothing revealed nothing except two mobile phones and a VHF radio. The radio would only work on one of the ridges, and their mobile phones had no signal. There was nothing else of any use, so we returned to our bivouac, packed and continued our ascent of the peak. It would take the best part of the night, climbing slowly in the dark without lights, but once over the top at eleven and a half thousand feet, we had a straight descent to where I hoped we'd find Sutherland's cabin.

After several hours the rain eased and the front blew through, leaving a half moon lighting our path up the steep slope to the ridge just below the peak of Rainbow Mountain. To be safe, we tied ourselves together with the rope John carried and arduously made the climb.

It took another two hours, but finally we crested the ridge.

The views in the bright moonlight were spectacular. Below us one of the high mountain lakes glistened darkly against the white rock and scattered trees. At any other time we would have sat and basked in the beauty, but we barely noticed as we scrambled carefully down the boulder field. It would be dawn soon and we needed to get there as soon as possible.

According to the coordinates, Sutherland's cabin was close to the lake, hidden in the rocks and trees. I sat down and John studied his GPS. We were about three hundred feet higher and less than a mile from the cabin.

The VHF radio I'd taken from the tent crackled to life.

"¿Jose?"

There was silence as the enquirer waited for a reply.

"¿Jose?" came the voice again and I figured Jose must be one of the men we'd dispatched.

"Si," I whispered, muffling my voice as much as possible.

"Jose. Acaba con ellos. He encontrado la cabina."

"Si. No hay problema," I whispered again, thinking I should have left the last part out.

"They found the cabin," John said. "Goddam son-of-a-bitch."

We started down towards the lake as fast as possible. Away to the east, dawn was beginning to break.

Gunshots echoed across the valley, bouncing off the sheer cliff walls. Six. Seven. Then silence.

I saw four men scrambling across the open rocks between the trees towards the lake. The cabin must be somewhere hidden out of our sight. John unslung his AR-15, lay down and steadied his breathing. His rifle barked once and the lead man fell in his tracks.

The others stopped. Uncertain. John's rifle barked again and a second man fell. That had the survivors ducking into cover, looking for John's position, but because of the way the sound echoed off the mountains, unsure of where to look.

I was up and scrambling down the slope before they poked their heads up, reaching a line of trees and slipping into cover, with John close behind.

"Take the left flank," I said. "I'll work my way around the lake edge."

He nodded and slipped quietly away. I waited until he had successfully worked his way behind the gunmen before moving.

If there were any backpackers camping close by, they would be wondering what was happening in their quiet peaceful world.

I heard two more gunshots to my left. Handguns, not John's AR-15.

Finally I caught sight of the cabin, cut into the mountainside as protection, with the front facing out across the lake. The ground dropped away in a vertical cliff, some sixty feet to the still waters below. I saw Sutherland behind a tree, crouched over. He fired into the trees, then staggered to the side door of the cabin, fell inside and slammed the door shut. One of the gunmen made a run for the door. My second round caught him in mid stride and he slammed into the ground, rolled and lay still.

I heard two more shots away to my left.

Then silence descended as the last echoes of gunfire faded with the dawn.

I ran crouching to the side door and knocked three times. Then twice more.

"Thomas?"

"Yes. Open up."

I heard the sound of the lock being turned, the door opened and Sutherland staggered backwards falling against the wall and sliding to the floor in pain.

"You badly hurt?" I asked stupidly. Any gunshot wound is bad and I could see blood on his lower left side.

"What do you think?"

"Let me take a look."

"Get Natasha and Dean and get the hell out of here. They're in the cellar. Trapdoor is over there under the chest." He pointed to a large wooden chest of drawers that stood against the wall. There seemed no way to move it. "There's a button on the right side."

"Let me look at this first."

Apart from stopping the bleeding, there was not much I could do. He had two bullet wounds in the side of his lower abdomen. Both going all the way through. He was lucky. It would hurt like hell, but if I could get him to a hospital soon, he wouldn't die.

"I messed up. I thought I could control this operation and flush Moresby out. Radley tried to change my mind but I thought, 'fuck you this is my country, I'll sort it out myself'. You were a lucky accident and I should have trusted you. You have to stop them Thomas."

"Who are 'they' Sutherland," I asked urgently.

"Wish I knew. My investigations stopped at Moresby. But there's someone higher. Another level." He grimaced. "Jesus. I'm not cut out for field work."

"That's the truth," I said, as I took field dressings from my backpack, dressed the exit and entry wounds, then wrapped a bandage around his abdomen to keep the dressings in place.

There was a sound outside and I flattened myself against the wall.

"Thomas, it's John. I'm coming in."

"Come forward."

He stepped sideways into the cabin and lowered his weapon.

"Anyone else out there?" I asked.

"Not as far as I could tell. But who knows if they'll send reinforcements. Natasha?" he asked, mind on his mission.

"In the cellar," I answered crossing to the chest of drawers, feeling for the button on the right side. The chest slid to one side and stone steps led downward.

"Natasha? It's John Shand. I'm coming down."

"Okay," came a muffled reply.

While John was busy with Dean and Natasha I went outside, climbed to a vantage point where I could watch the approaches to the cabin, and called Sarah on my secure sat phone.

"Need reinforcements?" she asked immediately.

"Just you. Sutherland's injured and I have two others to pick up."

"Natasha and Dean?"

"Safe and well."

"What are you going to do?"

"Walk out. You'll be too heavy at this altitude to lift us all out."

"We'll talk about that later. I'll be light on fuel, see you in three hours."

While John looked after the others, I went in search of a decent flat area for Sarah to land and found the third gunman I had taken out. Surprisingly he was still alive, but not for much longer. The round had hit his spine and he was unable to move, staring at me in fear as I knelt down beside him. I recognised him as one of Eliseo's personal henchmen. He shivered in the early morning air.

"Ayúdeme, por favor."

"Nothing I can do for you mate," I replied to his plea for help. "Where is Eliseo?"

"He tell us bring him girl. Visalia. Tonight."

"Exactly where?"

"I no remember. Eliseo put in phone."

A quick search of his pocket revealed a Samsung Galaxy III. It was open at the Google Earth app which I expanded until I saw a bookmark in Visalia. Closing in on it, I saw an address.

"North Ben Maddox Way?"

"Si. Small warehouse. Was tyre company, now empty. Ten o'clock tonight."

"How many men does he have with him?"

He was fading fast and I slapped him to get his attention.

"How many men?"

"One. Maybe two."

"Did he kill Morgan Alvarez?"

Even though he was dying I could see the fear in his eyes from my question. His breathing slowed and his eyes glazed over. I left him and continued to look for a reasonable landing area for the Explorer. We were at nearly eleven thousand feet and Sarah was going to have a handful, but I had no doubt as to her abilities. I found what I was looking for a few minutes walk from the cabin, where the scrappy pines petered out and opened onto a flat rocky area, about a half acre in size extending from the lake edge to the boulder field that led up to the ridge line we had crossed.

It was quiet. So quiet that it seemed the rest of the world did not exist, and I let my mind wander to Julie, feeling my throat constrict and wondering again what I had done to her. I half expected to hear Danny's voice in my head, but I was alone and never felt lonelier in my life. But my self-pity wasn't going to get the job done, so I cursed my weakness, brushed aside all thoughts, and went back to the cabin to wait for Sarah's call.

Dean and Natasha sat close together on the settee as John prowled the cabin looking out of the windows, checking for any movement.

"Do you have any pull with the local FBI in Visalia?" I asked Sutherland, after I'd checked his dressings.

He was pale and in pain but there wasn't much we could do about that. All we had were oxycodone tablets, and I didn't want to give him too many as he'd be going into surgery as soon as Sarah got him to the hospital.

"They'll listen to me. What do you have in mind?"

"Protection. I'm going after Eliseo Martinez tonight."

"He's in town?"

"Apparently he wants to take personal delivery of Natasha. With a bit of luck he doesn't know what happened here today."

"We need him alive, Thomas. Otherwise we'll never find out who's behind all this."

"You let me worry about that." I handed him my satellite phone. "Make the call."

John listened to the exchange. "Need back up?"

"You up for it?"

"Beats the hell out of baby sitting."

The words were out of his mouth before he realised and turned to Natasha with a mortified expression.

"No offence ma'am," he said quickly.

She smiled for the first time since we entered the cabin, and relaxed.

"None taken John. I'm thankful you came when you did."

"Just doing my job ma'am."

Natasha Gregory looked like her sister, but the resemblance ended there. She was quiet and gentle, unlike her sister's confrontational assertiveness that I'd seen on the video. I wondered if she knew her sister was dead. If she didn't, I wasn't going to be the one to break the news to her.

Sutherland finished his call and handed the phone back to me. "Your contact is Special Agent Larry Wise. He's our co-ordinator with MAGNET."

"MAGNET?"

"Multi-Agency Gang Enforcement Team. Operates in the Visalia area. It was set up six months ago." He closed his eyes and lay back in the armchair, pale, his eyes screwed up in pain. "There's a pen and paper on the desk. I'll give you his personal mobile number."

"There's one other thing we need to do."

"What's that?"

"Destroy this place and then have a news story tonight about a landslide that killed several people here. Our names should figure prominently. Well, yours and mine anyway."

"I can arrange that," Natasha said. "Well, my Dad can."

"Thank you. I was going to suggest that you call him. This is a secure phone." I handed it to her and went back outside with John.

"I brought the C4 and some dets," he said.

"Good. We can set up a blast over there." I pointed to an overhang behind the cabin. "That should take care of the cabin."

We busied ourselves for the next few hours calculating exactly where to lay the charges for maximum effect, before returning to the cabin.

"Dad has got it all arranged. It'll be on the late news tonight. Names but no photographs," Natasha informed us.

"Great."

My phone rang and Paul's voice cut through the helicopter noise.

"We're overhead Cerro Gordo Peak, Thomas, heading 270°."

"That's good and what the hell are you doing out of bed?"

"Got bored with daytime TV."

"Wait one."

John spread the map out and I quickly located the peak and calculated a new heading.

"Make your track 262°, you're about forty miles out. When you're overhead Moraine Lake, turn left to 233° for four miles, then turn right to 310° and slow down. Wind is light, no more than 2 knots. I'll guide you in from there."

"Roger. Call you when we're overhead Moraine Lake."

Sutherland was getting weaker by the minute and I checked his dressing again. Blood was still seeping from his wounds, but it was the shock that was getting to him from what was probably a ruptured bowel. Peritonitis could kill him within twelve hours. I wrapped him in a blanket and found some tea and made him a brew with lots of sugar. He would need to get to surgery pretty soon and the nearest place with a helipad was the Kaweah Delta Medical Centre in Visalia. I called the number Sutherland had given me, explained who I was, and asked

Special Agent Wise to alert the hospital that we would be bringing Sutherland in with gunshot wounds.

A sense of relief flooded over me when I got off the phone. I felt as if I was 'coming in from the cold' and working with official law enforcement agencies for the first time since this adventure began and that we now had a safety net. Perhaps my stupid plan about putting Jonas on TV had galvanised the Government into action.

Twenty minutes later Sarah brought the Explorer in exactly where I had marked the spot. Paul climbed out grinning, his left arm in a sling, and helped load Sutherland carefully on board followed by Dean and Natasha.

"Sarah reckons we can take you two as well."

"Okay. Just one thing we have to do."

John and I ran to where he had placed the timers and set them for four minutes. Then ran back to the helicopter. Paul climbed in the back with John and I settled into the co-pilot's seat and put on the headset.

"Let's see just how good you are. We're headed for Visalia."

"And hello to you too," Sarah retorted.

I looked at the gauges and she was right, the Explorer was low on fuel, but getting off the ground at this altitude with a full load and then climbing up over the ridge at 11,000ft wasn't going to be easy. The little helicopter shuddered as the rotors bit into the thin air and I could see she'd redlined the throttle being careful not to 'overcook' the engines as the EGT rose. Slowly we lifted off and she turned, dipped the nose and gained speed before lifting the collective and climbing, heading for the ridge.

Behind us the charges blew, sending rock high into the air. We scraped over the ridge with feet to spare, thankful that at this height there were no trees, then descended over Mineral King Valley, gaining speed before climbing again and crossing the far ridgeline on a direct route to the hospital. We had clearance all the way, courtesy of Special Agent Wise, and settled back for the fifteen-minute flight. Descending all the while once clear of the mountains.

"How's Julie?"

"Not good." Sarah wasn't one to sugar coat anything.

"How so?"

"She's got swelling on the brain. I don't know the medical terms except they've still got her in an induced coma. Her Dad's there with her."

"Jesus Christ what a mess."

"We're all volunteers Thomas. Kinda."

"Are we?" It was a rhetorical question and we fell silent as Sarah concentrated on listening to Visalia ATC, guiding her to the Helipad that had been recently built in the Kaweah Hospital parking lot.

TWENTY-THREE

We didn't belong in this part of Visalia. Small run-down auto repair shops, tyre retailers and fabrication shops lined the road, some of which had been torn down with new buildings in progress, but exactly what was being built wasn't yet clear. At night, gangs roamed the areas killing each other and trying to avoid the Multi-Agency Gang Enforcement Team.

Special Agent Larry Wise turned out to be in his mid thirties, ginger haired, slim, efficient, and all business. Unlike the caricature FBI agent he was dressed in a dark blue rugby style shirt, lightweight beige bomber jacket that hid his shoulder holster, suitably faded blue jeans and lightweight brown hiking boots.

We sat in a battered 2006 Buick Century, parked up out-of-sight in the building site close to the address Eliseo's gunman had in his phone, watching. In the rear seat, John and Paul checked their weapons. Paul had insisted on coming claiming that his arm was fine, which it wasn't, and that he could at the very least cover our backs. We both knew he wanted payback.

"The Team have organised two raids on houses about a mile away, just to cause a distraction while we go in."

"We?"

"My turf. Where you go, I go," he said, quietly but emphatically. "Who is it we're after?"

"Eliseo Martinez, also known as…"

"…El Cobra Poco," he finished my sentence. "I've been wanting to get my hands on that little bastard for some time, but we were told 'hands off'."

"He has friends in high places."

"Our instructions came from the DOJ (Department of Justice). Explains how he comes and goes like he owns the country."

"I'm sure that's exactly his plan. Take a look at the LA Mayoral election. And that's just the tip of the proverbial iceberg."

"I want him alive," Wise said with feeling.

"Me to," I lied. "But that may not be possible."

He looked at me sideways, made up his mind and nodded once.

"Seems you have friends in high place too."

Paul laughed without humour. "Only when those friends want something."

Special Agent Wise smiled and I could see his shoulders relax. We had a common connection. All of us. We were all engaged in violence and yet at moments like these, we felt the humanity, the fragility of life, and the need for trust and truth. Without each other we were dead men. Together we would come through in one piece and who knows, maybe what we did would be worth something.

"I'm going in," I said opening the door and stepping from the car. "Paul with me, you two cover the perimeter."

They followed without comment as sirens blared in the background with the start of the house raids.

It was 21:30hrs.

Paul picked the padlock and we slipped inside.

Everything had been cleared from the interior of the warehouse except for several chairs placed in the centre of the floor and chains hanging down from the steel roof beams.

This wasn't a warehouse it was a slaughterhouse. This was where Eliseo's men kept the local gang members in line with the cartel's wishes. What I found interesting is why he would come here himself, rather than have his men do the dirty work. There was a lot I didn't know about Eliseo Martinez. And I knew even less about his cartel.

The gunman's iPhone vibrated in my pocket.

"Si," I answered as gruffly as possible.

"Jose, ¿tiene el paquete?"

"Si."

"¿Esta en al almacén?"

I coughed. "Si, estemos esperando."

"Bueno. ¿Es el pacquete intacto?"

I grunted, paused. "Tal es un poco daño."

"Bastardo." Eliseo shouted and hung up. I hoped I had done enough to convince him I really was Jose.

"Eliseo?" Paul asked.

"Indeed. He's on his way."

"Impressive."

"What?"

"The Spanish."

"The result of a misspent youth bumming around California and Baja, way back when life wasn't so complicated. Anyway it's not that good, let's hope it fooled Eliseo."

"Is your friend John up to covering our arses?"

"Indeed he is."

"That's a relief," Paul grinned and stationed himself by the only window that looked out of the side of the building, from which he could see the road.

Ten minutes later a new yellow Lexus LFA pulled up outside and Eliseo Martinez stepped from the driver's door. It wasn't the most expensive car in the world but with a price tag of over $400,000 it was close. He only had one bodyguard with him who climbed out of the passenger seat, looked around defensively, hand inside his jacket, and walked behind Eliseo towards the side door.

I let them both enter before sticking my gun into the back of the bodyguard's neck, pulled it away as he froze for a second, then shot him as he turned pulling his gun from his jacket pocket.

The silenced Beretta made a soft plopping sound in the warehouse. The sound of the dead bodyguard hitting the floor was louder.

Eliseo spun around and backed away as Paul levelled the Glock at his face.

"Not what you were expecting, Eliseo?" I asked quietly.

He stiffened, surprise dislike and contempt written on his face. "You have too many lives, Tomas. That news report was a clever deception."

"One friendly coming in," Paul warned as Special Agent Wise walked in the door. He paid no attention to the bodyguard's corpse; he only had eyes for Eliseo.

"Ah. Special Agent Wise, how good to see you again," Eliseo smiled coldly. "It has been a long time."

"Too long, Eliseo, too long. I've been waiting for this day."

"What can I say? Your partner was sloppy. He died like a coward crying for his mother." Eliseo turned to me, dismissing Wise. "I was told before we met the first time that you did not speak Spanish, Tomas. I had forgotten that you did."

"An expensive mistake."

"What is it that you want? Not money, you already have enough. Perhaps Special Agent Wise needs a new house for his new bride? No he is a patriot to the core." He laughed and sat down on one of the chairs. "Perhaps you are looking for revenge maybe. For Morgan Alvarez and the lovely Julie, such a pity both had to die."

"Julie's not dead."

Eliseo shrugged and sighed, and nodded his head towards the dead bodyguard. "As you can see good help is so hard to find these days. But Miss Keskküla does enjoy her work, which I'm sure you will discover when she finds you."

I was finding it difficult to ignore his needling and concentrate on the job. "Why Morgan?"

"It was just business my friend. She was getting too close. I tried to warn her but these modern women just do not listen. What can I say?"

"You tortured her first."

"A warning to others. In my business a fine or a suspension just doesn't work." He was too relaxed and I stepped towards him, gun levelled. "Not so fast Tomas. You need information only I can give you," he said quickly.

"Perhaps I can get it from you by using your methods."

Eliseo's laugh turned into a squeal of pain as the round from my Beretta shattered his left knee.

He looked at me with fear and incredulity.

"You need me. Only I know what you want to know."

"Actually I don't need you. You gave me the answer I was looking for just now. The piece of the puzzle that just didn't fit."

"What do you mean?"

"Spanish," I said obliquely. "And you've outlived your usefulness."

Then I shot him between the eyes.

Special Agent Wise jumped forward but Paul held him back with his good arm. "What the hell did you do that for?" he shouted.

"For Morgan, Jake and for Julie."

"He was a valuable witness."

"He would have walked inside an hour if you'd taken him in."

"How do you know that?"

"Ask Sutherland, he'll fill you in on the details," I said, checking to make sure Eliseo was indeed dead. "Now it's time to go."

"Who the hell are you guys?"

"Surprisingly, we're the good ones," Paul said as we left the building. Sirens were still blaring as the MAGNET force swept up Eliseo's pack of vermin.

"You need to get a clean-up team in here now before anyone finds out what happened to Mr Martinez. We need that kept quiet for a few days."

"What's going on?" Special Agent Wise asked and then held up his hand resignedly. "I know, ask Sutherland."

After a good night's sleep in the Executive suite at the Marriott Hotel, I felt a little more human. Aching from hiking all over the Sierra's and sleeping rough, but otherwise in good shape. A phone call to the hospital the previous night yielded little information on Julie's condition and I was anxious to get back to Page. Sarah had already left with Dean and Natasha for the flight back, stopping at Visalia airport first to refuel, but I needed another conversation with Sutherland before Paul myself and John, who had asked Gregory for a temporary transfer to me, flew back to Page in the Mustang.

Special Agent Wise was already at the hospital when we got there.

"Apparently the Park Rangers found six bodies near Mineral King this morning. Know anything about that?"

"Guilty as charged, and I'm sure Sutherland will politely ask you keep it quiet for the moment, before releasing a statement that it was a gang turf war."

"Any connection with the 'gang turf war' in Big Bear and a ranch near Palm Desert?"

"Could be. Eliseo covered a lot of territory."

"Who the hell are you guys?"

"Sutherland didn't tell you?"

"He said this was National Security, but you're a Brit."

"Actually I have dual nationality, if that makes you feel better."

"And him?" he said, pointing at Paul.

"You really don't want to know."

Wise paused for a moment and leaned forward whispering. "If you hadn't shot the son-of-a-bitch then I would have, after I did to him what he did to my partner. Just so you know." He stepped back. "Now I've got a mountain of paperwork, thanks to you guys." He grinned suddenly, turned, and walked away down the corridor.

Sutherland was conscious with a nasal gastric catheter, an IV and several tubes leading under the covers to his abdomen from bags hanging on the side of the bed. Paul and John had stayed outside at my request.

"Wise told me what happened last night," he croaked with difficulty.

"As he should."

"What is it you want from me now?"

"Nimruz. You were there. It wasn't just a money drop, was it?"

Sutherland shook his head slightly. "No it wasn't. We had word that the Iranians were storing yellow cake there before transporting it across the border. They weren't. It was Moresby. And it wasn't yellow cake, it was spent fuel rods from the Pakistan nuclear program. Marika Keskküla was shipping them out to Estonia a little at a time. That's how she got started with her research. Her husband found out what she was doing with his money and he... well... died, as you know. Then she found other spent submarine fuel rods when she acquired the Suldiski Island facility."

"And Radley knew all this?"

"Not the Moresby connection. We kept that our little state secret on this side of the pond. Once you dealt with Keskküla's operation in Estonia we had to come clean. We didn't know what you might find in her facility."

"Do you know who Moresby really is?"

He shook his head. "No. I was getting close, but then this shit happened." He looked at me, his eyes narrowing. "But you do, don't you?"

"Maybe."

"Going to share?"

"Not just yet. I need to make sure. Besides, I don't think you need an 'international incident' right now."

"Plausible deniability?"

"That's a very common phrase in Government. But I do need access to a surveillance satellite without having to hack into the NSA's system, again."

Sutherland managed to grin, somewhat painfully. "They did get pissed. I'll see what I can do."

"I need it by this evening at the latest, otherwise the rabbit may run. Again."

I gave him the coordinates of the area I wanted the satellite photographs to cover, the secure encrypted email address I wanted the photos sent to, then left him shaking his head and reaching for the phone at his bedside.

Taking off from the Woodlake airport was going to be interesting. At 2,200ft it was 900ft shorter than the minimum stated in the manual, but I figured Cessna had allowed for an aborted take-off in the figures. Well, I was soon going to find out. The wind was coming from the west at ten knots, which would give me a little lift, but I made sure I had every inch on the runway, starting well before the threshold in the runoff area. Any cars driving along the road when I applied full power were going to be surprised.

John won the toss to ride up front with me, but was having second thoughts when he realised just how short the runway was with the trees at the end. After I called Visalia ATC and told them I was ready to take off, just for fun I put Bruce Springsteen on the stereo speakers singing *'I'm on Fire'* and had it blasting through the cabin. John's apprehension heightened when I advanced the throttles to full power, holding the shuddering little jet on the brakes until the engines reached their maximum thrust then released them. The Mustang bounded forward picking up speed rapidly.

"Get it right this time Thomas. I don't want to spend another two weeks in hospital in traction," Paul quipped, adding to John's discomfort.

The end of the runway hurtled towards us.

"He was kidding," I said, as John pushed himself back into the seat as far as he could, waiting for the inevitable. "Mind you, I've only done this once. And this is it."

I waited until the last moment to raise the nose, felt the main wheels lift off the runway, brought the gear up immediately to reduce drag and executed a climbing turn to port to avoid the trees.

"Holy crap you guys are nuts."

"Still want to be on this next one?"

"Wouldn't miss it for the world."

Visalia ATC cleared us to San Francisco area control, who in turn cleared us en route. We flew back over the scene of our recent adventure and fell silent as Bruce Springsteen died away into the hum of the engines and we each sank into our own private thoughts. Now that I'd switched on the autopilot I felt my shoulders relax and my thoughts turned again to Julie. Snapshots of her lying in the sun on the aft deck, floating in the anchorage off the island of Gozo just over a year ago, after the passage from Italy.

That's how long we'd known each other, and yet it seemed a lifetime away since we'd met in the bar in Capri. A year filled with the highest highs and the lowest lows. A year where our lives had not been our own, but controlled by others no matter how hard we tried to escape.

Before I knew it San Francisco area control were on the radio handing me over to Page ATC for the approach vectors to runway 15. I tore my mind off Julie and concentrated on reducing height by throttling back, establishing my glide slope, and adjusting the rate of descent with the speed brakes. The Mustang dropped from the clear blue sky towards the yellow desert and fractured canyons that became the spreading waters of Lake Powell, as if we were in a silent capsule returning from the edge of space, the engines a quiet hum in the background.

I smiled as John tensed, while I executed a steep descending turn onto finals.

"Relax John. We could land twice on this runway and still have room to spare."

He grinned and glanced at me sheepishly. "It's different riding up front."

I floated the jet just above the runway before touching down and slowing to turn off on the taxiway. Ground control directed me to a parking slot beyond the terminal building where I could see Sarah waiting. I introduced John, and Sarah led us to an SUV she'd rented for the short trip to the hotel where we could dump our kit. I left the others and drove with Sarah to the hospital on the outskirts of town.

"She's still in an induced coma, Thomas. Her Dad's with her."

"What's the problem?"

"He'll explain."

Professor Oldfield gave me a hug, tears in his eyes, as we met in Julie's room. He looked tired, defeated almost.

"What's going on with her, Professor? Nobody's telling me anything."

He took a deep breath, passed a hand over his eyes and eventually turned his eyes to meet mine.

"She didn't want you to know. It was the helicopter crash last year. Shrapnel entered her head, which is what caused her deafness. The surgeons didn't operate because they said the fragments were small and brain surgery risky. The fragments are from a DU weapon, Thomas. They have the same radioactive signature as the ammunition from Keskküla's facility in Estonia."

I had a flash of Julie holding her head and taking Tylenol, something she'd never done before. "That explains the headaches."

He nodded. "The radiation medication isn't pleasant."

Another flash of her face when I found her on the house boat, eyes not focusing, and seeming to wander independently of each other, before she slipped into unconsciousness.

"There was some internal bleeding on the brain where the fragments are," Oldfield continued. "They had to drill to release the pressure.

That's why she's in an induced coma. When the swelling reduces, they'll see what they can do."

"Jesus Christ, what have I done to her," was all I could say, as I looked at her.

"Nothing she didn't want to be a part of. You're good for each other. I have never seen her happier. She chose you."

If I had been Julie's father, I didn't think I could have been so magnanimous. I would have wanted to strangle me, or at the very least yell and scream.

"You still have a job to do Thomas. There's nothing you can do here."

He was right. She was getting the best care possible and there was nothing I could do, except hang around like a moping dog waiting for his owner to come home. I walked outside into the heat of the day feeling angry, violent, seething with a pent up rage that had no way of expression. Out-of-control emotion wasn't helping, as impotent frustration built steadily until the mental switch went off in my brain, the years of training kicking in.

Oldfield was right, I had a job to do and I regretted having given Eliseo a quick death for what he had done to my Julie, but he had only been a small part of the problem. I walked out into the desert until I reached the edge of the Colorado River and sat for a long time, staring down into its slow moving depths, as the dark water meandered through the canyon.

It was late afternoon by the time I returned to the hotel, hungry, thirsty, dusty and tired, but with my mind sorted out and a basic plan of action in my head.

Paul, Sarah, John and I gathered in the living room of the hotel suite after I'd showered and eaten. They sat watching me expectantly. I checked the email on Julie's iPad and downloaded the photos I asked Sutherland to get, then sat the iPad on the table for everyone to see.

"Isla Santa Cruz," I said quietly. "Near La Paz in Baja Sud. That's where we're going. The elusive Moresby's there. It's where he runs his empire from."

"How do you know?" Paul asked.

"Because he as good as told me." They all stared at me as if I had gone completely crazy. "It's a long story. Sarah, did Leila come through with the photo enhancement?"

"She did. Here you go." She handed me copies of the blown up photo and one of a particular badge. It was as I suspected. The name on the badge was Delgado. Then everything I suspected fell into place, but I knew that our window of opportunity was narrowing with every passing hour.

The best photograph of the island was taken from an oblique angle, the sun shining onto the huge glass picture window of the massive house set back into the cliff face of the island mountain. It had been built under an overhang, cantilevered out from the back of the cliff, the rock overhang itself becoming the roof. The photographs taken from above could not detect the house, just the one from the oblique angle, and even then it required a zoom to see it.

"Can't see anyway we can approach it, except from the far north side," Paul pointed out.

"Correct. And I'm pretty sure that's where we'll find the entrance. But he'll have that covered." I looked at John. "You're the expert climber. What do you think?"

"The cliff drops straight to the sea, no landing points there at all. But the face looks reasonable," he said cautiously. "Are these the only photos we can get?"

"Maybe not," I replied.

TWENTY-FOUR

Near La Paz - Baja - Mexico - September 5th 2013

Capitan Ernesto Rodriquez was a creature of habit, motoring back from the bay north of La Paz in his thirty-foot powerboat after his usual early morning fishing trip. I had flown the Mustang into La Paz late last night and was waiting on the dock as he guided his Sea Ray back into the slip.

"Cómo estás Señor Gunn. You're back from your business trip. I did not see your yacht."

"It's still in Loreto. I came to see you."

"Please come aboard."

I climbed onto the boat after first tying off his dock lines. He was inside the cabin, already brewing coffee.

"Is this an official visit Mr Gunn, or simply social?"

"Official."

He nodded. "Black or with milk and sugar?"

"Milk and sugar please."

"Please sit down. Tell me."

"Isla Santa Cruz. Tell me about it."

He took a deep breath and looked at me carefully. "You are not who I thought you were. I am correct?"

"That depends who you thought I was."

"I did research on you and it says you are the chief of Gunn Group Industries in the United Kingdom. A very large, very rich and very important company."

"I was. Past tense."

"What else are you?"

"Someone who was nearly drowned in these waters. And I believe someone with whom your Government would like you to cooperate."

"I did receive a call late last night, but they would not tell me exactly what it is you want."

"Information," I said quietly. "Isla Santa Cruz."

"It is a private island about which we were told not to ask questions."

"But I'm sure you do some judicious snooping when you're out 'fishing'."

"It is always good to know what surrounds you."

"Eliseo Martinez is dead. I killed him."

The shock registered on Rodriguez face just as I'd hoped.

"You killed him?"

"He murdered several of my friends and put Julie in a coma. So yes, I killed him and now I'm after the men who controlled him."

Rodriguez shifted uncomfortably in his seat.

"I am glad that he is dead. Perhaps that will make things easier here." He reached into a drawer and pulled out a series of photographs. "Yes, I having been looking at the island ever since you told me that you lost two men overboard."

Without thinking he slipped into Spanish. "No parece plausible y no sabía si estaba mintiendo a mí o que hay algo más está sucediendo." Then looked at me in apology.

"It's okay, I get it. You didn't know if I was telling the truth or whether I was just another lying son-of-a-bitch."

"Then my cousin in Loreto tells me that your yacht is being watched by cartel people."

"Will you help us?"

"Yes. I love my country. I love Baja. I would like to see an end to fear and violence."

"We can't guarantee that, but we can make a start. And to do that we need your boat."

"There is one condition. That I come with you. It is my boat after all and I am responsible for the waters around here."

"Okay."

He nodded and I called Sarah, Paul and John, who were busy having breakfast in the Mosaic restaurant.

"Mr Gunn, I want you to know that the money you found on the Bay-Cruiser really did go to an orphanage."

"I never doubted you," I lied.

The team ambled down the dock to the Sea Ray and for the rest of the day we went over the photographs Ernesto had taken, comparing them with the latest satellite images.

"I saw a helicopter land on the plateau near the peak yesterday, and there is a dock hidden in a natural cave on the north-east peninsula."

He laid the photographs down for me to see. They were taken with a zoom lens and were a little fuzzy, but I could make out a large dock inside the cave with what ironically looked to be a 67ft Nordhavn moored there. A rising breakwater, painted and textured to look like the rocks of the cave had been installed, which could be raised in bad weather, or simply to hide the dock from prying eyes. Ernesto had taken a sequence of photos showing it in the raised and lowered position.

"The yacht left two days ago, but I hear it will return tomorrow morning at slack tide. That is at 04:50hrs."

A direct approach to the dock wasn't going to be feasible, as the breakwater would be in the raised position until the yacht arrived, so I looked at the cliff below the house.

"How about going up there?" I asked John.

"Not a problem."

"That's easy for you to say," Paul quipped. John shrugged and grinned. "So what's my job?" Paul continued.

"I need you and Ernesto to stay on this boat and tell us when the Nordhavn arrives. John and I will gain entry from the helipad."

"There are many hammerheads in these waters Tomas," Ernesto said with concern.

"So nobody will expect us to swim then," I said, as cheerfully as I could.

Sarah rolled her eyes. "I'm glad all I do is fly."

We picked up wet suits, rebreather diving gear and two electric underwater sea scooters that I'd ordered the day before then checked our weapons, climbing gear and explosives. John and I went over the details of the climb, until I was sure I knew what I was doing. Once we gained entry we'd be making it up as we went along.

At 01:15hrs in the morning I slipped into the water a mile from Isla Santa Cruz, and with John hooked onto me we headed in towards the island. Paul stayed on the Sea Ray with Ernesto.

We couldn't use glow sticks or waterproof flashlights, instead relied on the GPS attached to the sea scooter to get us to our destination. John had a bang stick should any of the hammerheads take an interest in us. I was hoping they stayed at the El Bajo seamount, which seemed to be their preferred hangout.

Out of my peripheral vision I could see dark shapes moving slowly and sinuously around us, but the hum of the electric motor kept them at bay.

The trick to any successful surprise assault is to do the very thing that your enemy has discounted as being impossible. Of course the reason they think it's impossible, is because it is.

Or almost, as impossible wasn't a word we had in our vocabulary, although at this point as the gentle swell moved us inexorably towards the rocks below the cliff face, I really wished we did.

John swam past me as I cut the motor on the sea scooter, and rode the swell in towards the rocks we planned to use as a landing stage. He made it look easy scrambling onto the rocks like a mountain goat, securing himself quickly with the climbing rope hooked to an offset cam he'd inserted into a flared crack in the rock, then turned back to help me as I let go of the sea scooter and slammed into the rocks. He pulled me out of the water and we climbed up to the base of the cliff, out of the reach of the waves and I nursed my bruised body. My shoulder had taken the brunt of the hit and for a moment my arm was numb and useless, the pain excruciating.

John stared up at the house cantilevered out over the sea one hundred feet above us, smiled at me and started climbing. He was in his element, moving steadily and decisively, inserting cams into crevices in the rock as he climbed, hooking the rope to them. I belayed him from below, keeping the line loose so as not to exert any pressure, paying out as he climbed. He got halfway up and then signalled for me to follow him.

Truth is I never really took to climbing, only doing it as part of my training and really not getting into the discipline much, so going up a blind cliff face in the dark with just a moon to light the way was not my idea of fun. Unlike John, who was enjoying the climb.

I reached his spot without incident, and rested while he climbed the fifty feet to the base of the house. Again he secured himself, and I climbed up and reached for the iron beam, finding what I thought was a reasonable foothold. Then I felt the ground beneath my feet slip away in a shower of crumbling rock to the waters of the Sea of Cortez one hundred feet below, and was left dangling, clinging to the iron beam.

My grip was slipping.

John reached down and pulled me up until I had a better grasp on the beam, and pointed to his left.

There was a bigger cantilever beam supporting the front of the house, about eighteen inches wide, enough for me to lie on if I could get to it.

Slowly I inched my way along, each movement testing the strength in my fingers and I could feel them slipping. Somehow I made it, hauling my feet up onto the cantilever and rolling up so that I was lying on my stomach, arms wrapped around the iron, staring down in horror at the drop below.

John grinned at me, hanging by one hand and enjoying my discomfort. It was payback for the plane.

The beam was only five feet long, buried in the rock, running right back as the base of the house.

Slowly I crawled along the beam to the rock face, grateful to feel the solid support of mother earth. To my right, underneath the house, was a rock ridge, presumably carved out by the construction workers so they could work on the structure. It stretched across to the far side, a distance of about forty feet. There seemed to be some cuts in the rock that could be used as handholds. How far they went I had no idea, but as there was nothing on this side we had no choice.

Standing on a narrow ledge, with little or nothing to grab hold of, is not my idea of having a good time. John skipped across in no time and secured the rope. For me, each inch was a nightmare. I tried not to look down, but stared fixedly at my destination. I suffered from height vertigo when on cliffs or tall buildings, but strangely enough not when standing on the ramp of a C130 at 30,000ft waiting to jump.

When I got there, I climbed onto the beam and once more leaned back against the rock, before looking at the cliff face to my right.

I started up the wall, following John who danced along, but with each foot up the rock face I lost another square inch of skin from my hands and another fingernail. By the time I reached the ledge near the top, my hands were a mangled mess. John was already on top and waiting for me.

It was now 02:30hrs.

From my new vantage point there did not seem to be any obvious way into the house, but I had seen on the satellite images what appeared to be a steel plate on the summit, to the side of a carved out flat rectangular area that was the helipad.

After a short search I found what I was looking for. A trapdoor set into the rock.

The trapdoor opened easily on well-oiled hinges, revealing a dark, narrow staircase cut twenty feet down through solid rock. I stepped down, followed by John, who closed the trapdoor behind us. In the pitch dark I slowly descended the stairs until I felt the smooth surface of another dark room.

Feeling along the wall I found a switch, pressed it and blinked in the sudden brilliance of the light. It was a chamber that had a descending staircase on one side cut down through the island's core, and doors to an elevator opposite. There was a biometric pad to the side of the doors that meant access for us was impossible.

We started down the stairs and came to another chamber, which again had more descending stairs and another door. This looked like an emergency exit in case the elevator didn't work and the stairs were the only route in or out. There was a handle that I tried carefully, simply out of curiosity. It turned, I signalled John to turn the light off, and then opened the door.

One of Moresby's guards sat asleep in a chair just inside the room. He never woke up as John quickly dispatched him and carried his body back to the stairwell. They were obviously not expecting company.

The room beyond was laid out like a command centre. A bank of radios against the right wall. Television monitors on the left wall linked to Wall Street, the Stock Exchange and to the News Network. On the back wall a huge map of the world. Beside it, a three-dimensional computer image of the earth with plots of all the stationary and orbiting satellites.

A huge ebony desk stood in the middle of the floor, with a large leather swivel chair, empty, facing the door at the end of the room.

This was the nerve centre for a global empire. And I knew I was looking at the heart of RBM Defence Electronics. The next door opened to reveal a short passage with empty bedrooms and their en-suite bathrooms, leading to the main living room, a vast area with a huge glass wall that looked out over the Sea of Cortez. It was open plan, including the kitchen, dining room and entertainment area with a huge plasma screen TV and HiFi equipment. But they seemed small by comparison to the overwhelming view.

The walls were bare rock, rough, just as when carved out of the mountain, but covered with some type of plastic sealer that made the rock smooth to the touch. Behind me, to one side, were elevator doors.

There was a loft area, connected to the living room by a spiral wooden staircase, which I ascended slowly and entered a museum.

A military museum.

All the weapons of the different ages of man were represented here. Suits of armour stood against the walls and swords and shields, flintlock muskets and lances covered them. Modern assault rifles, machine guns, grenades and hand held rocket launchers filled the space in between, standing in racks and display cabinets, that were a tribute to the craftsmen's art.

"Holy crap," John whispered. "What the hell is this place?"

The centrepiece was a display dedicated to the Iraq War, a testament to one man's ego. All the weapons we had ever used were there. Not old but as new as the day they were manufactured. And interspersed amongst them, were photographs. Lots of photographs, and they all showed the face of the man I had seen in Purdue's files.

Then there was a photograph taken just before the Nimruz operation, the photo I'd asked Leila to enhance.

315

Nothing stirred in the house but I sensed that someone was here, so we quietly went back to the stairs, closing the door softly behind us and descended to the next level. This was the servant's quarters and they were asleep. A middle aged couple in the bedroom, probably the cook and caretaker who we immobilised, tied up and gagged. Ernesto could take them back to La Paz on his boat after we'd finished here.

We continued on our way down until we reached the cave dock.

The stairs emptied out to the end of a rock platform hewn from the rock wall, to which was attached a substantial floating dock kept in place by pilings driven into the sea floor at each end. There was a forty-foot Luhrs sport fishing boat docked at the elevator end, leaving plenty of space for the Nordhavn. I guessed it was Moresby's runabout, and no doubt what he'd used to escape from the Bay-Cruiser that night.

The breakwater was raised, a massive metal structure with large spherical bearings at each end and I figured it was similar to the London flood control gates that swivelled up from the seabed into position. It was no small engineering feat and would have cost a fortune, but if you've got trillions of dollars to play with it was a drop in a bucket. There was a small bunkhouse half way down the rock platform. John and I crept quietly towards it until we could peer inside the doorway. There was a table with a control panel for the breakwater, TV, telephone, two chairs and two bunk beds upon which slept two guards, snoring softly. We retreated back to the stairwell and up to the first level to assess the situation and make a plan.

It was 03:15hrs.

"We need Paul and Ernesto," I whispered.

"How do we get them in?"

"Open the breakwater."

"Of course. Why didn't I think of that?" John replied sarcastically.

"There are only two of us. With the two guards and his boat crew, Moresby will have at least five. We need Paul and Ernesto."

John nodded and we went back up to the helipad to call them. Timing was going to be everything.

"No problem, it's boring out here, there's only so much mariachi music I can take and the fish aren't biting," Paul said cheerfully. "See you in ten minutes."

We returned to the cave dock and quietly walked to the control hut. One of the guards stepped from the doorway rubbing his eyes, saw us and shouted before one round from John's AR-15 dropped him instantly. We could hear the other guard scrambling around inside the control room and a burst of fire came from the doorway aimed at nothing, but the rounds ricocheting off the walls were as dangerous as if they had been aimed. I flattened myself against the side of the door, poked the barrel of my automatic around the edge and fired six shots. There was a cry of pain so I rolled inside and shot the guard as he writhed on the bunk.

The gunfire echoes subsided and all was quiet again.

"Okay Thomas?"

"Okay. And you?"

"Yup. One of the ricochets grazed my cheek but I'm okay."

"Right. Let's get this breakwater open."

The control panel was simplicity itself. A green button to open the breakwater, and a red one to close it. I pressed the green button and slowly the massive steel structure began to move. I had no idea how long it would take to open, so after weighting the bodies with some anchor chain and tossing them into the water, we sat down to watch.

It took seven minutes before the electric motor whined to a halt and we could see the faint outline of the Sea Ray approaching. Ernesto had a Flir image intensifying camera installed on the boat hooked up to his chart-plotter and so could see clearly, especially with the light spilling from the door to the control room.

Within another five minutes the Sea Ray was docked. I looked at it, and then at Ernesto.

"You have a new boat," I said, pointing to the Luhrs.

He frowned. "I do not understand."

"We're going to have to sink this at the back of the cave," I pointed to his Sea Ray. "It'll give the game away otherwise."

Ernesto looked from one to the other and shrugged. "It will sit at the dock in the marina under confiscation until the owner claims it. And if after three months nothing, then..." He shrugged again and smiled slightly.

The Sea Ray slid quietly into the depths of the cave's deep dark water and I led everyone on a tour of Moresby's kingdom.

"I had no idea that something this big could have been built under my nose," Ernesto exclaimed, in genuine horrified amazement. "Madre de dios."

"What do you think we should do with this, Ernesto?"

He looked at me, searching my eyes for a clue to my meaning.

"I think it must cease to exist, Tomas."

"I agree. With your permission we'll destroy it. But not before we empty the place. Upstairs are some passengers for you to take back. I'm sure they will have some useful information."

He nodded, and John set to work with Paul laying charges then went outside to attach explosives to the structural beams.

By the time we had finished wiring the entire complex it was 04:10hrs.

The plan was simple. Paul and Ernesto would act as the guards when the yacht came in to dock. It was dark enough down in the dock for them to escape close scrutiny and Ernesto was of course fluent in Spanish. Once Moresby was in the elevator, they along with John would take out the crew.

I stayed in the house as they went down to the dock.

Of course the success of my plan depended on the fact that Moresby would be on the yacht and it wasn't just a maintenance crew refilling the pantry and freezer, or checking the breakwater machinery. I'd know in less than half an hour, so instead of worrying about it I crossed to the bar and helped myself to a glass of twenty-five year old Laphroaig single malt whisky, then sat down in the corner of the overstuffed settee so I could look out across the Sea of Cortez and in the distance saw the lights of the approaching Nordhavn. I leaned forward and pressed the button for the dock on the intercom panel set into the coffee table in front of me.

"They're on their way in. Maybe another fifteen minutes."

"Roger that."

The whisky was pleasant and I let it ease the tension that bound my shoulders as I watched the yacht motor towards the island and then disappear from view. Another ten minutes to wait, if my plan went the way I thought it would.

The elevator doors opened and Chaz Duprés entered the room followed by Ted Lieberman. A cleaner tidier Chaz Duprés, the beard fashionably trimmed and long grey hair gone. Surprisingly he was bald, unlike his photograph at Nimruz. Sensing my presence, he turned. Saw me, and then the gun. His first expression was shock, but he soon recovered, smiled and crossed to the liquor cabinet that I had already sampled. Lieberman stood frozen, staring at the gun.

"This is a surprise," Duprés said slowly, without the hint of a Texas drawl. "Mind if I pour myself a drink."

"Go ahead, it's your house after all, Chaz."

"Charles. I prefer Charles Delgado, the other was... well let's just say a little amusement for your sake."

"Not really. Duprés was Moresby's scientist at Nimruz. You had him killed. Who was the guy on the Bay-Cruiser?"

"An actor. Not very good one I grant you, but then you did not allow me much time, so I had to improvise. As you perhaps guessed, the real Moresby never made it out of Afghanistan. He was a secretive fellow, so I just kept him alive in the minds of those that wanted to fund his company. A little sleight-of-hand. Moresby, Duprés, me. One and the same."

"Who the hell is this guy, Charles?" Ted Lieberman growled, nervously looking at my gun.

"Let me introduce Thomas Gunn, Ted."

"You told me the bastard was dead."

"So I was led to believe by the television news reports. A landslide in Mineral King."

I shrugged. "It helps to have a TV company on your side. Simon Gregory is a little upset, as you can imagine."

"Gregory? What the hell's going on here," Lieberman demanded.

"Shut up Ted," Delgado retorted curtly.

Delgado selected the bottle of Laphroaig, poured a generous amount in a glass then sat down, watching me carefully.

"I did wonder if in fact you had managed to escape the little trap I set you at Sutherland's so-called secret cabin. You are a very resourceful man, Mr Gunn. Very resourceful. Now what?"

"Now I'm going to take you back to stand trial for murder, corruption and fraud."

He smiled and sipped calmly. "Your word against mine." He paused, with the glass halfway to his lips. "How did you know it was me and indeed where to find me?"

"Spanish. Eliseo Martinez confirmed my suspicions when he informed me that he was told I didn't speak Spanish. Only one person could have told him that. You."

"Ah yes, I remember. When we first met and I greeted you in Spanish, you did not react," Delgado said with a slight smile. "You would have made a good actor."

"And you would have made a lousy judge at the Oscars."

"And so just how did you find me?"

I held up the flash drive I found at Morgan's ranch and threw it to him. He caught it cleanly and looked at it.

"DC-243-8-110-2," I recited. "I didn't know what that meant when I found it, but I do now. DC stands for Devil's Cauldron and the numbers are the latitude and longitude of this island. It used to be called Isla Caldero del Diablo back in the times of the Conquistadors. Morgan Alvarez figured it out and put everything she knew on this drive. You knew that and wanted her dead, so you enlisted the services of your friend Marika Keskküla, who teamed up with Eliseo Martinez and his gang of killers."

"Neither Marika nor Eliseo could find this. Miss Alvarez was very cunning. Eliseo told me she had little to say to you before she died." He sipped his whisky and looked at me waiting for a reaction. There was nothing from me, so he continued. "So why don't you just kill me now that you've found me?" he said smugly, feeling comfortable and safe. "Why are we having a conversation?"

"I want to know why so many people had to die."

Charles Delgado smiled thinly. "Expedience. I can't afford anyone who might connect me to the fictional Moresby remaining alive to tell the tale. Simple really."

"And me? You could have finished me off on many occasions."

"You? You I wanted as a witness to 'Moresby's' death. And then I wanted you to dig into 'Moresby's' dealings as far as you could go. I knew you'd find out about Marika's little escapade with Pakistan's spent fuel rods and 'Moresby' stealing all that money the Government so carelessly flew into Iraq and Afghanistan. It added to the game. It is a game you know Mr Gunn. A very enjoyable game don't you think?"

"Which you engineered with the help of your friend here."

"So much cash and nobody in the administration cared where it went. Call it a re-assignment of assets."

"Of course you brought Mr Lieberman here for a brief holiday no doubt," I said sarcastically.

"Well, we were going to celebrate your timely death at Sutherland's cabin, and then all the loose ends would have been tied up and we could continue with our business."

"That being power through the money supply. The Federal Reserve. The World Bank. Just you in control, able to do anything you want?" I said rhetorically.

Again the thin smile. "That's right. But here you are. Very much alive. You really do make a habit of spoiling things, don't you? Games have rules Mr Gunn and you should have died in the mountains. But no, with you it's like playing 'Whack-a-Mole'. Think you're dead and you pop up somewhere else."

"That was your second mistake."

"What?"

"Thinking that because you thought I didn't even speak rudimentary Spanish, I was therefore a dumb idiot to be played with."

He shrugged. "I see no reason to change my mind."

"I'm taking you back."

"I believe you will try."

I stepped forward and hit him on the side of the neck, temporarily cutting off the blood supply to his brain and rendering him unconscious before he had time to react, then tied his hands with zip ties. I wanted to do a whole lot more to him, but that would do for now.

Lieberman stared at me in terror. "What are you going to do?"

"You are going to stand trial for fraud, extortion, and treason for your part in the Nimruz operation, after you tell me exactly where Marika Keskküla is."

"None of this was my idea. It was all Delgado. He's the brains."

"And whose idea was it to have my father killed, his or yours?"

He paled visibly.

"There's only so much he can do as Head of the World Bank, but the head of the Federal Reserve now that's a whole other proposition. The Fed sneezes and the world catches a cold. Isn't that right?"

Lieberman stopped shaking and stood up. His eyes were dark flecks of pure sinister sociopathic evil.

"You really think you can stop us?"

"That depends on who else there is. There are supposedly three of you. But only two here." I took Morgan's flash drive from Delgado's hand. "Perhaps the last name is on here. Perhaps there isn't a third person at all. Just another illusion in the deception."

The elevator motor whirred and John crossed the room, flattening himself against the wall. The motor stopped and the door opened.

"It's us Thomas," Paul said, staying in the car.

"Come on in." Paul, John and Ernesto stepped into the room. "Everything good down below?"

"Sweet as a nut," Paul replied. "They weren't expecting us. There's a nice trawler down there."

"That'll do."

"What are you planning?"

"A boat delivery. The one I never finished."

"What the hell does that mean?" Lieberman shouted.

"It means the country can't afford a scandal and a trial Mr Lieberman, there's too much at stake. Confidence in the Fed, the money supply, Wall Street. Besides, why should we keep self-serving power-hungry slime-balls like you and Delgado around. You're nothing but human waste. With you two gone, this ends."

"That's murder."

"Or pest control."

Lieberman lunged for Ernesto's gun and Paul shot him. Just once, putting a neat hole in his temple. Lieberman's lifeless body fell to the floor.

"What about him?" He pointed to Delgado.

"He comes with me. I deal with him alone. Clear all the files you can find from this place and then we'll blow it. Don't forget the servants. Ernesto is taking them back to La Paz."

Paul loosed the dock lines and I backed the big trawler out of the cave boat dock towards the open Sea of Cortez, the radar domes barely missing the roof arch on the rising tide.

As we passed the headland I knew that there was no way I was taking him back to the States. Delgado knew it too, as I untied him and forced him up the companionway steps, onto the deck behind the pilothouse.

"You can't do this," he said, watching me carefully. "You don't have it in you anymore. You said you were taking me back." But as he said it, I could see he didn't believe it.

"I lied. I'll give you the chance you never gave my friends."

"What does that mean?"

I took out my Böker Plus Ginger Fighter Tactical knife and placed it on the deck between us. "Take me out and you can sail anywhere you want. No doubt your friend Marika can arrange a diplomatic passport for you somewhere safe."

He went for the knife, picked it up and lunged at me.

It wasn't a fair contest as I took it from him after I'd broken his wrist. He screamed with pain and then stared at me, blood gurgling in his throat as the knife buried deep in his chest.

"The game ends here Mr Delgado," I said and twisted the knife.

His eyes widened in the realisation that he was dying, then rolled back in his head as blood gushed from his mouth.

I let him fall to the deck, tipped his body over the side for the hammerheads, and stared at the dark water rushing by with a feeling of growing emptiness and the need to be in Julie's arms, where I could ask for forgiveness and forget everything that had happened.

"It's over Julie. It's over. I'm coming home," I whispered quietly into the dawn and thought I heard a sigh on the wind carry across the sea and past me to the ocean beyond.

I headed the trawler towards the deep water of the Sea of Cortez, smashed the seacocks and went aft to lower the whaler as the trawler quickly began to settle, the sea rushing in through the holes in the bottom. When I was sure that she was sinking I motored away a short distance to watch.

Without much fuss the three million dollar motor yacht disappeared from view with just a bubbling sound, the surface of the water foaming as it sank to the bottom.

In the distance on Isla Caldero del Diablo, there was a low rumble that sounded like distant thunder.

Then there was nothing.

I turned the whaler and motored slowly towards La Paz as the sun rose on another stunning day on the Sea of Cortez.

Coming soon
The third book in the Thomas Gunn thriller series

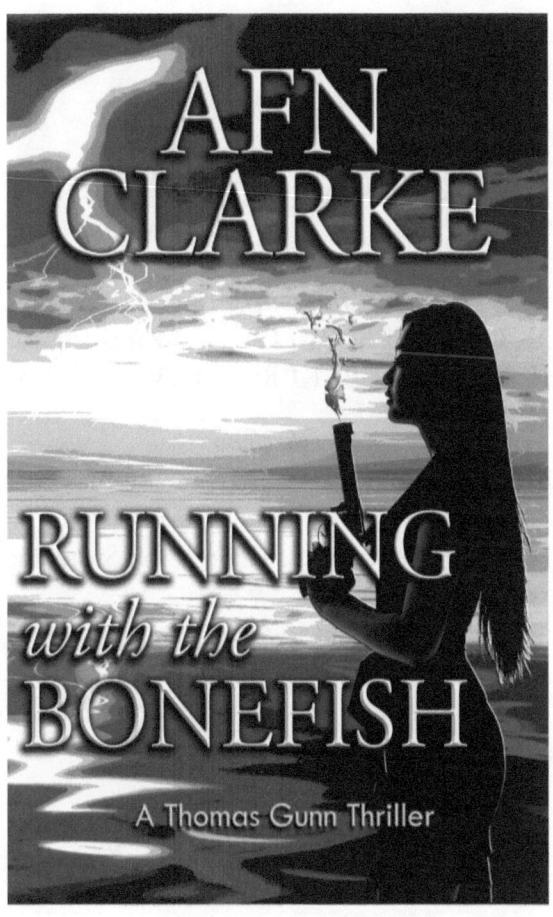

Other books by the author

autobiography
CONTACT

literary fiction
COLLISIONS
AN UNQUIET AMERICAN
DRY TORTUGAS

humour/satire
THE BOOK OF BAKER: Part One - Dreams from the Death Age
THE BOOK OF BAKER: Part Two - Armageddon

thrillers
THE ORANGE MOON AFFAIR (a Thomas Gunn thriller)

These books are available in the Amazon Book Store and Kindle Store

I hope you enjoyed this book and would very much appreciate it if you would post a review on my Amazon page. To learn about new releases, special offers and free books please leave your email address on my secure website.

www.afnclarke.com